MAN IN A WIRE CAGE

MARK PERAKH

A Critic's Choice paperback
from Lorevan Publishing, Inc.
New York, New York

Copyright © 1988 by Mark Perakh

All rights reserved. No part of this book may be reproduced in any form without the written permission of the publisher.

ISBN: 1-55547-257-5

First Critic's Choice edition: August, 1988

From LOREVAN PUBLISHING, INC.

Critic's Choice Paperbacks
31 E. 28th St.
New York, New York 10016

Manufactured in the United States of America

PART 1

Chapter 1

FROM TIME TO TIME BORIS PETROVICH TARUTIN TRAVELED from his city of Kalinin to small neighboring towns where he delivered lectures in local high schools. On the evening of this cold and cloudy November Friday, Tarutin found himself in drab Bologoe, on the shore of chilly Lake Bologoe.

His lecture lasted about two hours; usually he caught the last train and arrived back home in Kalinin around midnight. This time, however, one student, a homely-looking boy by the name of Litvin, asked countless questions. Tarutin had singled out this boy during his very first lecture in Bologoe, more than a year earlier; while many pupils hardly concealed their yawns, insatiable curiosity vibrated in Litvin's eyes. Today, excited by Litvin's grasp of the subtleties of Quantum Mechanics, Boris forgot about the time. Reluctantly, he quit finally and tossed his notes into a vinyl bag he used for both papers and sandwiches.

To make up for the delay and just for fun, Tarutin jogged all the way to the railway station. He inhaled the crisp air of the near-freezing evening, enjoying the long strides of his mountaineer's legs. At this hour, the streets of Bologoe were empty. Nobody noticed the long-legged man in a raincoat running on the pitted, bumpy sidewalks.

In the station hall, as by devil's design, a fat woman stood ahead of Boris at the cashier's counter. She could not properly count her rubles. When Boris finally got his ticket and hurried to the platform, the red light of the last car was disappearing behind dark trees.

So that was it. He was trapped in this forlorn town, on the edge of nothing, in the cold and dark night.

In the hall, a policeman, *Militsioner*, watched the few people still hanging around, then began driving the people out. In accordance with regulations, the station closed at 11 p.m. Nobody would be allowed to sleep on the floor. Tarutin glanced hesitantly at the policeman. The latter seemed to notice Tarutin's glance. Although Tarutin had not violated any regulations, he felt a chill in his stomach under the policeman's stare.

"Your documents, citizen."

"Yes, comrade Militsioner."

The policeman's coarse fingers flipped over the passport pages. First name, father's name, last name. Birthdate. The passport gave the man's age as thirty-three. Birthplace. Kalinin. Nationality. The ethnic origin was given as Russian.

The Militsioner compared the photograph with the original. Both had the same oblong pale countenance with widely set gray eyes, a slightly snubbed nose and a disobedient curl of russet hair. Then the policeman turned to the "Employment" section. Assistant Professor of Physics, Kalinin State University, Tarutin's sole place of employment during the last ten years.

"What are you doing in Bologoe?"

"Can't you see, here is my trip authorization, comrade Militsioner."

The policeman apparently lost interest; this Tarutin turned out not to be prospective prey.

"What shall I do now, comrade Militsioner? There are no trains until morning."

"I don't know about trains. You must leave the station." The policeman even made a gesture implying that in the event of a delay, he might apply force to kick the citizen out.

Tarutin walked slowly to the street.

He stood on the sidewalk looking into the dark chilly night. The huge door banged behind him. The iron clang of the lock testified that in this Soviet town the regulations were strictly enforced. The shadowy figures of the few people who had just left the station dissolved into the darkness, and the clatter of their heels on the cobblestones gradually subsided. The street was now empty and silent.

There was only one hotel in this town. Tarutin had passed it each time when walking back and forth to the school. Though he knew that all the space in the hotel was held for Party and Government functionaries possessing the official reservation, *bronya*, Tarutin had no other options. He sighed and headed to the hotel.

Not a single light shone in the street. From time to time, the moon threw its pale greenish light from behind fast-moving clouds.

He turned the corner. The hotel was dark. Only the entrance glowed faintly. Big letters on a shield attached to a pole permanently announced, "No vacancies." Those with *bronya* ignored the sign. Those without it hardly ever tried to get a bed. The sign seemed superfluous. But now Tarutin understood the expediency of maintaining the shield and the pole. In response to his knocks, the shadow behind the door, instead of explaining that the hotel was full,

5

inquired whether the stranger were literate or not. And if he were, then why the devil did he not read the clear Russian on the shield?

Boris shivered in his light coat and walked away. How was he to live through the long hours of this freezing night? Suddenly the door behind him clicked. Boris turned around. There was a male figure of formidable size against the dimly lit background of the half-opened door.

"G-get over h-here, d-do you h-hear me?"

Boris returned to the entrance. The very tall man seemed to be in his late forties, with a bald skull speckled with multiple scars, and a bristle on pock-marked cheeks. He shone a flashlight in the stranger's face.

"No vacancies; however . . ." stammered the big man. Boris nodded and turned to the street. But the big chap made an inviting gesture and Boris, rejoicing, entered the lobby.

In the weak light of the night lamp he saw people sleeping in chairs. Suitcases and sacks scattered over the floor. Every one of those sleeping kept a hand on his belongings. Snores and the odor of tobacco ashes, vodka and sweat struck the ears and nostrils. But it was warm here and Boris wished only to be permitted to join these people and to stretch his legs anywhere on the floor.

The big man still stared at Tarutin's face as if trying to penetrate the guest's mind. Boris Petrovich Tarutin had nothing to hide. He handed over his papers readily to the big man who apparently was the *Night Administrator*. The man inspected each document.

"However, are you from Kalinin?"

After Boris confirmed that he was, the stammerer asked, "However, you don't have any relatives or friends in Bologoe?"

Boris assured the clerk that this was indeed the case.

The clerk now turned to the "Personal Status" section of the passport.

"Not married, however?" he inquired, since there was no stamp with the spouse's name in the passport.

"No," Boris said, amused by the clerk's frequent improper use of the word "however," common in the speech of the Siberians.

"Don't you have any orders or medals, however?" the clerk asked.

"Medals? No . . . Why?" Boris was perplexed. The big man sighed and did not explain why he was interested in the guest's medals.

"You know, it's prohibited to allow more than twenty in the lobby." The big man's pock-marked face showed regret. "Maybe I can help you, however." He opened the door bearing the sign "Entrance Forbidden" and shouted, "Matveyevna!"

A woman appeared in the door, dressed to leave, a handknitted shawl over her head half covering her wrinkled face. She was probably the same age as the clerk but she looked ten years older. She smiled affably, showing gaps between her few remaining teeth.

"What do you want, Guran?" she said.

Boris knew Guran must have been a nickname. In the East Siberian vernacular, this word denoted everybody born east of Lake Baikal.

"Look, Matveyevna, this is Boris Petrovich, from Kalinin. He doesn't know, however, anybody in Bologoe. Would you accept him for the night?"

"Why, sweetheart, you shouldn't sleep in the street. I charge only one ruble. And you'll have a cup of tea." She smiled at Boris, but her fierce eyes contradicted her manner and servile tone. Probably she was much in need of this one ruble. As to her interrogating glance, here in the province they were all most distrustful.

The hotel door banged behind them and the cold night embraced Boris and the old woman. Although plump and stocky, she moved along the almost invisible sidewalk at an astonishingly fast pace. These old vixens were expected to be weak, to cough without any apparent reason and to moan when they had to lift something. Yet, this creature ran. Well, she must not be that old after all. Maybe the dim light in the hotel lobby had deceived him. He tried to stifle a faint alarm of anxiety ringing somewhere in the back of his mind.

The woman approached a dark, two-story wooden building which copied many such dilapidated structures lining the narrow curved street. The sweet odor of rotten wood and mildew hung over the neighborhood.

The house was tiny. It had only a door and a window on the ground floor and two windows upstairs.

"I'll make the tea now." She bent over the big Russian stove.

The kitchen looked calm and cozy with its dark corners where the cobwebs had remained untouched for years. As the common superstition held, a spider web was the sign from the *domovoy*, the house's spirit, that he was benevolently disposed towards the family.

The woman assembled pieces of wood on the stove grates, and soon yellow tongues of flame danced behind the cast-iron shutter. She moved deftly and noiselessly, removing dust from the benches, sorting out dishes and cutting a loaf of bread. Then she put on the shaky table a pot adorned with red poppies, and the aroma of currant leaves, used in this area instead of tea, filled the room.

"You know, sweetheart, we don't have sugar here."

"Thanks, *babushka*. I like it without sugar." Boris swallowed a few gulps of the pleasant warming potion.

It was about one o'clock. Deep silence embraced the house. The clang of dishes in the hands of the old creature and those mysterious creaks which can be heard in all wooden houses during the late hours, emphasized the silence of this chilly autumn night.

The woman finished her evening chores. She moved some old rags and revealed a huge axe. This was an axe like those used in the past by the traveling wood-cutters. They used to put a backpack with bread, salt, matches and *makhorka* tobacco on their shoulders and leave the village for the wilderness. They never parted with the axe. It was a universal tool. Using just such an axe, these woodsmen could topple a tree, build a hut and carve a fancy oakwood spoon with an ornamented handle. And if a fugitive from one of the many Russian jails, desperate from hunger and loneliness, attacked the lone lumberjack or hunter to take his food and tobacco, the axe was put into swift action. One swing and the assailant's head, severed cleanly from the torso, would roll away.

The woman crossed herself several times and her thin lips moved silently, apparently saying her prayers. Finally she led Boris upstairs.

It was pitch dark in the stairway. The old stairs creaked and the railing shook and rattled. The woman opened an invisible door and over her shoulder Boris perceived the pale rectangle of a window in the small room.

"You'll forgive me, sweetheart, we don't have light here. The bulb is dead. It was a small nice bulb, served a long time. And now it's dead. They only sell the large ones now, very expensive. In the old days we used candles, but I haven't seen them in ages."

Boris's eyes now faintly discerned something which must have been a bed. He stumbled over a chair and fell upon a cabinet.

Such cabinets could not be purchased anymore. This one was a remnant of sturdy old-fashioned furniture, once the pride of a thrifty merchant's wife. Built of iron-hard oak, its thick doors could withstand a canon ball. It was a rare relic. Almost all of such furniture had been burnt during the long winters of the twenties, thirties, forties, and fifties, when a supply of wood for heating lasted for only a few weeks.

"Now you undress, sweetheart, and lay your things neatly on the chair, and the jacket you hang over the chair's back."

"Yes, *Babushka*," said Boris astounded by the odd instruction.

"And what about medals? Do you have any?"

"Medals? I don't have any medals. Why?"

"Well, sweetheart. Just so you lay everything neatly . . . Good night."

Half asleep, Boris answered "Good night" and sat down on the bed. He took off his shoes. The woman quietly closed the door.

Then something went wrong. Boris heard the sound of a key in the lock.

As he used to do when encountering a baffling mathematical problem, Boris tried to construct in his mind some plausible explanation. Was it her habit to keep the door locked at all times? No. When they reached the door, it was not locked. Boris cautiously moved towards the door. The floor creaked so loudly that it was probably heard all over the house. He stopped. No other sound broke the dead silence. He seemed to hear his heart beating.

He stepped forward and his hand, extended, touched the knob. The door was locked.

He turned from the door. The pale rectangle of the window hung in the darkness. It took him three steps to get to the bed. Boris knelt there and his hands found the knob on the window. He tried to turn the knob. It did not yield. Then he clenched both hands on the knob and applied more force. The knob now turned with a screeching sound. The window folds opened and cold air struck his face. And then he understood why the sound of the opening window would not have worried the old wench; thick bars attached from the outside to the window's frame crossed the rectangle of a sky covered with fast moving clouds. Behind the clouds, a pale spot indicated the position of the moon. Boris closed the window.

Now he turned to the cabinet. He extended his hand and sensed the smoothness of the polished wood. Prepared to find the door locked, he turned the knob. The mammoth slab moved on its hinges and Boris peered into the black vault. He stood motionless, waiting for his eyes to adjust to the darkness. Then the moon crawled from behind the clouds and revealed the body of a man.

The man was naked. His head had apparently been hit by a heavy sharp tool. Before the moon had hidden again behind the moving clouds, Boris grasped a number of other details. A pair of boots. Old crumpled clothing on hooks. And a neatly folded military uniform on the cabinet's wooden floor. One of the shoulder straps was exposed, showing the two stars of a Lieutenant.

A thick metallic bar rested on wooden supports attached to the cabinet's walls. This bar once served to carry heavy fur coats. Boris pushed the bar from the supports and weighed it in his hand. It could be a weapon.

On the inner side of the cabinet's door horizontal levers were connected to a pair of vertical rods. Turning the knob placed outside the door counter clockwise, one could rotate the horizontal levers, lifting one vertical rod and lowering another. The rods then entered iron shanks clamped to the bottom and the ceiling of the cabinet, thus deadlocking the door. To open it, one had to turn the knob clockwise. But from inside, the rods could be moved up and down just by pressing on the horizontal levers. Boris knew this mechanism from his childhood. The kids loved to play hide-and-seek. To lock oneself in such a cabinet from inside was one of the most exciting adventures in those childhood games. He would have to play the game again.

He undressed and hung his coat and jacket on the chair. He folded his shirt and pants and laid them on the seat. He listened to the sounds, to the creaks of the wooden structure. He lifted the body of the unknown man. It was cold and heavy, as if made of clay and lead. He placed the body on the bed. He covered it with the blanket tucking the edges under the legs and arms. He turned the dead face to the window. Then he entered the cabinet. He pressed on the levers and the vertical rods slid snugly into the shanks. Now, as in hide-and-seek, he had locked himself in the oakwood fortress.

He leaned against the wall. And waited.

He waited through the long hours of this unreal night. Everything was silent. The stairs did not creak anymore, as if the old house itself fell asleep to skip the chill of the endless night hours. Long they are, the November nights in Northern Russia. And after endless waiting, the sounds of steps in the street echoed from the windows and walls. A key rasped in the lock and screeching hinges announced somebody's arrival. Steps sounded on the stairs. The door creaked slightly. Steps approached the bed. A powerful thud shook the house. And for several seconds afterwards, thin rattles traveled all through the house, gradually subsiding but still sending waves and trembles through the vibrating walls and cracked floorboards.

Then the visitor struck a match. The slot between the cabinet's door and its wall glowed faintly. The match's flame died and a hand touched the knob. Boris clenched the levers. He felt the force outside striving to control the knob. But the long arms of the inner levers increased with the force applied by Boris. The person outside apparently realized that the odds were against him. Boris heard steps and voices. Something clanged, and the grating sound testified that the person outside started to drill through the door. The sturdy oakwood hardly yielded to the bit. Then Boris heard the voice of the old wench, "Stop it, Guran. God has saved him from your axe, so let him go . . . He does not even have any *cockle-shells*, not a single medal. As to *bashli*, such a lad, he probably has in his pocket just a couple of rubles."

"D-devil w-with you," shouted Guran. So, this was the hotel clerk. He evidently had just finished his shift.

"Fetch the auger, however, old bitch."

The woman apparently obeyed and Guran resumed drilling.

The auger made its way through the door but met the steel rod. Guran cursed and started to drill in a different place. He made one more hole but the auger did not reach Boris's body.

"I tell you, Guran, God's saving him. Give up, you blood drinker."

"You old scold, we can't let him go. Were it just between me and God, I wouldn't do it for all the gold in Siberia. However, if I don't fulfill the quota, your God will not save us from Plague."

"Always this damned Plague. When will God punish him?" murmured the woman.

"Where is the axe, fuck your God-soul-cross-faith-ass-mother?"

A deafening thud shook the cabinet. Guran, with all his might, struck over and over at the trembling cabinet. The old wood slowly yielded slivers and chips. But Boris knew the outcome was predetermined. In a few short minutes, the huge axe would destroy the door. He heard some other thuds besides the blows of the axe. Was it his blood thumping in his temples? The last minutes of his life were running out. Boris dropped the bar and knelt. His only desire was to stop the deafening blows.

Suddenly the thuds stopped. For an instant, the silence was as deafening as the thunder of thuds before. Then he heard a peevishly shrill female voice shouting from outside, "You fucking hooligans! Children are sleeping, you whores! Dawn just coming. I am calling the Militsia."

Steps thundered down the stairs and a hush descended upon the room. Boris slowly straightened up, listening. The woman outside continued to curse and shout but her voice now came from a much farther distance. In the house everything was still.

Boris cautiously opened the cabinet's door. The room was empty. The window was already lit by dawn. The skull of the unknown Lieutenant, freshly smashed, rested on the pillow. The door was ajar. Boris pushed open the window folds and looked through the grating. The rusty remnants of a rain pipe, to his left, dangled from the overhang.

Then a noise came again from the ground floor, steps and undiscernable words. Boris shoved the metallic bar between the wooden window frame and the grating. He leaned his body upon the bar, the muscles on his back and shoulders bulging in strain. The approaching steps were at the door when the left side of the grating suddenly broke off the frame and displayed tips of rusted nails on the wooden boards which now dangled from the grating's left edge. The big man appeared in the door, the axe in his hand. Pushing aside the grating, Boris leapt through the window. Cold air scorched his skin. He found himself on the pavement among the fragments of ice crushed by his fall.

The house door swung open, and the big man appeared on the threshold. Boris rushed along the empty street, his bare feet slipping on frozen puddles. He was almost at the corner when a police van flew out from the side street, the brakes screeching, while two policemen in their violet coats pulled out guns and pushed Boris on the pavement.

"There are murderers back there," Boris shouted but the policemen dragged him over the cobblestones, his knees and ribs leaving a bloody trail on the icy bumps.

It was close to noon the next day, this last Sunday of November, when the iron clang of the cell door awoke Boris from oblivion. A policeman tossed a pile of clothes and the vinyl bag on the bespattered cement floor. He unlocked the handcuffs and ordered Boris to dress.

The dark corridor smelled of burnt buckwheat *kasha*, dirty clothing, sweat and rusty iron. This was the odor of a garrison barracks or a jail. Yet in a barracks it would also smell of munition oil. Boris knew this stench from his two years in compulsory military service.

Then a door leading into the inner quarters of the jail swung open, following the kick of a boot. Another policeman dragged in a female body. It looked like a pile of rags. And Boris recognized his hostess. A bloody strip hooped her mouth; her swollen eyes were closed. Unwittingly, Boris gasped. One of her eyes opened and peered at Boris's face. The woman opened her swollen lips and Boris discerned the words, "God bless you, sweetheart." The policeman cursed and pulled the woman into the next cell.

A Captain was sitting at a shabby desk shuffling files. A board above his head gave his name, Nikiforov. He pushed a form towards Boris who signed without reading it.

Captain Nikiforov looked tired and bored. Without glancing at Boris, he said with no expression on his red square face, "Citizen Tarutin, Boris Petrovich. The analysis has not shown signs of inebriation in your blood. The pertinent *organs* have made the decision. You are now being released to proceed to the place of your legal residence. After you have signed this form, any complaints regarding the treatment given to you in the Militsia will constitute a criminal slander punishable under clause 70 of the Criminal Code of the RSFSR. Moreover, you are forbidden, under the threat of criminal prosecution, to disclose to any person, including your immediate family, anything you have seen in the Chamber of the Preliminary Confinement. Have you understood that, citizen?"

"Yes, comrade Captain. I have understood. Thank you. Please, may I ask you, who those people are, this Guran and the woman? And the man in the cabinet, a Lieutenant? Why did they kill him?"

Captain Nikiforov stared at Boris. Then he grinned. Obviously enjoying the opportunity to show his access to confidential and important information, he said in a different, almost unofficial tone, "Look, this Lieutenant they had tricked into a box, he was a visitor, just like you. No acquaintances in this town. They never touched our local folks."

"But why?"

"Well, they did not shun anything, clothing, money. And," the Captain chuckled, "*cockle-shells.*" Here Nikiforov, as if he had stumbled over the word which slid from his tongue, stopped."

"But who is this Plague they mentioned, comrade Captain?"

The Captain's face again changed, he pursed his lips and returned to his cool official manner, "Whatever you need to know, citizen, the competent *organs* will let you know, at the proper time."

"But, as a victim, I am entitled to know . . ."

"You're not entitled to anything. Mind your business, citizen. Now go home and wait until you are summoned."

The first snow started to cover the dirty cobblestones. Boris was running along the curved streets of Bologoe to the railway station. After the stale atmosphere of the jail, the crisp air was giddying and beautiful. Inhaling deeply, Boris jumped over the giant puddle in front of the station. Far to the left, among the white-powdered fir trees, he saw the approaching string of green cars. This was the speed train Leningrad-Moscow. He had just a few minutes to make it.

Chapter 2

THE TRAIN ATTENDANT LOOKED SURPRISED WHEN, DURING the one-minute stop in Bologoe, two men boarded his car. This expensive speed train, on its entire route from Leningrad to Moscow, made only two stops, one in Bologoe and another in Kalinin. Not many people in Bologoe could afford tickets on this train.

Prompted by the luxurious musquash fur cap the first passenger wore, the attendant greeted this man with a servile bow. Such a cap could not be acquired other than through a special distribution store catering only to high-level officials. Because of this cap, the attendant even failed to notice that the man's coat was worn and of an average quality. The musquash cap had made this man look typical of the passengers on the train.

When this passenger rolled open the door of the car to step inside, warm air wafted from the well-heated interior. Then Tarutin handed over his ticket to the attendant. The latter suspiciously sized up Tarutin's crumpled overcoat, disheveled russet hair, creased vinyl bag. Tarutin smiled and touched the stubble on his cheeks. His ticket was in order, so the attendant reluctantly moved aside to let Boris into the car.

Unlike the local train where brown pallets covered with graffiti hung low over the heads of passengers sitting shoulder to shoulder on narrow wooden benches, here rows of soft bucket chairs lined a carpeted aisle.

Boris found an empty aisle seat right next to the entrance. The wheels started to rattle and the train, skirting curved rows of drab structures, sped up along the shore of the glinting lake. Boris stretched his legs under the seat in front of him and settled in. He saw somebody's head, with dark curly hair, above the seat in front of him. The window seat in that front row was empty. A gray briefcase of artificial leather, apparently belonging to the man with curly hair, rested in the rack. Such briefcases rarely could be purchased in stores. This one was familiar to Boris. A few months earlier, a commission from the Ministry of Higher Education came to inspect Kalinin State University. The commission had indicated as the main shortcoming, "excessive percentage of faculty members not participating to the full extent in the research programs directed towards the fulfillment of the five-year-plan goals." On the other hand, the commission emphasized the high level of Party propaganda activities and especially praised, for this important achievement, the University Party Secretary, Rodion Glebovich Baev.

Soon after the commission had reported its findings to the Minister, the latter awarded the University twenty of these gray briefcases and forty vinyl bags. The Rector, Professor Sergei Pavlovich Nekipalov, personally compiled the list of those entitled to purchase briefcases and bags which went for twenty rubles a briefcase and seven a bag. All twenty briefcases went to Full Professors. The bags fell into the hands of Assistant Professors, "Asses." Once such ass-bag rested now on Boris's knees.

A mascot dangled on the briefcase's wood-stuffed handle. This was Misha the Bear, the official mascot of the 1980 Moscow Olympics. During the months preceding the Games, members of teams which had won the University championships in Olympic sports were awarded such mascots as signs of honor. Only one person at the University was both a Full Professor eligible for a briefcase and a member of a winning sport team. This was Boris's friend, Professor Nikolai Ivanovich Galaunov, an eminent specialist in Technical Physics and a ski champion. But the dark curly hair above the seat back was quite different from the partially gray, frequently disheveled, blond hair of Galaunov. The man in the front seat was somebody else.

The man in the window seat in Boris's row gazed steadily out the window. Fir trees flickered past the foggy glass. Then a red-bricked station flashed by, the high speed of the train merging the letters on the board with the station name into an illegible black ripple. The man evidently tried to catch the station's name; he pressed his cheek to the chilly window glass, turning his head and squinting at the quickly disappearing ghostly image of an icy platform and of dark half-circular windows on a red background.

"That was Vyshny Volochek," Boris said without glancing at the window.

"Oh! And the next?"

"The next would be Likhoslavl. Karelians' realm."

"I see," the man said. "You know this area by heart, don't you?"

"I was born here."

"And lived here happily ever after?"

"Longer than that. It will soon be eleven centuries."

"You mean . . ." the man said.

"Yes, Tarutins have been living in this area from the times of Prince Rurik."

"Which makes it from the ninth century. So, Rurik was your ancestor?"

"He was not," Boris said. "When Rurik of Jutland came with his gang to these forests, the Tarutins already were among the chieftains of Slavs. Of Tverichi, to be specific. The Tarutins had been registered in the so-called sixth book of Russian nobility, along with the Pleshcheevs, Veresaevs and Bunins. We are supposed to have been here longer than the families descending from Rurik and his armbearers."

"So, Tarutin, is that your name? You gave a lecture last Friday at the school in Bologoe, true?"

"Yes. Why?"

"Then I know who you are. My son has told me a lot about you. He is just crazy about your lectures. My name is Litvin. Doctor Litvin."

"Oh, the little Litvin is your son. You must be proud of him. I would be happy to have him next year among my students at the University. An exceptionally bright boy."

"Just don't tell him that, Professor," Litvin said. "This is a small world. You know, unlike you, we are newcomers in these swamps. Originally we came from the Ukraine. I have been serving in the Army for quite a few years. Used to live everywhere, mainly in Siberia and the Far East. In all the rat holes. Recently succeeded in getting released. My first civilian job was in the Bologoe hospital. A rotten hospital, even aspirin was in shortage. Now I am going to Kalinin, to get a new assignment from the Region Health Authority. This time, hopefully, one which accounts for my specialization."

"As a surgeon?"

"Oh, no. Once I dreamed of becoming a surgeon. But . . . with my name, I was lucky to get into a medical institute at all. They opened a new medical institute, in Tyumen, that year. They had more openings than applicants. So I went from Kiev to Tyumen to become a doctor. But, still, I had no chance to choose my specialization. They assigned me to what nobody else wanted. Psychiatry. And that's where I am."

"And unhappy with that?" Boris said.

"Well, no. I am content . . . Psychiatry could be a great field. But . . ." Litvin stopped short, apparently deciding against saying too much and said instead, "Tarutin, this is a famous name. For instance, the composer, Pavel Tarutin . . ."

"He was my great-grandfather."

"Usually this goes down the line, from father to son, the talent."

"If a father has a chance to bring up his son. I don't remember my father. He died when I was small."

"Illness? Or an accident?"

"Neither . . ." and Boris looked at the doctor for the first time. The doctor returned the gaze. Seemingly, both men felt satisfied with this mutual inspection. Then Litvin said, "You see, my father perished in 1952. He was a writer. In Yiddish. A wholehearted admirer of Stalin and devoted communist. Stalin thanked him by shooting him in Lubianka's basement."

"My father," Boris said, "was picked up one night in 1953. Doctors' plot."

"What do you mean? He was not a Jew."

"No, but he was a brain surgeon."

"Wait a minute. Was he Professor Tarutin, the author of the Handbook of a Brain Surgeon?"

"You know the book . . ."

"Everybody knows it. An unsurpassed source . . . My God, I had no idea Professor Tarutin perished in this way. How did he manage to get mixed up in a Jewish predicament?"

"He just happened to be a descendant of the Tarutins and to marry a descendant of the Roksaevs. These are my mother's people. Also an ancient family. As the legend goes, they were descendants of a Tatar prince, Roksa. In the fifteenth century he was baptized and became a Russian Prince. With such a genealogy, my father admirably fitted the needs of Beria's henchmen, as one of two or three people with unmistakably non-Jewish names, added to a group of fifty or more doctors with obviously Jewish names. So the message was unequivocal; everybody in the country understood that the Jews were the target. On the other hand, a couple of Tarutins on the list of culprits could lend credibility to the explanations of the Western fools thirsting to whitewash Stalin's thugs—to prove that there was no anti-Semitic trend whatsoever, just a bunch of traitors caught in the middle of a devious plot."

"True. And after Stalin's demise . . ."

"My father was not among those who came back from jail. They delivered his clothing to my mother. With blood stains. She never recovered. She died two years later."

Suddenly Litvin put a finger to his lips and pointed at the front seat. Boris, too, noticed that the man with curly hair; this mysterious owner of the gray briefcase and the Olympic mascot seemed to be not quite indifferent to their conversation. He shifted several times in his chair, his shoulder now protruding into the aisle. This was not a comfortable position but it would be natural for a person trying to overhear, through the soft humming of the wheels, what was being said one row back. There was something familiar about the figure of this man, his narrow shoulder and the dark curly hair, but Boris could see too little to identify him. Boris shrugged, letting Litvin understand that whatever the reason for the man's obvious attempt to overhear their talk, just a casual curiosity or a professional zeal, they had not said anything secret. Times had changed after Stalin's death; nowadays, people would hardly be picked up just for a casual chat on a train, more so since it related to some thirty-year-old stories. Still, both now felt reluctant to talk.

"Your cap," Boris said, "it's a fine piece."

"Yes, one of my patients happened to be a clerk in a special store . . ." Then the conversation died.

It was almost dark when the train thundered over the bridge crossing the Volga. The dreary walls of barns and depots with lamps here and there threw pale triangles of light onto wire fences. Kalinin, which its four hundred thousand inhabitants still preferred to call Tver, as was its name for almost a thousand years.

Boris and Litvin descended into a tunnel leading from the platform to the street. The doctor was saying something and Boris seemed to listen. Suddenly Boris's heart stopped. In front of him was a slowly moving pair of beautifully shaped female legs. Very slowly, they ascended the stairs, and the symmetrical motion of the perfect calves, both tender and powerful, was full of mystery. The legs looked somewhat familiar. His heart filled with immense joy.

As the beautiful legs climbed the stairs Boris could not keep his eyes from their smooth motion. His eyes followed, embracing the slender ankles wrapped in thick blue woolen socks folded over the white-and-blue sport shoes; the glittering capron stockings contouring the muscles; the mysterious cavities on the back of round knees; the hand-knitted skirt and sweater tightly following the slim waist and wide sporty shoulders. Doctor Litvin followed Boris's stare and understandingly pursed his lips. "I see . . . Yes, these are magnificent legs . . . Good luck, Tarutin . . . So long."

They ascended from the tunnel and found themselves on a slippery pavement flickering in the light beams falling from streetcars and taxis. Now the girl was not on the stairs any more, and Boris saw that she was almost his height. Her auburn hair, cut short, stressed her colty look.

He knew he had seen these legs before. Probably she was a student at the University. She boarded a streetcar, and when she turned back to look at somebody, he saw her face, with dark childlike eyes, straight graceful nose, and full lips. Her glance caught Boris, apparently attracted by his unswerving stare, then she disappeared into the crowded streetcar.

Boris stood there until the tram, ringing and screeching on the shallow arc of rails skirting the yellow building of the Militsia, crawled away slowly. This tram was marked Marinovo, the remote Eastern suburb, location of a huge chemical plant. The tram's ringing gradually subsided behind the Militsia building. Boris breathed deeply and walked across the square, heading for the building of the Kalinin University, a few blocks from the railway, in Sadovy Pereulok.

The smell of burnt leaves reached him. He knew there were no leaves to burn at this time of year. In a few more minutes this odor would become denser; instead of leaves it would stink of rotten meat; a little later it would reach its full power, the stench spreading all over the city. These were mercaptanes, toxic chemicals appearing once every few hours in the blue-gray smoke pouring day and night from the tall brick chimney erected above the vast chemical plant in Marinovo, the suburb to which the tram had carried away the girl with the magnificent legs. At least twice a week, especially in winter when the wind blew from the East, there was no escape from the Marinovo plant's stench.

He walked the dark streets, stepping over the pits and bumps, and now, instead of the horrible weekend in Bologoe, the image of the girl with her short-cut heap of auburn hair, floated before his eyes. She was not alone at the railway station. Somebody had accompanied her.

The building in which the faculty of physics, the departments of languages and the University's Administration were located, was almost completely dark on this Sunday evening. Just a few windows and the entrance glowed.

Boris crossed the asphalt rectangle in front of the building and walked into the lobby. It was empty. Only the woman janitor, Alevtina, sat at her usual post, a shabby desk at the entrance. A black telephone was on the desk, the sole telephone in the building besides those in the offices of the Rector, Nekipalov, and of the Party Secretary, Baev. Alevtina seemed to be taking a nap. She half-opened her muddy eyes and said, "Ah, Boris Petrovich. Your man, Valushin, had been waiting for you since yesterday. Wouldn't go away." Then she opened her eyes wider and chuckled. Boris understood her glance, looked at his crumpled coat and touched the stubble on his cheeks. Alevtina touched his sleeve and said, "I won't tell anybody. You men, all of you, you need it often, this damned potion, vodka." She nodded several times showing that all men were cut from the same cloth, professors and peasants alike.

She did know men. Alevtina's moniker was "bookwoman," not because she was an avid reader, but because of her sexual arrangements. She had been given this nickname because an interested client, passing her desk, would place a book on the desk. Somewhere in the book was a five ruble bill. She fished the bill out and suggested the time. If the man agreed, he nodded and the deal was made. The room where she lived with her two daughters, fourteen and eleven years old, was just around the corner. She certainly knew all about men.

Alevtina was in her late thirties. Despite her partially gray hair, it was obvious that she was once a pretty woman.

She had large, firm breasts and Boris remembered how, years ago, challenging sparks in her pale blue eyes had made men's hearts beat a little faster.

Boris handed her a book from his bag. The book was in English. As Boris was not a client Alevtina looked with disbelief. Still, she leafed through the book. There was no money in it.

"This is Talin's book," Boris said. "Would you please give it to him first thing tomorrow morning? I borrowed it just for the day, but have had no chance to return it, so he might worry."

"Oh, I see." The expression of surprise left Alevtina's face. "But Talin's here. You better give it to him yourself, as I might forget." She closed her eyes to continue her nap.

Boris took the book belonging to the Acting Head of the English Department, Talin, and walked to the magnetic lab located on the ground floor, just opposite the entrance. He saw through the matted glass of the door that the lab's interior was brightly lit. So, his technician, Evgeny Valushin, was indeed waiting for him, despite it being Sunday and a late hour. They had to prepare the demonstration experiment on the Barkhausen effect for tomorrow's classes.

Chapter 3

BORIS SWUNG OPEN THE DOOR OF THE MAGNETIC LAB. The lanky figure of Valushin hurried behind benches that held black-painted magnetic devices. Valushin snatched up a ragged cloth and threw it over an object behind his body. The nickel-plated handles of amplifiers, resistance decades and an oscilloscope reflected the dazzling beam of a powerful mercury lamp. A big magnet stood on the floor exposing its red copper-wire coils. This magnet concealed the object Valushin had covered with the cloth.

Then Valushin looked at Boris. The pouches under Valushin's light-blue eyes made him look ten years older than twenty-seven. He recognized Boris and he half-smiled. Boris had never seen Valushin smile fully. Then Valushin, as he usually did when he met Boris, took the posture of a soldier in front of a commander.

"What's that you have there?" Boris asked, nodding towards the object covered by the spotty cloth.

"It's waiting for you," Valushin said in a raucous voice and removed the cloth revealing a canvas about a meter wide and seventy centimeters high, taut, on a home-made stand. "You've been out a long time. I was just finishing this."

The dazzling rays of the mercury lamp shone into Boris's eyes. He turned the lamp towards the yellow wall. Now, in its diffuse reflected light, he could scrutinize the painting. It was made in mute, dark colors, with a few contrasting bright spots. For a long while Boris stood motionless, comprehending his technician's creation.

"Zhenya, what do you call this?" he asked finally.

"Widows," Valushin said, nervously squeezing an unlit cigarette.

On the canvas was the interior of a rustic North-Russian hut, *izba*. A bare electric bulb hung drearily above a crude wooden table. In the corner where once traditionally hung an icon with Jesus or the Virgin, now hung a fly-specked likeness of Karl Marx tacked to an unpainted rough board. A candle stood on a small shelf in front of the picture. At the table, several women huddled, singing, their black mouths gaping wide, their souls given over to the song. Their gnarled hands either rested on the table or were tucked under ragged aprons. Widows of war. And of purges. Worn out, sinewy, black from their gloomy life, hard labor, miserable daily rounds. They poured out, in the song, their loneliness, their hopeless anguish, their incurable pain. A girl, about ten, stood in the foreground, leaning against the timbered wall. Thin as a blade of grass, innocent, listening to the widows' song, as if foreseeing her own future.

"Breathtaking," Boris said. "A cruel truth . . . And, of course, real anti-Soviet propaganda without a single word. No surprise, they won't give you an exhibition . . . Just to think of it, such a talent perishing."

"If you like it . . ." Valushin said.

"It's great. It's worth a million times more than all the

daubs for which Gerassimov, Serov, and all those ass-lickers from the Union of Soviet Painters get their prizes and awards. With such a talent, you shouldn't let yourself be a slave to vodka."

"Boris Petrovich, there's no cure. People like me, we are condemned," Valushin said calmly. "You know, *The Joy of Russia is drinking* . . . If I could have only one exhibition, only one, in all my life. Then I could die . . . Well, forget it. If you like this, take it. As a gift from Valushin. For everything you've done . . ."

"I haven't done anything. It's just crazy, such a masterpiece. How can I accept it?" Boris said.

"You have done what my own father wouldn't have done. You know, I had been kicked out of seventeen jobs. They put up with me only until my first drinking bout. As if I wanted them, those damned benders . . . You're the first boss I've ever had willing to tolerate my misfortune . . . And you hardly drink yourself . . . I don't need this canvas. Please, it's yours."

"Well, I'll take it, along with those other pieces you've given me before, just to hold. You may want to know that Professor Galaunov, Nikolai Ivanovich, has seen your paintings and admires them. He'll much appreciate this piece . . ."

Valushin carefully wrapped the canvas in several newspapers and tied them with a thin rope. Handing it over to Boris, Valushin said, "I better tell you, I don't think you'll be able to cover up for me much longer. Last Friday, this boar Baev, the Party Secretary, warned me that one more absence, even for one day, and I am out."

"Yes, he's a pig, everybody knows that." Boris frowned. "You think you'll have another bout soon?"

"I can feel it coming. It's always the same. First, vodka no longer seems loathsome. And the nightmares start . . ."

"Listen, Zhenya, I want you to help me to help you.

When you feel like you're on the edge . . . Before you take the first drink, just tell me . . . Promise?"

"I'll try, Boris Petrovich . . ."

"Good. Now, you probably want to smoke. Go ahead. In the meantime, I have to see Talin. And then we'll start to work."

Boris saw the tall figure hobble towards the corridor's corner. With a cigarette in hand, his clothes looking too large for him, Valushin disappeared around the corner, heading to the men's room located in the left wing of the building.

Boris walked up stairs lit by a dim emergency light. His footsteps resounded along the hollow corridors of the nearly deserted building.

From the landing, he saw that no light glowed behind the frosted glass of Talin's office door. Still, he went to the door and tried the knob. The office was locked. On a board beside the door, several announcements hung, some of them obviously old, already yellow and dusty. One of them was a note written in Talin's wide writing on a sheet torn out of a notebook—"Shall be back soon." There was no way of knowing whether this note was a recent one or from days ago. Was the doorwoman Alevtina wrong about Talin being in the building? Or had he left while Boris was talking to Valushin? Boris pushed the book under the door and walked away.

When Boris entered the magnetic lab again, Valushin, too, walked in.

"Before we start, I've got to eat something, I'm starved," Boris said.

Valushin quickly pulled out a drawer, "I have some bread here," he said. Boris thanked him and bit into the crumbling rye bread. The taste reminded him of how, years before, while working towards his Candidate of Sciences degree in this same magnetic lab, he used to chew such bread, almost all he could afford at that time, during the long hours of overnight experiments.

Then he drank water from the tap. They started now to assemble the set-up for tomorrow's lecture. Actually Valushin did all the manual work. After several months in the lab, he was able to set up the experiment on his own. He never did so, however, unless Boris watched, mainly because of a deeply ingrained sense of subordination; it was typical of the people suffering from the most common Russian disease, drinking.

Boris watched Valushin attach a tiny wire to the end of another, even thinner wire. The microscopic wire, lost in Valushin's hard fingers, met the center of the opposite wire clamped in a vise. Boris knew from his previous experience with Valushin's skills, a measurement with a precise caliper would not reveal a deviation from the perfect alignment. Then Valushin made an imperceptible movement with the other hand holding a soldering iron and the two wires converged into one piece, the point of connection becoming undiscernable from the rest of the wires' length.

Then Valushin took a sheet of transparent tracing paper and without using a rule, drew a set of coordinates, perfectly straight and mutually perpendicular. He wrote on the axes the graduation marks and units. When he was drawing lines and letters, his hands, unlike other times, did not shake. He looked with apparent satisfaction at the set-up he had finished and his sad face with its low-cut flaxen hair and deep creases on the cheeks, softened a little.

Then he went again to the rest room to smoke.

Boris stayed in the lab to test the set-up's performance. He watched the peaks of the Barkhausen effect on the round-shaped screen of the oscilloscope. It was an obsolete model purchased in a Moscow store which specialized in selling used or rejected Military equipment. As with all this equipment, the oscilloscope was expected to collapse time and again, but Valushin managed to keep it operational.

"You wanted to see Talin," Valushin said, walking back into the lab, "so I've checked in his office. He's not there. It's locked and dark."

They lifted the entire set-up, including the seventy kilograms of the oscilloscope, and placed it on a wheelcart, preparing it for the transfer to the lecture hall.

Suddenly, a deep thud sounded next door in the mechanical lab. Boris and Valushin glanced at each other. There was no light on the frosted glass of the connecting door. And no more sounds.

"What the devil was that?" Boris said.

Valushin walked to the connecting door and pushed it open. His hand touched the switch on the wall and the ceiling lights in wire baskets threw bright checkered patterns on the black-painted testing machines lined up along the yellow walls. Through the open connecting door, Boris saw the door from the corridor opening. Alevtina, the janitor, appeared there.

She stared into the lab and screamed. The shrill sound flew through the deserted corridors and echoed in remote corners and empty stairways. Boris rushed to the connecting doors.

Over Valushin's shoulder, he saw the rows of hardness testers, the Gagarin's press, the small impact tester. And, in the center of the row, the big Charpy impact tester. Once manually operated, this machine was recently upgraded by Valushin who had added to it an electronic circuit enabling one to use simple time-programming. A small black box atop the tester's stand held the electronic circuit. A set of zero-digits froze on its screen.

There was a man's body kneeling by the tester's stand. Its head, resting on the machine's table, was unnaturally twisted. The hands hung loosely as if they were just empty sleeves. The tester's pendulum hammer was down, its black-painted circular load half-covering the smashed head.

Now Boris recognized the man. This was the second most powerful man at Kalinin University, a former KGB officer, now the Secretary of the University Party Committee and a member of the region Party committee, *obkom*.

"It's Baev," Boris said, and Alevtina again started to scream, though not so loudly.

"Such a great man," she said, evidently by "great" meaning powerful. Indeed, the power this man possessed made incomprehensible his conversion into a motionless body, as if the enormous power over people's lives he wielded in life should have made him invulnerable even to the forces of death.

"Stop whining," Boris said to Alevtina. "Lock the entrance door. Nobody shall leave until the Militsia arrives. You hear me? Call the Militsia."

Alevtina did not respond. She stood at the door, hugging herself. Boris slapped her lightly on the cheek and pushed her towards the corridor. Then she obediently trotted away and Boris heard the heavy entrance door squeal followed by Alevtina nervously talking into the phone.

Valushin, two cigarettes in hand, walked back to the magnetic lab. Boris knelt down to the Charpy tester trying to figure out how Baev had managed to make his head a target for the pendulum hammer's six hundred-kilogram fall. The salty odor of blood mixed with the pervasive stench of mercaptanes that crept into the the building. Through the window, Boris saw that the snow again had started to fall and was gradually whitening the dark streets.

Chapter 4

THE NOISE OF APPROACHING CARS WAS MUTED AS ALWAYS when fresh snow covered the asphalt driveway. Engines snorted and died.

The knock at the entrance had the air of overbearing authority and Alevtina rushed to unlock the door. A Militsia officer walked in, accompanied by two more policemen, one tall and skinny, and the other thickset and short-legged, both in crumpled and dirty violet overcoats. A man wearing a white smock over his civilian winter coat, with a briefcase in hand, obviously an ambulance doctor, also walked in.

At first, Boris had an impression that the police officer was the same Captain Nikiforov he had met in Bologoe; he had the same red, square-shaped face with small eyes hidden in folds of fat. The officer announced his name which sounded like Nikiforov. Then Boris realized that the officer's name was not Nikiforov but Nifontov. He was older than Nikiforov and much fatter, with a belly sagging over his uniform belt which slanted forward over his puckering overcoat. And he was not a Captain but a Lieutenant.

"Who called the Militsia?" Nifontov asked, his narrow Mongolian-type eyes sizing up Alevtina, Boris and Valushin.

"That was *we*," Alevtina said. "*We* are the janitor here, Ponareva's *our* name." She stretched her hands along her hips and her eyes expressed the utmost readiness to be of help. "*We* are doing what *we were* told to do. *They* told me," and she pointed a finger at Boris. "*They are* a teacher here, Taluntin's *their* name, comrade Lieutenant." She never managed to pronounce names properly but Boris did not care to correct her. She did not mention Valushin, too insignificant a person to refer to.

"Good," the Lieutenant said. "Now, Kalugin, you tell me what happened."

"He is Tarutin, Boris Petrovich, not Kalugin and not Taluntin," Valushin said.

The Lieutenant looked Valushin up and down and said, "Shut up. You'll answer my questions when I tell you to open your mouth. You, doctor, follow me and this Kalugin man. And you, Kokin and Burda," he said to the policemen, "Check all over the building. Whoever you find, fetch them all here and keep them. Search every corner. This woman here, the janitor, will open every door for you. Go!"

The policemen, Kokin and Burda, shuffled away, preceded by Alevtina who walked with one shoulder forward, glancing back nervously at the policemen following behind.

In the mechanical lab, the body of Baev still knelt. The doctor glanced at the body and shrugged.

"It looks as if you don't need me here," the doctor said. "Your forensics expert is who you want here now."

"Is he dead?" Lieutenant Nifontov asked, staring dully at Baev's twisted head.

"Very intelligent question," the doctor said. "You see,

he's not a Militsioner, so he can hardly live with a pancake for a head."

"Write your conclusion, doctor, and get out of here," Nifontov said. "And you, Kalugin, tell me what happened."

"Alas, Lieutenant, I do not know too much. We had heard a sound, like 'bumm!' That's it. We came over here and it was like it is now."

"Bumm! That's all you can get from these intelligentsia people," the Lieutenant said. "Had you heard anything before that 'bumm'?"

"No, we did not. I think I understand what you mean. If there had been a struggle or whatever, we would have heard something. No. It was just this sudden 'bumm.'"

"Now, Kalugin, you work here? A Professor, ah? Then tell me what this machine is all about. How could this have happened?"

"Look, Lieutenant, this is an impact tester. We test here how different materials stand up to an impact. This lever, it hangs on a hinge. On the lever's lower end there is a load, this barbell. Now it is on Baev's head. By rotating this wheel, the lever is lifted. When it is vertical, the barbell is in its apex. Now look, here is an arrester, this short rod. It locks the pendulum in the upper position. If you pull the arrester out, the pendulum with the barbell swings down and hits the sample." Boris stopped talking. He realized suddenly that, prompted by the Lieutenant's question, he had gotten into his habit of a professional lecturer, accustomed to explain in detail how devices worked. He glanced at Baev's body and shuddered. But Nifontov seemed to listen with attention and Boris went on. "The sample is a bar of the material you want to test. You settle the sample in an anvil which is hidden now under Baev's head. Then you release the pendulum and let it fall. We used to do so manually. But, a couple of times, this barbell fell off the lever. Fortunately, nobody was hurt. But we realized it was unsafe. So, Valushin, my technician, has mounted this box which is a timer, coupled with an electromagnet. The magnet pulls the arrester out to let the pendulum fall. Now, you push these white buttons, and that's how you dial in the numbers. They appear on the screen, here. Say, you dial 10. Then ten seconds will elapse between the time you start and the actual fall of the load. So, you have ten seconds to move a few steps away. Now, if you use a regular sample, then the hammer's edge, after hitting the sample, goes through a slot in the anvil. Then the sound is just a crackle. But this time, Baev's head overlapped the slot, so the blow was transferred to the entire bench. That's why it was like the 'bumm' we heard."

"I see, you're a lecturer," Lieutenant Nifontov said. "Better tell me, if you didn't hear any noise, then you mean, this man, Baikin? . . . Baev. *Could* he have done this himself?"

"If he had wished to. All he had to do was to dial, say, ten seconds, then to push this red button, 'start.' This would have given him ten seconds, plenty of time to kneel at the bench and to settle his head upon the anvil. As simple as that."

The Lieutenant knelt himself and tried to look at Baev's head through the slot, from beneath the bench.

While explaining the operation of the impact tester, Boris had felt that something was wrong. Now he understood what it was. In the upper left corner of the timer's screen, there glowed a small letter. Usually this was an 's' which stood for 'seconds.' This time, instead of 's,' there was another letter. This was an 'm.' It meant minutes. Zhenya Valushin had the timer set up for a seconds-long delay. To readjust the timer from seconds to minutes, one had to unscrew the back cover on the timer's box and to replace a small potentiometer inside. The alternative potentiometer which would set the device for minutes instead of seconds, was kept in a drawer in the machine's stand.

In the tests Boris conducted with students, they never used the minutes-long delays. If Baev wanted to commit suicide, why would he bother to replace the potentiometer? Ten seconds was more than enough time to assume the position at the bench and to settle the head on the anvil. Moreover, as far as Boris knew, the former KGB Major, the Party Secretary of the University, lacked the knowledge and skill to tackle the timer. The timer had been changed by an expert who wished to increase the time span from the start button's depression till the hammer's fall. From ten seconds to ten minutes. Somebody for whom this difference between minutes and seconds was of importance. And, apparently, the person who had played with the timer should still be in the building.

In the lobby, Alevtina had turned all the lights on. The concrete floor gleamed dully under the bright beams.

A man entered the lobby from the left stairway. Professor Yosif Markovich Magidov, a theoretical physicist. He wore a winter-coat, with a time-rubbed fur collar, a hare fur cap and galoshes. He took off his metal-framed glasses and started to clean them with a handkerchief. His prominent eyes, the color of barley beer, blinked as if dazzled by the light. He was tall and lean, with dark brown curly hair and a pale narrow-boned face. Boris scarcely knew him except by name. Magidov kept his distance from everybody on the faculty. His science was all he seemed to care about. He rarely even spoke with other professors. Only those few students who selected Theoretical Physics as their major subject seemed to communicate at all with Magidov.

Magidov bowed silently to Boris and Valushin, and a woman appeared from the left stairway. Senior Lecturer Starkova. Big, flat-chested, raw-boned, with angular shoulders and a stern expression on her dried-up face, she looked at Magidov through slanted spectacles. Her lips twisted squeamishly. Magidov half-bowed. Starkova did not respond. Her yellow-tipped fingers pulled a cigarette from a silver case and, putting it into her mouth, she muttered, in a low voice, but loud enough to be overheard, "I guess it's some more Jewish skullduggery, our domestic Einsteins making trouble as always."

Magidov lowered his head and his pale cheeks flushed slightly.

Another woman entered the lobby, this time from the corridor in the side wing. Klava Turova, engineer in the Electron Microscopy lab. A roundish woman with dimpled soft cheeks and languishing eyes, with an airy heap of fair hair, vivaciousness written all over her pretty face. She smiled widely at Boris and wanted to say something, but Lieutenant Nifontov shouted, "Shut up! Not a single word without my permission. And you, Katurin, just keep clear of everybody."

Boris Tarutin shrugged, amused by this new distortion of his name. Apparently, Lieutenant Nifontov was not much better at remembering names than Alevtina.

Then Talin appeared from the right stairway. So Alevtina was right, Talin indeed was in. He was without a jacket, his short plump arms hugging his rotund body. His thick lips over a large rounded chin looked dry, and he wiped them with his short-fingered hands, his small blue eyes winking after the semidarkness of the stairway.

Professor Galaunov came down the stairs next. A robust man, if motionless, he would have looked bear-like, but in motion his body, even through the sloppily fitting clothes, displayed a play of well-trained muscles. When he walked, his long strides called to mind Peter the Great in Serov's famous painting. Peter the Great, however, shaved off his own beard and, moreover, forced the nobles to cut off their traditional beards thus ultimately humiliating the old Russian Princes and Boyars. But Galaunov's big nose, mouth and ears were buried in a curly blond beard. His bright blue eyes sparkled. A hand-knitted tri-colored scarf enveloped his thick neck and wide shoulders. Boris was one of the very few people who knew that knitting was among the hobbies of this ski champion and eminent physicist. He had knitted the scarf himself. Even fewer people shared with Boris the knowledge that the scarf's striped colors were those of the flag of pre-revolutionary Russia.

The policemen, Kokin and Burda, reappeared with Alevtina and announced that now everybody they could find on the premises was in the lobby.

Lieutenant Nifontov took Alevtina's seat and laid his brown-gloved hands upon the desk.

"Now, Lieutenant," Galaunov said, his roaring voice echoing from the remote corridors, "What the devil is all this about? I have been doing important work and that's why I am here at this time, as well, I guess, as everyone else. If you've anything to tell us, then do it fast."

Lieutenant Nifontov was not impressed. He sized up the tall figure of Galaunov who approached Alevtina's desk.

"You want it fast?" he said. "And if not? Then you'll sic your dog on my cat?" and he grinned, apparently fond of his joke.

"I see you've a cat," Galaunov said. "Poor creature. You must keep him in handcuffs at all times, to prevent him from fleeing." Galaunov sat down upon the desk. He was now face-to-face with the Lieutenant. He leaned upon his hand and his tri-colored scarf swung aside, revealing the lapels of his jacket, tight on his wide chest. Lieutenant Nifontov started to say something, which, from the expression of his reddened face, would be far from polite, but stopped with a half-opened mouth, staring at Galaunov's jacket lapels. He saw there three badges. One was a square-shaped silver platelet with the engraved words, "Master of Sport. USSR." The second was a smaller bronze lozenge, a relief of the Tver's ancient coat-of-arms on the background of the fancy domes of the famous Moscow Saint Basil cathedral. Members of the Kalinin chapter of the All-Russian Society for the Preservation of Russian Cultural Heritage wore this badge. But it was the third badge which attracted the Lieutenant's attention. This was a medal with a Lenin likeness on it. The sign of a Lenin Prize winner, the highest honor given by the Government for outstanding achievements in science or art.

Nifontov silently glanced at the badge. "Excuse me, comrade Lenin Prize winner," he said. "I apologize. Please, it's my duty to ask some questions. I'll not keep you a single second beyond the necessary minimum."

"The devil with your apologies. Go ahead, and fast. And start with the women."

"Of course, comrade Lenin Prize winner."

Galaunov climbed down from the desk and nodded to Klava. She approached the desk. Staring at her voluptuous body the Lieutenant tried to pull in his belly and to straighten his stooped shoulders. His face displayed a struggle between an impulse to meet her smile with his, and what he apparently considered his duty to stay formal.

"Your name, citizen," Nifontov said.

"Turova, Klavdiya. Better just Klava, Lieutenant," she said grinning and her breasts moved softly under her white, almost transparent blouse.

"Well, we'll record your full name, and now tell me what you wish to tell about the event . . ."

Before he finished the sentence, Klava already was answering. "I am sure, Lieutenant, you'll understand, you know I am a woman . . ." and when saying the word "woman," her shoulders made a twisting motion, and Nifontov almost repeated this movement with his slanted shoulders. "And if one is a man, you understand what I mean, Lieutenant. You won't condemn us, I am sure. Well, if you wish me to say, I was the beginning and the end of it. I alone. Since I am a woman . . ."

"Stop it, stop it," and Nifontov raised his brown-gloved hand as if trying to hamper the flow of Klava's words. "What the devil is all this about? We all see that you're a woman . . ."

Somebody from outside shook the door. Alevtina threw a questioning look at Nifontov.

"Kokin, see who's there," the Lieutenant said, reluctantly turning his head from Klava. The skinny policeman pulled the door open and a man appeared on the threshold. Puffs of fresh snow lay on his shoulders and on a musquash fur cap.

"Oh, *they* are Gavrik, Vilen Trofimovich," Alevtina said hastily, "Dean of the Faculty."

Vilen Trofimovich Gavrik stepped inside. Although he was as tall as Galaunov, Gavrik's body, even under his thick fur-lined winter coat, suggested bare bones without flesh. The students nicknamed him scarecrow. His shortcut, straight black hair started right above his unblinking eyes, which seemed to pierce through everybody at the same time, although he didn't glance at anybody directly. Three deep creases crossed his low forehead. His widely stretched thin lips looked as a pale slot sawed through flat cheeks which carried a permanent bluish shadow. A shade of a smile never left his face, but it appeared only in the corners of the lips, slightly flattening the wrinkles surrounding his mouth. His hands were his most noticeable feature. He had very thick palms and even thicker fingers. The thumbs, especially, were unnaturally thick. The little fingers, however, were very small, as if borrowed from other, female-like hands. He kept the four thick fingers apart and motionless, and only the tiny pinkies continuously moved as if they were separate entities artificially attached.

"What's going on here?" Gavrik asked in a raspy voice. His tone bore such an unmistakable air of authority that the Lieutenant jumped to his feet and touched the brim of his cap with his gloved hand. He did not, however, say anything, and seemed to be indecisive as to how to treat this tall chap whose title of Dean sounded obscure to the Militsiaman.

Gavrik brought from a pocket a small pad and unfolded its cardboard cover in front of the Lieutenant's eyes. Boris knew this was the *red booklet*, the certificate of a KGB officer. Although Gavrik had retired several years ago from active service in the KGB, as everybody knew, once a KGB officer, forever a KGB officer. Formal retirement was just a reassignment.

When the Lieutenant saw the *red booklet*, he stretched his body, lifted his shoulders, pulled in his stomach, and again jerked his gloved hand to the brim of his uniform cap. The moment of hesitation was over: now he unreservedly accepted Gavrik's superiority.

"I am Lieutenant Nifontov, comrade Dean," he said. "A body has been discovered on the premises. Possibly a suicide. Or maybe a murder."

"Body? Whose body? Where is it?" Gavrik moved his fierce eyes from face to face, scanning everybody in the lobby: Galaunov, leaning upon the wall, the tri-colored scarf again wrapped around his neck, and the shadow of his body stretching across the dully gleaming floor; Magidov, whose shoulders seemed even narrower than usually, with a lowered head, his eyes directed at the tips of his galoshes; Starkova, noiselessly ejecting loops of smoke through her large yellow teeth; the doctor still writing his report on a piece of paper laid upon his briefcase; Alevtina, whose widely opened eyes gazed at Gavrik, following the Dean's stare; Valushin, frozen in the corner, with an unlit cigarette clutched in his hand; the two policemen, one skinny and the other thickset, in their dirty coats, standing at attention at the entrance; Boris, keeping his hands behind his back and meeting Gavrik's stare with an equally unblinking gaze; Klava Turova not smiling anymore; Talin hugging himself.

"Whose body?" Gavrik repeated and Alevtina, swallowing something which seemed to clog her throat, said in an almost whispering voice, "Baev . . . Rodion Glebovich . . . There, in the *Metanical larbotrary* . . ."

Starkova, Galaunov, Talin, Klava Turova and Magidov jerked their heads. Somebody gasped.

Gavrik's face showed no feelings. After a heavy silence he chewed something in his mouth, his wide jaws bulging, and said, "Proceed, Lieutenant. I'll not interfere."

Nifontov, apparently relaxing, sat back down.

One by one, the eight people approached the desk and told their names and titles and answered the same question: where had they been both just before and at the time when the sudden thud sounded.

Then the Lieutenant ordered them to line up along the wall.

"Attention, citizens. I'll now read what I have written down from your words. All this will be handed over to the Investigator appointed by the Prosecutor's office. So, you will now listen and if anything is wrong, just lift a hand . . . So, we have established that at the time when something happened in the mechanical lab, there were eight people on the premises. All of you are here now. The sound occurred at or about eight o'clock. Now, the people in the building were as follows: Galaunov, Nikolai Ivanovich. Russian. 46 years old. Professor of Technical Physics. Claimed that he was in his office, room 412 on the fourth floor, did not hear any sounds of unusual character, does not know anything about the death of citizen Baev. Is that correct? So be it recorded. Now, Starkova, Anna Vassilyevna, Russian. 55 years old. Senior Lecturer, General Physics. Claimed she was also in her office, room 216, the second floor. Had heard a sound as if something fell but did not attach any significance to it. Does not know anything about the death of citizen Baev. Correct? You see, everything has been recorded exactly as you have told, no distortions. Well, now, Magidov, Yosif Markovich. Jew. 45 years old. Professor of Theoretical Physics. Claimed that he had not heard any sounds at any time. Claimed that he was not in the building at eight o'clock but arrived about thirty minutes after eight. Claimed that nobody was in the lobby at the time he entered the building. Claimed that he went from the entrance directly to his office and, before he even had time to take off his overcoat, a Militsioner, I believe this was Burda, came in and ordered him to come down here. Citizen Magidov, is that your exact statement? You still have a chance to admit, as everybody has done, that you were actually in the building at the time of the event. That you had your coat on because you intended to leave the building, isn't that true? Well, that's up to you, citizen Magidov, but you must understand that you've no proof you arrived after the event . . . Well, now, Talin, Oleg Nikiforovich. Acting Head of the English Department. Russian, 42 years old. Claimed that he was at all times in his office, room 227, from six o'clock until Burda sent him down here. Never left the office before that. Had heard the thud but did not think it was of significance . . ."

Boris glanced at Talin whose round face did not show any embarrassment. Boris knew Talin had not at all times been in his office. In particular, he was not there a few minutes before the thud's sound.

Nifontov continued, "Very good. Now, Turova, Klavdiya

Mikhailovna. Engineer, Electron Matroscopy . . . What? Microscopy? Well, Electron Microscopy lab. We don't have any distortions. Russian. 27 years old . . ." Nifontov stopped, lifted his eyes from the paper and glanced at Klava. Klava shifted her shoulders and her breasts rolled under the blouse. Nifontov sighed and continued, "Claimed that she was at all times in the Electron Matro . . . Microscopy lab, eh? Yes, we don't allow any distortions . . . So, she had heard the sound but did not realize its significance. Does not know anything about the death of citizen Baev. Very good . . . Now Valushin, Evgeny Ivanovich, Russian, 27 years old, Technical Associate, General Physics. Was the first person to discover the body of the deceased. Do you confirm that, Valushin? Good. Ponareva, Alevtina Semenovna. Russian, janitor on duty. Had heard the sound of a blow in the lab when she was at her post, here, in the lobby. Rushed to look at what had happened. Opened the door of the lab and saw Valushin standing in the door connecting the room with the next-door lab, is it magnetic? Correct? Now, she saw the body of the deceased and started to scream.

Then citizen Tarutin appeared from the Magnetic lab. Correct, Ponareva? Very good. Now, Tarutin, Boris Petrovich, 33 years old, Russian. Assistant Professor, General Physics. Had heard the sound of a blow in the next door lab, had sent Valushin to look. Through the opened connecting door, saw that Ponareva, the janitor, entered from the corridor and started to scream. Rushed to the connecting door and saw the body of the deceased at the impact tester machine. Is that correct? You see, everything has been written exactly as you've told, citizens. So, now, all of you, one by one, will come over here, write your addresses and the words, 'Written down correctly from my oral statement' and sign here. Well, let's go, citizens."

When Boris, in his turn, had signed the paper written by

the Lieutenant, a group of men with cases and cameras appeared in the door. Criminal experts.

Boris walked out. The wind had changed direction and swept away the odor of mercaptanes. The young snow glistened under the moonlight, its fresh scent filling his chest with a joyful sense of nature's beauty, and reminding him that only a couple of kilometers from this street, forests stretched around lakes already covered with thin fragile ice.

Boris crossed the street, turned the corner and entered the dark building of the student dorms. He shook away the snow sticking to his soles. The clock opposite the entrance showed eleven o'clock. With red and blue spots dancing before his eyes, and with the bruises on his ribs, knees and feet aching, he tiredly climbed the stairs, to his room on the fourth floor, which he had left nearly sixty hours before.

Chapter 5

THE NEXT EVENING, MONDAY, NOVEMBER 28, BORIS returned home after nine hours of classes.

He entered the corridor on the fourth floor. Dark windows, with scraps of dirty cotton jutting from chinks between the panes, were to his right. To his left stretched a row of dark-brown doors. There were twenty of them in this wing. Behind nineteen of them lived families of Professors, one room per family. The twentieth door was always ajar. This was a kitchen, one for all nineteen families.

A few steps from his room, Boris heard a child crying. It was Katya's child. She lived next door to Boris, and this child of hers, he cried all the time.

Then Boris saw a light under his door. Somebody was in his room. Boris pulled open the door and saw before him a pair of feet in gray socks, and the owner of the gray socks sleeping on Boris's sofa. The sofa stood along the right wall of the small oblong room, half-concealing the door leading to Katya's room. A wooden bar was nailed across this door. To mute the sounds of the child's cries, Boris had piled books in the wall recess containing the door.

Two pictures of Boris's parents hung on the left wall, opposite the sofa. Next to his parents hung Boris's skis, their curved tips wrapped in cloth. A small cabinet stood at the narrow window, next to the skis.

The man sleeping on the sofa was Artamon Sergeev. His right hand hung down, clutching a blue-labeled quarter-liter bottle of *Moskovskaya Osobaya*, "Moscow Special" vodka. Sergeev's jacket lay on the floor.

For a while Boris stood there looking at Sergeev. He had known this man about twenty-five years. Yes, it was in '59, when Boris was in the second grade, that a new boy had appeared in their class, a short, pale and slightly stooped boy, with the funny name of Artamon. The class supervisor had assigned to Artamon Sergeev the seat next to that of Boris Tarutin.

Artamon had missed several weeks of studies because of his transfer from another city in the middle of the school year. In this new school in Kalinin, he just could not catch up with mathematics. To pass the written tests, he "rolled over," as the school jargon went, all the solutions from Boris's pads. Boris didn't care, he was just not interested in this short-legged boy, ignorant of Boris's beloved mathematics. It was about two years later that Boris's attitude towards his seemingly dull schoolmate had drastically changed. It had happened when their history teacher, an obese, tired-looking woman, her pudgy hand making circles over the map of ancient Russia, solemnly narrated the glorious story of the heroic struggle of the Russian people against the Tatar-Mongol invasion. She described the bravery of the Tver's warriors who, shoulder to shoulder with their elder brothers, the sons of Moscow, protected the Motherland against the hordes of Tatar Khans. Suddenly she stopped her lecture and, hitting her left palm with her right fist, shouted, "Artamon Sergeev! What's wrong with you? Why are you wriggling there? Stand up! Are you not interested in the heroic struggle of our ancestors against the enemies of the Motherland?"

Artamon crawled slowly from behind the desk, his pale countenance becoming even paler.

"So, Sergeev, will you tell the class what's the matter with you?" and she pointed her thick finger at Artamon. He swallowed something and then said in a very low voice, "You said the people of Tver, which is now Kalinin where we live, followed the lead of Moscow. Together they fought the Tatars. Then why in 1327, when the people of Tver rose in rebellion against the Tatars, did Ivan Kalita, the Prince of Moscow, ally with the Khan of Tatars in the wars against Tver?"

Dead silence followed the words of the daredevil. The teacher stared with disbelief at the pale boy.

"Who taught you this?" she asked, almost whispering.

"I read this in the 'History of Russia' by Karamzin," Artamon said. Looking baffled and scared, the teacher seemed not to know the name of Karamzin, a famous Russian writer and historian. The bell announced recess and she retreated to the teachers' room.

Apparently she did not tell anybody about Artamon's impudence as he was not summoned to the school's director.

After that day, each time the teacher conducted the class in history, she nervously glanced, time and again, at Artamon, as if expecting from this dull-looking boy a new challenge. Indeed, a couple of weeks later, when she told the students that the glorious victory of the Russian arms in the Kulikov battle, in 1380, had put an end to the Tatars' sway over Russia, Artamon lifted his hand. The teacher stopped in the middle of her sentence, gazing with horror at the hand in the air. With the expression of a doomed victim, she faintly nodded, and, among the dead hush, Artamon said, "Karamzin states that the Kulikov battle had not led to the liberation from the Tatars' yoke. Just two years later, Khan Tokhtamysh invaded Russia. He burned Moscow to the ground and massacred 24,000 men and women of Moscow. Only a hundred years later, in 1480, we stopped paying tribute to the Khans."

The next day, the obese teacher disappeared. She transferred to another school, located on the opposite end of the city. And Boris looked now at his mate with different eyes. Artamon showed him the Karamzin's book and a pile of other books on history. And Boris also saw a neat stack of double-sized sheets on which Artamon had drawn wide tables with dates, names and comments. On these tables he matched the events which took place in different countries in any given year. At that time he had reached in his effort the middle of the 16th century. The names of Ivan the Terrible, Maximilian I, Charles V, Suleiman the Magnificent, and Leo X lined the sheet's width, inspiring in Boris a new respect for this strange boy and sparking his interest in history, alongside mathematics and physics.

The same year, one more event took place after which relations between Boris and Artamon took on a new dimension.

There was a trio of notorious hooligans in their class, Dronov, Tyushkin and Tereshko. It was the third year in a row that Dronov had stayed in the same grade. A bear-like, blotchy boy with the shadow of a beginning mustache and small drowsy eyes, Dronov was by far the biggest and most muscular lad in the class. Tyushkin and Tereshko, both sons of single mothers, who spent on vodka all of their meager salaries earned in the textile factory, were on the lowest rung of the class's unwritten hierarchy. To make up for this, Tyushkin and Tereshko stuck to Dronov as his permanent arm-bearers. The trio recognized in

Artamon Sergeev an easy target for their pranks. They took away Artamon's sandwiches, smeared his notebooks, broke his pencils, never missed a chance to pinch him, to push him, to pull his hair, to tear up his shirt. The rules of the school yard forbade anybody to interfere.

One day this came to an end. It happened during the long daily recess when the teachers hid behind the door of the teachers' room to devour their sandwiches and when all hell broke loose in the corridors. Boris walked into the toilet. It had a small anteroom with a faucet which never worked. Another door led from the anteroom to the toilet's main area. To Boris's surprise, this door did not yield to his push. Boris leaned his shoulder upon the door and, against somebody's resistance, flung it open. He saw Tyushkin there, who had tried to hold the door and was now staring at Boris with wide scared eyes. Three more boys were inside. Dronov, Tereshko, and Artamon Sergeev. Artamon's bony body was bent forward, his head squeezed between Tereshko's knees. Tereshko's wart-covered hands held Artamon's hands twisted behind the latter's back. Artamon's pants were down revealing his pale thin legs. Dronov stood behind Artamon, his pants also lowered, in a pose of preparation, his big palms on Artamon's buttocks.

Later, Boris could hardly remember the exact sequence of events. One moment he was standing at the door, dully staring at the four boys in their frozen poses, the next moment Tyushkin was on the dirty urine-sprinkled floor and Boris was flying forward, his lowered head targeted against Dronov's stomach. And the next moment, both Tyushkin and Tereshko had sneaked out, and Dronov, attempting to pull up his pants, was hobbling away from Boris. And a moment later, there were only two of them, Boris and Artamon, in the stinking room.

From that day on, the notorious trio not only never touched Artamon again, they invariably tried to get out of

Boris's way. From that day on, Artamon's affection for Boris started to develop into a strong attachment, one that strengthened throughout the years.

After graduation, when Boris enrolled in the University to study Physics, Artamon, instead of history, choose, to everybody's surprise, the faculty of law. It seemed that Artamon's parents, teachers in a suburban school, had insisted on that.

But Boris understood why Sergeev had chosen law; his goal certainly had been to achieve the status of Prosecutor. A Prosecutor is not afraid of anybody; everybody is afraid of a Prosecutor.

When Sergeev finished his studies, the only assignment he managed to get was that of a Notary in a remote rural area. Artamon languished there a few years until he had overcome his natural aversion to political activism, and, following the persistent advices of his parents, joined the Party. This indeed helped. In a couple of years he was finally given the position of Investigator at the Kalinin City Prosecutor's office.

It was not the first time Boris had found his former schoolmate in this room with a bottle of vodka. Every now and then Sergeev came here, usually in the evening, after long hours in the City Prosecutor's office. The janitors knew him well and he had obtained from them the key to Boris's room. He had no need to display his Investigator's badge which would have opened almost any door for him anyway.

He seemed especially eager to see Boris when an exciting case was assigned to him. Sergeev was able to solve complicated and ingeniously implemented crimes. He would stretch out on the sofa, slowly sipping from a bottle of *Moskovskaya Osobaya*, vodka bought at the special store catering to the Prosecutor's office personnel; he would set his feet on the faded gray sofa and talk.

There were two Sergeevs. One was known to his bosses in the Prosecutor's office and to his Party Secretary. This Sergeev accurately paid his monthly Party membership dues, 3% of his salary; on every election day he performed his *voter's duty* early in the morning, by casting his vote for the candidates of the *Great Block of communists and non-Party people*. He interrogated criminals. And he never said more than was necessary.

The second Sergeev was known only to Boris. This second Sergeev stretched on the sofa in this small oblong room and talked. He could talk for two, three, sometimes four hours—as long as the bottle lasted. About everything. Of course, about women. Unlike Boris, Artamon had never had a girlfriend. But every other month he found himself in love with one of the young secretaries who hardly ever suspected being the object of Sergeev's dreams. He talked about his supervisors. Most often about his immediate boss, Senior Investigator Lopoukhov, and about his much bigger boss, Region Prosecutor Gnida. He endlessly enjoyed making fun of their names. Lopoukhov, for Artamon, invariably was "Lopoukhi," *lop-eared*, which in the Tver vernacular also was a word for a dunderhead. As to Gnida's name, Artamon had no need to alter it since this unique name, meaning nit, already sounded like mockery. He talked about the cases he was assigned to and those he wished to be assigned to but was not. Most of the cases were dull stories involving fistfighting drunkards, wife beatings and pilfering in factories.

Rarely did his stories sound like detective novels and those that did, he embellished with vivid details, ignoring the rules of secrecy of the Prosecutor's office. Artamon knew these stories never slipped out of this room.

Artamon sighed and opened his eyes. "At last, it's you, old pirate," he said lowering his feet to a floor. "I thought you'd never come. Plenty of news! Get ready to tax your physico-mathematical brains."

"I hardly believe I still have any brains intact," Boris said. "Last Friday, I was but a few seconds short of saying good-by to my brains."

"Kidding? Oh, I see, you also have news! We shall swap stories, *in perpetuam rei memoriam*. But, first, what do you have to drink? Nothing? Shall I again drink this potion," Artamon said, waving the bottle in front of Boris's eyes, "without any snack like the lowest incurable drunkard?"

Boris opened the cabinet. Shirts, pants and socks were stacked on the upper shelf. On the bottom, there was mountaineering gear: an ice-axe, a rucksack, a folded cotton-stuffed sleeping bag. A few dinner plates, a ceramic tea pot, a can with Ceylon tea, and salt in a paper bag sat on the middle shelf. A half-loaf of black rye bread, wrapped in newspaper, partially displayed the words, MORE GRAIN INTO THE GRANARIES OF THE MOTHERLAND!

Artamon broke off a piece of bread, swallowed a mouthful of vodka from the bottle, shuddered, wrinkled his nose and said, "Uh, damned potion, *aqua viva*! . . . Well, now talk!"

"Last Friday," Boris said, "I went to Bologoe, as usual, to give a lecture . . ." He described his weekend in Bologoe. Artamon laid aside his bottle, his forehead wrinkling as he absorbed the story.

"There are peculiar points in this story," Artamon said and lay back down on the sofa. "First, you say, this man Guran, he had a lot of scars on his skull? I bet, he's an *urka*, professional criminal. Do you know how professional thieves find out whether a stranger is an *urka* or only pretends to be one? They shave his head and look for scars. If there are no scars or only a few of them, then he is not an *urka*. Anybody who belongs to the criminal world, at one time or another, takes part in settling scores among feuding gangs or is interrogated by *Pakhan*, a gang's Master. And on each such occasion, to encourage the fellow's cooperation he is hit repeatedly on the skull . . .

"Now, about his East-Siberian accent and vernacular, these multiple "howevers" in every improbable place. You see, you're not an expert in speech are you? Genuine experts, after listening to someone talk, could tell his place of origin within a radius of a hundred kilometers. But you could easily be confused by a quasi-Siberian accent. Probably, he is not of East-Siberian origin, but spent long years in Siberia, probably in camps and exiles. That is where he picked up his vernacular. You know, the word Guran denotes anybody born beyond Lake Baikal. There are a few million of them. Only for a man who is not a Guran but speaks or behaves like a Guran, such a nickname would be typical in the criminal world.

"Also, you say they used the word *bashli* for money. Well, it's not exactly the *urkas'* jargon. It's more the slang of those in the underground economy, of those just short of being professional thieves. By no means, though, is it the Siberian vernacular. Which lends more credibility to my theory."

"I see your point," Boris said. "And as I know, I better rely on your judgment in such matters. Now, what do you think about that mysterious Master of Guran, somebody they named Plague? He seemed to inspire great fear."

"More proof in favor of my theory," Artamon Sergeev said, looking at the ceiling and crossing his feet on the sofa's bolster. "You see, in the criminal world, a *Pakhan* has unlimited power over the life and death of his gang's members. And the death is never an easy one, *non nobis*. Now, Plague is a widely used nickname for a big Pakhan, a Master of a large, or of an especially successful gang.

"Now, there is one more peculiar feature in your story; *cockle-shells*, which means orders and medals."

"What was all that about medals?"

"My friend, you live far from the real world. Why do these stupid girls fall for you all the time? Medals and orders are the hottest items on the black market. In Tbilissi or in Baku, or, say, in Dushanbe, a Red Banner order went for two thousand rubles! Medals and orders all contain silver, gold, gems . . . Tangible, easily storable, everlasting security against life's vicissitudes . . . The underground wealthy, they sleep and dream that one day this regime will collapse, *post tenebras lux*. Then these gems and gold will regain their real value. Do you remember the story of Fleet Admiral Kireev?"

"Sure, didn't he die recently? A hero of the Patriotic war? I read the obituary in the newspaper signed by all the Kremlin big shots . . ." Boris sat down on the floor, leaned against the cabinet and stretched his long legs on the rug.

"Yes, that's him," Artamon said. "The Admiral's demise was not natural. He was murdered, together with his wife. A hammer was used as the weapon. They smashed the Admiral's and his wife's skulls, and the only thing they took from the Admiral's apartment was his dress uniform. Its chest was covered with a couple of kilograms of medals. Now, this murder occurred in the Admiral's apartment, in a thoroughly guarded compound, in one of the most exclusive neighborhoods of Moscow.

"You understand, the entire story never reached the newspapers; they just made a lot of fuss about his heroic feats during the war, *aere perennius*. So far, there is no information as to who the murderers were. As you might guess, we have no doubt it's the work of a well-established gang with help from the inside, and probably high connections . . . So, your story in Bologoe may have some sinister overtones. I think, it was your luck that the Militsia in Bologoe apparently had no connections to these medal-hunters . . . Well, I'll try to find out how the investigation in Bologoe progressed."

Artamon sipped vodka. He lay silent for a while, then sighed and said, "Now, my friend, there is one more story of which you know perhaps more than I do. I am assigned to investigate the death of your University's Party Secretary, this pig Baev."

Chapter 6

AN HOUR LATER, THEY HAD SWAPPED POSITIONS. NOW Boris was lying on the sofa while Artamon was sitting on the floor, leaning against the cabinet. The bottle Artamon had brought with him was as yet nearly untouched.

"Now," Artamon said, "Let me review all you've told me." He repeated the main points of the story Boris had just told him about the previous night's murder at the University.

"So," Artamon finished, "the Militsiamen had brought to the lobby whoever they had found on the premises."

"Right," Boris said. "Eight people including myself."

"Before we talk about these people, tell me a little about the building," Artamon said.

"Sure, what do you want to know? It's a four-story building, it has a central part and two side wings. The entrance is in the middle of the central part, but in both wings there are back doors. They are always locked . . ."

"And who has the keys?" Artamon said.

"I believe the man who has all the keys is the Chief Janitor. His name is Musaev."

"Could it be that he was in the building and left through a back door before the Militsia arrived?"

"Lieutenant Nifontov asked Alevtina about that and she was positive she saw nobody else."

"Good. What do you have in that building?"

"First, there is all the big *nachalstvo*, management," Boris said. "The Rector, Professor Nekipalov, has his office on the second floor, as well as one of the Prorectors. Baev, the Party Secretary, as well as Gavrik, Dean of the Faculty, also have their offices on this floor, in the other wing. The ground floor is just for the labs, mainly physics. The rest of the building is made up of classrooms and offices. We have quite a few departments—Theoretical Physics, General Physics, Experimental Physics, Technical and Applied Physics. Then, the Computational Center, and language departments. English, German . . ."

"Very good," Artamon said, his foot pushing the bottle away from him. "Now, tell me about those seven people. Did any of them have reason to hate Baev?"

"Anybody? . . . Everybody!" Boris said. "That pig Baev!"

"Including you?" Artamon said.

"Oh, yes. You know, he was a former KGB officer. Maybe, it was he who tortured my father . . ."

"Would you have killed him, given an opportunity?"

Boris glanced pensively at Artamon. "Yes," he said, "but, I didn't."

"Tell me one thing, Borka," Artamon said, his foot again moving the bottle closer to him. "I understand it is common knowledge that Baev was once in the KGB. Still, such information is not freely disseminated. How did you learn about his past?"

"Simple," Boris said. "Gorbatov told us . . ."

"Who the devil is Gorbatov?"

"Oh, he's the Head of the Department of Theoretical Physics. At twenty-six! One day he appeared out of nowhere, and the Dean announced, hey, friends, this is your new Department Head, comrade Gorbatov. Just like that. No usual procedure. His predecessor was dismissed, no reason given. No vote in the Council. The secret of Gorbatov's appointment is however simple. . . ."

"Wait, isn't he the son of the late General Gorbatov?"

"Yes, the Chairman of the Region KGB," Boris said. "The general is dead, but his buddies took care of his son. I have to admit, though, this Gorbatov is a rather knowledgeable physicist. He also is a good pianist. It looks like he did not take after his father. He inherited his father's big apartment, but not his father's philosophy, if the late butcher had any . . ."

"And this Gorbatov told everybody . . ." Artamon said.

". . . that Baev was once a KGB official. Yes."

"I am amazed," Artamon said, "that you liked the son of a KGB general. *Audi alteram partem* . . ." And Artamon again looked through the bottle.

"I don't like him. In fact, I barely get along with him. Fortunately, I am in another department, General Physics, and I am glad to have as the department head a little old flower, Andrei Ivanovich Vernov. He can't tell a Barkhausen effect from a Mossbauer effect, but, at 63, he can boast that he does not have a single enemy on the faculty . . ."

They again exchanged positions, Boris climbing down from the sofa and Artamon taking his place there, bottle in hand.

"So, Borka, tell me about the seven people who were in the building. There were three women among them . . ."

"And four men, true," Boris said.

"Let's start with the women," Artamon said, his hand

swinging the bottle. "First, this Klava Turova. You must know a lot about her, don't you?"

"You might say so, yes," Boris said. "Very pretty girl. The ass is a little flat, but she has great white boobs . . ."

"Don't forget the legs," Artamon said.

"The legs are what I can never forget," Boris said. "Yes, Klava has nice legs. But, after the legs I saw yesterday, at the railway station . . ."

"Please, no poems about female legs at the railway station that you'll never see again. Now, Borka, why did you quit making out with Klava?"

"You may not know it, but she has a nickname among the faculty, 'Weak at the front,' which means . . ."

"That she is readily available to anybody wearing pants," Artamon finished.

"Not to everybody, but to many," Boris said, "Though she never had an affair with a student, only faculty. You see, she is a lovely, friendly creature, and I like her very much. I discovered that while she used to spend a couple of nights a week with me, she also had similar arrangements with other men. I felt it was beyond what could make me happy."

"And no regrets?" Artamon said.

"Well, she is still more than willing to renew our sessions. I have to admit, those white boobs are very tempting. But no thanks . . ."

"Dirty old man," Artamon said, looking through the bottle. *Experientia docet stultus*. Tell me now, where did Klava stand with Baev."

"She hated his guts. It is no big secret that Klava's habit is to lock herself with a man in the electron microscopy lab. And it does not take much imagination to guess what they do there. A few months ago she applied for a course in electron microscopy. Afterwards she could have been promoted with a salary increase from 120 rubles to about 140 rubles a month. For her, this would have been a big deal. Andrei Ivanovich Vernov, the Department Head, approved her application. But Baev, as the Party Secretary, vetoed that decision. He said Klava's 'indecent' behavior deprived her of any privileges reserved for only the good sons and daughters of the Soviet people.''

"I see Baev was indeed a fervent protector of the morals of the Soviet people," Artamon said. *"Pro rege, lege, grege."*

"Much simpler than that," Boris said. "Baev felt he was entitled to share Klava's tits. He insisted, but she refused."

"So," Artamon said, "she is not that easily available."

"She is, unless she dislikes the man."

"So, as I understand it," Artamon said, "as long as Baev stayed the Party Secretary, Klava had no chance to improve her situation." Artamon started to rock the bottle on the rug. Boris shrugged.

"Now," Artamon said, "what about that other woman, the janitor?"

"Alevtina? Well, for her also, men are no strangers. Except, Klava does it for fun and Alevtina, for money. She has no husband, and two daughters. Baev wished to kick her out but the rector, Professor Nekipalov, for some reason resisted Baev's efforts."

"Ah," Artamon said, "so, this Alevtina is a Marxist . . ."

Boris nodded. In Kalinin, as well as in Moscow, ladies of the oldest profession, looking for customers, gathered around the Marx monument. The girls were referred to as Marxist girls.

"Now," Artamon continued, "your rector, Nekipalov, he was independent enough to withstand Baev's pressure, right?"

"Yes," Boris said. "He is also a member of the region party committee, professor of the party history and, moreover, he has a relative in Moscow, in the party Central Committee."

"Back to Alevtina," Artamon said. "I understand she had a reason to hate Baev . . ."

"And how!" Boris said. "Baev did his best to kick her out, not only from her job but from the city, and were it not for Nekipalov's interference, she might already be far away."

"If Nekipalov stopped protecting her, Baev could destroy Alevtina's life. Again, one blow of a hammer, and the worst threat to Alevtina's fragile existence would vanish."

"If you say so," Boris said gloomily.

"There was one more woman," Artamon said.

"Starkova, Anna Vassilyevna. This is quite a different story. She is 55 this year . . ."

"Women's pension age! I can see the scenario . . ."

"Yes. Nekipalov wanted her out."

"Nekipalov? The rector, not Baev?" Artamon said.

"Well, Nekipalov does not like dirty work. He loves to appear the good guy. Baev didn't care about his image."

"KGB upbringing. So, the rector wanted to get rid of this Starkova and he let Baev handle it. Why?" Artamon said.

"Starkova's story is not quite conventional," Boris said. "She had been working at the university for thirty years, as a lecturer, then as a senior lecturer. She had always been depicted as a model teacher, she faithfully followed the great decisions of the Party. She had developed some pet idea that Einstein erred in his theory of mass. When the Party started hunting Jews, she decided her time had arrived, and criticizing that Jew, Einstein, would bestow glory upon Anna Starkova. She wrote several articles containing what she considered a mortal blow to Einstein's theory."

"Was it indeed?"

"It was bullshit! Nobody in his right mind would consider Starkova's gibberish seriously. The department's big shots reluctantly published her delirious exercises in the University's proceedings. They added a footnote that the editors did not share Starkova's opinions. The volume with her articles became a collector's item. Moscow physicists made fun of this story, to the Kalinin University's disgrace . . ."

"*Sic transit gloria mundi* . . ." Artamon said.

"A few months ago we had a commission from the Ministry of Higher Education. They indicated that there were many faculty members not contributing enough to research. And, this time, it was the plain truth. Even my Department Head Vernov, is mortally afraid of research. Others give lectures without moving their eyes from notes prepared twenty years ago."

"My friend, is it not true that you, yourself, have abandoned your research?"

"Right, Artyusha. I have my reasons for whatever they're worth. Well, Nekipalov had to take measures to comply with the commission's findings. He selected Starkova as one of the victims. He thought that her being of pension age, plus her anti-Einstein escapade, would stifle any voices heard in her defense. An easy quarry. But, still, he played it through Baev, so Starkova directed her rage against that old KGB villain."

"A nice nest of spiders in this temple of science," Artamon said, toying again with the bottle. "So, for this nice Starkova lady, one blow with a hammer upon Baev's head would mean eliminating her personal enemy. A neat picture!"

"Enough about the women," Boris said. "Shall we switch to the men?"

The child behind the cardboard door renewed his cries. They heard Katya's muffled voice, singing a lullaby.

Chapter 7

"Tell me about your technician," Artamon said.

"Zhenya Valushin? You know about his drinking binges, don't you?"

"Is he still painting?" Artamon said.

"Better than ever. Look at this," and Boris reached behind the cabinet and brought out several framed canvases. He unwrapped one and laid it on the floor. Artamon stared at the painting for a while. "And he just gives these away! You know, Borka, one day this will be worth a fortune."

Boris nodded, wrapped the painting again and set the canvases back behind the cabinet.

"Obviously, his drinking bouts were known to Baev," Artamon said.

"Right. Zhenya Valushin has been in a very bad state. He feels the next bout of drinking is coming on. I have the impression that he has come close to suicide . . ."

"Or to a murder?" Artamon said. "Was he with you at all times that evening?"

"Except to smoke in the toilet. He went there a couple of times," Boris said.

"Since he was the man who installed the timer on that impact tester, isn't it natural to think he might have tampered with it?" Artamon said. "I mean, this alteration in the delay time, from ten seconds to ten minutes. You see, this timer is the witness; it testifies that we are not dealing with a suicide."

"Yes," Boris said, "I believe it was murder."

"And the killer must be one of these eight people, counting you among the suspects. Well, who's next? This friend of yours, Galaunov?"

"Galaunov is a fascinating man. He is a brilliant physicist, but what may be of special interest to you, Artyusha, he lately switched to history."

"Oh, *credo quia absurdum*," Artamon said. "Do you know, only in the city of Kalinin do fifty historians with diplomas work as janitors? And your brilliant friend has voluntarily plunged from the height of physics into the swamp of history."

"He's not competing with those who have diplomas. He has written a treatise on the history of socialism. It's now very popular in the *Samizdat*. He read through a heap of books and has developed an amazing theory that socialism is by no means anything new. It occurred, as he puts it, many times throughout the history of mankind. In ancient Egypt, the land, the crop, everything, belonged to the state, and the Pharaoh distributed all the goods through a state-operated system. Or, say, in Peru, before the conquistadors arrived, there was a socialist system for three hundred years. There is a difference, however, in that our beloved state is, indeed, the first in the history of mankind; not the first socialist state, but rather the first Propagandistic state . . ."

"Three years in jail," Artamon said, "for what you're

saying now. And why does the KGB tolerate this Galaunov's activity? I am sure the KGB is aware of his views and his contribution to the *Samizdat*."

"Maybe they don't want to crush a Lenin Prize Laureate."

"Sakharov had earned many more distinctions than your Galaunov," Artamon said. "And what happened to him? No, Borka, I think Galaunov has some sympathizers in the high strata of the Party. Or in the KGB. And what was his stand regarding Baev?"

"Contempt," Boris said. "Disgust."

"I imagine Baev must have been furious," Artamon said.

"Right. He threatened Nikolai Ivanovich Galaunov with transferring Galaunov's doctoral students to some other supervisor, someone more reliable from the Party viewpoint."

"And was he able to make good his threat?"

"Able and willing. To take students away from Professor Galaunov, a Lenin Prize winner, the pride of the Kalinin University . . . Baev might just as well have taken a hammer and hit Galaunov over the head."

"So, would it not be reasonable for Galaunov to be the first with a blow to Baev's head?" Artamon said.

The child behind the cardboard door was still crying, and a lullaby, muffled by the door and the heap of books, so that no words could be discerned, was still sounding in the next room.

"Who else was there, the head of the English Department?" Artamon said, playing with the bottle.

"Yes, Talin, Oleg Nikiforovich. I get English books from him sometimes. There is a funny thing about him. He considers himself a victim of Jewish plotters who have conspired to stop his career. It has been five years that he has been *acting* head, and he still can't get approved as permanent head of the Department. It is also true that on the Faculty of Languages there are still two Jews, professors. Both are highly acclaimed linguists. Both are old chaps on the verge of retirement. They would never dare to cast their votes in the Faculty Council against the Rector's instruction. Talin, however, attaches all the blame for the freeze in his promotion to these two cripples who are even scared of each other. The truth is that, where Talin seems to know English very well, he is just not suited to kiss the Rector's ass. So, Nekipalov persists in his search for somebody else who could be appointed department head. The funniest thing about Talin is that, while attributing his career's slow-down to those two Jews, he feverishly strives to prove that he is not an anti-Semite."

"You can't be serious," Artamon said. "Indeed, fools are neither sown nor cropped, by themselves they grow. And what has this to do with Baev?"

"Well, recently Talin's position at the University was drastically undermined. Baev just made mincemeat out of Talin. You see, Talin decided to divorce his wife of eight years. If you saw her, you wouldn't ask why. Talin once confided in me that he married her under duress. Once, eight years ago, he attended a party, drank in the genuine Russian manner, then found himself in bed with a girl he had never seen before. Whatever had happened during the night, the next morning the girl's parents appeared and accused him of raping their virgin daughter. You know about such stories in our enlightened Fatherland . . ."

"Alterum tantum," Artamon said. "So, after eight years he finally got up the courage . . ."

"To break up an exemplary Soviet family. Yes. But the woman . . ."

"Was too respectful of the morals of a Soviet man," Artamon said. *"Aut vincere aut mori."*

"Yes," Boris said. "She did what any average Soviet woman would do in such circumstances . . ."

"She complained to the Party Committee," Artamon said, nodding and chuckling.

"So, Baev called for a general meeting of the Party members, but he made it *open*. You can imagine, the rumor spread about the meeting's topic and the room was full. Baev publicly interrogated Talin, forced the poor guy to report on his sexual relations with other women, and demanded all the details. For over two hours, Talin stood in front of the crowd, answering questions, to Baev's full satisfaction. Talin was given respite only after he had solemnly promised to immediately restore his marital union and to cease his affairs with other women."

"Capiat qui capere possit," Artamon said. "Well, who's the last suspect? Is his name Magidov?"

"Yes," Boris said. "Yosif Markovich Magidov. I don't know much about this man. I can't remember ever talking with him. I think he's been at the University about twenty years. The only Jew on the Faculty of Physics who has survived the purges by Nekipalov."

"How so?" Artamon said.

"About twenty years ago, when he had just joined the faculty, he wrote several articles regarding the nature of electrons and positrons. You know, he's a theoretician. In those papers he spelled out some theory which sounded a little heretical at that time. The main point of his theory was that an electron could be treated as a positron moving backwards in time."

"Please, no treatise on Theoretical Physics," Artamon said, his hand with the bottle making slow circles in the air.

"Well, he didn't directly contradict any of the big shots in Theoretical Physics, so his work was never criticized. It was simply ignored," Boris said. "His doctoral degree was never approved, so he apparently was discouraged and quit doing research. Instead, he began to write textbooks. I think he is a clever guy. Indeed, as you understand, with a Jewish name like Yosif Markovich, it would be very difficult for him to pave the road through the jungles of the State Publishing House. So, while he had probably written the textbooks all by himself, he had always published them with two co-authors. These co-authors always had impeccable Russian names and, apparently, good connections in the General Authority of State Publishing Houses. Judging from what I know about Magidov's co-authors, while they have been receiving royalties and credits, they could scarcely have contributed a single sentence to those textbooks."

"And these textbooks, are they good?" Artamon asked.

"I would say, they are outstanding, especially the one dealing with magnetic fields. I can state this for fact; it's my area, you know."

"Was this enough to save Magidov from Nekipalov's hand?" Artamon said.

"Certainly not. He was slated for dismissal, but . . ."

"Ah, now the interesting part," Artamon said.

"Indeed it is. Not long ago, an American physicist, by the name of Freeman, was awarded the Nobel prize for his work in the field of elementary particles. So far so good. You know, we have only seven Nobel prize winners in our country. Each time an American wins the prize again, it's a thorn in the side for the bigwigs in the Academy of Sciences."

"And even more for the Party Central Committee."

"Oh, yes. So, Freeman had received his prize, while Yosif Markovich Magidov humbly continued to work on his next textbook. Then, one sunny day, an issue of the monthly *Achievements in Physics* arrived in the University library. And in that issue was a paper by the famous Academician Lerov. And in this paper Lerov stated, no more and no less, that the substance of Freeman's work, although Freeman might not have known it, repeated what twenty years before had been developed and published in an obscure *Proceedings of Kalinin University*, by an equally obscure physicist named Y.M. Magidov."

"I see. And that's what has saved your Magidov from dismissal?"

"Yes," Boris said. "You understand, academician Lerov is too much of a heavy-weight for our Kalinin jackals. Then, a Soviet scientist whose work turned out to be on a par with an achievement of an American Nobel prize winner, such a man couldn't be treated lightly anymore. Magidov was awarded the Doctor of Science degree, after a twenty-year delay."

"I guess our own bigwigs Nekipalov and Baev were hardly happy with these events," Artamon said, getting up from the sofa.

"Nekipalov, after he had succeeded in getting rid of almost every Jew on the faculty of Physics, except for Magidov, probably felt satisfied. As I read him, he did this not as much out of anti-Semitic feelings, but rather out of the desire to prove that he was a very efficient administrator. Were the Party line say, pro-Jewish, he would probably have done his best to employ as many as possible. Now, Baev hated Jews. For him, the sudden ascent of Magidov's star was like a knife in his heart." Boris sat down on the sofa and shook off his shoes.

"Well, did Baev continue his efforts to kick out the last Jew on the faculty?" Artamon said.

"Sure he did. I have heard rumors that Magidov has been negotiating with some Pedagogical institute, somewhere in the remotest corner of East Siberia, where they were thrilled by the chance to acquire a scientist of such caliber . . ."

"And Magidov wanted to escape there from the ubiquitous hands of the Baevs and Nekipalovs? These events are not attributes of place, they are attributes of time," Artamon said. *"O tempora! O mores!"* He uncorked the bottle and took a long gulp. "Ah! Bitter damned stuff." He sniffed the bread, following Russian drinkers' habit, and wrinkled his nose, shaking the bottle in front of Boris's face. "Tell me what you think. Which suspect is the guilty one."

"None," Boris said. "Yes, they all hated Baev. But I can't imagine any of them could murder the scoundrel . . . Actually, I do not know this man, Magidov, well enough. I can't speak for him. But the rest? Klava Turova, a gentle, friendly person, planning and executing a murder? Starkova? She is an old scold, and an illiterate physicist, but a murderer? Alevtina the janitor? No, none of the women seem able to plan such a murder. Although Baev was a wretch, very short and physically weak, still, for a woman to overpower a man . . ."

"Borka, you still remain as naive as you were at the school . . . Don't you know women kill husbands, lovers, bosses and even strangers? But, go ahead, what about the men?"

"Who's capable of killing the scoundrel? Zhenya Valushin? Of course, he spent some fifteen minutes, at the supposed time of the murder, out of the lab. But, you know, he is an alcoholic. Such people usually have no willpower. To murder a man, one needs some willpower, doesn't one? Talin? Yes, he was not in his office at the time of murder, and he lied to the police about his whereabouts at that time. However improbable as it sounds, he certainly seems to be a more logical suspect. Still, he hardly matches my image of a murderer. Galaunov? I think he simply considered Baev beneath him."

"Infra dignitatem," Artamon said, his voice showing the first signs of the vodka's effect.

"This leaves Magidov," Boris said. "Such a shy man, he looks as if he is afraid of his own shadow. Again, I don't know him at all."

"Great, my sober friend," Artamon said. "Now, before I get drunk, let me tell you that despite your general naivete regarding the suspects' ability to commit murder, you may have arrived at the right conclusion. What are the Russian tools of murder? Broken bottles. Kitchen knives. Bricks. But a machine? This impact tester? No, my dear friend! Too sophisticated! During all my tenure at the Prosecutor's office in this blessed city, I have never encountered a murderer who would have used anything more complicated than an axe. It just would be too non-Russian! And that's where this Jew comes in as the most natural suspect." And Artamon took one more gulp from the bottle. His speech was gradually becoming less crisp and he repeatedly combed his already shaggy hair with his fingers.

"Time to call it a day," Boris said. Artamon obediently donned his jacket and headed towards the door. His legs seemed unstable. Boris took Artamon's hand and led him into the corridor. It was clear outside, and no wind shook the bare branches of the birch trees lining the street. The giant disk of the dazzling moon hung in the cloudless sky, throwing rugged shadows of the two straggling figures upon the squeaking snow. At the door of his apartment, Artamon rummaged awkwardly in his pockets. He could not locate his keys. Boris frisked him and, pulling the keys from one of the pockets, said, "Hey, you really are drunk."

"Drunk and smart—twice blessed," were the last words Artamon said, as he disappeared behind the door.

PART 2
APPOINTING THE CULPRIT

Chapter 8

THE ALARM CLOCK WAS PERSISTENT. ARTAMON SIGHED AND opened his eyes. After the quarter-liter of vodka he had consumed the previous night, his mouth was dry and something was wringing his stomach. He found a jar of marinated cucumbers and swallowed several gulps of its pickle juice, the traditional Russian remedy for a hangover. Artamon felt better. Then he prepared tea in a ceramic pot, a strong, almost black steaming potion.

Outside, freezing air puffed into Artamon's face and he breathed deeply as the remnants of his hangover faded.

And then Artamon saw Lida. In her short winter coat revealing her knees, she stood on the sidewalk staring at the window of Artamon's apartment. Artamon's heart jumped. For several weeks Artamon had been certain he was in love with Lida, Lidochka, secretary of his boss, Senior Investigator Lopoukhov. Then she noticed Artamon and said, "Oh, comrade Sergeev. How good, you've come out. Comrade Lopoukhov wants you to hurry to the office, it's very urgent."

The four-story yellow building in which the City and Region Prosecutor's offices were located stood right on the quay facing the Volga. Several other, almost identical yellow structures, all built before 1917, lined the shallow arc of the Volga shore. Artamon rapidly crossed the bridge and, following Lida whose legs flashed in front of his eyes, entered the building.

Artamon's boss, Senior Investigator Lopoukhov, and the Region Prosecutor Gnida, stood in the lobby in winter coats and fur caps.

"Ah," Lopoukhov said, squinting at Sergeev from behind glasses. "We go to the *obkom*, immediately. Comrade Korytov wants to see us. He has sent a car to pick us up."

So, Ivan Platonovich Korytov himself, the First Secretary of the *obkom*, the Region Party Committee, the Kalinin region's Master and Lord, wished to talk personally to Gnida, Lopoukhov and Sergeev, no doubt in connection with Baev's death. Apparently, the Party bosses attached much significance to the demise of the University Party Secretary.

The hushed cough of a black Volga sedan vibrated slightly in the driveway. The number O-001 on its license plate indicated that the car was from the *obkom* garage. The chauffeur, a young man with an expression of disdain on his face, tapped ashes from his cigarette through the half-opened window.

In the marble-walled lobby of the *obkom* building, a solemn-looking guard meticulously checked the Party certificates of the three visitors. Then he pressed a button and a man in a black suit appeared from nowhere and led them to the elevator. On the fourth floor of the eight-story building, a guard led them towards an oakwood door. Neither the guard, nor any of the three men said a single word.

The doors opened without a sound and they entered a huge room. A man in a black suit and with a dark-brown tie, was sitting at a large desk with a row of telephones on it. There were two big doors to the left and one on the right. On it were white letters reading "I.P. Korytov." A red carpet stretched from the entrance to the center of this room and another red carpet from the center to the large door on the right.

The man behind the desk rechecked the Party certificates of Gnida, Lopoukhov and Sergeev. Then he took the receiver from the white telephone and talked in a very low voice. The door from the corridor opened and a man entered the room.

The visitors knew him. Mikhail Berkin, but to many in the upper strata of the region Party organization, he was just Misha. Misha's official position was *technical aide* to the First Secretary of the Region Party Committee.

Misha Berkin was unique. He was unique because he was a Party *apparatchik* despite his being a Jew. Actually, he was half-Jewish. His mother was a Russian peasant woman from a small village in the Kursk region. The hut in which she was born stood a few hundred meters from another hut in which Nikita Khrushchev was born and spent the early years of his life. As a child, Misha's grandfather used to go fishing together with the neighbor's son, Nikita, the future leader of the country.

As the rumor went, once, in the early sixties, there was a telephone call from the office of the First Secretary of the Party Central Committee, comrade Khrushchev, to the *obkom* of the remote Siberian region where at that time Ivan Platonovich Korytov was head of the Propaganda section. During this call, a young communist by the name of Berkin was highly recommended for the position of technical aide to the section head. With such a recommendation, the Party closed its eyes to the second half of

Misha's origin. After all, Misha's father was a communist with an impeccable reputation; during the war he served in the *Smersh*, the Army's dreaded secret security service. In Misha's passport, the fifth line indicating one's ethnic origin, read *Russian*. Ivan Platonovich Korytov, apparently, never regretted that Misha was assigned to be his aide.

For twenty years, Misha followed Korytov along the twisted path of his Party career. Now Misha Berkin was still with Korytov, and still a *technical aide*, because for a person imprudent enough to have a Jew for a father, there was no place on the ladder of the Party hierarchy. He was the only Jew in the Party *apparat*.

Officially, Misha had no decision-making power, but as *technical aide* the extent of Misha's real power was unlimited.

Artamon Sergeev happened to know firsthand of a case when Misha's unofficial power had changed the life of one family. There was an actor in the Kalinin City Theater by the name of Dudkin. Dudkin's only son, a lad of eighteen, got mixed up in a youth gang. Their escapades led them finally to a burglary; a guard in a storehouse was wounded and crippled. The gang was caught and Dudkin's son was sentenced to twenty years in jail.

This event crushed Dudkin and his wife. They felt their life had come to an end. Then somebody reminded Dudkin that Mikhail Mikhailovich Berkin, of the *obkom*, as rumors went, was a great fan of the theater and, moreover, of Dudkin's performances. Some friends introduced Dudkin to Misha. Misha agreed to help.

He started with a call to the Kalinin City jail where young Dudkin was waiting for the *etap*, transportation to a camp. The call came just in time: while the rest of the gang members were loaded into a *vagonzak*, a jail-car, and transferred to a remote camp, young Dudkin was assigned a job in the Kalinin jail kitchen.

Then Misha delivered a pass to Dudkin and his wife allowing them to enter the *obkom* building. They came to the *obkom* every day and waited in a room adjacent to Misha's personal office. It took several days, until Misha had found a proper slot in Korytov's schedule. When Misha had decided the time was right, he opened the door to Korytov's office and let the Dudkins step in. They followed Misha's instructions precisely. Once in Korytov's office, the Dudkins, without saying a word, prostrated themselves on the parquet floor at Korytov's feet. Stunned, Korytov helplessly glanced at Misha who was standing in the door. "What's this, Misha?" he said. "What's this? Misha, do something . . . Whatever this is!"

Misha nodded and the Dudkins immediately retired to Misha's room.

Now Misha dialed a number in the Region Court. The Chairman of the Court was on the line immediately, as a call from the *obkom* took precedence over any other business.

"Comrade Korytov is of the opinion," Misha said, "that it's advisable to look into Dudkin's case more carefully. Certainly, we have no intentions of interfering with the legal procedure . . ."

In two days, the Region Court had canceled the sentence of the People's Court in regard to young Dudkin. The lad was released immediately.

Now, in the *obkom*, Misha Berkin stood in front of Gnida, Lopoukhov and Sergeev.

In his early forties, of average height, with slanted shoulders and a beginning paunch, Misha had the pale visage of a man who shunned outdoor activities.

Unlike the men on duty, Misha Berkin did not wear a tie. A soft gray sweater with an open neck showed a pink shirt. The unbuttoned collar signified Misha's position. He was beyond the strict dress code prescriptions.

"Comrade Korytov will receive you in five minutes," Misha said.

One of the telephones rang. The man with the brown tie picked up the receiver, then nodded to Misha, who turned his face towards the entrance as the big door opened and a man entered the room.

Professor Sergei Pavlovich Nekipalov, Rector of the University, was a member of the Region Party Committee. A tall, spare man, with a bald cone-shaped head and thin gray mustache, he crossed the length of the red carpet. His narrow wrinkle-framed eyes bore a slightly sarcastic expression which made the solemnity of his countenance look like a mockery.

Nekipalov shook hands, first with Misha, then with Gnida, then with Lopoukhov and finally with Artamon. In silence they stood in the middle of the large empty room looking at the empty walls.

Then, again, a telephone rang and the man at the desk listened and nodded in response to Misha's glance. The entrance door opened and two more people walked in.

The first man wore a dark blue uniform with gilded shoulder straps bearing two large stars. This was Lieutenant General Timofei Georgievich Rashkov, the Chairman of the Region Committee of State Security, the KGB. His eyes hid behind a thick-glassed pince-nez with a dangling old-fashioned gilded chain.

The man who followed him was the KGB's Investigator Mordin, a big, wide-shouldered man with a thick nose, big lips and bushy dark brows.

Rashkov walked straight to the door displaying Korytov's name. Misha Berkin followed General Rashkov, and the others followed.

The six men entered a room the size of an average square in the town's center. A thick red carpet stretched across the parquet floor to the far end of the room where a long red-covered table stood with rows of high-backed chairs on both sides. Behind the far end of this table, there was an immense desk. Not a single sheet of paper spoiled its perfect, gleaming emptiness.

Ivan Platonovich Korytov was sitting behind the desk. Two large pictures in gilded frames hung on the wall behind him. One of them was Lenin, and the other, the First Secretary of the Party Central Committee.

Artamon Sergeev had never met Korytov. The region's Master, God and Czar, was a thickset, broad-shouldered man in his early sixties, with heavy jowls and a dense web of furrows on his cheeks. He wore a gray jacket tightly buttoned up to his fat neck, with big pockets on the chest. His white hands rested on the gleaming surface of his huge empty desk.

General Rashkov pulled out a chair from under the table, sat down, and laid a black folder on the desk. The other visitors remained standing, glancing timidly at Korytov until Misha made a gesture inviting them to take seats. They pulled out their chairs and sat down on the edges keeping their spines straight.

Suddenly Korytov hit the desk with his palm and shouted, "Pigs! Idiots! Siberia weeps for you." Everybody, but Misha and Rashkov, started.

"Where is the politico-educational work? Where is it? Is that what the Party teaches us? That any fucking bastard can kill a communist with impunity? And not just a communist, a Party Secretary!" He again moved his eyes around the table. After a while, he looked at Misha Berkin and said, in a calm and businesslike manner, "What will we do?"

In an almost inaudible voice Misha said, "Investigator Sergeev will report now on the factual situation. Comrade Sergeev, explain what is known about the death of our dear comrade Baev."

Artamon's pale visage became even paler. He opened his mouth but did not say anything. The eyes of the six men stared at him. Then he got up and, in a voice which was hardly louder than that of Misha Berkin, told about the events which had occurred at the University. When he named the eight people who were in the building the night of the murder, Misha and Rashkov took notes.

"Who's next?" Korytov said, looking at Misha.

"Rector Nekipalov will now tell us about the general situation at the University after the tragic death of dear comrade Baev," Misha said, in the same almost inaudible voice.

Rector Nekipalov jumped to his feet. Bending slightly forward and gazing at Korytov, he said, "All of the University's Party organization, as well as the Faculty, students and auxiliary personnel, deeply mourn the untimely death of our comrade, Rodion Glebovich Baev." He paused and continued. "So far, Dean Gavrik has temporarily taken over the duties of Party Secretary. He has been a Deputy Party secretary during the last two years. He is an honored communist, a highly experienced leader, and a former KGB officer." At this moment Nekipalov glanced at General Rashkov who nodded approvingly. "And he had been the closest friend and co-worker of our dear comrade Baev. I am seeking the approval of the *obkom* for this temporary arrangement, until the *obkom* will recommend to us a person as a permanent Secretary."

"The Party will let you know shortly about Gavrik's temporary assignment," Korytov said. "Now, Rashkov, what will we do?"

The KGB chairman nodded and said, "Ivan Platonovich, would you allow comrade Mordin, our investigator in charge of this heinous crime, to explain the viewpoint of the Region KGB? We have already discussed it with Moscow and . . ."

Before he had finished, Korytov pointed his finger at Mordin and nodded. Mordin awkwardly pushed away his chair and stood up. He coughed, covering his mouth with his hand and said, in a deep growl, "Our starting point is that, first, attempts to present what happened as a suicide must be suppressed. Party members, not to mention Party secretaries, do not commit suicide. This would be against the communist morals and the optimistic communist world outlook. Second, this must not be represented as a common crime without political motivation. No, we will treat it as a political crime committed by enemies of our people. We know who those enemies are. Mercenaries of the international circles, American capitalists and Zionists. Therefore, this must be handled by the KGB rather than by the Prosecutor's office. We are prepared to use the assistance of the Prosecutor's office under our guidance . . ."

Artamon, Lopoukhov, Gnida, Mordin, Rashkov and Korytov glanced at Misha Berkin. Misha's visage did not reveal any reaction to Mordin's words.

"This is beautiful," Korytov said. "Just tell me who this pig was, the murderer . . ."

"Yes, comrade Secretary," Mordin growled, "the KGB suggests that we concentrate our effort on this dissident Galaunov. We have enough evidence regarding his activities, but his status as a Lenin Prize winner has been impeding our work. We had to wait. Now is the appropriate moment to stop his anti-Party activities. If we connect him to the murder . . ."

"No. No," Korytov said. "I don't want to make Galaunov the culprit . . . I have told you, and more than once, that Galaunov, even though he occasionally rubs elbows with those snotty dissidents, is anyway a Russian, he is a patriot. Of course, he must be warned, his stupid behavior stopped. But not by making him a murderer. No, give me another murderer, a Zionist, some Finkelstein, or

Rabinovich, or Khaimovich . . . That will indeed be what the Party needs now . . . Well, what does the Prosecutor think?''

Mordin sat down slowly and Region Prosecutor Gnida stood up. For a while he chewed his thick lips. Then he rubbed his chin and said, ''We at the Prosecutor's office agree fully with your words. Zionists, beyond any doubt, were instrumental in this awful crime.''

Korytov nodded and senior investigator Lopoukhov, rising from the chair, spoke in a dry monotonous voice. ''Our opinion is that this case should not be played out as a political event. There must not be a hint that there are forces in our midst opposing our Great Party. Otherwise, how could the KGB have missed the existence of a terrorist body capable of killing a Party Secretary? No, this was a common crime with a vile, but still a common-type motive. We will share with our KGB colleagues all the information we unearth . . .''

Again, the six pairs of eyes gazed at Misha Berkin. And, again, Misha's face did not display any signs of either approval or disapproval.

''It's all nice and interesting, but who is the murderer?'' Korytov said.

''Yes, comrade First Secretary,'' Lopoukhov continued. ''As you indicated, the murderer must be a Zionist, even if the crime had a non-political motive. And there is only one natural suspect, and his name is Magidov, Yosif Markovich . . .''

''I see, very good, comrades . . . I'll tell you the opinion of the Region Party Committee after we take a break.'' Korytov walked rapidly to a door situated under the picture of Lenin. Misha walked to the other door, under the likeness of the Big Master. When they disappeared behind the doors, the five people sat down relaxing . . .

*   *   *

The door used by Korytov led to a short corridor with two doors to the left, two to the right and one at the corridor's end. The first door on the right led to the office of Misha Berkin. Ivan Platonovich Korytov walked into Misha's office. Misha was waiting inside.

Ivan Platonovich unbuttoned his collar and poured mineral water into a crystal glass. "What will we do?" he said.

Misha Berkin sat down on a leather-clad sofa and said, in a voice which this time was quite audible, "We will feed both the KGB and the Prosecutor's office a small slice, but to neither of them the whole pie. We cannot go the path Rashkov wants. For several reasons. One, too much fuss regarding the demise of that idiot Baev will reverberate in the Central Committee. And it's not the time to attract attention . . . I have a gut feeling that some purges are imminent. Better to stay quiet, to play down this whole story . . . Two, I feel that, for several months, this bastard Rashkov has been digging under the *obkom* . . ."

"A grave for himself he digs, I say this in the Party's name," Korytov interjected. "Those times when the KGB could threaten the Party leaders are gone . . ."

Misha nodded, and continued. "We don't want to give Rashkov a chance to turn this affair against the *obkom*. Hence, the investigation will be conducted by the Prosecutor's office. This story cannot be inflated to the level of a political event. On the other hand, we have to use this as a tool of the Party propaganda. So, this Magidov is an ideal scapegoat. A Zionist! Excellent. Officially, he had done this because of some base motive, whatever Gnida's guys come up with. The people must be told it was a Zionist plot. To this end, meetings of communists will be conducted, in large factories, at the University and so on. *Closed* meetings, of course. The communists will be warned not to spread around what they will be told in these meetings. They will be told that a Zionist, Magidov, connected to the imperialist-Zionist circles, has murdered a Party leader because of his hatred of all that is Russian. The communists will whisper to their spouses and lovers, under the covers, about what they will have learned in the meetings. The spouses and lovers will spread it further. But all this will be handled in a way of whispered rumors.''

"Great, Misha," Korytov said, "Great. Yes, I've made my decision. We will kill two hares by one shot: twist Rashkov's nose and gain a propaganda victory . . . Let's tell them about my decision.''

Chapter 9

THE FIVE VISITORS AND MISHA WALKED OUT. IVAN PLATOnovich Korytov glanced at his wristwatch. It was only 9:30; the entire day was still ahead.

His Seiko watch entertained him for a while. Those stinking foreigners had invented a fascinating gadget: the watch contained a calculator. Ivan Platonovich multiplied 2 times 2. It came out 4. Amused, Korytov tried once more. 2 times 2 was still 4. Korytov chuckled. However, he felt something bothering him. Yes, he knew what it was. Nonsense. A small accident which had happened that morning.

He and his guards had left the *Big Dacha* located in the forest on the shore of the picturesque Tvertsa river, as usual, in three identical black Volga sedans. In one was Korytov and his chauffeur Arkady. In the two other cars were his guards.

Every few minutes, the three cars swapped places in the motorcade; first the car with Korytov was ahead of the two other cars, then it was behind them, and then in between.

This arrangement was approved by the KGB's Department of the Party Leaders' security. They drove at 100 kilometers an hour, making left turns on red lights, rushing past bus stops and schools, and the Militsiamen regulating traffic jerked their hands to their caps as the three black cars with the *obkom*'s plates flashed by.

Then some stupid girl happened to cross the empty street when the three black cars flew out from behind a corner. The bumper of Korytov's car hit the girl. The chauffeur Arkady slammed on the brakes, and the other two cars stopped too. The guards immediately jumped out and surrounded Korytov's car. Korytov climbed out. Entering the second car, behind the guards' backs, he threw a quick glance at the girl slumped in the snow. Her legs were in *valenki*, traditional Russian felt boots. Between the *valenki*'s upper edge and the overcoat's lower hem, he saw a strip of her bony thigh in cheap cotton stockings.

This all happened in front of a meat store, where gray figures huddled at the entrance, sullenly waiting for the store to open. These figures had just started to turn their eyes to the three cars when Korytov's sedan had leapt forward, spraying fountains of smudged snow under the rear wheels. The second car swerved and also leapt forward, the guards jumping into it on the move. Arkady stayed behind the third car, to take care of the *GAI*, the traffic-controlling unit of the Militsia.

This stupid event was of no significance. Korytov's concern was not that Arkady could not deal with the *GAI*. Surely, Arkady had arranged everything perfectly. He held the rank of a KGB Lieutenant. Korytov was just curious, though, how exactly the young lad had handled the situation.

He picked up a receiver and ordered Arkady to his office.

Arkady's mustached visage showed no emotion. Lazily, he approached the desk, his fingers playing with car keys.

Korytov stared at Arkady. Arkady stared at Korytov. *Stinking boar*, thought Korytov. Arkady did not say a word. Korytov could not ask about the morning accident. The region's Master must only be concerned with matters of historical importance.

Arkady continued to play with the car keys. His boss stared at him. Then Korytov coughed, significantly. Arkady did not react. So, Korytov understood that his insolent chauffeur wouldn't tell, without being prodded directly, about the outcome of the morning accident. And the region master gave up.

"At ten thirty," Korytov said, "you'll meet Alla Shumilova at the train station and drive her to the Big Dacha. Is that clear? And today, the engine was awfully noisy, didn't you notice?"

"Uh huh," Arkady nodded. "You've told me already about this Shumilova girl. I know. And I'll tell the chief mechanic, he'll lose his bonus this month."

Korytov waved his hand dismissing the insolent chauffeur.

He closed his eyes. In less than an hour, Alla Shumilova will be in Kalinin . . . Alla Shumilova . . .

It was over forty years ago, but Ivan vividly remembered how, as an awkward youth with a clean-shaven skull, his bony arms stretching from the sleeves of a second-term uniform, he arrived in the Tank School. On the third day, the school commander, a limping Colonel with an obviously Jewish face, after observing Ivan perform his exercises, said, "This one, maybe he could be taught to graze cows." No, this was war time, and the school was allowed no rejects. In three months Ivan graduated from the school as a tank driver, alone with the humiliating Lance-Corporal rank, among three hundred Senior Sergeants and Junior Lieutenants.

The Colonel, apparently, had had keen vision: Ivan's fate ultimately led him to an encounter with a cow.

The tank battalion was ordered to move through a forest, on a narrow clay road among centuries-old oak-trees. Ivan's tank moved in the middle of the column-of-route. The tank bounced sideways, roared over bumps, cruelly dove into pits. Clutching the levers, Ivan feverishly strove to follow the abrupt swings of the deep grooves in the road. His whole world shrank down now to his vision slit. A roaring mass of the front tank rolled ahead, shooting arcs of clay from under its screaming caterpillar tracks. Suddenly the image of the tank ahead disappeared. Darkness fell upon the vision slit. Ivan did not hear the tank commander cursing and swearing; Ivan clenched the levers in a mortal grip. The tank bumped, shook and continued its motion, led by the deep grooves in the hard clay, until the commander crawled from his turret close enough to Ivan to tear Ivan's hands from the levers.

They opened the hatch and understood what had happened. Trying to save their cattle from the vicissitudes of war, Polish peasants had hid them in the forests. One cow had crossed the road right in front of Ivan's tank. The tank's low hull had rolled under the cow's rump and lifted it. With the thighs of its hindlegs caught on the tank's hood, the cow continued to run on its forelegs, pushed ahead by the rolling mass of metal; the cow's body covered Ivan's vision slit.

Ivan had become the division's overnight celebrity. The regiment's commander said, "I don't need a tank man kissing cows' asses. Make him an orderly, to anybody, at once."

So Ivan became an orderly, moving from one officer to another, none of them willing to put up with him for more than a couple of weeks. Finally, he was assigned to the head of the division's Political Department, one Major Vasily Shumilov who made a point of educating and bringing up backward people. He would take personal pride in making a *man* out of that village bumpkin, Ivan Korytov.

Indeed, even Ivan's appearance changed quickly. Instead of puttees, he now wore boots like an officer. Soon thereafter Major Shumilov recommended him to the Party.

As the orderly of the Political Department's head, Ivan did not take part in battles. He cleaned Shumilov's uniform, waxed his boots, cut bread for the Major and poured tea. And, occasionally, before inspections by the corps PolitDep's big shots, Ivan took care of the Major's multiple medals. Rubbing the medals with chalk powder, breathing upon them and then polishing them with cloth, Ivan would place the medals upon his chest and look into a fragment of a mirror he carried in his sack.

When the Army had forced its way across the Oder River, a shower of decorations followed this victory. Major Shumilov had used this occasion to prove that his methods of reforming village bumpkins had indeed worked. He recommended that his orderly Ivan Korytov receive a medal for the exemplary implementation of duties.

Then a lieutenant who served as Shumilov's aide happened to step on a mine. The General decided not to replace the lieutenant with anybody else; in the latest battle over the Oder the division suffered a heavy toll and every remaining able-bodied man had to fight. So, Shumilov had Ivan Korytov promoted to the position of his aide, with the rank of Junior Lieutenant.

As the PolitDep was authorized to award medals, Ivan could now, time and time again, decorate himself with this or that medal. He soon had a full set.

The red light on the white telephone blinked persistently. This line could be used only by Korytov's deputy, the Second Secretary Kurchin. This fat fool Kurchin must have known, that if Ivan Platonovich did not answer, then Ivan Platonovich was occupied by some important matter.

Korytov never answered Kurchin's calls at once. First, a Party leader must never be immediately accessible: twenty-four hours a day, a Party leader is occupied by matters of immense significance. Second, Korytov could hardly put up with his deputy. Kurchin, a native of Kalinin, surely resented in his heart the superiority of Korytov's position; Ivan Platonovich was for him an alien. Third, Korytov felt more comfortable communicating with everybody through Misha, especially if a decision had to be made. Ivan Platonovich had delegated responsibility to Kurchin only for overseeing three areas of secondary significance, namely primary education, social maintenance and health protection.

Unfortunately, there was no way to avoid direct calls from Kurchin. Korytov sighed and picked up the receiver.

Calmly but pressingly, Kurchin requested a definite answer as to whether he might approve a Doctor Litvin for the position of chief physician for the Golokomlya Mental Hospital. This madhouse was situated on the island of Golokomlya, in the middle of Lake Seliger. The previous chief physician had died, and the Region Health Authority was having trouble finding a doctor who would accept the position. Those bastards-doctors, they did not want to live and work far from the big cities, to spend long winters on the remote island. The legendary beauty of the lake did not, in their opinion, compensate for the absence of what they called "culture." The chief physicians who had served in Golokomlya were all bitter drunkards and pilferers.

Now, said Kurchin, at last here was a chance to have a decent person in Golokomlya. This was an important position, in view of the recent trend to treat dissidents as psychiatric cases. Doctor Litvin, Kurchin said, has good credentials; he is not a Party member, but he has served many years in the army, and is eager to get the job.

Both Kurchin and Korytov knew that as a Jew, Litvin would not have an opportunity to switch to a better location. This appointment would solve the Golokomlya problem for a few years to come.

It was a difficult decision, to appoint a Jew to a managerial position. Still, Kurchin and Korytov knew that a position in such a hole as Golokomlya would not be envied by any other doctor. Korytov knew also that Kurchin could not handle this matter through Misha Berkin; unlike his boss, Misha could not afford to support the appointment of even a single Jew to any position whatsoever.

Korytov sighed and said, "I have made the decision. Tell them in the Health Authority, that if they take responsibility for this Litvin . . . I presume, you've checked with the KGB? Let him take over Golokomlya . . . Except, they must keep an eye on him . . ."

Korytov glanced at his watch. Fifteen before ten. In just a few minutes Alla Shumilova would be in Kalinin. Korytov's heart jumped. Alla Shumilova . . . If it's true what his former boss Major Shumilov had written in his letter, and Alla indeed resembled her mother that closely, then he must meet today a replica of Sonia Pitkina . . .

It was some forty years ago. In Ivan's division, there was a famous scout, a dare-devil, by the name of Sonia Pitkina. A redhead with wild aquamarine eyes, she walked holding her head high among privates and colonels alike in an impudent manner, aware that much would be forgiven her because of her fame. The Marshall himself pinned the Order of Glory on her khaki shirt. She always carried the common weapon of a scout, a long, sharp, German-made knife.

Korytov could not understand what fascinated him more: the fiery eyes, small waist and jutting breasts of the tomboy scout; the aura of uncanny fame and strings of decorations; or her indifference to the Junior Lieutenant of the PolitDep. Soon, she became aware of Korytov's persistent stares. Many officers were seeking her favors. Nobody was known to succeed. Major Shumilov's homely aide would hardly ever dare approach the wild scout, but it was his commander who encouraged him.

Major Shumilov was a handsome man, nicknamed Cossack, although he was a native of the industrial city of Tula. This nickname was given to the broad-shouldered Major because of his black Cossack-like mustache. And also because of the Cossack-like, swift manner in which he gained women's favors.

Somebody had told the Major that his aide was suffering from unrequited passion. Shumilov thought that Ivan was striving to win the favor of some of the regiment's telephone girls known to readily spread their sturdy legs under any bush, between attacks and marches.

"Women fall for the brave," Major Shumilov told his aide. "They believe you're brave if you just take them this way," and he made a twisting motion with his steelworker's wide-palmed hand.

Then the division was transferred to the near rear for a short rest between two offensives. Ivan waxed his boots, brushed his teeth and sprinkled his hair with perfume he had found in a German house. Emanating the sharp odor of the perfume, he walked to a clearing in the forest where the tents of the divisional reconnaissance fluttered under the cool spring wind. It was breakfast time and Sonia Pitkina was bound to walk from her tent to the mess-hall.

She appeared on the path, the knife on her belt, the young breasts pushing out the khaki shirt like two more sharp knives. She glanced at the sparkling boots of the PolitDep's Junior Lieutenant and then at the row of medals on Ivan's chest. She chuckled. She yanked her knife swiftly and cut off the entire row of Ivan's medals which fell into Sonia's palm. Grinning, she weighed the medals in her hand.

"Oh, how light," Sonia said. She shoved the medals

into Ivan's hand and walked away. A bunch of nearby soldiers watched Sonia's prank, grinning.

Even now, after over forty years, the scene in the German forest stood vividly before Ivan's eyes: Sonia's gleaming boots as she walked over a slushy path among gnarled pines; grinning soldiers enjoying Ivan's humiliation. He seemed even to smell now the strong odor of his German perfume which mixed with the scents of smoke and freshly baked bread wafting from the mess-hall. All this re-emerged sharply in Ivan's mind now, cramping his heart with pains of impotent fury.

The war was over. That summer of 1945 their division was stationed in Berlin. The feeling of escape from the death which had been hunting Ivan during the endless war, overwhelmed him now. And that summer Ivan had his first woman.

She was a lithesome German girl by the name of Zitta, redheaded, with a freckled nose, like Sonia Pitkina. Unlike Sonia, Zitta was shy, and tender like a child.

Ivan occupied a six-room apartment in a Berlin suburb, Koepenick. The apartment's huge windows faced a quiet street lined with lime trees. The building on the opposite side housed the District Commandant's office.

The apartment was full of beautiful furniture. The bed was nearly the size of the entire room in his parents' hut back in the small Urals village where Ivan had spent his early years until, at seventeen, he was called up for the Defense of the Motherland.

On this bed, where several generations of Germans had given birth, made love and died, he saw, for the first time in his life, a naked female body, with a protruding net of ribs, tiny buttocks, pale nipples and a mysterious triangle of red hair between fragile legs.

Before going to bed, Ivan laid out a meal on the oakwood

table: a slab of butter, a long loaf of brown German bread, salted herring and a pack of German cigarettes. Watching how Zitta devoured the food, how she inhaled the smoke, closing her eyes, Ivan tried not to think that this was the real reason for her coming.

He managed to bring Zitta to this apartment only three times. On the third evening, Zitta had just taken off her gray skirt, showing the play of tender muscles on white thighs above the edge of glistening stockings, when loud knocks rattled the front door. Frozen, Ivan nodded towards the balcony. Obediently, Zitta sneaked into the darkness.

At the door was a Lieutenant with two more soldiers, red fillets displayed on their sleeves. The Commandant's patrol.

"Where are the German women?" the Lieutenant said.

"Which women? I don't know of women . . ."

The Lieutenant pointed towards the widow. Behind it glittered the windows of the Commandant's office which looked right into Ivan's apartment.

The Lieutenant moved his eyes around the room and stopped at the balcony door. They took Zitta with them. Ivan knew she would be subjected to a medical examination and, regardless of the results, expelled from the city.

They led Ivan to the Commandant's office. They took away his belt and everything found in his pockets but the cigarettes. Ivan did not smoke; the cigarettes, a part of his lieutenant's ration, served as universal currency in occupied post-war Germany.

They led Ivan to the basement and locked him up with a bunch of soldiers, all without belts. These bastards at once snatched away all of Ivan's cigarettes. Ivan stretched on the cold cement. He spent almost two days in that basement until Major Shumilov had learned of his whereabouts and arranged for his release.

In a couple of days, while urinating, Ivan felt an itch.

He discovered, to his horror, something slimy on his underpants. He rushed to a night dispensary, tens of which were maintained at that time all over town. The attendant glanced at Ivan standing there with his pants down, shook his head and handed over a piece of paper with an address. Of a doctor.

A former SS-physician, the doctor slapped Ivan on the shoulder with impudent familiarity. Although the doctor's Russian was not any better than Ivan's German, the doctor managed to explain what would be the price of the treatment, by drawing pictures of cigarettes, herrings and slabs of butter. What he charged was close to a Lieutenant's entire monthly ration.

This Nazi doctor administered some German drugs called Uleodron and Cybazol. The drugs seemed to start suppressing the disease. Ivan probably would have been cured fully, had this Nazi bastard been given two or three more days. But the treatment was abruptly stopped when the results of Zitta's examination arrived. Then, even Major Shumilov could not override the regulations. Under escort, Ivan was sent to the city of Pirna.

In this picturesque German town there was an ancient castle hanging in the sky above the Elbe's streams. It was converted into a VD hospital for the Soviet Army personnel. The thousands of Soviet soldiers and officers who gathered there, in the Army's apt vernacular, became *The Blue Division*.

They had neither Uleodron nor Cybazol in this place. The nurses said that in the section for higher officers there was in use some miraculous imported drug called penicillin. But for the rank and file they used some loathsome stuff. After a shot one felt as if the sky were the size of a kopek.

The first two days nobody treated Ivan. Whatever the Nazi doctor had achieved was now in vain. The disease went deeper into Ivan's body. All that these farriers could do now was to stop the spreading of the infection. It took over three weeks.

What Ivan did not know on the day of his release from the *Blue Division*, was that although his healers had cured Ivan's clap, he would never be able to father a child.

Two days later, back in Berlin, Major Shumilov, twisting the ends of his luxurious Cossack mustache, waved a folder in front of Ivan, with the papers sent from the commandant's office and from Pirna.

"I will not allow my comrade-in-arms, a communist, to forfeit his entire career because of some German harlot," Shumilov said, and he threw the papers into the fireplace where, despite the soft warmth of a German August, scarlet pine logs smoldered, warming up the major's wounded knee.

"Now, Vania, you must find a nice woman," Shumilov said. "Like I have done. Yes, Vania, enough's enough, no more chasing women. I'll marry Sonia. Sonia Pitkina . . . What's the matter with you? Hey, this boy is indeed attached to me. Look at his excitement! Well, Vania . . . You need to relax after what has happened to you . . ."

Soon thereafter, the paths of Ivan and Major Shumilov parted. Vasily Shumilov and Sonia, released from the Army, moved to the city of Tula. Before his departure, Shumilov secured for Ivan a coveted enrollment in a Party School.

In the Party school, the teachers soon discovered that Korytov did not have the brains to be a giant in Marxist-Leninist theory. They had kept him in the school, however, since his dream of obtaining a Party school diploma made him dig stubbornly into the cumbersome and hopelessly obscure works of Lenin, and toil over the decisions of the Party congresses. Ivan's diligence has been whipped up by the two images which stood permanently before his eyes. One was of his native drab village where whining winter winds swept away the snow exposing the black frozen soil to the cruel Urals sky. And the other, of neat German towns, warm lights in the windows of cozy cottages, soft furniture. He knew there were beautiful cottages and soft furniture in Russia also. But these belonged to the selected few, and among the selected, the most selected were those in the *Nomenklatura*. To become one of them—this had been the sole goal of his life and the only reason for the communist Korytov's unreserved readiness to follow his superior's directives without the slightest hesitation, whatever those directives would be.

In the classroom of the Party School, the neighbor at Ivan's elbow happened to be a stooped fellow by the name of Kalyazin. Unlike Ivan, Kalyazin had come to the school after he had occupied a high position in the Party *Nomenklatura*. After finishing school he was expected to rise even higher. This guy had no friends among the students. Even among those seasoned Party professionals, the deadly glance of Kalyazin's watery eyes singled him out. "This guy will go far," Ivan thought. During recesses, he fetched tea and sandwiches for Kalyazin from the canteen; he wrapped Kalyazin's books in newspapers to preserve them; he cleaned Kalyazin's suit and shoes.

Once, in the summertime, the students of the Party school were sent to a *kolkhoz* in the Tambov region, to take part in the harvest. To be sure, they were not to do any manual labor; their task was to provide assistance to the local Party committees in the Party propaganda work among the peasants.

On the way to Tambov, their train made a short stop in Tula. At that time, Ivan's former boss Shumilov headed up a section at Tula city Party committee. Shumilov and Sonia came to meet Ivan at the railway station. When Ivan saw Sonia's red hair through the car window, he felt his heart fall; the pain was still there. He hid in the car's toilet until the train's wheels rattled once again.

It was not long thereafter that Ivan realized, he was lucky that Sonia had rejected him. When, in 1945, the Marshal shook Sonia's hand, kissed her forehead, and handed over the Order of Glory, who could have imagined then, that all this would be of no consequence only three years later. What counted in 1948, was that Sonia was a Jewess. In Ivan's Urals village there had been no Jews; it had never occurred to Ivan that Sonia could not be Russian. When Ivan's former boss and benefactor Shumilov was dismissed from his job in the Party because of his wife, Ivan suddenly became aware of his own inherent advantage: he was the salt of the earth, a son of the Great Russian people. Shaken by his dismissal, Shumilov had gone to Uzbekistan where nobody knew him.

Then Ivan lost track of Shumilov. But he had learned a lesson: in a Party career, marriage could kill one's chances. Also, it could provide chances as well.

It was on May 1st, when the column of the Party School marched through the streets which were decorated with slogans and flags. In this school's column, there were not only students: many had brought relatives with them. Among them was Ksenia, the sister of Kalyazin.

In her late twenties, about five years older than Ivan, she was a squat woman, with very fat formless legs and greasy hair of an uncertain color. She used to keep her mouth half-opened, and, if asked something, immediately covered her lips with her hand, in the awkward manner of a peasant woman. Ivan watched her during the three hours of the march. This was his chance.

He came to Kalyazin's apartment wearing all of his medals, and, without preliminaries, said to the stunned woman, "I love you. I want to marry you."

His marriage had worked all right for his career.

Kalyazin's ascencion was rapid, and his brother-in-law Korytov followed Kalyazin along the meandering path of a Party official. Now Kalyazin was a big shot in the Party Central Committee, and in line to go higher, maybe right into the Politbureau. And Korytov was a Master of a region. And not just a region, but the Kalinin region, next door to Moscow. And, hopefully, also in line to go higher . . .

As to his relations with Ksenia, here their marriage did not work at all. But what was the importance of that? She did not want sex. So what? With her, Ivan didn't want it either. Then they both discovered that Ivan could not have his own children. Ksenia wept for a year, then acquiesced to her fate. Party officials do not divorce!

Several times, at Ksenia's insistence, they had attempted to adopt a child. They went to orphanages, but all those babies did was cry and pee into diapers. Korytov felt nauseated looking at them. Once they even brought home a girl, kept her for three days, then, fed up with the whines and smells, sent her back. And Ksenia gave up.

She had otherwise learned to enjoy all that came with Korytov's status: *dacha*, servants, cars, special distribution stores; and what she had loved above everything—trips abroad.

How many years had passed since he had last heard of Shumilov? Twenty-five? Thirty-five? Suddenly, several months before, there came a letter. It was addressed to the Kalinin *obkom*. Misha decided it deserved the Master's attention.

Vasily Shumilov had read in the newspapers that Ivan Platonovich Korytov, the First Secretary of the Kalinin region Party committee, had been awarded the Order of Lenin for his great achievements in the service of the Communist Party and the Motherland. Shumilov had decided to write Ivan a letter, to congratulate his former protege. In this letter, he had also told a little about himself.

Shumilov had worked all those years in Uzbekistan, in the ancient city of Samarkand, as a metal craftsman in a locomotive factory, before his recent transfer to pension. He and Sonia had had a son, Igor, and a daughter, Alla. Igor was recently killed in Afganistan. Post mortem, Igor's Red Banner Order was given to the family to keep. The daughter, Alla, was born when Shumilov and Sonia were in their late forties. She had recently turned thirteen. As Shumilov had mentioned in his letter, Alla was a copy of her mother, another wild-eyed redhead.

Shumilov had also mentioned that his heart was gradually yielding to the burden of his years. Not expecting to live for long, he hoped he might meet his former pupil once again, to chat about the glorious days of the Great Patriotic War.

Korytov had not answered the letter. But for reasons he did not himself understand, he had instructed Misha Berkin to keep track of the retired metal craftsman's whereabouts and health. Was it because of young Sonia Pitkina's reincarnation in her thirteen-year-old daughter?

Recently, Misha reported to Korytov about Shumilov's death. Korytov then showed the late Major's letter to Ksenia. He described the late Major as a great man, a hero of the Patriotic war. He told Ksenia that during the war he and Shumilov had slept under one greatcoat and more than once had saved each other's lives. He said that the girl's mother (he seemed not to recall the mother's name) was also in the Army during the war. He let Ksenia digest the information. Yes, this foolish old woman fell for the bait easily. She thought it was her idea to invite Alla. She was happy that she had managed to persuade Ivan Platonovich. Ivan knew the old fool imagined that this might be a chance to adopt a nice little girl.

They decided to invite Alla. Just for a visit. Misha, as always, arranged everything. Sonia Shumilova's pension, fifty-five rubles a month, could barely provide everyday meals for her and her daughter Alla, so Sonia readily agreed to send Alla to Kalinin, to visit with Shumilov's former comrade-in-arms, now a prominent Party leader.

Korytov glanced at his wristwatch, then dialed a number on an electronic device and the door at the corridor's end rolled into the wall. In his private office, he again dialed a number on a device attached to the wall. The door rolled back separating his private quarters from the rest of the building. Besides this thick oakwood door, his quarters were protected by a steel partition. He pushed a button, the huge steel slab moved from a hidden recess and slid into thick shanks bolted to the concrete plate underlying the floor. This steel slab was designed to withstand a bomb explosion.

He touched the cool steel surface of the partition, then walked back to one of the rooms next to his private office. In this room there was a large bed, several easy chairs, and a couch. A matted glass door led to a bathroom where warm water whirled in an oval marble bath the size of the entire hut of his childhood.

Korytov picked up a receiver. "Please, Annushka, send Lisa, I have some dictation to do."

Soon, he saw on a TV screen the face of the woman standing behind the door. He pressed a button and Lisa, the stenographer, entered the room. In her early twenties, she was a buxom, round-breasted woman. Red boots snugly encased her shapely legs.

"What will we do?" Korytov asked. Lisa giggled. Korytov lay down on the couch. Lisa knelt and unbuttoned his pants. He tried to concentrate on what she was doing. He felt Lisa's warm lips, yes, but nothing else. She used her fingers, skillfully and gently. It did no good. Then

Lisa undressed Korytov. When he was naked, she turned a lamp from him and directed the light beam at herself. She undressed herself, and her round breasts softly rolled as she took off her blouse, then her skirt and stayed in her boots and stockings, their gleam stressing the whiteness of her thighs. To his annoyance, all that occupied his thoughts at that moment was a letter from the Party Central Committee regarding the necessity of increasing egg production in *kolkhozs*.

Lisa massaged Korytov's stomach and legs. Then she bowed again to his thighs. She used her hands and tongue, she pressed her breasts to Korytov's body, she kissed his lips. It did no good.

"You're not in the mood, Ivan Platonovich," she said. "Maybe I had better call Lena."

Korytov nodded.

Lena, a tall scrawny girl, also a stenographer, appeared in a few minutes. She joined Lisa, and now they worked on Korytov's body from two sides, with highly professional skill. It didn't work. And Korytov gave up.

He dismissed the women. Then he sat in his personal office, in his rocking chair, and thought of the arrival of Sonia . . . yes, of course, of Alla, Sonia's thirteen-year-old duplicate.

Chapter 10

THE CLANGING OF THE BELL DIED. IN THE LOW-CEILINGED classroom, forty pairs of thirteen-year-old eyes stared at the teacher, a dark-skinned Uzbek woman. She had her hair tips bleached blond, contrasting with the natural glossy-black portions near the roots.

"So, children," the teacher said with a heavy Uzbek accent, "As you know, our Russian language is rich, musical and expressive. Great masters of the great Russian literature, like Pushkin, Tolstoy, Turgenev, Sholokhov, have shown us, with great examples, the great use of the great Russian language."

The forty pupils of the sixth grade listened silently to what they had been told at least once every day.

"Now, children, I shall read aloud a story by Pushkin entitled 'The Shot.' You will listen carefully and afterwards you will tell me what this story is about." She opened a battered book with a dark blue binding. "We were stationed in the town of N-. The life of an officer in the army is known. Drill and riding school in the morning.

Dinner at the Colonel's or in a Jewish tavern. Punch and cards in the evening . . ."

When she had finished the story, she moved her eyes around the class. "Now, who will tell us what this story says about Silvio and the Count? Who? Nobody can tell us?" She glanced with expectation at her favorites, Uzbek girls, but none of them volunteered to speak. She switched her glance to the Uzbek boys, to no avail.

The door of the classroom opened. The children jumped to their feet. This was an inspection visit and the deputy director was a Russian woman. Her small contemptuous eyes had a drilling look. She waved her hand, allowing the children to sit down, and proceeded to the last row. The teacher glanced at her wristwatch. It was about fifteen minutes before the bell was to ring. Sadly, the teacher looked around, but in the presence of the deputy director her favorites were even less eager to talk.

The teacher sighed and pointed her finger at a redheaded girl in the last row. "Alla Shumilova, tell us the gist of the famous story 'The Shot' by Pushkin."

Alla Shumilova climbed from behind the bench which seemed to be too small for her. When standing, she was taller than the teacher. The time-rubbed cotton blouse revealed the angular bones of her scrawny shoulders. She took a deep breath and began, " 'The Shot,' a story by Aleksandr Sergeevich Pushkin . . . We were stationed in the town of N-. The life of an officer in the army is known. In the morning, drill and riding school. Dinner at the Colonel's or in a Jewish tavern. In the evening, punch and cards . . ."

The teacher, looking at the book's pages, followed Alla's narration line by line, throwing occasional glances at the deputy director. The latter listened in silence, nodding when some sentence which was familiar to her sounded in the girl's narration.

Somewhere in the middle of the story, the bell rang, and the deputy director approached the teacher. She took the book, looked at its pages and said, "As usual?"

"Yes, once she has listened to a poem or a story, she memorizes it at once, just like that, as if printed in her mind, word by word. Such memory . . ."

"Purely mechanical," the deputy director said. "I wonder if she has understood a single word she has mechanically repeated. Well, tell her to go to my office, right away." And she walked out without glancing at the children who again jumped to their feet as she disappeared behind the door.

The deputy director looked Alla Shumilova up and down. The tall girl, with her hands behind her waist, calmly met the woman's inquisitive glance. The girl's dress, albeit colorless after countless launderings, was impeccably clean and ironed.

"The hands," the deputy director said. Alla extended her hands, palms upwards, towards the desk. The palms were clean, no ink spots on the middle finger, no traces of chalk. The deputy Director sighed and said, "Your mother had a conversation with me. She requested your release as of tomorrow, to go to Kalinin for a visit. You know, it would be against regulations, such a release being almost three weeks before the New Year vacations. But . . . your mother, you know . . . With the Order of Glory and all those other decorations . . . Well, in this case we must make an exception. Unless . . . Do you understand that you will miss important lessons? If you do not want to go, I will tell your mother . . ." She looked at Alla with expectation, but the girl continued to stare calmly at the woman, in silence.

"You'll be back right after the New Year," her mother said. "And, you'll see Moscow. The subway! Maybe, even the Kremlin! Besides, as I've told you, Ivan Platonovich

Korytov is a very important man. You'll live in his house for a few weeks, and you'll have all kinds of fruit, like oranges, and chocolate. And you'll see real snow. And you'll ski and skate. And by the time you come back, I hope I'll have whitewashed the rooms. Now, wipe your tears, and kiss me. It's the time for you to board your train."

Alla wiped her eyes with her sleeve. She had decided she wouldn't weep anymore. She would be as strong as her mother had always been.

Erect like her mother and her gait firm, she walked to the car marked number 12, carrying in her hand a small bundle with her belongings: a few textbooks, a spare cotton dress, a ceramic cup containing the Uzbek cheese *suzma* and two photographs, one of her mother and father, shoulder to shoulder, both wearing the full sets of their wartime decorations, and another of her late brother Igor, taken just before he left for Afganistan.

The trip to Moscow would take over three days and nights even though this was a speed train which rushed for three, four hours straight without stopping. The car, its invisible iron parts jingling, gradually warmed up. Many men took off their coats, then their shirts, their sweat glistening on their hairy skin. Next to Alla, four men laid upon their knees an old wooden suitcase and scattered battered oily cards on it. Whoever lost a game had to run outside during short stops to try and get beer in the station canteens even though they knew the errands would probably be in vain.

Alla sat motionless, afraid of losing her seat. The men ignored her.

The bare desert, rusty-brownish like a camel's skin, ran backwards behind the dirty windows. Yellow booths flashed by, and dogs on chains jumped madly; railroaders stood, in discolored old uniforms, with flags, once green and now a faded white; children pottered about on the sandy ground and some of them waved their small hands at the dashing train, though not a single passenger waved back. And slogans made of neatly laid sloping stones flashed each time the same message: "Glory to our Great Party."

Her thirst became almost unbearable, but Alla did not dare ask the men to let her out. She was lucky, though; the men quarreled, they swore, and two of them shook each other, their hands on each other's shoulders. The two others tried to stop the fight, so they had to put the suitcase on the vibrating floor. Alla laid her bundle on the pallet to show that the place was occupied, and sneaked into the aisle. In the bathroom, she pressed a brass button, and tepid water slowly oozed from the tap. She drank, from her palms, filling them several times, then splashed water on her face, moistened her hair and walked back to her seat.

Back in the stall, the men still fought. One of them wiped his mouth with his hand, blood smearing his gnarled fingers. And there was no longer an empty place on the pallet. Another man had settled there. He was taking a nap, his nose whistling, a smoldering cigarette hanging from his hand. Alla's bundle was under his feet.

For a while, Alla stared at the new man. Then she pulled her bundle from under the man's feet. He did not move. With the bundle in hand, Alla scrambled through the corridor to the car's end. There, in a small cubicle, the woman conductor slept, fully clothed, even with her boots on. Alla touched the conductor's foot. "Auntie," Alla said, "I want my seat. I've bought a ticket."

"Big deal," the conductor said, yawning. "Whoever is without a ticket goes to the Militsia. We have no seats assigned. First come, sit. Numbered seats are in the compartmented cars only, see?"

"Auntie, I did have a seat. I just went to get a drink, and some loafer took it and . . ."

"Devil knows, who lets children travel alone. This car's not for children. Not a minute to relax . . . Where was your seat?"

Once in Alla's stall, the conductor looked at the sleeping man and shouted, "You, boar, get up. You don't have the right to abuse children." She shook the man, but the man just moaned, apparently dead drunk. A woman on the second level pallet, her head in a warm shawl, bent down and said reproachfully, "Don't you see, the man is drunk. Have a heart!"

The conductor spat on the floor and walked away.

"Auntie, what about me?" Alla said, following the woman. The conductor looked at her pensively and said, "We will be in Tashkent soon, in just a couple of hours. Many will get out there, so don't miss your chance." She turned away but then stopped and looked again at Alla. "Listen, girlie, how old you are? Thirteen? Come on, let's go to my cabin. You'll wait there a while."

Alla sat down on the conductor's bed which was covered with a dusty blue blanket. The conductor went somewhere. The train rattled, and the same yellow-brown desert with rare spots of dust-clad gardens and checked booths flashed in the windows, with the same slogans on the slopes glorifying the Great Party.

The conductor appeared in the door and said, "That's her." Some woman who looked pretty old to Alla, maybe close to thirty, with bleached blonde stylish hair, glanced at Alla over the conductor's shoulder. The woman held a handkerchief to her nose and breathed through it. A smell of perfume wafted into the cubicle. The woman looked Alla up and down and then nodded.

"Let's go, girlie," the conductor said. "There is a better space for you, thanks to this nice woman."

"Call me Aunt Rita," the nice woman said.

On a shaky bridge connecting the cars, the train's roar struck their ears and their skirts billowed under cool gusts of the head wind.

The next car was different. There was a narrow corridor along the car wall and not a single person in it. In compartments separated from the corridor by sliding doors, people, many of them wearing striped pajamas, lay on pallets, some of them reading books, but most just staring at the ceiling. Then Aunt Rita and Alla passed two more such cars.

In the fourth car, the conductor said, "That's it, girlie." She twisted Alla's nose slightly and leaned against the wall.

Aunt Rita rolled back the compartment door and said, "So, my girl, what's your name? Alla? Nice name. But I'll call you Inna, eh? You see, Inna, I have an empty pallet for you. You make take it. No payment for it. No! Just, I may need some help once in a while."

Alla looked into the compartment. There were four pallets in it, two on the upper and two on the lower level. A plastic bag with yarn sat on the left lower pallet, thick knitting needles jutting from the skeins. Next to the yarn, a small leather cosmetic bag trembled, responding to the train's jolts. This apparently was Aunt Rita's place. On the opposite pallet slept a fat Colonel, his uniform shirt unbuttoned on his hairy chest. On the right upper pallet lay a boy about twelve. The left upper pallet was empty.

Before Aunt Rita could change her mind, Alla hurriedly said, "I can do whatever needed. I can knit and I can bring drinks from the stations and . . ."

"Very good," Aunt Rita said. "Relax now. Up there." In no time Alla was on the upper pallet. She stretched her legs and pulled her skirt over her knees, glancing stealthily at the boy on the opposite bed. He did not look at her.

*   *   *

When Alla woke up, the window was dark. Two oranges rocked in a saucer and Alla stared at them for a while. She had never seen real oranges before, just pictures of them. The Colonel on the lower pallet was now sitting, a bottle of vodka in one hand and a cigarette in the other. He lifted the bottle and poured vodka in his mouth, spilling it on his shirt. The boy on the upper pallet was now sleeping.

The door rolled open and Aunt Rita appeared. She wrinkled her nose and said, "Comrade officer, please no smoking. The child has a headache, and he also has polypi."

The Colonel raised his eyes at the woman and said calmly, "Go to hell."

Aunt Rita jerked her head in disgust. The Colonel threw his cigarette on the floor and tried to set his heel on it, but his shoe, instead of hitting the cigarette, just twisted the rubber carpet. Apparently, he had already had too much of *Moskovskaya Osobaya*. The hot rubber started to stink and Aunt Rita said, pointing at the smoldering butt, "Inna, my girl, take away this abominable thing." And she put her handkerchief to her nose.

When Alla returned to the compartment, the Colonel was holding the bottle over his gaping mouth. The bottle was empty. He jerked it to the floor and stared at Alla.

"What an abominable pig," Aunt Rita said. "Don't worry though. I know, he'll get out soon, in Kzyl-Orda. We will be comfortable then. Now, how old did you say you are? Thirteen? I envy you."

The next morning, the two oranges still rocked on the folding table and Alla looked at them with admiration.

Then Aunt Rita took Alla and the boy, Nika, to the dining car. They asked for the menu. There was only one selection: udder with noodles.

"Would you eat this?" Aunt Rita asked. Surprised, Alla

nodded; it did not occur to her that one might refuse to eat whatever selection was available.

"So, good, I will order it for you, Inna. Nika suffers from a bad appetite, so I must always invent something with which to tempt him. Myself, I am prone to ulcers, so I can't have noodles. Nika, we'll have tea, and some food we saved from Moscow."

When the tea arrived, Aunt Rita unwrapped what turned out to be something pink, with a nice salty smell. Aunt Rita noticed Alla's furtive stare and said, "I see, you wonder what this is. It's just *balyk,* cured salmon filet."

A short bald man entered the compartment. "Without going into details which are of no interest to you, my love, I have *pushed,* last Monday in Dushanbe, a bagful of cockle-shells . . ." said Comrade Ivanov.

It was funny, Alla mused, that adults could also be interested in cockle-shells. Back home, she had a small collection of cockle-shells. Her brother Igor had brought them back as a gift, that summer when he had gone to make some money working at the salt extraction plant, somewhere on the Aral Sea. This was right before he was called up to the military service, to end his yet unstarted life in Afganistan. How did comrade Ivanov "push" the cockle-shells, Alla wondered. Was it a kind of a game?

"It was a fine bagful," comrade Ivanov continued. "With one golden crab, worth five thousand alone, and a pile of red banners . . ."

Alla was confused again. She did not know that there was a cockle-shell named "golden crab," not to mention "red banner." Five thousand rubles? Her mother's pension was only fifty-five rubles per month.

"I have done favors for you, Vova," Aunt Rita said. "You owe me that much, to introduce me once to Plague. I bet he has a job for me too. There is enough for both of us, I'm sure. As a woman, I would . . ."

"There is never enough, my dear woman. Besides, I myself have never even talked to Plague personally. I don't even know what he looks like."

Why do adults always speak in riddles, Alla thought. She knew that the plague was a disease which was once a scourge on the people, in particular in the old Samarkand. Soviet scientists, the best in the world, had eliminated it. So, how could anyone be talking *to* a plague?

Comrade Ivanov and Aunt Rita continued to talk, but, as usual when listening to an adult conversation which she could not understand, Alla soon lapsed into a state where she both listened and did not hear. While the adults spoke, she thought of the things she loved, the lines of her beloved poems sounding in her mind, the beautiful lines of Pushkin, Lermontov, Fet, Tyutchev . . . She knew however, that even though she seemed not to listen, she would remember every word. She had grown accustomed to this instant memory of hers which, she knew, usually stunned people. Was it true that, as the school's deputy director put it, hers was just a 'mechanical' memory? Alla did not know the answer. She knew, though, that her thirteen-year-old mind, indeed, did not understand many of the things it continuously absorbed.

When Rita and the children returned to their compartment, Rita moved the curtain aside. Behind the dirty pane, white waves of sand floated, combed by oblique winds. The train was approaching Kzyl-Orda. A few servicemen waited on the platform. The Colonel walked out, rocking on unstable legs. The soldiers took him by his elbows and led him to a van waiting in a small garden. Here, in Kzyl-Orda, began the roads leading to Tyuratam, the site of the Cosmodrom, with its launching platforms for rockets.

The oranges still rocked rhythmically in the saucer. Alla gently touched an orange, the tips of her fingers exploring its surface, both rough and soft. Then she sniffed her fingers to find out if the beautiful smell of the orange had stayed on her skin.

Soon after the train left Kzyl-Orda, a conductor walked along the row of compartments, taking notes of the unoccupied spaces. Aunt Rita talked to him briefly. He nodded, and she handed him something. Then he passed their compartment by.

"Now, he'll not put anyone in our compartment, at least until the Ural River," she said.

And again, behind the dirty panes, sands floated backwards and the dark blue arc of the Aral sea fled away to the dusty horizon.

Then comrade Ivanov appeared at the compartment's door. "My dearest friend," he said, his golden teeth sparkling. "Here is your *bashli*, if you will," and he fetched an envelope from his pocket. Aunt Rita half opened it. "Well, I trust you, Vova," she said.

"That's all you can do, my love."

"Nika, please," Aunt Rita said, "will you now swap beds with Uncle Volodia? Just for a little while."

The boy looked calmly at Aunt Rita and said, "Sure, why not. Please, *bashli*. Five pieces."

Aunt Rita pursed her lips and shoved a five ruble bill into Nika's hand. Nika calmly scooped up the bill and walked to the corridor. Rita followed him. Comrade Ivanov, alias Uncle Volodia, stepped inside and pulled the door closed. The lock clicked.

What could it mean, Alla thought, and some vague fear ran along her spine. Uncle Volodia stared at her, not grinning anymore. "Don't be afraid of me," he said. "I never abuse little girls." He sat down next to Alla, and shadows of poles flickering behind the window flashed over his white-pink face. Suddenly he jerked his hand and Alla felt his fingers slide between her legs. She gasped and leapt into the corner, but Uncle Volodia's second hand caught her neck. The next moment she could no longer move as Uncle Volodia pushed her onto the pallet, his knee pressing upon her stomach. His hand pulled down her slips but could not remove them. He tore up the slips, throwing aside their halves. His hand now covered Alla's mouth, as the other hand hastily moved between her knees.

Paralyzing fear swept over Alla's body. She could not comprehend what he wanted from her. She knew this would be something unbearably humiliating.

Ivanov's face was now quite close to Alla's eyes. Its color had changed to dark red. He breathed heavily, the odor of wine and sweet perfume causing spasms of nausea in Alla's stomach. She could hardly breathe. Instinctively, she tightly crossed her legs, as Ivanov's hand futilely searched its way between her thighs.

"Wait, my sweet, I never abuse little girls," Uncle Volodia again muttered. He removed his hand from Alla's mouth; he needed both hands to handle her legs. She felt how his wet trembling fingers ran over the hair triangle between her thighs.

Her weakening hands tried to push aside the weight of Uncle Volodia's body. She said suddenly, "Let me reach Kalinin. Ivan Platonovich will put you *where crayfishes spend winters.*"

Why had she used this common threatening adage, and why had she said these words about Ivan Platonovich, which seemed out of place? Was it just because in despair one grasps at a straw?

The man's smothering weight seemed suddenly to lift, as Comrade Ivanov propped his torso on his half-bent arms. His white-pink face still hung close to Alla's eyes, but a small gap now appeared between his and Alla's chest.

"Who is Ivan Platonovich?" he said. Behind the tone of derision which he tried to make apparent, there was in his voice a faint inflection of uncertainty, poorly hidden.

"Ivan Platonovich Korytov is a member of the Party Central Committee. And he is the First Secretary of the Kalinin region Party committee. And he is my mother's best friend."

After a short pause Alla felt the gap between hers and uncle Volodia's body slowly expand. Then Ivanov stood up between the pallets, buttoned up his pants, and squinted pensively at Alla. "You have made it up, have you not?" he said, his voice now betraying fully his anxiety and fear. And he walked out.

Alla heard how he said, in the corridor, "Rita, you behave like an imbecile. You must check first who you're dealing with. I would have never taken such a risk, if I knew a higher-up could be involved. Give back my *bashli*, at once. And if this small viper of a girl is telling the truth, you're in trouble. But remember, I have never been on this train, is that clear? Otherwise, blame yourself!" And he walked away.

Aunt Rita dashed into the compartment. "Inna, my dear girl, it's a misunderstanding," she said, hastily helping Alla put her dress in order. "My God, he is an awful man. Believe me, I did not know . . . And your slips, my God, what a swine . . . Inna, my girl." Aunt Rita wiped then Alla's forehead with her perfumed handkerchief.

"My name is Alla. And don't you touch me . . ."

"My child, where will you go? I have paid for this place, why should it stay empty now? At least, take this . . . What do you mean? Everybody needs money . . ."

"Let me out, you old pig."

"My God, I am a young woman! Why do you talk that rudely to me? Today's children! What is the world coming to? Who will build communism?"

On the swinging bridge between the coaches, amidst the train's roar, a chilly wind struck Alla's face and legs. Gray snow lay on the North Kazakhstan plain still running backwards on both sides of the train. She hurried through the second car, then through one more. Once again, her trembling legs stepped over the swinging iron gangway. Then she was back in her car. There, tens of legs dangled from the pallets, and half-naked bodies moved like ghosts in the humid smoke.

The woman conductor stared at her. She did not ask what had happened. Instead, she asked, "D'you have any money, girlie?"

"Yes, I have," Alla said. She slipped her hand between her blouse and the skirt's cotton belt. There, in a pocket her mother had sewn to the inside of her skirt, she had a three ruble bill. The woman stared at the bill, then into Alla's eyes. Some feeling which, it seemed, surprised even herself, blinked in the woman's eyes. "No," she said, "Keep it. When I am on duty, you may sleep on my bed."

"Thank you, Auntie. You know, my mother's best friend is Ivan Platonovich Korytov."

"Is he? Everybody has friends," the conductor said. To Alla's disappointment, this woman apparently had never heard the name Ivan Platonovich Korytov.

Chapter 11

IT WAS EARLY MORNING, ON NOVEMBER 28, WHEN THE train, carrying sand and dust from endless Kazakhstan deserts on the grayish-green walls of its carriages, arrived in Moscow. Snow flakes danced slowly in the air and melted on the platform's asphalt. Thousands of feet pouring into the black gate of the Kazan terminal chomped on slippery slush. Inside, the high-ceilinged hall was filled with the drone of a gray and black crowd; kids slept on the floor, people ate, drank, argued, and fought for a place at the cashiers' windows.

Round-faced women in dirty white smocks worn over bundles of warm clothing, sold, right from wheeled benches, jam-stuffed rolls. Amazed by the easy availability of such good food, Alla bought one roll for 20 kopeks and, chewing it, walked out to the huge Komsomolskaya square.

It was an early hour, but streams of cars roared without interruption. While Alla peered at the cars and at the gilded dome high in the clouds, people pushed her, elbowed her, cursed at her for standing in their way. Then she saw a woman, again in a dirty-white smock over a thick cotton-wadded coat, selling *eskimo,* chocolate-clad ice creams on wooden sticks. The price was 22 kopeks. Alla hesitated. Besides her emergency fund, the three ruble bill, she now had only 30 kopeks. The temptation was too strong. She bought the *eskimo* and consumed it slowly, to prolong the pleasure.

In the car of the local Moscow-Kalinin train, crowds of people sat on every available spot, stood in aisles, leaned against the seat backs. They carried sacks, bags and cases with cheese, eggs, meat and other food they had purchased in Moscow stores. With her small bundle in hand, Alla managed to grab a seat by the window.

A group of Gypsies settled next to her. They played cards, they sang, they argued. Then two of them quarreled and almost started a fistfight, but at once changed their minds; they kissed each other and continued to play.

Dark forests ran behind the window. Station names blinked by. Alla knew that she would remember them as well as every word of conversations around her to which she barely listened.

In two and one half hours, the big letters "Kalinin" appeared on the station building.

She alighted to a platform which was covered with a thin layer of trampled new snow. The people poured into tunnels. A mustached lad, playing with a bunch of keys hanging from his finger, walked by. "Alla Shumilova," he said lazily, without glancing at her. And he made a sign with his chin, to follow him.

When she climbed into a glistening black car, the lad's eyes scanned her. "They will feed you up a little," he said.

It was the first time in Alla's life that she had ridden in a car. Her hands sank into a soft blue cloth covering the seats. They drove first through drab streets where hundreds of small dark houses jostled each other, then they crossed a new construction area, where she saw four-story standard houses, exactly like those in Samarkand's new quarters.

The car passed a long brick fence and dashed onto a road which ran first through an open field, and then between two walls of fir trees. A small black-water river with fragile ice scales dove under a bridge. Then Alla saw, to her astonishment, a Militsioner standing in the middle of a forest. Then her heart jumped as the car seemed to dash right towards a high wall. But a second before the car was to hit the wall, a gate she did not see before rolled aside and without slowing down, the car rolled into a giant garden.

A woman, with a white shawl casually thrown over her gray hair, stood at the carved oakwood door of a two-story red brick mansion. She looked Alla up and down. Alla waited for a while, and then said, "Ksenia Sidorovna? I am Alla . . ."

The woman continued to gaze at Alla. Finally she said, "You can call me Aunt Masha. I am in charge of everything in this house. Ksenia Sidorovna Korytova is in Africa. International Congress of Female Workers for Peace and Democracy. She will be coming back in a few days. And Ivan Platonovich will be coming home some time in the evening. I'll show you to your room now. Just don't ever forget to wipe your feet thoroughly whenever you enter this house."

The huge door of carved dark wood moved without a sound.

"We have twenty-seven rooms in this house," Aunt Masha said, calm pride sounding in her husky voice. "Not to mention two kitchens." She led Alla through a vast entrance hall. They crossed a thick mauve carpet leading to wide stairs. Holding her bundle in hand, Alla stared at a chandelier. It was the size of the entire two-room apartment where the Shumilovs lived. The chandelier hung from a high, frosted glass dome.

Then Alla saw an ornamented table on carved legs, which held a big wooden bowl filled with oranges. Their aroma, wafting through the hall, excited Alla.

Aunt Masha turned into a corridor where, along its right wall, paintings in gilded frames hung between white and gold carved doors. The corridor's left wall was all windows. Through the transparent layer of a silky screen, between the half-drawn heavy mauve curtains, Alla could see, outside, the meticulously swept asphalt paths among snow-powdered fir trees.

At the corridor's end, Aunt Masha opened a door.

"Oh, what's that?" Alla said. Inside a big square-shaped room, blue water in a large indoor pool reflected the dark contours of fir trees drawn up in rows behind the glass walls.

"How many people live here?"

Aunt Masha stopped walking. "What do you mean, girl? In this house live Ivan Platonovich Korytov and Ksenia Sidorovna Korytova. We, the personnel, all live there." She pointed through the window towards the garden where, behind the trees, a red roof could be discerned. "Also, in this house we keep a set of rooms for comrade Kalyazin and his family, in the event they may want to visit Ksenia Sidorovna. She's comrade Kalyazin's sister, you know. Three years ago comrade Kalyazin visited with us for two days. You know, comrade Kalyazin *are* in the Central Committee, in Moscow. Now, this will be your place."

She opened a door leading to a corner room. "Now, if you are hungry, go down to the kitchen, and the cook will take care of you." Aunt Masha left before Alla could muster up the courage to ask for new underwear.

She laid her bundle on the dark blue cushion of a

rocking chair. She tried the mattress on the wide bed. It was firm and springy. And then, for a while, she listened to the deep, soothing, all-embracing silence. The stress of her three-day trip was behind her. A new, exciting life lay ahead where there would be no lines for food, a cook in a kitchen *taking care of her,* and no overcrowded streetcars.

The smell of oranges. It seemed to follow her. Alla cautiously opened the door and peered into the corridor. It was empty. Trying to take noiseless steps, she walked downstairs. The corridor there was also empty. She listened for sounds, but there were none.

In the deserted hall, she took an orange and inhaled its delicious aroma. There were plenty of oranges there. If she took one, would anyone ever notice? No, she must not . . . She would wait until the oranges were offered her. She put the orange back in the bowl.

She went back to her room. It was time to write a letter to her mother.

Chapter 12

IT WAS ABOUT FOUR O'CLOCK WHEN THE DOOR OF ALLA'S room flew open. Aunt Masha stood on the threshold, breathing heavily, as if she had just run up the stairs. She said, "Ivan Platonovich *are* here, much earlier than usual . . ." She did not finish the sentence, and stepped aside hurriedly. A man was behind her. She retreated to the corridor, the man moved inside, and Masha carefully closed the door behind him.

Ivan Platonovich Korytov stared at Alla. She knew this man used to be her father's comrade-in-arms. She had imagined Korytov looking just like her father—a tall, wide-shouldered, warm-hearted man, with powerful, skilled, tool-hardened hands. When she gazed now at Ivan Platonovich Korytov, what startled her most was not his squat wide-hipped body, nor his short neck with its folds of wrinkled skin, nor even the cold sight of his narrow brown eyes. Two things seemed to be his most startling features. One was his womanlike hands, small and very white. And the other, his wide jaws, protruding sideways, permanently moving as if chewing something viscid.

When he entered the room, Alla got up from the desk. She saw, to her embarrassment, that she was taller than this man. He noticed it too. He said, "Over forty years . . . yes, you're very much like Sonia. She was also tall, but it looks like you'll be taller. Shumilov's contribution . . ."

He walked to a chair, sat down, and crossed his legs. Alla continued to stand at the desk. She felt tears about to appear in her eyes.

"You know, your parents and I had been together fighting the German invaders. Now, as your father is not with us anymore, I'll be your father." He waited for a reaction but the girl remained silent, her aquamarine eyes strangely glistening, and her lips slightly quivering.

"Now, come over here, little daughter," Korytov said and his white feminine fingers made a scooping motion, inviting Alla to approach him. She hesitated.

"Over here," he said in a slightly rougher manner. Alla took a few steps towards him and stopped.

"No, right here," and his fingers again made the same scooping motion. She took a few steps more. Not saying anything else, he continued making the same movement with his fingers. She took two more steps, and now he extended his hand and took her arm. He pulled her slightly to his chair.

"I am your father now," Korytov said. "Besides, in this house, and in the entire region, everybody obeys my orders. You must abide by the rules of this house."

She failed to understand what this man was saying, his weird pretension to be her father filling her with confusion and vague fear.

"Those obeying the rules are awarded . . ." Korytov's hand lightly rubbed Alla's shoulder. She heard his voice, but his words did not convey any message to her.

"You know, I am in the mood, at last," Korytov said. "But I see, you are not in the mood, my little girl . . . This time, however, you will not cut off my decorations."

She did not comprehend what he meant.

Walking towards the door, Korytov asked over his slanted shoulder, "Do you need anything? Your dresses, whatever you women need, Ksenia will take care of these things, when she comes back. And in the meantime . . ."

"Aunt Masha told me Ksenia Sidorovna will be coming back in three weeks . . . I want to go home before that. I want to go back to school . . ."

"Silly girl, what have you come here for? The school isn't going anywhere. After the New Year, you'll go to the best school in Kalinin. Have you seen our park? Did you ever skate in a rink? You may try now. We have here a skating instructor. I'll send him now." And his squat figure with its wide hips disappeared behind the door.

The dark blue shadows cast by the fir trees lay across the gleaming skating rink. The sky was slowly darkening and bright lamps on high poles threw wide panels of light on the ice which was slightly powdered with fresh snow. The thermometer at the rink's gate read minus eight degrees. The air smelled of pines and, strangely, of apples.

The skating instructor turned out to be the chauffeur, Arkady, who had driven Alla from the station. He lent her his ski pants, dark blue with orange stripes, and a sweater, mauve with a black deer head pattern. Both pieces were too large by several sizes. But the warm sensation of the soft woolen fabrics, especially pleasing after two days without underwear, was comforting.

Her ankles, unaccustomed to skates, did not obey her; time and again she fell, but Arkady, his mustache clad in sparkling icy powder, never let her hit the ice, though he seemed to be not much of a talker. In his posture and unhurried movements Alla sensed a mixture of self-assurance and mocking indifference.

Were it not for her aching ankles, she would not have noticed how two hours had elapsed. But her feet completely ceased to serve her, forcing her to reluctantly end the lesson.

She asked permission to hold onto the borrowed clothes, and Arkady, with the same mocking half-smile, lazily agreed.

She walked back into the house, her legs quivering, the floor falling somewhere before her. In her room, she took off the sweater, her cheeks burning after two hours spent against the freezing breath of the winter air.

The lamp on the desk, under a velvety shade the color of ripe raspberries, shone softly upon the thick mauve carpet and the deep, lavishly upholstered chair. Suddenly Ivan Platonovich Korytov was behind her.

He wore a dark red gown with two large pompons at the ends of the wide cloth belt.

"My nice girl," he said, extending his white small hand towards Alla. "Come over here, my small . . ." He sat down into the deep softness of the chair and pulled Alla's hand, forcing her to sit on the chair's arm.

"So, my nice little girl, I think you've been deprived of what every father does for a little daughter when she is of your age. I'll do it for you, my girl. You just listen and obey." He took Alla's hand and pulled it closer to himself. She felt his hands tremble, and, she, too, started to shiver. After a long pause, still trembling, he said, in a husky whisper, "Do you know what this is?" He moved aside the flaps of his gown.

There was a bundle of gray hair and in it, a pale slack sprout lay to which he pulled the girl's hand.

"My sweet girl," he whispered, "Do it for me." He

grasped her hand harder, forcing the girl's fingers to rub his slowly erecting flesh.

She did not know why her cheeks burned. Was it because of the two hours on the skating rink or because of this touch of Korytov's swelling flesh.

Tears again filled her eyes. Her whole body now shook. Hating both him and herself, she obediently moved her cold fingers back and forth along the gradually lengthening and hardening jut, both repelled and mysteriously attracted.

The old man unbuttoned her blouse. His small soft fingers made slow motions over her tiny sharp breasts. He squeezed her nipple between his fingers. He moaned.

She heard a faint ringing, from the pocket of the man's gown. Korytov defiantly shook his head. He grabbed Alla's hand, as if trying to increase the force she applied. It rang again. And again. And she sensed the tautness of the man's flesh subside. And then it turned flaccid.

Korytov sobbed. Then he angrily pushed Alla aside, jumped to his feet, pulled out from the gown's pocket a small black box, pressed a button on it and shouted, "Yes, what the devil do you want? You, Misha? About Gavrik? Can't it wait until tomorrow? I'll tell you later!" And he switched off the device.

He ran around the room, circling it at a fast pace, his fists clenched, the flaps of his gown flying like wings. Alla huddled in the chair, afraid to button up.

"Today, at last, I was in the mood," Korytov said. "Nobody has empathy for me." And he walked out.

For a while she sat there, her hand still sensing the warmth of the man's silk-skinned sprout. The shocking discovery that the old man's loathsome penis shamefully attracted her, caused her to feel faintly nauseated.

She walked into the bathroom. When she opened its door, she gasped. Soft milky light poured onto swirling blue water in a huge marble bowl of the bath; stacks of fluffy white and pink towels of different sizes rested on marble benches. A warm steam rising from the bath embraced her shivering body . . .

In their apartment in Samarkand, the Shumilovs did not have a bathroom. The lavatory was in the yard, a wooden booth with a cardboard door on screeching rusty hinges. It housed boards bridging over a pit dug in the sandy soil. The boards had oval holes in them.

To bathe, they went, once a week, to *banya,* a public bathhouse. There, after an hour in a queue, one was given an aluminum bowl and access to taps with hot and cold water, in a big steam-filled room, where tens of naked bodies poured water on themselves, rubbed their legs and each other's backs and beat up their scarlet bodies with tissues of birch twigs.

She was alone now in this huge bathroom, her long-legged body with its tiny sharp breasts reflected all around in mirrors.

She had never before had a chance to see herself like that, full-length in a mirror. She stared at her body. She liked her tender neck which carried gracefully her red-haired head. She was upset by her legs whose thighs, she thought, were too thin and whose calves were too bulky and muscular. "Soccer player legs," she said to herself.

She descended the marble stairs into the bath. Warm waves of clear water splashed gently upon her white arms and lightly freckled shoulders.

Then she suddenly woke up from the unreal luxury of this marble retreat to the reality of what had happened just a few minutes before.

She wrapped her body in a big towel and cautiously opened the door. The room seemed to be deserted. She walked in. She saw Korytov.

Now he wore another gown, black and gold, with a

widely opened chest. He stood at the desk holding the letter Alla had written to her mother.

"Ah, it's you . . . Listen, my little, this will not do, what you've written here. Why should you bother your mother with those idiotic stories of what occurred in the train. You must advise your mother that you have arrived safe and are doing fine. Well, I'll see that it's done. Do you have a telephone there, in Samarkand? . . . No, I thought not. Now, follow me. Just as you are in that towel." He walked to the door urging her to follow him.

While walking along the corridor, she saw through the windows two figures in long coats and wide fur caps, ambulating in the garden, one of them leading a large German shepherd on a leash. The guards on duty, they made their tour, their faces dully lit by the greenish moonlight while their shadows slid over dark shrubs. And Alla's heart fell again, as if the guards' task was not to protect the mansion against uninvited visitors, but rather to seal it off from the world stretching beyond those high walls.

They entered what apparently was Korytov's bedroom. She never saw a bed that wide.

Korytov picked up a receiver.

"Korytov speaking . . . Now, just do what I tell you. Call the Samarkand obkom, over the direct line. Tell them Korytov requests to send a messenger to comrade Shumilova. What's your address, little one? Write down the address, I'll dictate . . . Understood? The message is that her daughter is well and happy and sends her love. Do it at once. It's night there? So what? Do it at once!"

He replaced the receiver and looked at Alla. "What will we do?" he said. And he once more flung open the folds of his gown.

They were sitting on the bed, the old man moaning and the girl's hand rubbing between his thighs.

"So, they harp I am not in the mood anymore, those fat

foolish wenches," Korytov mumbled. "Look here, I am in the mood . . . My little daughter . . ."

His left hand embraced Alla's waist, pushing against her ribs, forcing her to tilt towards him. His right hand slid under the girl's knee pushing her leg up. And then she found herself straddling his naked thighs.

The towel now fell from her shoulders. Korytov's wet lips caught her nipple. He jerked her hand away from between his thighs.

"What are you doing?" she groaned.

"All fathers do this . . ."

"You're not my father . . ."

A sharp sudden pain forced her to try to pull away, the man held her in an iron grip as he entered her. She could only swing her head backwards, moaning, trying to push him away.

Breathing heavily, the old man groaned, "Oh, Sonia, oh, Sonia, Sonia . . ."

She jumped up, grabbed the towel, and walked to the door. Korytov did not open his eyes.

Dragging the towel over the wide marble stairs, she descended to the immense hall, dark and deserted. The slapping sounds of her bare feet resounded and died somewhere above the huge chandelier.

She took an orange from the bowl and bit into it. Unexpectedly bitter, the rind's taste made her shiver. She tore away the peel and tossed it over her shoulder. She devoured the orange and took another. The juice flowed on her chin. She rubbed it with the towel's edge. Her eyes were filled with tears.

She bit into one orange after another, the dripping juice smearing the towel. She hurled the peels sideways, strewing them over the obliquely angled strips of moonlight stretched across the gleaming parquet.

Then the pale visage of the old man, his sharpened nose

and strained smile reappeared in her mind. "Is he alive?" she wondered with sudden anxiety. She wrapped the wet stained towel around her waist and walked upstairs. She did not know whether she hoped to find the old man dead or alive.

She opened Korytov's bedroom door slightly and heard him saying, apparently over the phone, "So, Misha, as I've promised, I am telling you now, I agree with you. You may call the Rector, that cocksucker Nekipalov. Tell him the Party has approved the appointment of that man who is now their dean of the faculty, Gavrik . . . Is he Vilen Trofimovich? So, Vilen Trofimovich Gavrik, as a temporary Party Secretary, replacing that idiot, Baev . . . Anything from the Central Committee? Any news about Rashkov's skullduggeries? What is Kurchin doing? Nothing so far? Good, Misha, keep watching. So long, Misha . . ."

She closed the door quietly and walked to her room. Her bare feet felt the coolness of the parquet in that wide corridor with its dark paintings in heavy frames.

Chapter 13

IT WAS EARLY MORNING, WEDNESDAY, NOVEMBER 30, when Vilen Trofimovich Gavrik, Dean of the Faculty of Physics and the new Acting Secretary of the University's Party Committee, arrived at the University building.

Alevtina, the janitor, glanced at Gavrik's boots to find if they were wet and she would have extra work cleaning the floor. Gavrik did not leave a wet trail. Apparently, it was still cold enough at that early hour to keep the snow hard.

Gavrik walked upstairs and entered his office, in the left wing of the second floor. He took off his *shuba*, the fur-lined coat, and his musquash fur cap, and hung them inside a closet. He glanced at his wristwatch. It was ten before seven. He still had a few minutes before streams of people would flow into the building. He took a brush from a drawer and thoroughly combed his glossy black hair. Instead of heading to the front stairway he walked along the unlit corridor of the wing, then descended the back stairs.

Once in the corridor of the ground floor, he walked towards the entrance hall, staying close to the wall and passing the row of matted glass doors. Behind three of these doors was the Computer Center.

Recently, the big computer had arrived in the Kalinin State University. Three rooms on the ground floor were allocated for it, despite the objections of many physicists who were kicked out of the three labs to make room for it. These physicists insisted that this machine would be of no use.

The obsolete computer had been kept for over ten years in an inconspicuous gray building hidden in the maze of narrow bystreets on the Volga's left bank. A small signboard at the entrance said that the organization in the gray building was the "District Authority of Bread Production." The building, besides its two visible floors of modest offices, had four more levels underground, containing labs and shops. Here, over two thousand engineers and technicians had been studying and emulating the designs of Western-made missiles. The missile specimens had been supplied by the KGB Department specializing in stealing and smuggling the latest samples of Western rocket technology.

In all the official documents, this institution was referred to as "Organization P.O. Box 2139."

For ten years, the electronic wizards in "The Hole" had held an uninterrupted vigil, keeping the Mammoth, as the old computer was known, operational. Recently, the KGB boys had managed to accomplish an ingenious operation, a real feat. They had smuggled from America, via Sweden, an entire IBM System/370 computer. At last, the Institute in the gray building could get rid of the Mammoth.

Before the Party had transferred Captain Gavrik of the KGB to the University, *to strenghten the Party's guiding role in the Faculty,* he had worked for a couple of years in

"The Hole." Though now at the University, Gavrik was still in touch with his former co-workers at the Missile Institute. When he had learned that the Mammoth was to be given away, he managed to arrange for the machine's transfer to the University. It would be a nice show piece for the faculty, Gavrik thought. The faculty which Gavrik used to refer to as "*my* faculty."

During the eight months that the machine was at the University, the technicians could not make it work. It didn't much matter, because the machine, working or not, could be proudly displayed to visitors.

When he began his career, back in the fifties, as a warder, first in a prison and later in a camp, Vilen Gavrik went through a special course for warders and guards which taught the recognition of faces and figures. After endless drills, Vilen Gavrik had forever stored in his memory those classifications of noses (7 types with 21 subtypes), mouths (9 types with 32 subtypes), chins, cheeks, foreheads, hair colors, gaits, and special features which enabled trained warders to instantly recognize a person, even in a crowd. This professional skill served Gavrik well in his present position as Dean and reinforced his conviction that any job or activity was significant only to the extent that it contained police work.

It used to upset Gavrik that not every person entering the building belonged to *his* faculty. Students of the Faculty of Languages, secretaries of the Rector's office, there were too many of them not dependent upon Dean Gavrik. Starting today, it was going to change. Party Secretary Gavrik would introduce the proper order, as close as possible to the perfect order inherent in the institutions maintained by the KGB.

He did not need paper and pencil for his morning watch. He knew every face and name, be it a faculty member or a student. He would remember those running, those flinging their books, those shouting over their shoulders instead of walking in quietly and orderly, as should be the behavior of every good Soviet student.

Later, in his office, Gavrik would spread over his desk big sheets listing the names of all the students and professors. These sheets contained vital information. If a professor failed to appear at a Party meeting, or did not show up for the May 1st demonstration it was recorded here.

Rector Nekipalov walked in. Gavrik saw through the chink how Nekipalov brushed off puffs of snow from his shoulders and cap and stopped at the janitor's desk. He said something to the janitor.

The Rector walked to the stairway and Alevtina trotted outside. For a while, the post at the entrance was empty. Then Alevtina reappeared. A man accompanied her—short, limping, with a red nose and a stubble on his cheeks. He wore a *vatnik*, cotton-wadded stitched coat, and *valenki*, dirty felt boots clad in worn galoshes. This was the chief janitor, a Tartar by the name of Jildibek Musaev.

Musaev sat down, and settled his arms on the desk. Alevtina trotted upstairs.

On the second floor, Gavrik approached a small, locked door which bore no sign, but Gavrik had a key. He entered the anteroom and without switching on the light latched the door behind him. In the darkness his hand found the handle on the second door.

Now he was in a small lavatory reserved exclusively for the University elite. His hand touched the cover of the toilet bowl; it was down. Gavrik climbed upon the bowl's seat. Now his head was at the level of a grating that shielded the ventilation duct's opening. There he could heard voices from the rector's office.

One was the hoarse, wheezing voice of Alevtina the

janitor. The other, the falsetto of Nekipalov, the Rector. "Yes, Alevtina," the Rector said. "Again and again, I see you have amazing tits." Now the Rector's hand must be inside her blouse.

"So, what do you want today, Sergei Pavlovich?" Alevtina said.

"What will it be? You silly woman, is *this* not enough of a reason to see you? Your sugary jugs."

"Just tell me, what is it that you want today, Sergei Pavlovich."

After a pause, the Rector said, "Well, how do you know there's something I want besides your spreading your legs?"

"Because you never fuck at this time—so early. Also, because you like sex only on those days when your wife is on the night shift in the hospital. Not on Wednesday."

"How many times have I told you, never mention my wife. Well, here is what I wish to ask you about. That night, when Baev was stuffed into a box, you must have noticed when Magidov came in. You know, he's a liar. Everybody has admitted being in the building when somebody played that trick on Baev. Only that shitty physicist, that wily Jew, tried to dodge. Who could believe him? So, what do you know? When did he come in?"

"I did not see him come in, Sergei Pavlovich . . . No, I did not . . . So, may I go now?"

"Not so fast, you have all the time in the world. Musaev will wait for you there, at the entrance. Now, think harder. Don't you understand, it's important for you to remember if Magidov was in the building . . . You don't want to talk? Certainly, if he's guilty, and I am pretty sure he is, the *organs* will prove it without you. But, if you testify, this will simplify the task of the *organs*. And, isn't this your duty, as a Soviet woman, to help the investigation?"

"Sure, I would like to help. Just, I did not see him come in. I don't know . . . You want the truth?"

"Stupid question. The Party always wants the truth and nothing but the truth. That's what the Party teaches us. So, what can you now recall?"

"Yes, Sergei Pavlovich, I can tell you about Magidov . . . You see, I recall that I had cursed him in my mind when he came into the lobby, after the Militsiamen had found those seven people in the building . . ."

"You cursed that Jew in your mind? Very good. Go ahead."

"Yes, his galoshes were wet. So, I thought, this bastard had not wiped his feet, so I would have to clean up after him . . ."

"Stop it, you fool. Who's interested in his wet feet? The Party Secretary was murdered and you're talking rubbish . . ."

"Yes, Sergei Pavlovich, but, I just think if he had been in the building for more than a few minutes, his galoshes would have dried out. I think Magidov is telling the truth, that he came in later, after Baev was already dead . . ."

"That's what happens when one treats a fool like a reasonable person . . . What do you think, are you an investigator? A philosopher? Karl Marx? Spinoza? You *think*? Don't you know the proverb about a turkey? *A turkey tried hard to think, but the result was that it had just croaked*. Listen, Alevtina. Forget what you've said here. It's all rubbish . . . Galoshes!"

"Yes, Sergei Pavlovich, I am stupid. But, I just thought you wanted to find out who had really killed Rodion Glebovich. Don't be angry with me. Will you fuck now?"

"Get out of here. You make me nervous."

"I knew you wouldn't do it now. Not on a Wednesday morning . . ."

Entering the lobby, Gavrik saw Alevtina once again take her usual place at the entrance, and the chief janitor Musaev walk to the exit.

"Jildibek," called Gavrik in low voice. Despite the noise in the lobby, Jildibek Musaev sharply turned his head.

"Do you have all your keys with you?" Gavrik asked. Musaev nodded.

"Good, then let's go and open Baev's office. I want to look at the furniture before I move in there."

Musaev unlocked a door which still held a black board with white letters spelling "Rodion Glebovich Baev. Secretary, the University Party Committee." Gavrik scratched the sign, the wide long nails of his thick fingers leaving a deep impression on the paint.

"What are you waiting for, Jildibek? Away with that, you know which name must be here from now on."

"Yes, Vilen Trofimovich," Musaev said with a heavy Tartar accent. "It will be done."

The desk in the Party Secretary's office was larger than the Dean's. It would easily accomodate all of Gavrik's fact sheets.

"Look here, look," Musaev said as he opened the door of a wall closet.

"What the devil do you see there?" Gavrik said.

"Nothing. It's empty."

"So?"

"Vilen Trofimovich, yesterday, when I came here to check my inventory, this same closet held Baev's dress uniform jacket. You know, with the Major's stars on the shoulders and the decorations on the chest. My God, all those medals. That jacket was as heavy as if loaded with lead. And it is not here any longer. Empty . . . Oh, you don't think I have taken it, do you? . . ."

After a long pause Gavrik said, "No, I don't. Look, nobody has keys to this room. So, if you haven't taken it, it means there was no jacket here. Right? I think, the vodka has made you confuse yesterday with whatever happened maybe a month ago. Once you might have seen that jacket here, and those medals. But not yesterday. I am sure Baev took his jacket home some time ago."

"Yes . . . I don't know. I just think . . ." Musaev said.

"You *think*? Are you an investigator? A philosopher? Karl Marx? Spinoza? Do you *think*? Don't you know the proverb about a turkey? *A turkey had tried to think, but as a result it had just croaked.*"

"Yes, I see now . . . It must have been that damned vodka. Thank you, Vilen Trofimovich . . ."

"Good. Forget about this jacket nonsense. Now, Jildibek, you have furniture in stock. Leave the desk here and I will select the rest myself."

Holding the bunch of keys in his hand, Musaev hobbled away. Gavrik sat on the desk. A photograph in a carved frame stood there. In the photograph, there was a group of KGB officers, standing in front of a huge flag hanging from a pole. Only one man in the photograph was in civilian dress. Andropov. When this shot was taken, he was Chairman of the KGB. In the photo, he was pinning a medal to the uniform jacket of a short officer with a bald skull. Baev.

Gavrik looked at the photograph for a while. Then his large nails scratched it, leaving a cross-shaped trail over Baev's face. He removed the picture from the frame, tore it up and threw the scraps into the garbage can.

He looked at his watch. Ten to nine. The meeting of the Faculty Council was scheduled for nine o'clock. It was the duty of Vilen Trofimovich Gavrik, in his capacity as Faculty Dean, to serve as Chairman of the Faculty Council.

Today the Council meeting would be devoted to only one matter. It was going to be, however, one of those enjoyable occasions which would allow Gavrik an opportunity to exercise his power over other people's lives.

Chapter 14

WHEN DEAN GAVRIK WALKED IN, THE FACULTY COUNCIL members had already gathered in the "professors" room, and were sitting at a long table covered with an ink-stained, brown cloth. Dean Gavrik took his place at the head of the table and slowly moved his eyes from face to face. None of the faculty members looked at Gavrik's face. Some of them pretended to peruse notes they held on the table, and others looked at Gavrik's hands.

Besides Gavrik, there were twenty-four Council members: the Secretary of the faculty's Party Bureau; the Chairman of the faculty's Trade Union Bureau; the Secretary of the faculty's *Komsomol*, the Communist Youth Union Bureau; the faculty's librarian; the representative of students. And nineteen professors.

The rector wanted to expel senior lecturer Starkova and the Council was expected to fulfil the rector's desire. No one in the room had any doubts as to the results of the voting, but Starkova's countenance held a defiant expression. Apparently, she still could not believe that after all her years as an exemplary lecturer, a disciplined member of the *collective*, and an active executor of all tasks imposed by the Party Committee, Trade Union Bureau and the Administration, she would be kicked out.

Everybody knew were it anybody else to be expelled from the faculty today, Starkova would accept it as normal and would dutifully cast her ballot in accordance with the recommendations conveyed by the Rector, the Dean, or the Party Secretary. She had done so more than once in the past. Today it was her own future being decided upon in this room, and she was unable to acquiesce to an obviously base and arbitrary decision. Her face displayed a mixture of humiliation and rage.

"Comrades council members," Gavrik said in a raspy voice. "Today we have to discuss the application of Anna Vassilyevna Starkova for a reconfirmation in her position of Senior Lecturer for the next five years. You all know the procedure. The Applications Commission has completed its work and we will now listen to their conclusions. Andrei Ivanovich, you have the floor."

Andrei Ivanovich Vernov, head of the Department of General Physics and Chairman of the Application Commission, coughed and said calmly, "The Applications Commission, in its meeting on Friday, November 25, has considered both the application of Senior Lecturer Starkova and the recommendation of the Department of General Physics. The department is of the opinion that it is time for Anna Vassilyevna to retire. The Application Commission has decided to concur with the department's recommendation. The Commission's decision must now be approved by the Council, via secret ballot."

"What have you based your recommendation upon?" Starkova said suddenly, her dry voice trembling noticeably.

Andrei Ivanovich Vernov glanced at Gavrik. Gavrik nodded.

"Well, Anna Vassilyevna," Vernov said, "we simply think it's the proper time for you to retire. And certainly, the faculty will properly honor you for your work, and wish you many happy years of earned rest. Since you're of pension age, and our State cares for the people of that age . . ."

"And what is *your age*, Andrei Ivanovich?" Starkova said. Several people shrugged as if annoyed by the victim's impertinent behavior which would only delay the meeting's close. She was expected to accept her fate with expressions of gratitude to the Party and to the Government which provided pensions and a happy retirement. Of course, her pension, which would be about one-third of her salary, would not even pay for food. And she was still in good health and full of vigor and could continue to work for years to come.

Andrei Ivanovich again glanced at Gavrik, but this time Gavrik shook his head and Andrei Ivanovich did not answer the question about his age. Everybody knew he was 63, eight years older than Starkova.

"Does anybody want to express an opinion?" Gavrik said. He moved his eyes around the room. Nobody seemed to have the desire to speak up.

Dean Gavrik was about to start the election of the Counting Commission which would count the ballots. Then he noticed a hand in the air. It belonged to assistant professor Tarutin. What the devil could it mean?

"Yes, comrade Tarutin," Gavrik said. "Do you want to say something?"

Boris Tarutin slowly got up. He seemed ill at ease. "I would like to say . . . I will vote in favor of Starkova's application."

All eyes turned towards Boris. Such an utterance had never been heard within these walls, but the heavens did not crack above the daredevil . . . Andrei Ivanovich Vernov lowered his head. Something glistened in Starkova's eyes. Professor Magidov looked amused, while Professor Galaunov, staring at Boris, shook his head in disapproval. The face of Gorbatov, the young Head of the Department of Theoretical Physics, displayed contempt. And a few other people even opened their mouths, gaping silently at Boris. Only Gavrik seemed not to react, though his tiny pinkies tapping the table now moved even faster.

"And may I request an explanation as to why you would vote against the opinion of all your colleagues?" Gavrik said. "The opinion supported by both the Rector's office and the Party Organization."

Now, after overcoming his fear and saying his first words which had stunned everyone, Boris felt the stress of anticipation vanish. Saying the rest was suddenly easy.

"Yes, I would like to explain . . ." Boris said. "Unlike Andrei Ivanovich and some others here, I have never been on friendly terms with comrade Starkova."

Several people nodded.

"I see many people here know that. In fact, I don't even like comrade Starkova as a person, so, I don't have any personal reason to help her. Moreover, I consider the articles comrade Starkova has published, regarding Einstein's theory of mass, an insult to science . . ."

This time, Galaunov, Gorbatov and Magidov nodded in approval, but Andrei Ivanovich Vernov reproachfully shook his head. Gavrik's pinkies accelerated their incessant movement.

"Then why will I vote for her? Well, comrade Starkova has been working in this building for thirty years. Always praised . . . Whatever my opinion of her as a physicist . . . I feel I don't have the right to contribute by my vote to the expulsion of a colleague, whatever my personal attitude towards her might be. Thank you." Boris sat down.

A few minutes later, the Counting Commission was elected and the voting forms distributed.

While the Counting Commission hid in another room for the ballot count, the Council members chatted, walked around. Nobody mentioned Boris's speech. Nobody talked to Boris. The people seemed not to notice him. Then he saw Starkova approaching him, her flat raw-boned face paler than usual, a cigarette in her trembling hand. Probably she wanted to thank him. Boris hurriedly left the room. The last thing he wanted was Starkova's gratitude. Then Galaunov came out of the room and caught Boris at the elbow.

"What the devil has possessed you, my young friend?" Galaunov said. Boris shrugged.

"Do you feel better now?" Galaunov continued. Boris shook his head.

"I could understand it, Boris, were it for a good cause. But this Starkova, she is the shame of our faculty. You know that, don't you?"

"Yes. But to kick the woman out, isn't that also a shame? I just don't know which is more important. Before last Friday, I probably would have been in favor of kicking out a poor physicist. Not any more. I don't know, what's really more important—Physics, or clear conscience."

"I see your point," Galaunov said pensively. He put his hand upon his chest, where, Boris knew, Galaunov wore a cross under his shirt. "Maybe, you're right, Boris. And what happened last Friday?"

Boris told him about his weekend in Bologoe.

"You see, Boris, God has saved you from that axe. You have been given a new life. As a gift from God. Think, what must you do now with this gift. Russia needs you. And to start with, you must revive you research. With your talent . . ."

"I don't know," Boris said. "I would first like to find out who those murderers are . . ."

The Counting Commission reappeared and announced the results of the ballot count: twenty-two votes against Starkova's application, three for her application. Everybody knew, of the votes in her favor, Starkova had cast one herself. The second vote belonged to Boris Tarutin. Who could be the third? Who took the risk of hiding behind the secret ballot? As everybody knew, in their country, the secret ballot was never too secret . . .

Boris walked out. In front of the building, he saw the slightly stooped figure of Artamon Sergeev. The investigator waved his hand. He seemed to be in a jovial mood.

"So, my friend. The ice has been broken . . . My investigation of that pig Baev's murder is going to rev up. It's the most important assignment I have ever had."

"So, you have made progress? Congratulations," Boris said.

"Well, by process of elimination, we have come to the conclusion that Yosif Markovich Magidov, your Jewish theoretical physicist, is the only probable suspect . . ."

"I see," Boris said. "So, you've found proof."

"Not exactly what can be considered proof—our legal system does allow us in some cases, especially those with political implications, to play down the role of the *onus probandi*, the burden of proof. This approach, in particular, had been much promoted by Vyshinsky, the late Prosecutor General of the USSR. But you see, logically, everything points towards Magidov. What I really don't know is whether his motivation was indeed rooted in Zionism. I am rather prone to believe it was more of a personal hatred. But that's secondary."

"Well, I hope you find your proof," Boris said.

"*I* will. *Secundum artum*. Region Prosecutor Gnida has signed the order. Tomorrow morning we are going to visit citizen Magidov in Marinovo to search the premises. This may reveal something in the way of proof . . . Some *incriminating evidence*. And then we will book him. And then he will be happy to tell us what, where, how, and why. *Quantum sufficit*. Now, Borka, are you ready to eat? Let me take you to our canteen, in the Prosecutor's office. Let's hurry, my friend. They may run out of schnitzels if we're late.''

PART 3
ON THE RUN

Chapter 15

It was still dark on the morning of Thursday, December 1, when two Volga sedans rolled slowly along the deserted street in the workers' suburb of Marinovo. Garlands of icicles hung from the buildings' rusty overhangs.

A janitor sweeping the sidewalk stopped for a moment. He unbent his back and watched the two cars, a rare sight in this neighborhood.

The black car stopped at the curb. The beige car continued to roll, then stopped. Now the cars were on both sides of the building with the number 27 painted on its yellow wall. All the apartments in this building, as well as in the neighboring ones, were occupied by the workers and engineers on the Marinovo chemical plant.

Four people left the beige car and a lone man from the black car. They did not switch off the engines.

Artamon Sergeev, his hands in the pockets of his gray overcoat, glanced at the predawn moon as the five men gathered at the building entrance for a short conference. The team was headed up by the Senior Investigator of the

City Prosecutor's office, Igor Konstantinovich Lopoukhov. A tall, slightly hunched man, with a thin white mustache above very thin lips, his lower lip protruding over his narrow hard chin, he wore a fur-collared *shuba* which looked imposing.

Artamon Sergeev was here in his capacity as the investigator in charge of the case. Two more men on the team were junior operatives of the City Prosecutor's office. The fifth man, a nondescript lad about thirty, with a permanent smug expression had arrived alone in the black car. He was the *observer* from the KGB referred to by others as Comrade Timofeev.

"Very good," Lopoukhov said pointing his gloved finger at the janitor who was leaning upon his snow shovel. "We have here one *poniatoi*. And we will pick another from one of the apartments." The law required them to conduct a house search in the presence of two *poniatoi*, witnesses picked at random from among average citizens not involved in the case. Janitors were a good choice. All of them were police informants anyway, so they did not cause any trouble. According to the unwritten rules, for the second *poniatoi* a woman was preferred.

The janitor had no doubts, certainly, that the people arriving in the two cars could only be *nachalstvo*, bigwigs. Dragging his shovel, he obediently trudged towards the five men. Then all of them marched up the narrow stairway smelling of cats.

On the third-floor landing there were three doors painted red, on each a tacked piece of paper listing the tenants' names.

"Y.M. Magidov" was found opposite the stairs. A string of four names appeared on the door to the right; there was a large apartment, with four families, one family per room. A string of five names appeared on the door to the left. There, in four rooms lived five families. Probably, in one of those families a daughter's husband had moved in. And no wonder, Artamon thought; these chemical plant workers were lucky people—the plant supplied them all with accommodations. And there was a kitchen and a toilet in each of these apartments.

The second *poniatoi* selected was a woman named Maria, from the apartment to the right. When the team walked in, this middle-aged woman was serving breakfast for herself, her husband Kuzma, and their son Valery, a tow-headed boy of 19. Kuzma had come home from the night shift just a few minutes earlier. Valery, the son, was about to leave for the vocational school at the chemical plant.

There was a tired expression on Maria's round face.

The other families in the apartment were still asleep at that time; the people in those families were working the second shift that week, in the afternoon. So, at that hour, Kuzma's family had the kitchen all to themselves.

Lopoukhov explained to the woman that she was being called up to fulfill her citizen's duty as a *poniatoi* for the search of the apartment of citizen Magidov. In his monotonous voice, the senior investigator described the *poniatoi*'s duties: she was to watch the procedure; not to interfere in anything; not to ask any questions; to sign the *protocol* stating that the search had conformed to the requirements of the law; not to disclose to anybody, including the members of her family, whatever she might see during the search.

The woman nodded at each sentence, displaying her unreserved readiness to be an exemplary Soviet citizen. This unexpected break in the monotony of Maria's daily rounds created an excitement which now glistened in her watery-blue eyes.

The boy, Valery, seemed dumbfounded. He stared at the team members with scared wide eyes; his pale lips, with a shadow of a never shaved mustache, trembled.

"I am not surprised," Kuzma the husband said, his black warted fingers, with cracked thick nails, clutching a rusty fork. "No. I am not surprised. I've said many times, one day those two people there, next door, they are going to be put where they belong."

"Shut up, you windbag," his wife said, covering her unkempt yellow hair with a shawl.

"No, no, let the comrade speak," comrade Timofeev of the KGB interjected. "Go ahead, comrade. What is this about your neighbors?" And, turning to Lopoukhov, Timofeev added, "You know, the working class has a class intuition. They may not be educated, but they have a gut feeling about alien elements."

"Yes, comrades," Kuzma said, apparently encouraged. "You see, all of us here, the working class, we live here, four families in this apartment. Decently. Right? And they, those Jews, the Magidovs, there are only two of them. In a two-room apartment. Why? He is an intelligentsia man. So what? Big deal that they do not drink. Not even on Sunday. Yes, I drink, and my friend Yegor drinks. He's there, in that room. We are the working class, we pay for drinks with our earned rubles, not with stolen ones. So, I say . . ."

"I tell you, comrades, he's a windbag, the whole plant knows it," the woman said. "What do you know, Kuzma?" she seemed disturbed by her husband's jabber. Their life experiences had taught them never to volunteer opinions. It was too easy to fall into a trap; one never knows what those higher-ups really have in mind. "You know, *their* wife," Maria said waving her hand towards the wall separating the kitchen from the Magidov's apartment, "Magidov's wife, she used to work at our plant. She was head of the analytical lab. Then, ten years ago, they got this apartment from the plant. I believe it was three years ago, that she died . . ." The woman hesitated and then added in a whisper, "In an explosion . . . When that big explosion in our plant . . ." She stopped, evidently afraid she had already said too much. Since nobody seemed to react, she regained her composure and said, "So, they still live here, Magidov the widower and *their* daughter. Irina's her name."

When she named Magidov's daughter, Maria's son Valery opened his mouth, as if trying to say something, but apparently did not dare . . .

"So, they still live there," the woman continued, "Even though he is not with the plant, this Magidov. He is a teacher somewhere. Well, why I am telling you all this? You must know."

"True. Hair's long, wit's short," Kuzma the windbag said, closing one eye while his second eye squinted contemptuously at his wife.

Before the team left the apartment, the youth, Valery, asked one of the junior operatives, "I apologize . . . What is it that the Magidov's have committed?"

The operative thought for a while, then whispered, "Zionist plot!"

"Ah!" Valery gasped. "And Irina too? Magidov's daughter?"

"M-m . . . No, I think it is only this old man Magidov . . . But I warn you, not a single word to anybody, understand?"

The team gathered again on the landing, the junior operatives facing Magidov's door, Sergeev next to them, then Lopoukhov, one stair down, then the woman and the janitor, one more stair down, and Timofeev of the KGB in the rear, leaning flat against the wall and nervously clenching his hand around an object bulging in his pocket.

One of the junior operatives, who had the reputation of being a recklessly brave man, deeply inhaled the stale air of the stairway and knocked at the door.

After a pause which to every team member seemed

endlessly long, they heard shuffling footsteps. A man's crisp voice said, "Who's there?"

"Relatives," the brave operative barked and, probably to prove that the visitors were indeed just relatives, again knocked at the door, this time several times and much harder.

There was a silence, and then the same voice said, "I don't have relatives. What do you want?"

"This is the Militsia. Open at once," Lopoukhov said producing his Investigator's badge, and then held it before the peephole in the door.

The door clicked open and the junior operatives leapt into the apartment, pushing aside the tall man standing in his nightgown.

The jolt this man experienced caused his glasses to fall from his thin bony nose. His eyes blinked in embarrassment as the seven people filled the small anteroom. A bare twenty-five-watt bulb threw its weak light upon the man's brown curly hair.

Artamon Sergeev picked up the eye glasses and handed them over to the man. Artamon's hand touched Magidov's long-fingered hand. It was an odd sensation, a near-tangible stream of overflowing energy emanating from the man's fingers. Artamon peered into the man's eyes, deep in the dark-brown wells, black sparkles pulsated mysteriously, manifestations of powerful thinking machine. Artamon shuddered. He withdrew his hand, shook his head, as if to shake off the disturbing sensation of the hidden nervous energy of that calm-looking man.

Senior Investigator Lopoukhov placed his gilded-framed glasses on his nose and said, "Citizen Magidov, Yosif Markovich?"

"Yes, I am Magidov," the man answered, betraying neither fear nor nervousness. "What is the reason for your intrusion?"

"Here is the order signed by the region Prosecutor Gnida." Lopoukhov waved a piece of paper in front of Magidov's eyes. "It authorizes this team to search your apartment and your office and if need be, to perform a personal search of your body. First, I suggest that you surrender whatever weapons you have in your possession, be they firearms, such as guns, rifles and the like, or stilettos, daggers, sabers and the like."

"I have no weapons in my possession," Magidov said in the same calm manner. The junior operatives relaxed. The KGB's comrade Timofeev pulled his hand out of his pocket.

"And what am I accused of?" Magidov said.

"At this time you are not accused of anything, citizen Magidov," Lopoukhov said. "We have in our possession, information indicating that you may keep in your apartment anti-Soviet literature. I suggest that you voluntarily surrender such material, books, leaflets, manuscripts, diaries, notebooks, letters, and the like, of anti-Soviet character."

"I do not have any anti-Soviet material in my possession," Magidov said, his voice not betraying any anxiety.

"Let *us* decide, what is anti-Soviet material, citizen Magidov," comrade Timofeev interjected, putting a cigarette in his mouth. "Where do you hide your Bible?"

Magidov smiled and said, "I do not have a Bible in my possession, citizen."

"Then we shall state that you refuse to voluntarily surrender weapons and anti-Soviet material. This will be reflected in the protocol of the search. We will now proceed," Lopoukhov said. The door separating the anteroom from the rest of the apartment half-opened and a girl's face appeared. Apparently she was sleeping when the voices and footsteps filled the small apartment. Her dark eyes stared in amazement at the group crowded in the anteroom.

"The house search," Magidov said, his voice tense for the first time. The girl's childishly bright brown eyes filled quickly with comprehension. She started to close the door, but one of the operatives quickly set his foot between the door and the wall.

"Now, after the region prosecutor's order has been announced," Lopoukhov said, "nobody in the household shall be allowed to stay alone in any room, auxiliary areas and the like."

"But I am undressed, citizens," the girl said, her voice as crisp as Magidov's, but with a softer ring of a *kolokolchik*, the traditional tiny bell the Russians once used to hang on a sleigh's harness.

"Since the Prosecutor's order mentions only citizen Magidov, Yosif Markovich, but not you," Lopoukhov said to the girl, "you may call us comrades."

"Very well, citizens," the girl said. "You see, I am undressed."

"After the prosecutor's order has been announced, no member of the household shall be allowed to be alone in any room."

"But I am undressed—I demand that you let me put on—"

"After the order of the prosecutor has been announced, no member of the household . . ."

The junior operative stared at Lopoukhov, apparently anticipating permission to apply force for upholding the rules.

"I demand that you allow me to don—"

"Permit me, Igor Konstantinovich," Artamon Sergeev said. "I think, we may request that this woman, Maria, the *poniatoi*, might accompany this girl, to her room. Then the regulations would not be transgressed—And this girl-comrade, I gather she is Magidova, she will dress—"

Lopoukhov glanced at Maria and his dry face softened. Then he turned to the girl in the door.

"Citizen Magidov, who is this girl?" Lopoukhov said.

"My daughter. Irina," Magidov said.

Lopoukhov made a sign with his hand. The junior operative reluctantly removed his foot, letting Maria enter the girl's room.

After the junior operatives searched the clothing on hooks in the anteroom, they walked into the apartment which had two rooms, one about eighteen and the other fourteen square meters, a small kitchen, and a bathroom. Lopoukhov ordered Magidov and his daughter to take seats in the bigger room. They were not to move without permission.

Books dominated this room. Books filled shelves which sagged under the excessive weight. Books were piled under the window, along the walls, and even under Magidov's bed where the blanket and sheets remained in disarray. In this sea of books, the small island of a desk at the window, with a portable typewriter on it, looked lost, its ink-stained unpainted surface strewn with hundreds of sheets speckled with formulas and sketches.

Comrade Timofeev touched the sheets on the desk with disdain and said, "Yes, how messy they all are, this Jewish nation."

They hammered the walls searching for a hidden recess. Artamon Sergeev, Lopoukhov and comrade Timofeev leafed through the books. All of these volumes seemed to be professional books of a physicist. There were hundreds of dissertation abstracts and special magazines, with numerous scraps of paper inserted between the pages.

"They keep thousands of books in this place," the brave junior operative said. "What do they need them for? Can a person read all these books in a lifetime? It would take the entire day just to leaf through them."

"No comments, comrade. Just do your job," Lopoukhov said.

Magidov watched calmly as the visitors went through the books, shaking them to remove the bookmarks. They callously ignored him, he who had collected these books over the years and for whom each of these books was a part of his heart.

From time to time Artamon glanced at the physicist and his daughter. Irina's eyes were darker than those of her father, while Magidov's eyes did not have the childish brightness of his daughter's. Irina's youthful, softly drawn face with its tender full lips was dominated by her large, widely set bright eyes.

At first impression their glance was shy, but each time Artamon's eyes met with the eyes of either of the Magidovs, he felt the same disturbing sensation. It was as if he touched an open, throbbing wound and at the same time as if he had been exposed to a sharply penetrating laser.

Book after book, the team members went through the shelves. The junior operatives finished hammering the walls. Now they switched to the bed. They meticulously examined the sheets and the blanket. They pierced through the mattress with long iron needles, their standard equipment. They tore up the pillow's cover, its feathers spreading all over the mattress. Magidov and Irina remained silent and composed, not betraying any feeling as their belongings were being destroyed. Both *poniatois* also sat silent and motionless, their faces blank, only their eyes following the team members. The man was still in his working garb, a smeared tarpaulin coat with a rabbit fur cap resting on his knees. The woman still wore her thick gray shawl, drawn low over her forehead.

About eleven, the team members started leaving the apartment, one at a time, to get some food. Artamon's turn came close to one o'clock. Before leaving, Artamon asked Lopoukhov, "Igor Konstantinovich, what about the *poniatoi*? Shall I bring them something to eat?"

Lopoukhov nodded gloomily. Artamon walked out. He went first to the apartment next door. Evidently, all four families occupying the apartment had gathered in the kitchen. This dozen breathing men, women and children had created an atmosphere of a *parnaya,* a Russian steam-bath. Kuzma, the windbag, was sitting at the kitchen table. Despite the humid heat in the kitchen, he still had on his working garb, a thick cotton-wadded, oil-speckled coat. He was interpreting to his neighbors the meaning of the word "Zionist" which he pronounced as "ze-enist." When Artamon entered the kitchen, Kuzma was saying, "So, I am telling you, and I bet this is true, they just wanted to named 'Jews,' but the people used 'Yid' instead. So, to put it in order, there was a decision, to name them 'ze-enists.' "

So, comrade Timofeev of the KGB was right; despite the lack of education, the working class had perfectly understood the real meaning of the events in the next door apartment.

At Artamon's request, Kuzma fetched from the shelf a bowl containing a few cold cooked potatoes, a half-loaf of rye bread and a salt celler. Artamon ordered Kuzma to go to the janitor's quarters and get some food for his wife. Then Artamon walked back to Magidov's place, gave the food to the woman-*poniatoi* and left again.

When Artamon came back to Magidov's apartment, the search was in full swing. The disordered heaps of books had swelled on the floor during Artamon's absence. Magidov and his daughter sat in the same position, hands upon knees, silently watching. Now Senior Investigator Lopoukhov left to eat.

Artamon approached Irina. He pulled a small package from his pocket. It was a sandwich wrapped in a newspaper. Artamon offered the sandwich to Irina. She unwrapped the paper, glanced at the sandwich and shook her head. Artamon expected that. People usually can hardly eat in such situations. They usually want to drink. Only water, again and again, but their mouths still remain very dry. He laid the sandwich upon the girl's knees.

Then he stepped over to Magidov and took from his pocket one more sandwich. Magidov smiled and took the small pack. He calmly unwrapped it and took a bite from the sandwich. Artamon knew it was a hard task for Magidov to swallow anything but water. The physicist ate slowly but stubbornly and did not stop until he was through with his meal. Then he said something to his daughter. She nodded and also started to eat. She ate in the same stubborn way, looking straight ahead, until she too was done. Neither Magidov nor his daughter thanked Artamon.

It was about three o'clock when they had nearly finished going through all the books in the larger room. Only two drawers in Magidov's desk remained uninspected. Lopoukhov glanced at his wristwatch and said, "I think, we may split up now. Only keep the doors ajar, so the *poniatois* and Magidov can watch both rooms at once."

Now Lopoukhov, Artamon Sergeev and two junior operatives moved to the smaller room. Comrade Timofeev stayed in the larger room, to finish searching the desk. The smaller room had a narrow bed, a very small desk, one chair, and shelves with about fifty books divided almost evenly between Russian and English. The Russian books were mostly on running with a few on skiing. Several were novels, translations from English. Steinbeck. Salinger. Asimov. All these novels had been published by the State Publishing House of Foreign Literature, officially permitted for reading and therefore of no interest to the prosecution. One of the shelves held albums with photographs of Irina, all taken professionally. The photos showed her running, her beautifully shaped legs, too muscled for Artamon's taste, caught in motion in various stages of wide swings and leaps. And on the wall, a dozen prize certificates hung, attesting to Irina Magidova's prominence on the University's team of long-distance runners.

Lopoukhov took down a couple of English books, glanced at the titles and weighed them in his hand. "Comrade Sergeev," he said, "you shall carry out the task of examining these objects. I shall inspect the adjacent domains."

Artamon believed Lopoukhov knew not a single word in any language but Russian officialese. Now Lopoukhov hurried to inspect "the adjacent domains" which meant the kitchen, but he did not want to reveal his ignorance of English.

These English books were all published in Moscow. They were mainly textbooks for students of English, all officially approved for the Universities. Yes, Artamon knew from the briefing at the Prosecutor's office that Magidov's daughter, Irina, twenty years old, was a student at the University, in the Department of English. And the University's champion in long distance running.

As far as Artamon knew, his boss, Lopoukhov, would hardly rely on Artamon's conclusion, and the non-Russian books would be taken to the office for an expert's examination. Therefore, Artamon leafed through the books perfunctorily.

"Comrade Lopoukhov! Comrades, over here!" the KGB's Timofeev shouted. Lopoukhov and Artamon rushed to the larger room. Magidov, still sitting at the wall, stared at the KGB man exultantly waving his hand which held a small paperback book.

"Look here, comrade Senior Investigator," triumphant comrade Timofeev exclaimed. "Here, I have it! The incriminating evidence! Ah? And you, citizen Magidov, we really wanted to trust you. But you have chosen to attempt a deception. You think you are able to deceive the Soviet State? The Motherland? That which has given you the education, this apartment, everything of what the people in capitalist countries can only dream. And you have chosen the way of betrayal."

Lopoukhov took the small book from Timofeev's hand. He stared at it and frowned. He exchanged glances with Timofeev. Now the entire group gathered in the room, everybody gazing with curiosity at the *Incriminating Evidence*. Lopoukhov handed the book over to Artamon.

The tattered book appeared to be in two languages. Every even page was in Russian and every odd page in an unknown language, whose characters looked very odd, quite different from any language Artamon had ever encountered. The first page had a Russian title "MORI. Hebrew Textbook for Russian-speaking beginners."

"So, citizen Magidov, you indeed have been harboring anti-Soviet material," Lopoukhov said.

"It is not anti-Soviet material. It is a Hebrew textbook. There is no law prohibiting the study of foreign languages," Magidov said, his voice still calm, but his hands, resting on his knees, quivering slightly.

"*We* define what is anti-Soviet material," Comrade Timofeev said, grinning. And, turning his head to the *poniatois* he added, "You see, comrades, this book has been published in Israel, by imperialists and Zionists. Would a genuine Soviet man keep such a book?"

Both *poniatois* nodded and then shook their heads in disapproval of citizen Magidov's shameful behavior. Artamon Sergeev's eyes again met those of Irina Magidova. There was something new in those eyes, resentment, defiance, disbelief.

"Well, comrades," Lopoukhov said, and unfolded a

piece of paper. "I think we are now able to implement the next step of our task. I will now announce, citizen Magidov, the order of the region Prosecutor."

The junior operatives moved closer to Magidov and took places on both sides of him. Magidov's face became even paler. Irina put her hand on her chest. The voice of Lopoukhov, solemn and dry, portended something sinister.

"The region Prosecutor has signed the order, to subject citizen Magidov, Yosif Markovich, Jew, non-Party man, born in 1938 in the city of Minsk, Belorussian SSR, Professor of Theoretical Physics at the Kalinin State University, having the resident at 27 Lazo pereulok, Marinovo district, city of Kalinin, as of today, December 1, to a preliminary arrest, as a preventive measure, for the purpose of ensuring the proper investigation of said Magidov's possible involvement in the murder of citizen Baev, Rodion Glebovich, which occurred on November 27 in the University building, 25 Sadovy pereulok, city of Kalinin."

Irina gasped. Both witnesses, the woman and the janitor, opened their mouths and stared at Magidov with horror. Dead silence ensued.

Chapter 16

IRINA REMAINED SITTING AT THE KITCHEN TABLE AS THE NOISE of the two cars moved away. She stared at the wall, with her hands on her knees and her shoulders downcast.

In the mandatory course of Marxism-Leninism that all students went through, regardless of their specialization, their professor cited the odd statement by Karl Marx that in the history of mankind everything had occurred twice: the first time as a tragedy, and the second time as a farce. Irina could hardly judge whether this statement was true for the entire history of mankind. It seemed, however, to reflect what had happened to her and her father.

History indeed seemed to repeat itself. Irina knew from the stories told by older people that thirty, thirty-five years ago visits of the KGB's thugs after which the apartments looked as after a *pogrom* was a matter of routine. Then, fathers, mothers, older brothers disappeared without a trace, in the monstrous Gulag abyss. It happened to her mother's family and the family's fate was a part of the immense tragedy which had fallen upon the entire nation.

After Stalin's demise, it had changed. Regular people, those who did not speak up against the authorities, could sleep without the fear of being picked at random. House searches, harassment and arrests were now reserved for *dissidents*.

As to the rest, paying lip service one was now allowed to live one's small life.

Unless one was a Jew.

The boundaries of the measured freedom shrunk manifold in the case of a Jew, and the sense of security for a Jew was all but unknown.

Today it was Yosif Magidov's turn to experience the fall of the sword of Domocles hanging over Jewish heads. This event with Magidov was certainly much more of a farce than a tragedy.

So floated Irina's thoughts while she sat powerlessly in her kitchen. She got up, stepped over pans scattered on the floor, over piles of disarrayed papers with formulas and sketches, over slashed pillows, over torn notebooks, over broken plants, shirts, socks, stockings, shoes and underpants.

Somebody knocked at the door with impatience. Could those pigs have returned? Maybe they had decided to take her, too, like her father?

Irina turned the key in the door. The door swung open and pushing Irina aside, people poured in. They rushed into the rooms, chuckled, giggled, squealed. Then she saw it was not really a big crowd. Just five people. Two men and three women.

They were Magidovs' neighbors. Maria who had served as a *poniatoi* during the house search, her husband Kuzma the windbag. And Yegor, Kuzma's co-tenant in the next door apartment. And Yegor's wife and one more woman.

Kuzma's Maria made a soccer-player's motion and kicked up a bundle of clothing from the floor.

Yegor's Maria caught the bundle hurled by Kuzma's

Maria. She fished out Irina's bra and, giggling, put it over her knitted blouse.

Kuzma the windbag yanked open the pinewood door of a small cabinet hanging on the kitchen wall. Yegor, a paunchy chap in his early fifties, followed Kuzma into the kitchen. Yegor's reputation was of a wise man, a reputation based mainly on the way he conducted discussions. He usually kept silent, his yellow eyes peering unswervingly at those who talked. Kuzma and Yegor were among the few who communicated with the Magidovs regularly. Invariably, on Friday evenings either Kuzma or Yegor would knock at Magidov's door and usually it was Irina who opened. These men always had the same problem: they needed one ruble, to be returned next week. For a drink. Irina usually had a ruble ready. They were honest people. Some time during the next week the ruble would be dutifully returned, with thanks, only to be borrowed again, the following Friday. Yegor's and Kuzma's wives, were not supposed to be aware of these transactions.

The third woman who came with them was also a tenant in the next door apartment. The sight of Yegor's Maria trying the bra apparently encouraged her; she picked up a skirt from the bundle of clothing and ran to the smaller room to try it on.

"What are you doing?" Irina said.

Continuing to rummage in the cabinet, Kuzma said, "As you are Ze-enists, and we are the working class, whatever you have here, it's not yours anymore. Nor is this apartment. Now it will be given to the working class. Whatever you have here, you have no right to it."

Yegor the Wise nodded but did not say anything.

At this moment, the wide-hipped woman appeared from the smaller room, wearing Irina's gray woolen skirt.

It was the dress uniform skirt of the University runners team. Trying to don the skirt, the woman forced it over her hips. The skirt burst along the side seam. Her naked thigh with its net of dark veins flashed between the skirt's split flaps.

Glancing at the woman, Irina chuckled unwillingly. She could not stop it. The three women froze looking with astonishment at the laughing girl. They chuckled also, then stopped. They looked at Irina, then, swearing and cursing, screaming and whining, all three women fell on Irina, pinching her, and scratching her neck, face, and arms with their nails.

"You, stinking Ze-enist, fucking whore, you dare to scoff at us, you shitty harlot."

"A-a," Kuzma shouted, and the three women let Irina's hands loose. "Look what's here," Kuzma said waving a half bottle of Armenian cognac he had unearthed in the kitchen cabinet. "I knew I would find it."

The wide-hipped woman locked the entrance door from inside and put the key into her mouth and a bulge appeared in her cheek.

The women left Irina alone. Now they had a lot of nice things to look for—panties, stockings and shoes. They all walked into the larger room, taking with them the piles of clothing. The men settled in the kitchen. Nothing in the world could now distract them from the bottle.

Irina walked into her room and sat down on the bed. Her heart pounded as though she'd run a thousand-meter race. She felt a chilling sensation in her stomach. She touched her scratched cheek where the slowly drying blood had reached her chin. She picked up a handkerchief from the floor and tried to rub away the blood. She heard the squealing voices of the women who were stealing her clothing and shoes.

The door into the kitchen was half-open. Irina could see Yegor sitting at the table, his thick working coat puckering on his slanted uneven shoulders. Kuzma talked, making short breaks to gulp slugs of cognac. They fetched bread and the chunk of Danish cheese Irina' father had brought from his recent trip to Leningrad.

Irina felt a pain in her left arm. She rolled up the sleeve and saw two half-moon shaped strings of red bruises where one of the women had bitten her.

The feeling of impotence overwhelmed her. How long would the intruders stay? Besides the books, there were not many worldly goods among the Magidovs' possessions. The neighbors from the next door apartments were hardly interested in books.

Finally, the women finished examining the garments in the larger room. All three of them, wearing different pieces of Irina's belongings, walked into the smaller room.

"Look, she's here, this Ze-enist, whore," Yegor's Maria said. She chuckled and touched her bulging cheek where she apparently still held the key.

"Yes, sweetie, where would she go?" Kuzma's Maria said, "She likes us here, does she not?"

"You, women, hush!" Kuzma barked from the kitchen. "Because of your squeals, I cannot hear what Yegor says."

Yegor nodded but did not say anything.

The men banged their glasses at each other and drank. Yegor spat on the floor. The men sniffed the bread and cheese but did not eat.

"I tell you," Kuzma said, "since they are Ze-enists, there will be the decision soon, maybe even tomorrow, to make all the Ze-enists to give up all they have illegally acquired, and so we are just doing now what is our full right."

Yegor nodded and did not say anything.

"Especially, that now they plot to murder. Murderers they are, those physicists," Kuzma continued, gulping one more slug of cognac. "I've suspected that all along."

Yegor nodded but did not say anything.

"Look here," Kuzma's Maria said, fetching Irina's running shoes from the pile on the floor.

Wearing these shoes, Irina had won the University's championship. One of her father's colleagues, a Leningrad physicist who was once allowed to attend a conference abroad, has brought these shoes from the Netherlands at her father's request.

Irina watched how Kuzma's Maria tried to squeeze her thick foot into the running shoe. The foot did not want to go in. A wave of fury suddenly flooded Irina's eyes. She sprang up from the bed.

"Look at the whore!" the wide-hipped woman shouted, but she was late. Irina's hands grabbed the shoulders of both Marias. She pulled the women up, their heads dangling powerlessly, then she pushed them sideways. Both women slumped on the floor.

Irina snatched up her running shoes, then slapped the wide-hipped woman's cheek with the shoes, and the key fell into Irina's hand. Irina stepped over the prone body of Kuzma's Maria, while the woman's scared eyes gazed up at the girl's legs flashing above Maria's face.

Irina unlocked the door. She heard Yegor's Maria shrieking, "Yegor! The Ze-enist has murdered me."

"Shut up, you fool," were the first words Yegor had uttered all evening. "If you're murdered, then why are you yelling," Yegor added, proving by this logical notion that his reputation as a wise man was not completely unfounded. Kuzma laughed loudly.

Irina ran downstairs. On the ground floor, in the entrance door, Kuzma's son Valery stood, shaking snow off his soles. Apparently, he had just come back from his vocational school.

The bruises and blood on Irina's face, and her uncovered hair waving as she ran past him in a blouse and skirt, without a coat, running shoes in hand, baffled the youth.

He knew enough to figure out what happened upstairs. His face wrinkled in pain. "Bastards," Valery said through the teeth. "What bastards! I hate you. Such a girl, such beauty! What have you done to her?"

Chapter 17

HARD SNOW SQUEAKED UNDER IRINA'S FEET. AT THE DOOR of a food store an old woman in a *tulup*, toe-long sheepskin garb, sat on a folding tarpaulin stool. She stared in amazement at the rapidly walking young woman in a white blouse, a short skirt and light house shoes, a pair of running shoes in her hand.

Suddenly, Irina felt the cold, her body shivering as the frost's chilling hand reaching through her thin cotton blouse. Her cheeks still burned, and the hands quivered after her outburst at the three women. She had to calm down and warm up. She knew the best way to do that. Run!

Her first strides were cautious, but soon her skilled runner's legs had found the proper pace, her feet surefooted on the icy ground. It took just a couple of minutes till the rows of the apartment buildings ended and the street became a rough road crossing a big waste ground. Here, no artificial lights spoiled the darkness of the early night. In the western sky, the stunningly radiant Venus hung low over the scarlet glow of the city's lights. The city of Kalinin lay there, a few kilometers from the suburb of Marinovo.

And as she ran, the events of this unreal day faded gradually from her mind. The house search; the significant glances of the searchers and the witnesses when they had discovered that *incriminating evidence*, the Hebrew textbook; her father's pale face when the Prosecution's official announced the arrest to ensure the proper investigation of a murder; the chuckling neighbors hurling up Irina's clothing in the ransacked apartment; the expression of sympathetic pain on the milky face of that scrawny boy Valery. It all had happened. The aching bruises and scratches on her face and arms testified to that, but when she ran, the only true reality was the springy stride of her perfectly trained legs. The deep inhalations of the crisp air in the freezing night, the huge bright stars faithfully following Irina along the hard snowy path.

When she stopped on a wooden bridge over the Lazur river, her breathing was even, her skin warm and no rage wrung her heart. A black sheet of rough ice under the bridge hid the narrow frost-bound Lazur. To her right, where the Lazur's streams fell into the Volga, the mighty river withstood the forces of cold. The huge stars twinkled on the Volga's black water. As it happened each time when she faced the beauty of this land of forests and lakes, her heart filled with a powerful sensation of life throbbing in her athletic body.

She had to decide what to do next. She had to go back to the apartment, if only to pick up her passport, her student's card and her mother's photograph. Would the neighbors leave anything intact in their excitement? She could not stand another encounter with them. She was not afraid of them, she just couldn't imagine looking at their faces, ashamed at the outburst of her sudden anger. She knew too well that those people had been abused by life and viciously misled as to the source of their misery.

She would spend this night with a friend. Of all her friends, Esther Bronsky's apartment seemed to be the closest.

The next leg of her run ended at a four-story house on a small street on the Volga's left bank.

Esther Bronsky unlatched the door. She looked at Irina's face and gasped. In the heavily crammed antechamber, Irina smelled fried potatoes. The Bronskys had apparently just finished their supper.

"What happened?" Esther asked, her roundish face expressing perplexity and compassion.

"I am afraid that I cannot go home tonight," Irina said. "May I stay with you, just for this night?"

"Ira, what kind of a question is that? You know we'd be happy to have you with us."

"Yes, I know. That's why I am here."

"Let's go in, Irka. Are you hungry? Tea? A sandwich? But look at these bruises! First thing, you need first aid."

They walked into a small kitchen where Esther's parents sat at a round table, tea in cups steaming in front of them. They had only three chairs in that kitchen, there was no space for one more. Doctor Bronsky, Esther's father, a very short, paunchy man of about fifty, jumped up and offered his chair to Irina. He saw the bruises on Irina's cheeks and forehead. He did not ask anything as he fetched his doctor's bag. His fingers gently touched Irina's cheeks. Doctor Bronsky rolled up the sleeve of Irina's blouse.

"I hope whatever creature had bitten your arm, did not have rabies." Bronsky kidded as Irina felt the burning touch of a disinfecting ointment.

The doctor said, "Don't worry, your scratches will heal up before your wedding." And the doctor chuckled again.

Esther's mother, a tiny white-haired woman, offered Irina a sandwich and tea. Like the doctor she did not ask any questions. The tea was very sweet. It was always this way at the Bronsky's. But this was genuine Ceylon tea which the doctor's patients supplied from a special store.

After the run in the chilly night, the warmth in this cramped apartment and the hot sweet tea made Irina drowsy. In the small room, one of the two in the apartment, Irina and Esther settled on a sofa.

"Well, Irka, I must boast a little. You know, this conference of young scientists of the Kalinin region. My presentation was awarded a favorable citation. It's an excerpt from my dissertation, so, my Prof says he has no reservations now. I'll successfully complete my diss in no time, probably by the middle of the next year. Certainly, it will still be just a prelude to the real task, which is to locate a place willing to accept my diss for approval. Now, if you don't want to tell me what has happened with you, I am not going ask you."

"My father was arrested today."

"Your father? Why?"

"They ransacked our apartment. Took away a Hebrew textbook. They said it was incriminating evidence—something about Zionism . . ."

"Oh, no." Esther's face became pale. She swept a hand across her forehead. "Zionism? Say, it's not true." Genuine fear sounded in Esther's voice.

"Moreover, they said, they suspect my father was involved in the murder of the University Party Secretary, Baev."

Esther opened her mouth and stared at Irina, all the color disappearing from her cheeks. She stood up, leaned against the wall, sat down again. Her eyes slowly filled with tears. Finally she said, "It's awful. "I must tell my parents." She rushed to the kitchen.

Irina leaned against the wall, looking at Esther's desk piled with notepads and books about mollusks and shellfish. Photographs of mollusks lay scattered over the desk.

Esther slowly walked in.

"Listen, Ira," she said in an uncertain voice. "You

know how much I want to help you. First thing, you need some clothing. So, please take my sweater, the gray and violet one I knitted last fall. And a shawl. Sorry that your feet are a size larger than I wear. Would you try all this now? Or, maybe, we'll have more tea now?"

"Thank you." Irina stood up. "To make it short, you want me to leave."

The door opened and Doctor Bronsky trundled in. His face was flabby now, his short fingers squeezing the lapels of his house jacket. He coughed.

"Irina, you know how we like you. I never wanted a better friend for my Esther. You should understand. We are loyal Soviet people. We don't want to get mixed up in anything like Zionism. You know, if you can't go back home, try some Russian family, who wouldn't be suspected of Zionism."

"Thank you, Doctor," Irina said, "I certainly will leave at once. Thanks again, it was excellent tea."

Doctor Bronsky sighed and trundled out.

"Ira, you must understand, I can't go against my father," Esther said. "You don't know, years ago, after the *Doctors' plot* my grandfather was kicked out of his job at the Medical Institute. And my grandfather, he treated Marshal Topolyev. But even Topolyev could not help. My grandfather then had three heart attacks and became a virtual cripple. You've seen him, you know. And my father also has heart condition. We just cannot afford—"

"I understand, Esta. I am sorry. I hope your father will have no problem with his heart because of my visit."

"Ira, I don't want to pretend. I'm scared. In our family four generations had been physicians. But I was not admitted. They had statistics; too many Jews in the medical profession. They wouldn't say this; officially I did not pass the exams. But, on the exams, they gave me a problem which did not have a solution. You know about such stories. I was admitted to Biology, though. Luckily for me, they did not have enough applicants. What effort it took to achieve the next step, the *aspirantura,* the Candidate of Sciences course. It was a miracle that I was admitted. Even though Kalinin is not like Kiev, still, I think there are only two Jews in Kalinin allowed to take the Candidate of Sciences course. I am one of two exceptions. I can't forget that. It's so fragile, my future. If my dissertation is a success, even the faintest jolt can break up all I have achieved. And this time it would be forever . . ."

"Yes, Esta, of course I understand. I know your story. And many other stories as well. Well, now I have my own story. I'll leave now."

"Do me a favor, take the sweater and the shawl." Esther's voice broke and her body trembled as she began to sob.

"Esta, everything will work out. One day, there will be a celebration in our street." Irina hugged Esther when the door opened again and Doctor Bronsky walked in and embraced his daughter.

When Irina was on the stairs she heard Esther shout, "Ira, I am ashamed to let you go. Forgive me if you can."

After she left Esther's apartment, she had tried three more places. The first family she tried was a young married couple, the Fedotovs, both fellow runners. They listened to her story. They apologized profusely, saying they had just received a message that Fedotov's sister and her child would arrive shortly to spend the New Year vacation with them. They just did not have space for one more guest. Sure enough, Irina thought, they wanted to stay alone, to jump into their narrow bed as soon as she left. They had only been married for three weeks.

Olga and Aleksei, fellow-students in English, always seemed to like her. They did not listen to the full story. Aleksei interrupted her and said in an iron voice that he didn't want the intrusion of a person connected to a criminal in their decent Soviet home. Olga nodded.

The third family were physicists, both Professors at the Polytechnic. They happened to be her father's co-authors, had published a textbook under the three names: N. Stepanov, A. Stepanova and Y. Magidov. After the Stepanovs had heard Irina's story, they lost their voices. They did not speak, desperate to find her coming was just a bad dream. She left chuckling at the sight of their horrified faces.

She stood in front of the University dorm building, breathing on her icy hands which stuck out of the sleeves of Esther's sweater. There was nobody in this building to provide shelter for Irina Magidova. Here lived a librarian at the University, Katya, with her infant son. It was because of her child, whom Katya had to bring up without a husband, that the University let Katya live here. Before she became a mother, Katya used to be Irina's main competitor in long distance running. She did not run anymore.

Katya's window on the fourth floor was lit, so she was not asleep. At Katya's she could at least get a cup of tea. She decided to have that cup of tea and chat about Katya's child. What could she do next. Katya might have a key to the library. It would be a solution.

Irina ran past the janitor. It was too late for visits in the dormitory, but the old woman-janitor was too sleepy and too lazy to move. She had seen Irina more than once in this building and knew the girl was a Professor's daughter.

Katya was awake. She had managed to lull her son to sleep, now she sat on a stool, her hands holding a cup of tea. Her small room, with old newspapers tacked to the window frame, smelled heavily of dirty diapers and cheap soap. A hot plate sat on the floor.

"Irka, what a pleasure," Katya said, hugging Irina. "What's that, with your face? Hooligans? Or you have fallen on the track?"

"You can say so, yes," Irina said. "May I have a cup of tea? I am dying of thirst."

Katya put a kettle on the hot plate and plugged in the cord. The odor of burnt milk wafted across the small room. While water heated up, Irina told the story of the house search, her father's arrest and her neighbors' intrusion. The embarrassment Katya apparently felt because of the behavior of Irina's neighbors showed on Katya's face. Katya came to Kalinin from the city of Krasnoyarsk, in East Siberia, where Russian people had been mixing with Mongolians for several centuries.

"You'll stay here, with me," Katya said calmly, taking the boiling kettle from the scarlet hot plate.

Somebody knocked lightly at the door.

"Who's that, at this time?" Katya looked anxiously at the sleeping boy and unlatched the door. "Oh! Boris," she said, her voice losing its tiredness, jovially vibrating from deep in her chest.

"Poor Katya," Irina thought to herself. "Some scoundrel leaves her with a child, but she wants very much to have a husband." An unexpected guest was the last thing Irina was prepared to face at this time.

Katya glanced over her shoulder at Irina. "Come in, Boris," she said. "I have a friend with me for the night, Irina. Ira, meet my next door neighbor, Boris Tarutin."

Chapter 18

ADA RYZHIK HAD BEEN WITH THE UNIVERSITY AS LONG AS anybody could remember. A diminutive hunchback of uncertain age, one leg shorter than the other, she was popular with every Professor. The department Heads just told her the overall number of teaching hours a Professor was assigned for a given semester. Scheduling these hours was entirely up to Ada.

From her tiny cubicle in a corner of the fourth floor, Ada prescribed with an iron will where each Professor would take exams, deliver lectures and conduct labs.

Very few exceptions had been known. One was Ada's immediate boss, Dean Gavrik. During his eighteen months at the University as a Dean, he had no teaching duties. When the inspection commission from the Ministry mentioned unofficially, that a Dean, even if appointed for political reasons, was expected to teach. So, Gavrik was assigned to teach a lab in electronics.

Gavrik's class schedule had been readjusted every week to fit his convenience. Ada Ryzhik followed Gavrik's instructions regarding his schedule, taking revenge instead on everybody else.

Except for Boris Tarutin. Whereas every Professor, received a note from Ada indicating his schedule, Ada always asked Boris first what his preferences would be and did her best to accommodate him.

Nobody knew the reason for this special treatment. Just that each time Ada Ryzhik met Boris, the lumps on her face seemed to flatten and a radiant expression lit her face, because Boris always smiled at her and stopped to chat.

In those years when, fresh from achieving his Candidate of Sciences degree, Boris wanted to continue his research on magnetic films, Ada, responding to Boris's request, used to pack all his classes into two days, Monday and Tuesday, leaving the rest of the week for uninterrupted research.

Lately, Boris's research had become all but non-existent. Department Head Vernov had increased the teaching load assigned to Assistant Tarutin to over thirty hours a week.

Research or no research, Ada Ryzhik continued packing together Boris's classes even though there was no way to schedule thirty hours in two or even three days. She did her best. No classes on Friday and Saturday. On Thursday Boris had eight hours of labs and four hours of evening lectures. It was in the Evening Division, for those working people who, fighting tiredness, came to the University after a working day, desperately striving for a diploma which would improve their station in life.

It was close to eleven pm on this Thursday when Boris left the University's building. After all these hours his tongue felt numb and his lungs craved fresh air. He walked slowly, enjoying the light freezing wind. By the time he approached the dormitory his chest had filled with the refreshing air of the winter night.

When he arrived home he opened the cabinet. There

was no tea left in the can. He could drink water or he could try to borrow some tea from a neighbor.

Suddenly he heard voices through the cardboard door. So, Katya, his next door neighbor was not yet asleep; she had a visitor. Boris could not discern words, only that it was a woman's voice. Still, he hesitated. Usually, when Katya saw Boris, she slanted eyes of that shy and reticent woman filled with the unmistakable flame of invitation. She seemed to be a very nice person, this hapless single mother. Boris could not offer her anything beyond neighborly sympathy. Since a friend was with Katya it probably would not be inappropriate to ask to borrow some tea.

When Katya opened the door and saw Boris her face beamed. Over her shoulder Boris saw the visitor, a tall girl, with fresh bruises on her face and a black eye. At first he was puzzled then, his heart jumped with excitement. This was the girl he saw last Sunday at the railway station. Those magnificent legs.

"Katya, sorry, I am out of tea . . ."

"Sure, come in, Boris," Katya said. "I have a friend with me for the night, Irina. Ira, meet my next door neighbor, Boris Tarutin."

Irina nodded. Her dark eyes slid over Boris's face, and she frowned slightly as if she was making an effort to recognize him.

Katya fetched a can from under the table, shook it, black tea dropping on a sheet torn from a newspaper. In one more minute she would hand over the tea then Boris would leave and this chance would never come again. Katya's hands rolled up the paper into a small packet while Boris still stood silent, his eyes staring at Irina.

She felt his stare and again lifted her eyes and met his which were begging for a response. Even in the dim light of the small table lamp Boris could see that the girl's eyes had undergone a change, the expression of confusion was now replaced by a spark of interest.

"Here's your tea." Katya stopped in the middle of the sentence and her eyes opened wide as she looked from Boris to Irina. "I see, you seem to know each other . . ."

Neither Boris nor Irina answered.

"Well," Katya said, "maybe you just sit down, Boris, and we have tea together . . ."

"Yes," Boris said and continued standing at the door, holding his hands behind his back.

Irina chuckled. "I don't think we know each other. But I could've seen you at the University, couldn't I?" she said.

"You certainly know Irina's father, Professor Magidov, don't you?" Katya said. "I may as well tell you, he's been arrested today. They think he has something to do with Baev's murder."

Boris felt drums beating in his temples. Professor Magidov, the only probable suspect in Baev's murder. And this girl, by a miracle appearing in Katya's room.

"Yes," Boris said. "I know about this. I mean, about the investigators suspecting Professor Magidov."

Irina's face darkened. "It's nonsense," she said. "My father can't stand the sight of blood. Last summer we went to visit with my aunt, in Poltava. She wanted to prepare a traditional Jewish dinner, and she managed to buy a hen from some peasants, to make a chicken soup. She asked my father to chop off the hen's head. He took a knife, picked up the hen and threw up. He could not. Would you believe he could have murdered a human being?"

I believe you, Irina," Boris said. "Irina," he repeated. "Irina . . ."

Suddenly, Irina's shoulders trembled, her mouth curved and she turned her face away from Boris.

"That's it, Boris," Katya said. "We, women, we weep. Our tears, they are cheap."

The child, Lioshka, moved in his crib and opened his eyes. Katya put him on her lap. Disturbed by the voices, he wouldn't fall asleep again. He cried and Katya could not pacify him. She glanced apologetically at Boris and Irina.

"I think, we'd better go," Boris said taking Irina's hand.

"Yes," Irina said. "It looks that Katya will have a problem with Lioshka if I stay. Where shall we go?"

"First, to my room. We'll have tea and you may spend this night there. I must watch an overnight experiment in the lab."

Boris did not have an overnight experiment. Still, the bench in the lab was there and he would not have a problem sleeping on it.

Irina briefly told the story of her day, but then they continued to talk, jumping from one seemingly insignificant topic to another.

"I wonder, Irina, why your name sounds more Russian than Jewish."

"Not really. 'Magid' means herald in Hebrew, or, if you prefer the more modern version, spokesman."

"But this Russian ending, 'ov' . . ."

"Right. You may not know it, but Jews had no last names until 1801. That year, Czar Aleksandr the First ordered that every Jew be given a last name. As it happened, the clerks registering these new names often Russified them."

"That means your family came to this land before 1801. And some crazy xenophobes still view Russian Jews as aliens."

"I believe it's more complicated, Boris. I believe the hatred of Jews in this country is not the hatred of aliens who have come from other places. No, it's animosity nurtured by the descendants of the conquerors towards the descendants of the indigenous people, the previous owners of this country. Those ancient wars are long forgotten, but the bigotry transferred through generations, has evidently outlasted the memory."

"How can it be true? Everybody knows Jews came to Russia not that long ago."

"That's not correct. Do you know about Khazars?"

"Sure, I studied history. Turkish tribes. Our ancestors fought them centuries ago. You recall, in Pushkin's poem, The Song on Prophetic Oleg:

*'As if this is today, Prophetic Oleg prepares,
To take revenge on stupid Khazars'* . . ."

"Yes," Irina continued. "Of course, I remember.

*'For their wild foray, he doomed
Their villages and fields
To sword and fire.'*

You are right, Boris. The Khazars were a mix of Turkish and Finno-Hungarian tribes. There are several things your school has never told you. First, that the Khazars lived in what today is the Ukraine and a good portion of Southern Russia, for many centuries before the gangs of *Rus* came with 'sword and fire.' Second, at some time in the eighth century the Khazars had adopted the Jewish religion. I believe your ancestors at that time were pagans and the word 'Khazar' was tantamount to 'Jew' . . ."

"So, when they fought Khazars, they fought Jews."

"Oh, you see it now. Then, in tenth century, when Russians adopted Christianity, this centuries-old hatred of an adversary must have acquired a new, religious tint."

"But what had become of the Khazars?"

History is silent about that. Obviously, millions of Khazars could not have evaporated."

"You mean the Jews of Russia, are the descendants of Khazars?"

"Partially. Yes. I believe we bear in our veins a good portion of 'Khazars,' which is Turkish and Finno-Hungarian blood. Well mixed with the Semitic, and Polish, Russian and what not. Which does not make us any more acceptable to this country. Semitic, Turkish, or Hungarian, what is the difference?"

"So, if you're right, then you really have deep roots in this soil."

"The roots which my father only wishes to cut off. He has said, it has been too long that we have been vying to impose our love on this country. It's time to realize, love cannot be forced."

"I've heard, however, your father had been negotiating with some Pedagogical institute in East Siberia."

"In Eniseisk. Yes," Irina said. "But this was just a cover-up. In Eniseisk, there is no railway, no libraries, no physicists. No conferences, seminars. It would be death for an active scientist. No, his aspirations lay in the opposite corner of the world. A few days ago he traveled to Leningrad. I don't know why I am tell you that. I don't know. I trust you, Boris. I just need to talk to somebody."

"You may trust me, Irina."

"He went to Leningrad to meet an old couple, pensioners. They had received a visa to leave for Israel. He gave them our address and personal data, which is necessary to receive an official invitation from Israel. Without such an invitation one is not allowed to apply for a visa."

"But I've heard there is practically no emigration allowed with or without an invitation."

"Yes, it's nearly non-existent. But the same situation

had occurred before the wave of emigration which was allowed in the seventies. So, if the new Kremlin bosses will have a need to use Jews once again for concessions from the West, one more wave of emigration may become possible. My father wants to be prepared."

"Your father, is he a Zionist after all?"

"No. He's just a scientist. Theoretical physics is his creed and his Motherland. And, maybe, even his family. It was different when my mother was alive. Three years ago there was a terrible explosion in the Chemical plant. They delivered sealed coffins to the families. We had received one with mama's body. They did not allow us to open it. Thereafter, my father lost interest in everything. Sometimes he spends a day without talking with me. I know he loves me. I think his obsession is with that theory of elementary particles he had been working on."

"And his wish to leave this country?"

"Oh, his dream is to meet personally other physicists like Freeman in America, and others. He is famous and he has been invited to attend international congresses on theoretical physics but was never allowed to go. Even to East Germany or Poland. He feels strangled."

"It's close to one o'clock," Boris said, "You, probably, want to sleep."

"I'm not tired. Not so far. But you ought to go to your lab, those experiments—"

"Well, they can wait. What bothers me, Irina, is your documents. Those people, your neighbors, who knows what can they do with your papers. I think we ought to go there and see what we can salvage."

"Now? And you say 'we'—you mean—"

"Sure, I love to walk in the moonlight. Ready?"

"I am."

Chapter 19

BORIS AND IRINA WALKED ALONG THE VOLGA. THE DESERTED streets lay in stillness, only the squeaks of their footsteps on hard snow echoed from the dark gateways.

"At this pace, we'll arrive in Marinovo tomorrow," Irina said.

"No tram or bus at this time."

"We have our legs."

"Oh, yes, Irina, you've *legs*."

"Don't you? Haven't you ever run?"

"Well, I'm a mountaineer. We move at a snail's pace. As the proverb says, the slower you go—"

"The farther you arrive. The credo of slackers."

"Then, let's run," Boris said.

His first strides were cautious. Irina kept pace without signs of stress. Boris increased his speed slightly, glancing sideways at the girl. Her hands, sticking out of the sleeves of Irina's sweater, flashed rhythmically in the yellow moonlight. Boris increased speed a little more. Irina's dark figure kept close to him without a gap. He lengthened his stride. He had legs trained in mountaineering ascents. But the girl did not seem to feel any difference. She followed right at his elbow, her breathing as even as before. Now Boris ran without restraint, inhaling the freezing air at every fourth stride. To his amazement the girl's breathing remained even.

"You're a runner," Boris said, whirls of steam leaving his lips. "That's where I saw you, on the running strip, in the stadium."

They crossed the bridge over the Lazur and ran into the waste ground, the dark silhouettes of Marinovo buildings arising amid the heaps of snow.

"What's that?" Irina pointed at something which looked like a big fork driven obliquely into snow, a few steps from the path, the fork's two-prong shadow crossing the wavy snow drifts. They stopped. In the faint moonlight, they discerned footprints leading to the odd fork-shaped jut.

"It looks like legs," Boris said.

The waste ground gleamed in the moonlight. It was completely deserted, its Western edge lost under the scarlet glow of the city's lights. The pair of legs in *valenki*, jutting from moonlit snow, looked incongruous and preposterous.

"Oh, no!" Boris said. "One more body. Look at the blood," and he pointed at the dark spot in the snow, the size of a car wheel, right under the body.

"He's alive," Irina said, kneeling at the snowdrift. "Can't you hear him snoring? Dead drunk, I guess."

Indeed, they saw now faint swirls of steam rising from the man half-buried in snow. The man groaned.

"He'll freeze to death in an hour," Irina said.

"He'll not, he's lucky," Boris said.

"Only because we happened to run into him at this hour," Irina said.

Boris turned the body, pulling the man's head out of snow.

"Oh, I know him," Irina said. "He's our neighbor. Lives in the same apartment with Kuzma and Yegor. It was his wife who came to ransack our place with Kuzma and Yegor and their wives. Now I understand why he did not take part, he was drunk. They carried him in.

The woman-guard sitting at the entrance to the food store watched the couple carrying a body. She did not seem curious; relatives dragging home a dead drunk man, this was a common picture in the workers' district.

There was no light in the stairway. On the landing of the third floor, they laid the man down, his head touching the door of his apartment. The door to Magidovs' apartment was unlocked. Boris knocked at the neighbors' door, then he and Irina stepped into Magidovs' anteroom and slowly closed the door behind them. They heard how the door of the neighboring apartment squeaked and a woman's voice shrilly sounded in the stairway. The woman cursed her husband and dragged him into the apartment.

Through the kitchen door they saw the edges of a broken window sparkling in the moonlight. Clothing was strewn over the floor, plants were turned over and trampled. There were with bundles of sheets and torn up pillows, upon smeared and mutilated books.

"Is this what a *pogrom* looks like?" Boris said. He picked up a book from the floor. It was "Quantum Mechanics" by Fok.

"Look, Boris," Irina said, "the money is here. In this open box, they did not touch it. All's here, forty-two rubles. Oh, look, here's my uniform skirt. That woman wore it. It's back here now. They didn't take anything with them. Except for cognac. They finished that off."

"It's not a theft for a Russian to get a drink. Boris said. "As to the rest, maybe somebody scared them away."

"Maybe they are just honest people, after all? Don't want what doesn't belong to them? Just to make a pogrom for fun. Like children. Those Prosecutor's boys had already ransacked the apartment before the friendly visit of our neighbors."

He saw at his feet a diploma of parchment with a golden border, stained by a footprint. It was Irina Magidova's certificate of a University champion.

"Here are my documents," Irina said, opening a briefcase made of artificial leather. Misha the Bear, the Olympic mascot of 1980, dangled from the wood-stuffed handle.

Professor's briefcase. Sure, wasn't Magidov a Full Professor at the University? And wasn't his daughter a University champion, entitled to that sign of honor, Misha the Olympic mascot? The warm, vibrating car of the speed train from Leningrad to Moscow re-emerged in his mind; the rack with a briefcase on it and a dangling Olympic mascot; somebody's curly-haired, familiar head in the front chair. Last Sunday on the way from Bologoe.

"When was it that your father traveled to Leningrad to see those people leaving for Israel?"

"Last Sunday, why?"

"Yes, I thought so," Boris said. "I believe, I traveled in the same car with your father. Just as I boarded the train in Bologoe I saw you at the railway. Did you meet your father at the station?"

"I did. What's the matter? Is that important?"

"I don't know, it may be. I saw you boarding a tram."

"Did you watch me? There was such a crowd at the station. How could it happen that you've remembered me?"

"Legs."

"Legs?"

"Never mind. Tell me, was your father with you when you boarded the tram?"

"Of course, he was. Why?"

"Irina, it may be very important. Where did you go from the station?"

"Where? Right here, I had prepared stuffed cabbage, father's favorite. It was a pity that he refused to share the dinner with me. He was looking for a particular notebook containing his formulas. He said the attempts to recall where he might have left them had bothered him during his trip."

"I see," Boris said. "So he wanted to check in his office, at the University."

"Right. How do you know? Yes, he could not eat until he found the notebook."

"Could've been in his office," Boris said. "When did he leave the apartment for the University?"

"Maybe fifteen minutes after we came home."

"How long from the station to Marinovo?"

"I think about thirty-five, maybe forty minutes."

"That's what I thought," Boris said. "And it takes about the same time to ride from here to the University. Right? Our train arrived in Kalinin ten before seven. Ten minutes from the platform to the street to board a tram. Plus forty minutes on the tram to Marinovo. Plus fifteen he had spent here. Plus forty minutes to ride back to the University. How much altogether? My God, that makes it eight thirty. That's what Prof Magidov said, that he came to the University about eight-thirty. Half an hour after we had discovered the body of Baev. Do you understand, Irina? This proves that your father, Professor Magidov, has an a-l-i-b-i!"

"Alibi, my God. How lucky I was to meet you. Boris, maybe some people can be found who saw my father in the tram after eight o'clock. This would mean—"

"—that your father is innocent."

She found her red overcoat, a knitted hat the color of

dark wine, and a matching scarf. She put on her red-brown shoes with high heels. In these shoes she was almost as tall as Boris.

In this coat and hat, she changed from a colty tomboy to a tender, almost fragile little girl; in her soft face with its large dark eyes and full lips, vulnerability showed through a thin mask of toughness.

"How will you get home, Boris?" she said, looking into Boris's eyes, trying to give her words a sound of calmness, but her voice and her eyes betrayed her. She was shaken by this havoc, by the encounter with the neighbors.

"I'll not let you stay alone," Boris said. "At least not for this night. It's three o'clock. If we hurry, we can still have some sleep. Tomorrow we'll have a lot of work to do."

She changed into light shoes to run on snow. They ran shoulder-to-shoulder all the way back.

In the dorm building, the janitor half-opened her eyes, shrugged and fell asleep again.

"I am going to the lab now," Boris said.

"You'll stay right here. On this sofa. I am accustomed to sleeping with all my clothing on. We do this every time they send students to *kolkhoz* to pick potatoes or tomatoes."

"Then you sleep on the sofa, and I, on the floor," Boris said. "In mountains, we sleep in whatever position the night catches us, sometimes hanging on a rock wall."

"Good," Irina said. "I'll take the sofa and you, the blanket and the pillow."

The tiredness took its toll; Irina fell asleep covered by her coat, her head resting on Esther's rolled-up sweater.

Boris stretched his legs on the rug. He could not sleep listening to the even breathing of the girl. After the runs between this building and Marinovo, their bodies emanated a slight odor of sweat. There was no place for them to take a shower, at least not until tomorrow. But this animal odor did not disturb Boris. It was the odor of a gymnastic hall and of a tent fluttering under mountain wind, on a sheer Caucasus slope, and of a ski trail, and of everything tied in his senses to the joys of health and youth.

Legs. Irina's legs, they were right at the tips of his fingers. The temptation was unbearable. He listened to Irina's breathing. It was even and calm. He cautiously extended his hand. It touched Irina's calf, half-covered by her coat. His hand sensed the slipperiness of her capron stocking. And the springy relief of her runner's muscles. His heart plunged. He felt a lack of air.

"My God," he said to himself, "Thank you for this life. For this moment, blessed it be . . ."

Irina sighed and moved, straightening her knees. Boris froze. Then he moved his hand away from her leg.

"I am stealing the pleasure," he thought. He smiled. And for some time afterwards, he still lay smiling, listening to Irina's faint breathing. Only when the scraping sound of a shovel sweeping snow from sidewalks announced that for janitors the new day had started already, sleep finally took over Boris.

Chapter 20

A KNOCK AT THE DOOR ROUSED BORIS. HE RAISED HIS head and met Irina's questioning glance. He made a reassuring gesture with his palm, slid from under the blanket and moved towards the door.

She sprang up. In one continuous movement her feet slipped into her shoes, her hands passed through her coat's sleeves and she set her hat low over her forehead, covering the disheveled heap of auburn hair.

"What the devil, old friend, will you open today?" the voice of Artamon Sergeev shouted from the corridor. Boris opened the door to stare at the slightly stooped Artamon in a gray overcoat with a rabbit-fur cap set low above his eyes. He spotted the girl and his face showed his surprise.

"Tell her, Boris," Artamon said stepping over the threshold, "tell her that I am not a monster. Why do you not speak? Tell her at least that I am your friend."

"You are," Boris said. "Twenty-five years. Irina, meet Artamon Sergeev, my lifetime friend."

Irina's face showed complete confusion. Obviously, she

could not reconcile the two images of Artamon Sergeev. Boris almost sensed the thoughts running in her mind. Artamon Sergeev. Investigator of the Prosecutor's office. One of those scoundrels who had ransacked her apartment and then accused and arrested her father. Yes, this Sergeev pretended to appear the good guy. Those sandwiches he brought yesterday for her and her father. She wouldn't be sold that cheap. Sandwiches or no sandwiches, he was an enemy. And Boris turned out to be Sergeev's friend.

It was only a few seconds of confusion and hesitation. Then she made her decision. Her cheeks became even paler and black fires sparkled in her eyes.

"Thank you for the sofa. And for tea. And for accompanying me last night. I must leave now." And before Boris made a move, she sprinted out and the door clicked behind her.

Boris leaped to the door but Artamon grabbed Boris's waist displaying unexpected power.

"Stop, Borka, Let her go. Do you not understand what it means? Her father is a suspect in a murder. He's a Zionist. If you've banged her last night, great, so let this be the end to it, are you not satisfied?"

"You let me loose at once or I'll break your arms," Boris said in a suddenly very low voice. Stunned, Artamon unclasped his hands and stepped back.

"Listen, Artamon," Boris said, already in the door. "Magidov is innocent and I can prove it. I am a witness! And now you help me to stop her before she is too far away. Or, forget that you have been my friend."

"I see, it's not like it was with all those broads before," Artamon muttered. "This time it looks very serious indeed."

While Boris ran towards the main stairway, Artamon jogged to the back stairs. In a few minutes they met each other in the street. Irina was not in sight. Artamon spread his hands in a gesture of impotence.

Although he ran out in only a shirt and socks, Boris did not feel the bite of cold. He rushed to the corner, crossed the street, then ran back to the opposite corner. Nowhere did he see the tall figure of the girl in a claret-red coat and a knitted hat.

He ran around the block, jumping over the hoar-frosted hedges. He skirted some snow heaps, sprang over others, his long legs swinging in giant leaps. He did not see Irina anywhere. Suddenly he felt his knees and elbows stinging in the hardening grip of fierce cold. He turned back to the entrance. She must have been somewhere around . . ."

"That's him." Artamon said. "Well, my friend, here is your pass to life." He pointed at Irina.

"Irina! Where did you find her?"

"Well, my friend, I am not crazy like you are, in your high spirit and the blinding emotional state. *Amor vincit omnia*, love wins over everything, including one's ability to think logically. Luckily, I am still sober. Instead of jumping back and forth, I asked the janitor about this fast-legged gal. The janitor did not see her run out. It was just reasonable to guess she must still have been in the building. My friend and patron, even if you believe that the lady of your dreams flies in the air, I know she walks on earth. After last night she must have needed a visit to a restroom."

Boris stared at Irina's pale face, while Artamon, trying to disguise his embarrassment, continued, "The first thing I said to her was what you've refused to say; that I am not an animal but a plain bureaucrat of modest talents, doing my job and not always enjoying what I do. Secondly, that if, instead of me, somebody else would do that job, this would be hardly beneficial to anyone's *papa*."

"I see."

"Yes, my crazy friend. And I said to her that if one wants to help one's *papa*, one must not put one's resentment above the *papa*'s fate. And I said to her, that if one has proof, or a hint of proof, then I am the man to talk to about it.

"And I said to her that if one wants to talk with Artamon Artamonovich Sergeev, the best avenue to reach him is through you. And I also said to her that you would hang yourself on that birch tree if she is not back in three minutes."

Boris saw now that Irina's eyes fixed on his feet in snow covered cotton socks.

"I see. Irina, did he say all this to you?"

Irina just blushed as her hand touched the stubble on Boris's cheek.

"You must go in," she said. "Barefoot in the snow, you may catch cold."

"Will you run away again?"

"No."

In the corridor of the fourth floor, they heard Katya's child crying. "I was ungrateful yesterday," Irina said. "I didn't even thank Katya for her offer to stay with her. I'll do it now," and she knocked at Katya's door.

The door to Boris's room was still ajar. They walked in and Boris took his socks off and wrapped his bare feet in a blanket. Artamon leaned against the cabinet, a pensive expression frozen on his face.

"Before your gal comes in, we have a couple of minutes to talk *jannis clausis*, behind the closed door. I view your sexual obsession, as a kind of a 'beautiful madness.' However fascinating your feelings are, you cannot keep her in your room. It is probably a Punchinello's secret already. Janitors have big eyes and long tongues. If you wish to be of any help to her, put her anywhere but your room."

"I understand. I have an idea about how to find an accommodation for her."

"If you do, it would be the most ingenious idea you've come up with. Now, where is this proof of yours regarding Magidov."

While Boris was telling about the briefcase, the Olympic mascot, and the time needed to ride on a tram to Marinovo and back, Artamon nodded.

"I must tell you, Borya, your infantile naivete regarding what you call proof, may force me forget that you sometimes look like an intelligent creature. Say I accept your testimony at face value and forward your arguments to my bosses. They would dismiss me at once. For the sake of argument, assume that they agree to consider this testimony. They would asked me: 'Your witness had not actually seen and recognized the suspect in that train; he only saw the two items, a briefcase and mascot. Is there only one such gray briefcase in the country? Is there only one such Olympic mascot? Do you know how many such briefcases could've been sold in Leningrad? Or in Moscow? Even if Magidov had traveled in that train, couldn't he arrive in the University building before eight o'clock? What proof do you have that he went from the railway station to Marinovo? Just the word of a girl whose legs have driven your friend Boris crazy? Is a daughter an unbiased witness in a case involving a father? Shall we explain the fundamentals of the Soviet judicial system to you, comrade Investigator Sergeev?' So, you see, Boris, all what you've told me, from the legal standpoint, is just an *aegri somnia*, sick man's dreams."

"I see," Boris said. "Then enlighten me; what would be considered proof?"

"Oh, in this particular case, virtually nothing. Let's say, Magidov is not guilty of this murder, although I do not see how it can be possible, there's just no other suspect in view. Let's imagine the moment we release him the KGB picks him up. This Hebrew book is enough of a hook for them. Of course, you may argue that for the book he may draw two years, and for the murder of a Party leader, a very long sentence."

"Forget about the KGB. What would be sufficient proof for your bosses to dismiss the case against Magidov?"

"Oh, my stubborn friend. Well, if you bring me another culprit, with a complete confession corroborated by independent testimonies. Try, *andentes fortuna juvet*, the fortune favors the bold . . ."

"What are the results of the forensic examination?"

"Nothing sensational," Artamon said. "Baev's death was caused by a blow upon his head inflicted with a blunt tool. The time of death was not earlier than six o'clock, but it could've been eight o'clock as well. What I came to you for had nothing to do with this story. I just couldn't imagine this Magidova gal would be here. What is it that has driven you crazy? Just her legs?"

"So, what have you come for?" Boris said.

"Boris, was it just her legs?"

"Look at me, Artamon. Into my eyes. I think, you're struck by this girl as well, aren't you?"

"It's nonsense. Of course, not. How can you fantasize this way? No!. Yes. Yes, the devil. Does it show? It's not sexual. There is something in her eyes. Yesterday, during the house search, those crazy eyes of hers hit me. But, *experto crede*, trust an expert. You've drowned indeed."

"Drowned and happy," Boris said. "Now, Artyukh, you owe me at least that much, to check for me what those tram drivers may recall about that Sunday evening. Will you?"

"Just for you I will. Do you understand what you're trying to do to me? As long as I believe that Magidov is guilty, I conduct this investigation enjoying my job. As soon as I lose that belief, the same job becomes a self-rape. Luckily, it's quite unlikely that Magidov is telling the truth."

"I know it's truth, whatever your legal twists regarding my testimony," Boris said.

"My gullible friend, you yourself told me that immediately after you had discovered Baev's body, you ordered your janitor."

"Alevtina. Yes."

"To lock the door. Did she?"

"Yes—So what?"

"I am sure you've already grasped what I am driving at. After she had the door locked, it could only be opened from inside, true? Now, when, about eight-forty, the Militsia and the ambulance arrived, was the door still locked?"

"Yes. It was."

"Aha! So, let's even assume that Alevtina, the janitor, had abandoned her post at the door for a few minutes, somewhere between eight and eight-forty. Magidov indeed could have come without meeting anybody in the lobby. Still, how could he have entered through a locked door?"

After a silence, Boris said slowly, "Irina has told the truth. Magidov could not have come to the University before eight-thirty. I don't know how he walked in. Maybe Alevtina had not actually locked the door. Or, maybe somebody had opened it for Magidov."

"Maybe this and maybe that. Very convincing," Artamon said. "Well, I have to go now. What I came for was to suggest a ski tour for the two of us. Our trade-union committee has distributed tickets to the ski-train for this Sunday and I managed to get two."

"It's all in vain. Now this girl stands between you and me. So, I'll stay home Sunday. I will study the sixteenth-century habits in Russian princedoms."

"Sorry, Artamon, I'll make up for this Sunday."

Artamon nodded dolefully and walked out.

Chapter 21

He used the remnants of *Krasnodar* tea borrowed from Katya. When his old kettle, a veteran of Caucasus mountain travels, whistled on the scarlet hot plate, Irina walked in, with her auburn hair already combed neatly. Her fresh cheeks glowed, apparently after cold water and a hard towel. She carried her coat over her arm.

Boris had to force himself not to stare at Irina's taut small breasts stretching the blue-and-violet diagonal stripes of the sweater which was too small for her.

They drank the tea with bread, gnawing at small chunks of hard sugar, *rafinad*. He glanced surreptitiously, time and again, at the capron stockings encasing Irina's knees.

She had caught his glances, and a slight smile moved the corners of her bright lips. But her eyes remained sad.

"Thanks, Boris. I'll go now to the Prosecutor's office, and as for a meeting with my father."

"Good luck," Boris said. "I have to attend to some business which is near the Prosecutor's office. It shouldn't take long. If you're out of the Prosecutor's office before I'm done with my business, please wait for me on the Volga quay."

"What about your work?" Irina said.

"I do not have classes today, thanks to Ada Ryzhik. Let's hurry, Irina. The winter day is short."

One hour later, when she left the building of the Prosecutor's office, her shoulders were stooped, tears drying on her cool cheeks.

She walked along the deserted quay. A string of people appeared on the river's opposite bank taking off their clothing. They jumped into the freezing water. Members of a "Walruses" group.

Pangs of sudden envy wrung her heart. They were happy there, these "Walruses," the bodies of men and women splashing in icy water. The pleasure of the burning touches of ice and chilly water on their flame-hot crimson skin, this was all they cared about. How far from her was their joy.

Boris came around the corner, the lone figure on this bank of the Volga. He walked rapidly, the flaps of his raincoat swinging behind him, his cap still in his hand, a russet curl stirring in the air, his gray eyes glistening in excitement.

"I've done it. Here it is." He waved a piece of paper.

"What's that?"

"Blue Lakes. I've got a pass."

"Blue Lakes? It is a near-by village, isn't it."

"Yes. Next to Bologoe. But not just a village. A Trade Union's resthouse. I've got a pass. And what about you, have they given you the permission to see your father?"

"No." Her eyes again filled with tears. "The woman in the Department of Prisons Supervision, she said that, instead of trying to see my father, I ought to think how to fulfill my duty and help the Prosecution as a good daughter of Soviet people is expected to do."

"We should've anticipated that."

"She said I must be ashamed to shed tears when the most just system in the world makes an effort to re-educate a person erring in his ways. Then she softened a little and said that I might be allowed to see my father in three or five, or seven, or ten days. Not counting Sundays and holidays."

"Yes, Irina. I have learned from Artamon's stories, relatives aren't allowed visits to an inmate who is in an initial stage of the investigation. The length of this initial period depends on the degree of his cooperation. They believe that depriving one of seeing relatives makes one easier to interrogate."

"My God, you don't think he'll spend that long in the jail? And he needs his papers, to continue his work. It's his life. Boris, he's not guilty."

"That is what we must prove."

"Where do we start, Boris?"

"You must start with patience for a few days. I am going to talk with everybody who was in the University building the night we found Baev's body. I don't believe any of those people could've committed this murder, but maybe one of them will recall something which might provide a clue. Such information may help us to find out who killed that pig Baev. The best assistance you can give me now is to wait patiently somewhere. That's what this pass to blue Lakes is for."

"It has no name on it," Irina said, staring at the paper entitling its owner to spend a twelve day shift in the resthouse Blue Lakes.

"We'll write in your name now. This shift started eight days ago. This pass had been kept as a reserve in the event some higher-up might wish to go there. They always keep a few passes for such occasions."

"I have never been in a resthouse. It is so hard to get a pass."

"Neither have I," Boris said. "But now you'll spend the three remaining days of this shift."

"How did you manage it?"

"There is a woman in the City Council of the Trade Unions by the name of Tatiana, who is in charge of all these resthouses. Her niece, a student of mine, attempted three times to pass exams in Physics. No hope. So, Tatiana had approached me a few months ago and solicited my help. Of course, she promised a favor in return. I always had an aversion to *blat*, so I said no. I just agreed."

"When this Tatiana had approached you a few months ago," Irina said, "did she offer you a pass to a resthouse as a matching favor for your assistance with her niece's exams?"

"No. At that time, her payment would be herself."

"Oh. I see. Is she beautiful?"

"Reasonably pretty. Big blue eyes."

"And now."

"Unlike before, I decided that I must agree to help her niece. It has occurred to me that Tatiana could possibly provide this pass. And it worked. I don't feel any twinges of remorse. I will push Tatiana's dumb niece through the exam's filter. And we must hurry now, to catch the train. You go to Blue Lakes now, for three days, counting today."

In the station hall, they rushed to a counter where sandwiches with herring and bottles with a saccharin-sweet drink redolent of soap had been offered to passengers, twenty-five kopeks a sandwich and forty-five a bottle.

The green cars of the local train, humming under gusts of wind, stretched along the platform. Irina stood on the landing, her stockings gleaming before Boris's eyes. He remained on the platform, captivated by her. His eyes slid time and again to her legs.

The train made a leap, its buffers clanging; it stopped, then moved again, gradually increasing speed, and the conductor on the landing of the last car flung his yellow flag. Irina waved her hand, a wan smile on her lips. Suddenly, before he could comprehend the reasoning behind his actions, Boris ran a few strides, caught the railing and jumped onto the car's landing.

"I've no classes today. I may as well accompany you to Bologoe. I want anyway to attend to some business there."

They entered the car's crowded aisle, found seats next to a window and squeezed together into the corner. Through the dirty pane, the white winter threw soft ivory stripes upon Irina's legs and thighs pressed against Boris's. The snowfall, beginning outside, looked festive, portending a fresh ski trail for tomorrow.

"Those rules regarding visits to the jail," Boris said. "You know that inmates, on the one hand, and jailers, on the other, live in different time systems. For an inmate, every minute is a lost minute of his life. In the investigators' time system, it's just a wink of nothing, a minute slipping by without being noticed. It's about fifteen hours since your father's arrest? For him and for you, it's an eternity. The prosecutors lived through the same fifteen hours in a different time system. Eight hours was for sleep, two for meals, three for entertainment, and whatnot. For them your father's case is still where they left it yesterday."

"Do you, as a physicist, always build a theory for every situation?" Her tone suggested she was poking fun at Boris but her eyes burned with a warm flame, contradicting her words.

"Sometimes it makes life easier," Boris said.

"If you find a label for an event, you can acquiesce in the event, is that what you mean?"

"In Physics, one can at least attach a label to every

object," Boris said. "This is not the case with languages. I respect languages very much, though their vagueness is their power. And why have you chosen English?"

"Well, theoretically, a specialist in English may work as an interpreter, one of those accompanying sportsmen and musicians and whoever is sent abroad. You must understand that for a Jewish girl it's a zero chance option. Then, one may become a translator in some publishing house. Translators from Russian into English rank high. Again, I've no chance to get into such position. They all come from the special school in Moscow. In this school, only sons of higher-ups have been admitted. They study English from the cradle. Then, there are translators from English into Russian. This is a lower rung. Still, not within my reach. All I can expect is the lot of a school teacher in some remote hamlet."

"Then, why have you chosen English as a profession?"

"When I was eighteen, I thought English would open the world for me. In the classes on Russian literature they analyze every novel and poem from the viewpoint of its usefulness for building communism. I thought I would find a respite in reading English and American books."

"And."

"I have not yet had a chance to see genuine foreign books. We have access only to those officially approved and printed in Moscow. My teacher, Professor Talin, manages to get books from abroad. He never would admit this, of course, and he would not let us see them."

"So, Irina, you have become disenchanted with your chosen vocation."

"Wrong. Enchanted, more than ever. Especially after we decided to leave this country one day, whatever effort it takes. My English shall be my weapon in another world."

"A foreign language as a weapon in the struggle of life," Boris said. "Isn't this a quote from Karl Marx?"

"Indeed. I apologize for the words of Marx."

"You don't have much of a respect for Marxism, do you?"

"No, and you?"

"Neither do I." Boris said.

"I became immune to their ideological garbage only about a year ago."

"Which means you matured earlier than I did, Irina. I picked up a notebook in your apartment, yesterday. Your father's formulas. I wanted to save it for him. I was under the impression that your father had only been writing textbooks. Now I see from this notes, he's been working on Quantum Chromo Dynamics. It's the hottest area in today's Physics and he seems to have made stunning progress. He has evidently determined the forces between the elementary particles called quarks. And then encountered a preposterous obstacle. He needs a decent computer which the school does not have."

"Computer," Irina said. "A wonderful machine. I wish I knew more about it."

"That's an area where we hopelessly lag behind the West. They now have computers in almost every house. And you, I bet, have never seen a computer except for the obsolete monster we have at our university. It is not working anyway. As to the kind of computer your father would need, we don't have such machines in Kalinin."

"And in Moscow?"

"Even in Moscow the best computer available is not good enough to do the calculations your father needs. The one computer capable of this task is in America. It's called Cray-1 supercomputer. I wonder, isn't this the real reason your father wants to get out of this country? To get access to Cray?"

"Maybe," Irina said. "There are a dozen reasons for us to leave. The first is that we just feel there is no air for us to breathe."

"Then you need no more reasons. I understand your feelings. My father perished over thirty years ago, wrongfully accused of doing something he never did."

"Oh, Boris." She squeezed his hand with her warm long fingers. "We are of the same ilk, aren't we?"

The snowfall was over when they alighted. The arched windows of the Bologoe station, covered by thick layers of ice, gleamed in the low sun. Behind the station's red brick building, a few trucks drove by. Two were sitting with their engines running. For five rubles one of the drivers agreed to take Irina to the resthouse at Blue Lakes, about twenty kilometers from the station.

"We have to part now, Irina."

"Yes, Boris. Thanks for everything."

"Tatiana told me that on Monday morning, when the shift is over, there will be a bus from Blue Lakes to the station. I'll try to meet you in Kalinin, hopefully with some helpful information."

The driver, a drowsy-looking Karelian, offered Irina a seat in the cabin. The engine roared and the truck leapt forward, its wheels slipping in yellow slush. Its front wheels rolled upon the deep trails dug in the road. Unexpectedly, Boris found himself taking several wide leaps and, catching the platform's railing in one powerful motion, he yanked his body over the planking. The brakes screeched. Irina's head appeared in the cabin's window.

"It's just four o'clock," Boris said. "I better go with you to look at Blue Lakes. I've never seen a resthouse."

The cabin's door swung open, and Irina smiled at him, and moved into the back.

A few barrels loaded with lubrication oil for tractors, rocked on the platform. The bumpy road meandered past slim pines, their needles powdered white, their branches sinking down in the black brooks which fed into the ice-forged lakes. The truck bounced along, its engine revving up on ascending curves. Holding onto each other, Boris and Irina leaned against the cabin, their slightly bent legs cushioning jolts, their backs to the wind.

"You better take the seat in the cabin," Boris said.

"I feel better here," she said and snuggled closer. It took a little over one hour till the truck made a sharp turn and stopped before a snow-powdered gate.

"Blue Lakes," the driver said. Irina jumped down and Boris followed. The driver threw a questioning look at Boris, then at Irina, nodded, then revving his engine, disappeared behind the tall pines.

"How will you return to the station?" Irina said, her cap in her hand, the low sun highlighting her auburn hair.

"It's only a twenty-kilometer walk," Boris said. "Isn't this beauty worth it?" He spread his hands in a wide motion, embracing the lake, the rows of pines and Irina. Thin plumes of smoke rose above the snow-loaded roofs, scarring the transparent blueness of the sky.

There were five iron beds in the room assigned to Irina, plus two chairs and a cabinet. The four women in this room, all middle-aged and plump, were seated on one of the beds playing cards. To make the slots between beds a little wider, they had pushed the fifth bed into a corner. They seemed disappointed that for the remaining three days there would be one more occupant. All four women sized up Irina and then Boris.

"Men are not allowed in women's rooms," said one of the women.

A bell rang. The women abandoned their cards, grabbed their shawls and rushed outside. People were trudging rapidly towards the mess hall. The smell of porridge seeped out through the mess hall's door.

Irina walked into the mess hall and then reappeared within minutes with a bowl of porridge for Boris.

After the supper, the mess hall became a club. Couples

danced there to the sounds of an old record player, the tunes floating and fading. Outside, reflections of the winter stars twinkled on the gleaming lakes. Then a bell rang. Lights went off and long shadows of the low-roofed structures stretched across clearings among dark pines.

They stood at the entrance to Irina's ward. "I'll spend the night in the mess hall," Boris said. "Unless they've locked it."

"There's no lock, I've checked. Take my pillow and blanket."

"Then, it's time to part."

"Good night, Boris, and thanks again." She touched his face and then kissed him on the cheek.

It was dawn when Boris walked out of the mess hall. At the door of Irina's room, he set down the blanket and the pillow. He listened to the silence.

On the hard snowy road his footsteps crunched while the chill made him shiver. To warm up he ran, inhaling deeply. In about an hour, the sun rose in the Eastern sky, then golden sparks sprinkled the needles of tall pines.

Then the buildings of Bologoe appeared across a wide open space. On the crescent-shaped lake to his left, ice glinted in the low sun. Then he crossed the double tracks of the railway and walked into a curved city street.

PART 4

Chapter 22

AFTER HIS TWENTY KILOMETER RUN FROM BLUE LAKES to Bologoe, he fell asleep in the train and woke up only when the train attendant shook his shoulder.

"Why the devil had Talin lied to the Militsia?" Boris reflected. "I know firsthand that a few minutes before the pendulum fell on Baev's head, Talin was not in his office. He was not there when I pushed his book under his door. Then, again, he was not there an hour later when Zhenia Valushin look at his place. Talin must have had a serious reason to lie to the Militsia about his whereabouts on that evening. Talin knows something I would like to learn about."

As he thought of Talin now, Talin's image seemed to change in Boris's mind. Then he recalled one event which he had inadvertently witnessed two years earlier. The secretary of the English Department could not locate documents Talin had ordered her to prepare. The woman was positive she had given those documents to Talin ready for his signature. Talin denied that and accused the woman of negligence. In desperation, the secretary found a moment when Talin was out of the office, opened a drawer in his desk and was searching for the documents when Talin and Boris walked in. Talin's face changed from softness to rage and fury. He seemed to be on the verge of beating the woman, but he contained his temper and only his short hands continued to fold and unfold as if crumpling balls of viscid dough.

Boris had ascribed that unusual fit of rage to Talin's fear that the secretary might discover books smuggled from the West. As Boris knew Talin read such books stealthily. Just having those books was a risky venture.

With time, the impact of that event had almost completely vanished from Boris's mind. Now, however, Talin's face, distorted with a rage re-emerged in Boris's mind. It seemed that Talin was not as meek as he seemed to be.

Boris approached the University building as a flow of students poured out of the doors. The building emptied rapidly. When Boris walked into the office of the English Department, Talin was standing at the window.

"Ah, Boris Petrovich," Talin said. "Take my seat, I wish to stand."

"Well, then let's talk."

"Only for you, Boris. You're right on time, I have finally received the whole bunch. I'll show you, this time it's something special."

"What are you talking about?" Boris said.

"What? I am talking about those books from America. I told you, remember? A set of books, all on the same subject. How Americans view Russia."

"Oh." Boris sighed and sat down on Talin's hard chair. This digression from Baev's murder came as a respite from the anxiety he had felt during the last hours.

"Not that I can give them to you, but I'll show you."

Talin unlocked a drawer, pulled out some books. "Look, Boris Petrovich, look but don't ask how I acquired these books. This book is by Delia and Ferdinand Kuhn, 'Russia on Our Mind.' And this, 'An American in the Gulag,' by Alexander Dolgun. Great, eh? I can't believe it. And here's Robert Kaiser, 'Russia, the People and the Power,' and here's Hedrick Smith, 'The Russians.' And here are a couple of novels written by Americans about Russia. Cruz Smith and Viertel. Eh? I hardly can wait to lock myself in and read."

"So, what have they written about Russia?" Boris said.

"Ah, that's the question! Indeed, what they have written. Everything! From very keen observations to laughable nonsense. Can you imagine, this Kuhn couple spent seven days in our country, traveled on a train and think they have discovered Russia. Nevertheless, some of their comments are sharp indeed. Okay, look at Kaiser or Smith, or Shipler. Each of them has spent several years in Moscow."

"And?"

"No doubt they are sharp-eyed guys, they noticed many features of our life which the average Russian may not be aware of. Hedrick Smith has described the system of special distribution stores and how they are masked and disguised. Very good. There are in these books also some ridiculous errors."

"Like what?"

"Well, when they speak of Russia, they actually mean Moscow. Moscow was the only place they could have observed in some depth. But you and I know that Moscow is not Russia."

"Well, it's funny," Boris said. "But I would forgive such errors if the book is truthful in principle."

"Boris, I beg you, please, not a single hint to anybody that you've seen these books in my possession. Or I go straight to jail."

"Of course, I've never even heard about these books," Boris said. "Don't worry. Now, let's talk real business, Oleg Nikiforovich."

"Why so official? Why not just Oleg?"

"I am here, if you forgive me, to question you. I have no choice, Oleg."

"Yes, Boris, you do not look like a born interrogator. I am curious. Would you explain."

Boris sighed and said, "Why did you lie to the Militsia? Where had you been on that Sunday evening when we found Baev dead?"

Talin opened his mouth. He stayed silent for a while.

"What foolish joke is this?" he said finally. "You know that I had been in my office on that Sunday evening, don't you?"

"What I know, is that you were not in this office."

Talin's face seemed to lose color and shape, converting into a flabby mask. "You're crazy, Boris," he mumbled.

"I hope not. Now, will you tell the truth?"

"I don't know anything about that scoundrel's murder, if that's what you allude to."

"No allusions, Oleg. I am interested in learning what occurred on that evening."

"You know as much as I do, Boris. What is the reason for your interest, anyway?"

"An innocent man is in jail, accused of murder."

"Everybody thinks that he's not innocent," Talin said.

"I have proof," said Boris. "Magidov was not in this building at the time of the murder. But my word alone would not suffice. I need corroborating testimony. Anybody's testimony. It could be your testimony, Oleg. If you know something."

"To save your Magidov, what do you want me to do? To confess that I have committed a murder?"

"Why did you lie to the police? You were not in this

office, Oleg Nikiforovich. I had checked it myself. So did my technician Zhenia Valushin."

Talin's face showed a struggle of conflicts. Then he wiped his lips with his tongue and said, "You're nearly the only man in this place I can talk to frankly." Then he muttered, "Yes, I was not in this office, Boris. But I can't tell where I had been."

"Ridiculous as it is, you sound as if you're protecting the reputation of a woman."

As if the word 'woman' had open a valve, words poured from Talin's mouth. "It was a woman, Boris, a woman. Only, she hardly would care to keep it secret. It is I who cannot admit it. After that Party meeting. Remember? When Baev had publicly raped me, psychologically, in front of fifty rows of spectators, I had solemnly promised no more affairs. And it was my luck that when I was with the woman, that Baev chose to be murdered—at the same time the devil brought you to my office."

The voice of Talin had now an unmistakable ring of truth.

"I am not asking who the woman was," Boris said. "You were with Klava, in the electron microscopy lab, true?"

"Ah, you see, you know it yourself. Yes, Boris. When that scoundrel was being killed, I was without my pants." Talin's voice, in an odd way, sounded a ludicrous note of pride, as if the confession brought some relaxation of the stress he had endured during the week.

"Well, we must try to find out who killed Baev," Boris said. "I know Magidov couldn't do it, he was physically in another place. From the police's viewpoint, besides Magidov, the possible murderers are you, Klava, Alevtina the janitor, Galaunov, Starkova, myself and my technician Valushin."

"Good that you have not forgotten yourself," Talin said with a strained smile.

"Well, I happen to know, I didn't do it. I am going to talk with Klava now. Theoretically, she is on the list of possible murderers as well as you and I. Of course, I am confident she had nothing to do with it. Maybe, she noticed something of significance. Even if she had been with you. With or without pants."

Chapter 23

"YES, I AM INDEED NAIVE, I AM STUPID, I DON'T UNDERstand people at all," Boris mused walking towards the house Klava Turova lived in. This four-story, four-entrance concrete-block house, one of the twelve, had been built recently over an old cemetery. Fragments of gravestones and half-rotten wooden crosses jutted from the piles of debris.

"I thought I had a basic understanding of women's behavior. I could not imagine Klava would fall for this flabby roll of fat, Talin. That voluptuous body of hers has made her omnivorous. Why does this discovery of her involvement with Talin hurt me? Haven't I, myself, chosen to give up my relationship with Klava? Hey, Boris Tarutin, are you jealous? What imbecility! Especially now that I have met Irina."

Klava opened the door. There could be no mistake, as soon as she had recognized Boris, her eyes lit up. Her dimpled cheeks flashed and her white teeth sparkled in a bright smile.

"My God, it's Boris," she said. "I have waited so long for this minute. I knew you would come back one day. And, at last, you're here."

She took Boris's hand and led him into her small room. She closed the door and latched it as she used to do in those days when Boris had been a frequent visitor in this apartment. The sound of the latch served as a sign for Klava's relatives; they would never interfere with whatever was going on in her room.

There was a narrow bed in the room covered with an army-type broadcloth blanket, almost colorless because of its age but impeccably laid without the slightest wrinkle. Photographs hung on the walls, several generations of Klava's ancestors. On the small table stood an elegant ceramic bowl, holding pink and white paper roses. Both the bowl and the paper flowers had been made by Klava.

As happened always when Boris entered the coziness and neatness which dominated this room despite its utter poverty, made him relax.

He knew he had to be strong not to yield to Klava's passion.

"You may unlatch the door, Klava," he said. "I must talk to you about some business. It's very serious."

"You are always very serious," Klava said. "The latch will not gag your mouth, will it?" and her green eyes smiled. She took again Boris's hand and sat down on the bed.

Boris sighed. "Let's talk," he said.

"We will," Klava said. She pulled Boris's hand to her breast and he felt her springy nipple in his palm. Then she made a wriggling motion and her second breast, full and tender, touched Boris's arm. She peered right into Boris's eyes, her eyes now half-closed, were flames twinkling behind long fluffy eyelashes.

"No, Klava, please."

"We will not," she muttered. "Not at all," and her hand touched Boris's crotch.

"My God, Klava, stop it." But Klava's hand was already inside his pants. She made an imperceptible motion and her skirt flew up and the sight of her slightly spread, plump thighs struck Boris's eyes. He felt her body tremble leaning against his thighs.

Klava moaned. With her cheek tightly pressed against his stomach, and her eyes staring upwards, at his face, she pulled down his pants and then bent backwards, dragging Boris with her. His lips touched her hot throbbing nipple and he realized that he had lost the last remnants of will, completely yielding to the overwhelming desire.

"We will not, we will not," she repeated as she removed her clothing and his.

"That's what I love in you, Boris," she said as they lay flat on the bed. "This staying power of yours. You are just great, Borka."

A half-smile curved Boris's lips. "Klava, Klava," he said. "Why have I done that? I have met another girl but there has been nothing between us so far. Maybe, never will."

"Don't be silly, Boris. You know me, I believe there's nothing wrong with sex. So it's great if you have met some nice girl. I am sure she must be lovely. I wish both of you happiness. What harm has it done her or you that we can enjoy an hour of pleasure? Or didn't you enjoy it?"

"I did. Very much. But I came here determined not to let it happen, but I couldn't stand up to the temptation, Which was breathtaking. I am human and nothing human is alien to me. If this cannot justify, maybe it can at least explain what I've done."

Klava giggled happily. "No harm to anybody and nothing to justify. And, Boris, let's do it again," she said, embracing Boris's waist as her warm lips touched his mouth.

One hour later Klava brought two cups of tea from the kitchen. They sat naked on the bed sipping.

"Will you ever settle down, have children, Klava?"

"Sure I will. One day. You know, I am crazy. Each time I am with a man I dream to become pregnant. But I can't afford to have a child without a husband. As for a husband, where would we live? Until my brothers have finished school and start making a living on their own there's no way for me to marry. You wouldn't marry me, would you?"

"Not now. No. But before, I could have if you promised to stop your affairs with other men."

"Ah, you see. You want to own me. No, I can't promise it. I wouldn't be able to keep such a promise anyway. And I am not ashamed, whatever say about all these Baevs and Gavriks and even such nice, honest and friendly hypocrites as you, Borya."

"Let's talk about that Sunday night when Baev was killed."

"What about it?" Klava said.

"Were you alone that evening in your lab?"

"Boris, have you talked with Oleg Talin?" She giggled. "What did he say to you?"

"It doesn't matter what *he* said . . ."

"It looks as if it does. Are you jealous?"

"My God, no."

"You know that you ought not be jealous. I did not want to tell about Talin, because his wife might find out. What kind of woman is she? He says he has never seen her naked."

"So he was with you after all."

"If he has admitted this himself. Why should I deny it?

"I never would guess that you could fall for Talin."

"Hey, Boris, he's a man, isn't he? He does the same thing you do. Of course, you're better. Had you been available that Sunday evening I certainly would've prefered you. But you have been avoiding me because of your silly male pride. So, you're jealous, after all." She grinned with satisfaction and her hand touched Boris's hair.

"I just wanted to be sure Talin was with you that evening. You see, he lied to the police."

"Sure, because of his wife."

"Yes. But I thought he might have lied because he had seen something and was scared to admit it."

She laughed and her hand fondled Boris's earlobe. "No, he was with me proving his manhood. Why are you so interested? Whoever dispatched him has earned a place in the paradise."

"I do not regret Baev's demise," Boris said "What I regret is that an innocent man is in jail and suffers."

"Yes," Klava said, her hand rubbing now lightly Boris's neck. "I have heard about Magidov. They say he is a Zionist. What's wrong with that? I am a Russian, I wouldn't like to go away from my country, right? But he's a Jew. If he wants to leave for Israel, why not to let him go?"

"Yes, Klava, I agree, but, now he's accused of a murder he couldn't have committed."

"Wait a minute, Boris. Don't you know who killed Baev?"

"Do you?" Boris stood up holding Klava's hand.

"Of course, I know," she said.

Boris stared at her, holding her hand. After a pause she said, "I saw him. In the corridor."

"Which corridor? When?"

"A good man did it, why should I harm him? You see, I was with Talin in Electron Microscopy. Talin was afraid that somebody could have seen him walk in, so we not only latched the door, we also switched off the light. But there is an emergency light burning opposite the lab's door. If anybody walks in the corridor I can see his or her shadow on the door's frosted glass."

"Oh!"

"Yes, just a few minutes before the thud somebody was in the corridor running towards the back stairs."

"But you could not possible know whose shadow it was," Boris said, clutching Klava's hand.

"At that time I could not. It occurred to me later when everybody had gathered in the lobby with that Militsia man. You see, the person who was running in the corridor was very tall. So, when the Militsia explained what the thud meant, I realized that there was only one man tall enough to fit the shadow's size."

"Klava, you mean—"

"Sure, why not? It must've been Professor Galaunov."

"Galaunov? Klava, he couldn't have done it. He is not a murderer, he's a devout Christian."

"So what? You say this as if Christians had never killed in the name of God. Couldn't he consider the elimination of Baev a God-pleasing act?" Klava's eyes smiled again. "Look, why would he run in that corridor, in our wing, if he had nothing to hide? If he were the killer, however, then it would be natural for him."

"Yes," Boris said. "It sounds logical. Theoretically Galaunov could've dealt with Baev then dragged the body to the Mechanical lab, readjusted the timer on the impact tester from seconds to minutes, creating enough time to escape safely. But Kolia Galaunov would never do such a thing."

"Ask him about it."

"I will," Boris said.

"He's your friend isn't he?"

"Yes, Galaunov is my friend. And if he knows something relevant to Baev's murder he will tell about it."

Chapter 24

Boris knew that on a Saturday evening Nikolai Ivanovich Galaunov would not stay in town. He would have gone to Redkino where his parents still lived. At dawn, Galaunov would set out on a ski run. He would be back in Kalinin not earlier than Sunday evening.

"I must wait until tomorrow," Boris mused walking towards the University. He crossed the wooden bridge hanging low over the black waters of the Tmaka river.

His skin and muscles and blood still held the deep sensation of Klava's hugging hands, of her warm full breasts, of her silky firm thighs and her pulsating body. He did not want this sensation. Irina's dark eyes burned reproachfully in his mind. He knew it was absurd. Whatever had happened between him and Klava wouldn't hurt Irina. Unexpectedly, it had hurt him. I was as if something pierced the integrity of his feelings towards Irina, feelings he himself did not yet understand.

He walked into the "Professors" house, a four-story, gray structure erected two blocks from the University.

About 50 Professors' families lived there, envied by the University staff who had been allocated single rooms in dorms, like Boris, or not allocated anything.

Back in his room, Boris switched the light off and in a few minutes fell asleep. It was apparently the middle of the night when he suddenly woke up. A street lamp laid an oblique lozenge of yellow on the wall of his room. On this spot, the tips of his skis on the wall, the only item in the room which was visible at this time, seemed to convey some message. Yes, he knew what this message was. He wouldn't have enough patience to wait until Sunday evening, he had to catch Galaunov at dawn, somewhere on the ski trail.

With his skis over his shoulder, he walked the dark deserted streets of Kalinin, to the railway. It would take half an hour on the train to Redkino. Later, closer to Moscow, the train would be crowded.

Redkino station was covered with snow, the long structures of a chemical plant lit by swinging triangles of light from high poles. Boris knew the shortest way to the small hamlet where Galaunov's hut was situated and the familiar path led him among black spruces. When he approached Galaunov's hut, the eastern sky had changed from black to gray.

He came in time. Nikolai Galaunov stood in the passage to his parents' hut a white woolen sweater snugly encasing his body. The sweet aroma of red paste on the surface of his skis was mixed with the heavy smell of cow manure coming from a near-by shed.

Obeying the desire to cut short any preliminaries and to get to the core of the job he had to do, he said, without greeting Galaunov, "Nikolai, I have a very serious matter to discuss with you before you start your run."

"Good morning, Boris," Galaunov growled. "I don't know of anything in the world more serious than a ski run on a December Sunday morning."

Boris felt a sudden relief. He welcomed the delay granted by Galaunov's words. Reluctantly he said, "Please, Nikolai, it's important."

"No, no and no. I am the host and you're the guest. You must abide by the rules of this place. One does not come to an alien monastery with one's own statute. And I see your skis, so you're good and ready. Follow me. I bet you'll not catch me on the trail despite your young age. We'll discuss your problem after we are back."

Boris knew nothing in the world could compete in Galaunov's mind with the appeal of a fresh ski trail. And if a few days earlier Nikolai Galaunov had killed Baev, how could he avoid now displaying any signs of remorse?

As long as the trail ran over more or less flat fields, it seemed indeed hopeless to compete with Galaunov. The giant strides of his powerful legs carried him at high speed, the poles flickering on both sides of his big body which seemed to have lost its weight.

When the trail wound uphill, Boris's younger heart and body, trained in mountaineering, gave him an edge. And when the trail ran downhill, the mountaineer's dexterity which Boris had developed on the slopes of the Caucasus range, allowed him to catch up with his partner.

After an hour they made a short stop in a small oval clearing among dark blue spruces. Their faces red after the fast run, lungs deeply inhaling the sparkling air.

They returned to Galaunov's hut about one o'clock. Boris's legs and arms hummed after the hours on the ski runs; in the closed warmth of the hut his cheeks flamed, his tongue and lips bone dry.

"Hey, Mom," Galaunov said. "How about some milk for our guest?"

Galaunov's mother, a half-bent old woman, ran hurriedly to the cow shed. She returned carrying a jar filled with fresh milk. She poured it, still warm, into big ceramic mugs.

"Now, my friend," Galaunov said, sitting on a bench and stretching his legs under a pine plank table. "Before you tell me about your problem, I wish to interrogate you. You owe me an explanation about why you abandoned your research work. It was such elegant research. Your method for the determination of vertical anisotropy in thin magnetic films, those two angles you invented, the inverse polar angle and the azimuthal angle, all of that was just beautiful. You are wasting your talent."

"It is not a pleasure trying to exonerate myself," Boris said. "Since you insist, and to get it over with, I'll tell you what you can call 'Pictures from the life of a Soviet scientist.'

"Picture number one," Boris went on. "A Soviet scientist, by the name of Boris Tarutin, young but promising, is writing a requisition. He needs a chart recorder to measure magnetic anisotropy. He makes such requests at least once every year during the last five years. He never obtains a recorder. The response to his request is that recorders are allocated strictly in accordance with a quota. During those years scientist Tarutin learns that he is not important enough to be included in the quota. He also learns that those who got it did so mainly through *blat*."

"I know all this, Boris," Galaunov said, gulping milk from his mug. "I have the same story to tell. So what? It's no reason to stop doing research."

"Well, let's look at picture number two," Boris said. "Scientist Tarutin, still young and still promising, albeit already less young and less promising, exhibits a prototype of a device he had invented, a device for the anisotropy measurement, in a conference in Moscow. Two guys from Czechoslovakia attending this conference are Drobel and Vorak. Smart guys, sharp-eyed. They see Tarutin's device. They praise it. They request explanations and Tarutin delivers them. Well, in about one year, While Tarutin, still young and promising, spends twelve hours a day attempting to build by hand a primitive device to substitute for the recorder, a paper appears in a magazine published in the West, a paper by Drobel and Vorak. They suggest in this paper a device to measure anisotropy. Nice device. They even refer to some Mr. Tarutin, but the reference is made in such vague terms that nobody would suspect Drobel and Vorak had actually borrowed the principle and the design's details from this obscure boy Tarutin. It also becomes evident that these two smart guys did not understand some subtle features of Tarutin's device. So, the version they have described is inferior to what Tarutin has made with his own hands.''

"So, Boris, your ego suffered. No big deal."

"Sure it suffered. Now, scientist Tarutin wants to tell the world that the idea he had worked out can provide something more productive than Drobel and Vorak could ever imagine. Scientist Tarutin writes a paper. He lays out all the theory for the method he had suggested. Naturally, he wants to publish his paper in the same magazine where the article of the two Czechs appeared. No! For two years, the paper travels through hundreds of levels of the mature Soviet bureaucracy. Finally, somewhere in the Ministry, the decision is made, not to allow Tarutin to send his paper abroad.''

"My papers have also been killed, more than once," Galaunov said.

"Now, one more feature in the life of a Soviet scientist," Boris continued. "This Tarutin has received, four times, personal invitations to attend scientific conferences. Once in France, once in Italy, once in East Germany, once in Yugoslavia. He has never been allowed to go, even to East Germany. In the case of East Germany, an explanation was given: a shortage of the foreign currency. In the three other cases, no explanations whatsoever. Tarutin is made to understand that travel abroad is a privilege only for those who enjoy support of the KGB."

"Drink your milk, Boris, relax."

"Are you losing interest? There are however pictures number three and four and . . ."

"Let's get the rest," Galaunov said.

"Picture number three. A big American company pays some money to Drobel and Vorak and acquires the rights for their device. This company is headed up by an old multimillionaire who had been cultivating relations with the Kremlin's top brass for fifty years, and has made millions trading Russian icons, furs and what not. This company builds the device and sells it under some trade name. No mention whatsoever is made regarding the already not so young and even less promising Soviet scientist who is still waiting for a recorder."

"How's the milk?" Galaunov said.

"Milk is great. Shall I continue? Picture number four. A few years ago, scientist Tarutin used to supervise a couple of students working towards Candidate of Science degree. Then, one day, they were taken away from this young and promising scientist. He was told that the Ministry had established a quota determining how many aspirants the University may keep for each year. Not enough aspirant's openings to supply every potential supervisor. So, the priority is given to Party members and such prominent scientists as, say, Lenin Prize winner Galaunov, as long as Galaunov is politically reliable. They don't know that Galaunov wears a cross under his shirt."

"Boris, this all is true. Still, doesn't research carry its own reward?"

"It does. I have enjoyed my research, Nikolai. Now, picture number five. Still almost young and still slightly promising scientist Tarutin submits a research proposal relating to a study of a new type of magnetic films. The Party Secretary comrade Baev, who knows as much about magnetic films as about the sex life of whales, summons Tarutin and interrogates him and the usefulness of Tarutin's research for the politico-educational activity at the University."

Galaunov's mother ran suddenly into the hut. "Fast, Kolia, Boris, fast, hide the milk." She grabbed the jar and put it under a bed. Boris and Galaunov pushed their mugs behind their backs. They knew what could have happened.

A man walked in, in a tarpaulin overcoat, with an unkempt gray beard. He grinned widely displaying his yellow chipped teeth. The *kolkhoz* Chairman.

"Milkpeople, eh?" he said. "From the city, ah?"

"Be afraid of God," Galaunov's mother said, bowing even lower. "You know, *they* are my son, and *they*," she pointed at Boris, "*they* are my son's friend. No milk, we know the rules."

The Chairman peered suspiciously at the men. "Well," he said finally. "Just remember, not a drop of milk to anybody until you have fulfilled your yearly quota. You owe the state four hundred liters this year, but so far you turned on only 360 and the year is almost over."

The Chairman left; the jar and the mugs reappeared.

"Back to Baev's control over your research proposal," Galaunov said, "Couldn't you just have ignored all his shit?"

"That's why somebody killed him?" Boris said. "Nikolai, I am terrified to say this, some people think there may be some indication of your involvement."

Galaunov continued drinking milk, his face not betraying

any embarrassment. After a pause, Boris continued, "We have to do something. They have Magidov in jail. If you've seen anything related to Baev's demise, please speak up. Why did you run there, in the corridor, on that Sunday evening?"

"What? In which corridor?" Galaunov put aside his mug and looked at Boris. His bright blue eyes, and his half-opened lips all became a display of genuine astonishment.

"Didn't you run to the back stairs in the left wing's corridor?" Boris muttered, staring at Galaunov's perplexed countenance. "Just a few minutes before the pendulum fell on Baev's head?"

"Who told you this nonsense?" Galaunov looked for a while calmly at Boris's embarrassed face. "Well, Boris, my friend, somebody has misled you. I don't need to prove anything. To make you feel better, look here." He stretched his collar and fetched from under his white sweater a small wooden cross on a thin silver chain. "You know, Boris, the old Russian custom. Look, I kiss this cross, to tell you that I never ran in that left wing's corridor, neither before nor after the pendulum's fall." He pressed the cross to his lips.

"Oh, thanks, Kolia." Boris said. "I must apologize. It was somebody else running in the corridor. We need to find out who. You know, they have an innocent man in jail."

"Yes, Boris," Galaunov said. "They have put Magidov into jail in order to inflame anti-Jewish hysteria."

"Nikolai, but your own ultra-Russianism."

"Hey, stop it, Boris. My feelings as a Russian patriot have nothing to do with anti-Jewish skullduggeries. If a Jew wants to go to Israel, let him go. However, if a Jew wants to live in Russia, very good. If he considers himself a Russian, then he's a Russian. Like you and myself. Our language, our culture, our common sufferings, that's what make us Russians."

"I feel the same way. I have never formulated it in so many words," Boris said. "Though, unlike you, I am not obsessed with all this old Russian stuff. Now, what do you think, who killed that pig Baev?"

"You want to know?" Galaunov said. "I thought you knew. I thought, this was the actual reason for your odd voting in the council."

"What do you mean? Starkova?"

"It looks—I emphasize, *looks*, as though she may have been the perpetrator of that murder. About half an hour before that impact tester's struck Baev's head, I happened to walk next to Starkova's office."

"You did," Boris said meekly.

"Yes. The door of her office was slightly ajar. And I overheard voices."

"You did."

"Yes. One was the voice of Starkova. The other was that of Baev."

"Was it?"

"No doubt about it. Starkova said something, like it would not be impossible to revert the decision regarding her dismissal. She was in a rage, Baev said that there is no force in the world capable of opposing the will of the Communist Party. I just walked by, I did not listen what they said afterwards."

"I see," Boris said. "She tried to win Baev's support. He wouldn't budge. So, in her rage she hit him on the head. But how could she have dragged his body downstairs, and how would she know how to readjust the timer?"

"She is a rather big woman. As to the timer, we have no proof that it was played with because of Baev's murder. Couldn't some of the technicians or students replace the potentiometer? It's no big deal, they could've done it out of curiosity. You know, there are such curious infants among our students. As two-year-old toddlers, they cut open dolls' stomachs, to see what's inside. At twenty, they replace potentiometers to see what would happen. And, since a man has been killed, whoever had played with the timer may be afraid to admit he did it."

"You may be right," Boris said. "Do you really believe Starkova did it?"

"To believe is perhaps a little too strong a word," Galaunov said. "But given the personality of this charming woman, she seems capable of killing somebody she hates, especially if the situation inflames her rage more than anybody else among the eight of us."

"Nikolai, however hard it is to believe, I feel prone to share your impression," Boris said.

"Boria, you also don't want to ignore that she had been with Baev right before his mysterious encounter with the impact tester."

"Which means, that even if somebody else killed Baev, Starkova still may know something which may be a clue," Boris said. "There is a train to Kalinin shortly. Let's see if Anna Starkova had anything to do with the scoundrel's murder."

Chapter 25

THE FAMILIAR STENCH OF THE MARINOVO CHEMICAL PLANT greeted Boris when he alighted from the train.

He did not know where Starkova lived. He knew that tomorrow she would hardly be at the University; there would be no classes on Monday, December 5, the Day of the Soviet Constitution.

Every day added to the sufferings of an innocent man. Boris had to find Starkova. All he could think of was to inquire with Andrei Ivanovich Vernov, his Department Head. Vernov used to be on friendly terms with Senior Lecturer Starkova; he must know her address.

Andrei Ivanovich Vernov was gone for the weekend. His wife had no knowledge of Starkova's whereabouts. She wanted to be of help, however. Vernov's wife recalled how Starkova had boasted that she managed to buy eggs regularly from some store next to her house. The reason for this unusual selection of good food was the store's location next door to the foreigners' compound.

There was only one such place in Kalinin. The remote

Western suburb of Migalovo. Assuming the store was walking distance from Starkova's house, he could locate the store and then to walk through all the nearby apartment houses reading tenants' lists at entrances.

About forty minutes later, he stood at the tram's end-station in Migalovo. The Foreigner's compound stretched to his right behind a high wall with barbed wire on top. To his left were blocks of apartment houses.

The people walking the streets of Migalovo also differed from regular citizens seen in Kalinin. While Boris walked from the tram station, he had the impression that Migalovo had two kinds of people. One, Russians in uniform, the blue edgings of their shoulder straps and wing-shaped badges were Air Force. Pilots from the Air Force base.

The second kind of inhabitants were foreigners. Mainly Arabs and blacks from Africa.

And there was the brightly lit store. Its entrance lay opposite the cast-iron gate of the foreigner's compound. Unlike other stores where often no food could be found except for the fakes displayed in windows, in this store real meat was for sale. A big chap with a gloomy face stood at the entrance. He shooed away a woman who evidently had come to this store attracted by the rumors.

As soon as Boris pushed open the store's door, two young girls hurried towards him. Blondes with brightly lipsticked mouths, all in short coats of artificial fur, on high heels wearing genuine blue jeans. The girls stopped and then walked away lazily. They had recognized a compatriot and lost interest. The quarry they wanted were foreigners.

When foreigners entered this store, it was to hunt for young, blue-eyed blondes eager to serve the guests from another world, in exchange for imported cigarettes, records, even for jeans. These blondes wouldn't sell their bodies for the pitiful rubles of a Soviet citizen.

Some of these blondes bore the nickname "swallows." Besides the payment from their foreign customers, they were paid by the KGB on a regular basis. These "swallows," trained to pump their foreign customers had been allowed to pursue their trade on the premises of this food store.

Boris looked around weighing his chances of obtaining information.

Boris targeted a woman clerk at the bread department. As he headed towards her, a colleague at the next counter started talking.

Neither clerk looked at him. He waited patiently. The women did not seem to hurry. Lazily, they discussed the drinking habits of their husbands. Finally, one of them squinted at Boris and, with a professional expression of aloofness, said, "Yes?"

"I apologize," Boris said, using the most suave tone he could muster. "I am looking for an acquaintance of mine, maybe you can give me some directions."

"Does she work here?" the woman asked, her voice immediately acquiring a different, almost friendly tone. Both women now looked Boris up and down with obvious curiosity.

"I am afraid, not." Boris said.

"Ah." The women again turned their faces away, their interest evaporating. "This is not an information bureau." Then a second thought seemed to occur to one of the clerks. "Are you not from the *OBKhS*?" and the second woman immediately glanced again at Boris. Did he work for the *OBKhS*, the Department for the Struggle Against the Embezzlement of the Socialist Property?

"It is very important," Boris said. "Her name is Anna Vassilyevna Starkova, a tall, big woman, angular shoulders, she's 55 this year, lives a few blocks from here, wears glasses in iron frames, smokes cigarettes."

"Nobody smokes in this store, citizen. Strictly forbidden. Boris walked out. He started walking through the houses.

In about an hour, shivering in the wind, he had gone through ten houses. The name of Starkova did not appear on any of the lists.

He had also checked the names on the mailboxes installed in the passages. Sometimes people in one family had more then one name and placed a second name not appearing in the official list, on a mailbox. Boris suspected this could be the case with Starkova. As a lecturer at the University, not connected in any way to the Air Force, she wouldn't live in this district unless the apartment belonged to some other member of her family.

He had asked passers-by. None of them could help. He had tried also to knock at apartments to question tenants. Some of them did not even want to see him, answering from behind the locked doors.

His hopes of locating Starkova were encouraged when a girl of about twelve said that this smoking woman was the aunt of twins in her class. The girl was happy to show him the apartment. Indeed, there were twins densely freckled and an aunt. And she smoked indeed, but she was not Starkova.

Now he stood in front of one more house, reading names.

Suddenly, something blinked in his mind. His eyes had scanned the list of tenants in search of the word "Starkova" and ignored all other names. Now he realized that some familiar name had flashed by. He moved his eyes up. Yes, Ryzhik. Ada Ryzhik? The Commander of Professors' schedules? He climbed up the stairs and knocked on Ryzhik's door. A young woman opened, her face bearing a resemblance to Ada Ryzhik, only younger and prettier.

"I am looking for Ada Ryzhik, I am from the University."

"Aunt Ada? Oh, she does not live here. She lives in Kalyaeva Street."

In a few minutes, after he had thanked Ada's niece for the offer to have a cup of tea, Boris left the apartment with Ada's address.

It was close to eight pm when he knocked at the door of a small house some thirty kilometers from Migalovo district.

Ada Ryzhik stood in the door. Her face show perplexity. She was obviously pleased to see Boris.

The small room was impeccably clean. Hundreds of photographs covered all the walls. To Boris's amazement, he saw the faces of the University professors. Many were of the older generation, some retired and some dead. Boris saw his own likeness in the central part of this amazing collection.

"My family," the hunchback said having spotted Boris's curious gaze. She moved her eyes with satisfaction over the photographs. "What happened, Boris?" she said, her eyes staring now at her guest.

"Excuse me for the intrusion," Boris said.

"I am delighted if I can be of any help," the hunchback said, her eyes showing excitement.

"Yes, I have two questions, Ada. Or, requests if you will. ."

"Nothing will please me more."

"Next Tuesday, I have ten hours scheduled. Ada, it's very important, I need the entire day free. Under any conditions, I would replace, at any time of your choice, any of our lecturers or in labs."

"Ten hours, not an easy task. Let's see, one of your labs, electricity, we can just abolish." She went through Boris's schedule without looking at any paper.

"Don't worry, I'll take care of the schedules," she said. "Now, I would like to offer you tea, special formulation . . ."

"Tea would be great," Boris said. "Thanks for the schedule. Now, my second request. I hope you might know Starkova's address."

"Anna Vassilyevna? That Sergeant of a woman? I know, of course. I know everybody's address. It's a part of my job."

"I need to see her. Urgently," Boris said.

"She lives in Migalovo." And when Ada told him Starkova's exact address, Boris realized that in his search he had actually walked through Starkova's house. Her name did not appear there as she lived in her son-in-law's apartment. He was an officer in the Air Force.

"If you knew how important this is, Ada," Boris said. "I don't want you to think I wouldn't enjoy your tea. You have my word, some other time I'll taste it. Thank you again very much for the schedule. You've done a very important job. Maybe, you've helped to free an innocent man from jail."

"Ah . . . Who?" Her face showed a growing understanding, lighting up her eyes as Boris shook her hand and ran out.

It was after ten pm when Anna Starkova, with a cigarette in her hand, looked in astonishment at Boris Tarutin standing on the threshold of her son-in-law's apartment.

"What winds have brought you here at this time?" she said.

"May we talk inside?"

"Yes. Whatever are the reasons you're here, you're most welcome in my place," Starkova said. "I was looking for an opportunity to thank you for your valiant behavior in the Council. I'll never forget it. There are not many brave people nowadays."

Boris frowned. "Please, Anna Vassilyevna, forget it. I must ask you about something very important."

"Yes. Sit down, I'll make tea."

"No, thanks. Just tell me, I understand you had a conversation with Baev just shortly before he was murdered. An argument, I believe."

Starkova inhaled the smoke. "So, you know that Baev was going to help me."

"To help you? You had that conversation with Baev in your office about seven-thirty, last Sunday?"

"What conversation? I had met him on Friday. Not on Sunday."

"There're witnesses that you've talked with Baev in your office, just before he was killed. Somebody overheard you and Baev talking."

"What are you talking about? Oh, I see. It's my hobby. Look," She fetched a small tape recorder.

"Do you know what this is Boris Petrovich?"

"No."

"Not many people in Kalinin have seen it. I bought it from a foreigner, a cadet at the Military School. I paid four hundred rubles, two-months income."

"Isn't it a miniature tape-recorder?"

"Right, it is," Starkova said. "Japanese. A real wonder. It has a tiny cassette. It's my hobby. And in my situation, useful."

"And what does it have to do with Baev's affair?"

"Everything. My expulsion from the University was the result of a Jewish conspiracy."

"Come on, Anna Vassilyevna. You are venting such obvious nonsense. Baev or Gavrik, or Nekipalov, what do they have in common with Jews."

"You're too young, Boris. You don't properly understand Jewish slyness. But I knew, Baev just happened to be a blind tool of those Jewish plotters. On Friday we had had a meeting. And he understood the extent of this threat. He promised to help me. His death ruined my chance to stay at the University. This Jew Magidov killed him because he learned somehow that Baev decided to help me."

"Let's put aside all this conspiracy stuff," Boris said. "Did you talk with Baev on Sunday?"

"No. On Friday."

"But you were overheard."

"Not me. The tape recorder. I came to the University on Sunday, to sort out my belongings in the office, just in case Baev wouldn't be able to help, I wanted to prepare everything for moving out. I went through these tapes to see what was of importance. I played my conversation with Baev which I had recorded on Friday. On Sunday, somebody heard it when I played it and did not realize it was a recording . . ."

"You did not see Baev on that Sunday evening before his body was found under the impact tester. Still, you had reason to hate Baev, hadn't you?"

"Just because of his stupidity. I had succeeded in winning his support though, finally. Listen."

She pushed a button and two voices sounded clearly from the small device for a few minutes, the voice of Starkova talked about conspiracies. Baev grunted approvingly. Then he said, "Yes, comrade Starkova. I understand your concern regarding the Zionist threat. You think precisely in the way a good Soviet citizen is expected to think. The Party fully supports the initiative of citizens directed towards discovering all these Zionists who manage to hide in mice holes." After a few more sentences he said, "I am sure the Party will correct the situation. I'll stop the procedure regarding your dismissal. I'll talk to comrade Nekipalov. We certainly have some people we must get rid of. Not you."

Then Starkova said, "Thank you very much, Rodion Glebovich. I was right, I believed in the Party and the Party is now helping me."

And then Boris listened to Starkova's words apparently overheard by Galaunov, "You probably understand, Rodion Glebovich, that because of this awful injustice I have been in a rage. I was in a mood to do something drastic, to punish those responsible." And Baev's voice answered, "There's no force in the world capable of resisting the will of the Party." And he added few more words which Galaunov apparently did not hear, "Go to work, comrade Starkova, and don't worry. The Party will protect you from Zionists."

Now you see, Boris Petrovich. By killing Baev, the Jews eliminated the one chance that I could remain at the University. Gavrik who has now replaced Baev, he does not want even to talk with me. Just because Baev wanted to support me, was enough of a reason for Gavrik not to."

"Everybody knows Gavrik and Baev had been colleagues and friends," Boris said.

"Maybe. Friends often envy each other's success. Don't you see?"

"I see," Boris said. "I am now where I started. No progress. No clues as to who could kill Baev. Believe me, Anna Vassilievna, Magidov had nothing to do with this murder. He has an alibi."

"Jews always come out clean of any dirt they pile up for others. Alibi! Sure, he had an alibi prepared," Starkova said with a deep feeling.

"Thank you again for your valiant voting in the Council," she shouted when Boris ran down the stairs. "You alone, Boris, stood up to those Jewish plotters!"

Heading home, Boris thought, "After listening to Starkova's paranoid delusions, I need lots of fresh air."

Chapter 26

THE MORNING OF MONDAY, DECEMBER 5, BROUGHT A LIGHT frost, the kind when the air smells of fruit, the snow squeaks under foot and sparrows gather in small flocks close to restaurant kitchen doors. The platform of the Kalinin station was unusually deserted; on that holiday morning people enjoyed the opportunity to sleep a little longer.

Boris stood at the platform's edge, looking toward the approaching train which was expected to bring Irina from Blue Lakes. His heart shrank with guilt. He hadn't anticipated it; he was not a boy anymore. He was afraid he would have to pay somehow for those two hours with Klava.

And how would Irina meet him now? What had occurred in her heart and mind during the two days apart? His mood swung up and down. Now he was confident that joy would light up her eyes the moment she saw him. Then he switched to the fear that she would appear remote, fed up with his attention. To his dismay, he could not anticipate what his own feelings would be.

All that had happened between himself and Irina just a few days ago seemed unreal now, like an odd dream in which something immensely delightful was interlaced with grief and pain. He had not gone through such anguish since he was sixteen.

Then, for the first time in his life, he fell in love with a girl in his class. Everything about her was absolutely, perfectly beautiful. Beyond any doubt, there never had existed and never could appear again on earth such an impeccable beauty. Her hair, her eyes, her voice, her dresses, her books, sandwiches, and the very spot she touched with her hands excelled everything else in the world. Her face was in his mind day and night. Any minute he had to spend without seeing her was lost time.

The force of his young passion had swayed the girl. Astounded and a little frightened, reluctant at the first but increasingly with satisfaction, she accepted the religious devotion of Boris Tarutin. Whatever life would offer her in the future, she never would forget her encounter with such genuine, burning passion.

Then her parents transferred to the Far East. He felt he would die without her. Surprisingly, he survived. When he met her again five years later he tried to revive that former passion. It was impossible. He could not imagine what in the world he had found in those earlier days, in this plain, boring, girl of limited intelligence.

He had never again experienced that all-embracing delight at seeing a girl. He had girlfriends afterwards and he liked them, some of them more than the others. None had ever inspired such a flame as his first love.

It was different with Irina. He was not 16 anymore. But for the first time in 17 years he had discovered he was still capable of waiting for a girl with a mixture of fear and hope.

The train, clanking with its buffers, slowed down. And there she was on the coach's landing, more beautiful than he imagined. The bruises on her face had already paled but a light-blue crescent still remained in place of the recent black eye.

Evidently she was not sure Boris would meet her. When she saw him on the platform, gaiety lit up her face and dark childish eyes.

But some subtle barrier had developed between them. He did not dare take her hand. They walked a few steps in silence. Then he said, "How was it?"

"The place was beautiful. I walked in the forest for hours and hours. I did not want to speak with anybody. I felt better in the woods, alone. I am still terribly worried. I am afraid to ask. Have you unearthed anything?"

Her voice trembled. He knew it must have been an effort on her part to stay in those forests without knowing anything about the events which would affect her life. She had relied upon him.

"Irina, I have gone through all the avenues available. So far, no progress. I am where I started. The people I talked with don't seem to have any clues. I have to talk with Alevtina the janitor and Zhenia Valushin but I hardly expect them to tell me anything I don't know."

She stopped walking and turned her face towards Boris, tears glistening in her eyes. Her jaw was set and her voice sounded firm. "So, my father has to remain in jail. Why? Because the fifth line in his passport spells 'Jew.' Nothing has changed in two thousand years. We always pay the price for sins others commit. Thank you, Boris, for your help. I am going on to the Prosecutor's office. I want to talk to your friend, Sergeev. It would be better for everybody if we part company now, Boris. Our continuing cooperation would be harmful for you."

Boris's heart sank. "What are you saying, Irina?"

He knew he couldn't let it end this way. He did not believe she was serious. He wouldn't let his life be deprived of what had become its pivotal axis during the last days. The fight for the exoneration of the innocently condemned man and for this dark-eyed girl brought into his life, he wouldn't give up.

"Irina, I won't impose myself on you but I ask that you allow me to stay with you in this affair."

He saw in her eyes an expression of relief—as if she was afraid he would not say these words. She leaned forward and kissed him.

"The Prosecutor's office is closed today, Constitution Day," Boris said. "We'll go to Artamon's place, to have a talk with him."

Irina smiled, took Boris's hand and interlaced it with hers.

"Let's first drop in at Valushin's place, then at the University," Boris said. "Both are on the way to Artamon. We'll save time and push ahead my search for possible clues."

Evgeny Valushin, Boris's technician, lived somewhere in the labyrinth of curved, narrow passages which extended south of the Tmaka river.

Boris had been in Valushin's home a year earlier when Boris had found his technician in the lab heavily intoxicated; Valushin had been hit with one of his regular drinking bouts. Chief janitor Musaev, breaking the rules, unlocked a back door in the University building and then Boris and Musaev dragged Valushin out and loaded him into a taxi and brought him home.

It was after that event that Valushin started showing Boris his paintings and giving him some as gifts.

For a while, Boris and Irina walked along the Tmaka. Then they entered the maze of small houses.

Many of these old houses had one-of-a-kind, beautifully carved overhangs, doors and shutters. Artists from Moscow used to visit to copy the patterns of these old carvings. This place was an invaluable museum under the sky.

They stopped in front of Valushin's house, a tiny, dilapidated, timber-walled hut. The snow had never been shoveled aside.

Nobody answered Boris's knocks. He waited, then pushed open the door. A smell of paint, old clothing, rotting wood and desolation wafted from the inside. They walked into the semi-dark room, the floor boards creaking under their feet.

They saw piles of cold ashes in front of a big stove which occupied two thirds of the room. "He's not here," Boris said. "It's disturbing. He has nowhere to go, no relatives in this city. His wife abandoned him a few years ago, couldn't put up with his alcoholism. Where can he be?"

"Look here," Irina said, pointing to a corner where a homemade stand held a canvas still smelling of fresh paint. Boris took the painting from the stand and held it to the window.

In the left lower corner of the canvas, Valushin's signature appeared, a few letters in a beautifully implemented ancient Slavic ligature. Valushin had also attached a small wooden board to the canvas's lower right corner, with the picture's title, "The Artist's Sunday."

In the painting they saw a maze of roofs. Thousands of roofs of different shapes and colors, stretched from the viewer's observation point outwards. The buildings under the roofs could not be seen but their slanted shadows fell upon the lower roofs, creating a powerful illusion of a giddyingly menacing height.

To Boris and Irina it was undoubtedly a skyline of Kalinin. There was a feature in the picture giving the display of roofs the quality of a fantastic realm despite its similarity to the actual Kalinin's landscape; on the upper right edge a dark-blue fairy-tale sea started right at the buildings' walls and stretched to the remote arc of the horizon.

It was undoubtedly Valushin's self-portrait. He lay on his back, right in the middle of the central roof. In each of his hands, he held tissues of unlit cigarettes. A giant white rose jutted from his hair. His eyes were half-closed, as if dazzled by the bright sky's azure. The corners of his sad mouth curved down. And he was completely naked. The triangle of the fair hair between his thighs was depicted with the true-to-life precision. His thighs tightly held between them a bottle of vodka dripping from its uncorked neck onto his hairless legs.

They looked at the picture for a while, sensing the powerful impact of Valushin's almost schizophrenic defiance of plain reality for the sake of a blatant expression of his anguish.

"We take it with us." Boris said. "In this unlocked house, it will not last long." They found some rags and carefully wrapped the frame and canvas.

They walked into the University building. Alevtina Ponareva, the janitor, was there, at the entrance. Her eyes, drowsy as usual, opened wider when she saw Boris and Irina holding hands. A slight smile moved her mouth as she scanned Irina and nodded approvingly.

"Please, Irina, wait for me in the Magnetic lab, I have to talk to this woman."

"You make such a nice pair," Alevtina said, "Pleasure to look at. Both stand tall, one's russet, another auburn, gray eyes, dark-brown eyes, very nice, very nice," and she moved her eyes from Irina's legs, along her waist, up to Irina's head as if appraising the girl's physical attributes.

"Nice gal," Alevtina said again as Irina walked away. "The tits not that large," and she glanced at her own firm, big breasts protruding from inside her velvet coat. "It's not a big deal, you'll feed her a little, they will grow," she said very seriously.

"Thanks, you've encouraged me," Boris said. "I would like to ask you a couple of questions."

"Sure. I can tell you everything about girls."

"Not now. Tell me, Alevtina, about that Sunday evening when Baev was murdered."

"All of you want to talk about this thing. I keep having bad dreams after Sunday. I can't stand dead bodies. What do you want?"

"First when I told you to lock the entrance door did you do that? Was the door actually locked?"

"I did as you told me. You know I did, don't you?"

"Did you check lock?"

"I just did what you told me. Yes, it clicked, sure it did."

"Good. Now, after you called the Militsia, did you leave your post for a while?"

"'I have never been reproached, the Chief janitor knows. I am here, like a soldier. Maybe I go for three minutes to a—"

"So, at some time, between the moment you locked the door and the moment the Militsia arrived, you happened to be away from this post for several minutes. Nothing wrong about it. I am just trying to establish what happened."

"Yes, I am always doing what I am told."

"When you came back, was the door still locked?"

"Yes, yes, sure. I was only away three minutes, nothing could've happened. I have told them I did not see Magidov coming. I don't know anything."

"One more thing, Alevtina. Are you sure there was nobody in the building except for the eight of us?" Alevtina's face changed, her eyes downcast. She did not say anything.

"Who was it, Alevtina?"

The janitor did not answer.

"I see, there was somebody else."

"If you know, why you're asking me? I don't know anything. You better ask her yourself." and she gasped. "I am stupid," she said finally.

"So, it was a woman?" Boris said. "I thought it had to be a very tall man."

Alevtina lifted her eyes, her face showing astonishment. She did not say anything, her lips pursed in an expression of defiance.

"I would like to tell you this much, Alevtina. An innocent man is accused and condemned."

"I know. If you mean Magidov, he must have come here after we found Baev."

"Do you know that?"

"I have told them I had not seen him coming. Just, his galoshes were still wet, so he could not have been inside for more than a few minutes."

"You're a very smart woman, Alevtina."

"I know I am smart. Just, I have no education . . . ."

"So, would you tell me who was in the building besides the eight of us?"

"I don't know anything. Leave me alone, comrade Taluntin." The expression on her face indicated that she would refuse to tell anything else.

A drab figure appeared in the entrance. Valushin. He

was without a hat, shaggy hair hoar-frosted, soft stubble on his face, hands trembling.

"Zhenia," Boris said, turning to his technician. It has come, your disease."

Valushin nodded.

"Have you had a drink already?" Boris said. Valushin shook his head. You're just looking for something to drink." Valushin nodded again.

"Will you do what I tell you, Zhenia. Will you?" Valushin smiled faintly.

"Good heavens," Alevtina said, "what Vodka does to people."

"Please, Alevtina, fetch Irina from the Magnetic lab," Boris said.

Alevtina hurried to the lab. In a couple of minutes she reappeared with Irina in tow. Valushin glanced at the painting in Irina's hands. He did not say anything. In this state, on the verge of a fall into a drinking binge, and at the same time smothering his fear of alcohol, the outcome was predictable.

They led Evgeny Valushin out, across the street, into the dorm building, into Boris's room. "You stay here, Zhenia until it's over. You have bread and water here but in this state you will hardly eat anything or even drink water, will you?" Valushin, who still held Boris's hand, shook his head.

"I have to leave the town until tomorrow," Boris went on. "So, I'll lock you in this room. I'll leave a key with my neighbor, Katya, she's behind this door. In the case of an emergency all you have to do is to knock. You can even talk to her through the door. I'll instruct her not to yield to your cries or complaints or whatever else you might try in order to get out. Except for a real emergency, like a fire. Do you understand, Zhenia?" Valushin still held Boris's hand. He nodded, a curved smile trembling on his lips.

"Before I leave with Irina, I will take you to the men's room. Try your best there, it will be the last time you'll have a chance to use it until my return. Since you don't eat and drink in this state, I hope you'll endure without he restroom until tomorrow. It's cruel, but it's the only medicine for you now. I wish to ask you a couple of questions. Are you able to answer?" Valushin nodded.

"Listen carefully. That Sunday evening when Baev was murdered, you went to the restroom a couple of times, to smoke. Right?"

Valushin nodded. Irina's face displayed such tension that Valushin, as absorbed as he was in his inner pain, stared at her.

"Zhenia, I know that I did not kill Baev. And you know that. Magidov has an alibi. Starkova had a vital personal interest that Baev stay alive. You saw how Alevtina reacted to the discovery of Baev's body. I think she had nothing to do with this murder. Professor Galaunov, Oleg Talin and Klava Turova apparently had nothing to do with this murder. This leaves only you."

Irina's fingers interlaced now in a nervous clasp. Valushin trembled, then he grabbed Boris's hand. "Unless there was somebody else in the building," Boris said.

"Yes. There was," were the first words Valushin said. "With a bag."

"A bag?" Boris and Irina said simultaneously.

"So, you know who that woman was?" Boris said.

"Woman?" Valushin repeated, looking nonplussed. "I did not see a woman."

"What or whom did you see?"

"He ran in the corridor. With a bag in his hand. I had just opened the toilet door and he peered at me and then ran towards the back stairs."

"A tall man! The shadow Klava saw," Boris said. "Do you know him?"

"Do I know him? We all know him."

"What about this bag, Zhenia? You seem to be much impressed by this bag, why?"

Valushin said, "Officers don't carry bags." Soviet officers in the army, the police or the KGB never carried bags. The statutes prohibited an officer in uniform to carry anything which was not a part of the uniform. It became a deeply ingrained habit, and even a retired officer never carried anything like a bag even in civilian attire.

"So, who the devil was this man with a bag?"

"What do you want from me?" Valushin moaned. "You know everything. I can't stand it anymore. I need a drink, one drop! Only one drop!"

"Zhenia, no drinks, however hard it is for you. And you must tell us who this man was. Are you afraid of him?"

"He saw me, he would know."

"If he has seen you then whatever you say now would not change it. It's better if we know who he is. Who was that man?"

"Gavrik," Valushin said, his hands falling into his lap.

"Gavrik," Boris repeated. "A tall man running in the corridor. It matches. Wait, if he was in the building, then how could he appear later from the outside when the Militsia was already in?"

"Gavrik, the scarecrow?" Irina said. "He looks sinister, doesn't he?"

"If the man was Gavrik," Boris said, "then his being in the building hardly adds to our knowledge. Whichever way he had used to get out, nobody would suspect him in Baev's death. He was Baev's closest friend and colleague. They had served together for many years, fellow officers.

There was also one more woman in the building. Who? And what had she to do with all these events?"

"But Gavrik's bag," Irina said. "Why did he carry a bag, and what could have been in it? And how did he get out undetected and re-emerge later pretending that he had been somewhere else? I don't know about a woman, but this scarecrow Gavrik does not look innocent to me."

Artamon in shorts stared in disbelief at Boris and Irina standing at his door. He glanced at the girl, half-closed the door, then reappeared with a blanket wrapped around his legs.

"You're celebrating the day of Soviet Constitution indeed," Boris said. "Nice, sweet sleep, eh?"

Artamon combed his shaggy hair with his fingers. "You have not listened to me, Borka," he said. "You seek trouble indeed. Since you're here anyway, better come in."

"Irina wants to talk to you, Artamon, in your capacity of Investigator in charge of her father's case."

"She should come to the office officially. Not here. If anybody had seen you coming."

"I am to blame," Boris said. "I brought her. Could she be allowed to visit her father in jail?"

"You don't understand the situation, my friend," Artamon said. "This case is not conducted as a conventional criminal case. The KGB pokes its nose in and my bosses watch every step. Every move is weighed thoroughly by Lopoukhov and Gnida. Normally, visits to jail are completely under the jurisdiction of the investigator-in-charge. Not in this case. I cannot make any decision on my own."

"I see," Boris said. "Tell me, do you accept that Magidov has an alibi?"

"You think amateurishly, Boris. If you want to let me be of any help, you must disassociate yourself from Irina.

I am sorry. It's not a secret that Boris is my friend. If the slightest rumor surfaces regarding your connection with him, I shall be kicked off the case. This hardly would be to anybody's advantage."

"Artamon, she must stay somewhere," Boris said. "Not in my place. I am going to take her to Ostashkov."

"To your aunt Galina?"

"Right. Today. We'll take a bus in half an hour. We are here for two reasons. One, I didn't realize that you have no power to let her see her father. Second, I have found that on Sunday evening two more people had been in the building. One was some mysterious woman, I don't know who. And the second person was Gavrik. He's Dean of the Faculty and has now replaced Baev."

"I know him," Artamon said. "How do you know he was in the building? Didn't he arrive later, as you've told me yourself . . ."

"Zhenia Valushin saw him running in the corridor a few minutes before we found the body."

"Valushin? Your alcoholic? Was he sober on that evening?"

"Yes, Artamon, he was clear as glass."

"Well, Boris, then tell me, was he sober when he was telling you about having seen Gavrik? Didn't you tell me he was on the verge of a drinking bout?"

"True. He's in a very bad state, but."

"So, my friend, he could have a delirious hallucination, if not on that evening, then in telling the story. Moreover, what if Gavrik was in the building? You were there as well."

"I was," Boris said.

"Don't you realize Gavrik is the last person in the world to be suspected?"

"I think you consider Gavrik, on the account of his position, and untouchable big shot. You hate the notion you might be forced to raise hell if he turns out to be a suspect. And that's the hour of truth in our relations, Artamon."

"Why do you say that? Boris, why do you say that?" Artamon shouted while Boris and Irina ran downstairs. "As I've promised, I am going to investigate Magidov's possible alibi. Boris! Please."

It took five hours on a bus to reach the town of Ostashkov. They arrived when darkness had already cut off the view of Lake Seliger. From the bus station they headed right to the house of Boris's grand-aunt Galina Roksaeva. For a while they ran along the frozen lake's shore and beheld the faintly twinkling spots of light, reflections of giant winter stars, quivering on the rough ice.

Chapter 27

THEY WALKED IN THE MIDDLE OF A NARROW STREET HEMMED in by two rows of low dark buildings, with heavy snow on their roofs. Shimmering strips of light glowed faintly through the slots between closed shutters.

"I am a little scared," Irina said. "Without invitation, without warning, to fall on a woman and to tell her, hey, this girl will stay with you."

"That's because you've never met my aunt Galina," Boris said. "In fact, she is my mother's aunt."

"Why do you call her aunt? How old is she?"

"She is over eighty," Boris said.

"Good heavens!"

"I call her aunt because that's what I used to call her as a child. She raised me. I lived with her for twelve years from 1956 through '68. On her meager pension she made my education possible."

"You admire her, don't you?"

"I do. She is an amazing creature," Boris said. "Artamon

says I am very naive. It may be true. But Aunt Galina is an incarnation of naivete. After all the cruel lessons her life has taught her, she still assumes everybody is a good person."

"Cruel lessons?" Irina said.

"Her life is a Russian novel with a most improbable plot."

"It sounds intriguing," Irina said. "Tell me about her."

"She was born to a wealthy family, the Princes Roksaevs. They lived in their hereditary estates around Torzhok, Kashin, and Ostashkov. For centuries, they had been prominent in many field as surgeons, writers and navy officers. The entire family had been known as liberals. They built schools for peasant children and hospitals where the poor could get free medical care and they volunteered to work in villages during epidemics."

"And were they rewarded for all of that in 1917?" Irina said.

"Well, during the revolution in 1917, everybody was the enemy. Instead of wasting time sorting out suspected people, the Red and the White armies promptly shot whoever did not seem to be on their side. For instance, Aunt Galina's older sister worked as a nurse in an old-fashioned hospital, where the doctors and nurses had not grown to understand the 'logic of the class struggle.' They never asked a wounded person whether one belonged to the Whites or to the Reds. Once a detachment of the Red Guard came, raped all the nurses and then shot all of them together with the doctors. It was a lesson, not to treat the 'class enemy.' "

"It was an efficient way to cure political immaturity, wasn't it?" Irina said. "But what about your grand-aunt Galina?"

"She was a maverick even in the Roksaevs family. At the age of fifteen, she came to the conclusion that all this building schools and volunteering as nurses was a half-measure. What had to be done was to share their wealth with the poor and then to plunge into revolutionary work, to fight for the radiant future when there will be no poor and no rich, everybody equal to everybody else."

"I understand," Irina said. "Where a Russian general would be equal to a Jewish cobbler, and a crocodile to a hare. Did she share her wealth with poor?"

"She never had a chance. In 1917 she was only sixteen. Roksaevs' estates were burned and most of Galina's relatives were shot by the Reds. She disappeared from her home and joined an underground group of the Bolsheviks. When the Civil war erupted, she turned up in a Red cavalry unit. She was tall and strong and wore male clothing. She smoked *makhorka* and swore and drank vodka. And she handled her rifle and saber like a professional. Her Browning gun bore an engraving attesting that it was a personal present from her commander, a hard-boiled ex-sailor by the name of Kalinets. When needed she could ride a horse for ten or fifteen hours at a time."

"She must be a very masculine-like woman."

"You might think so. During those years of the Civil war, her comrades used to joke about the absence of a beard on her face. They had never suspected she was not a man. They were mistaken just as you are now, Irina. She was then and is now very much of a woman.

"Once, in one of the cavalry battles in the Urals, they retreated under an attack by a crack regiment of the Whites. She happened to gallop on her mare a few steps ahead of her commander, Kalinets. She saw his gelding pass her but Kalinets was not in the saddle. She turned and saw him lying on the ground in blood and dirt. While the rest of the detachment galloped towards a village she, alone, turned her horse and under a hail of bullets, rushed back towards the attacking Whites. One bullet hit her in her left shoulder, another scratched her neck. She reached Kalinets as the attacking unit was closing on her. In front of the unit galloped a young officer his hand extended with a gun. She saw the gun's barrel looking straight into her eyes. She jumped down, lifted Kalinets's body and placed him over the mare's back.

"Her *budionnovka*, the pointed-top cap fell off. Her hair, although cut short but obviously a woman's hair, stirred in the air. When she was in the saddle again, she saw that the White officer had lowered his gun. He could've shot her but did not.

"She managed to reach the Red trenches and Kalinets lived. He lost his right hand, however. Galina's wounds, turned out to be relatively light. She was given the Order of the Warrior's Red banner for that event. She married Kalinets after the war."

"My God, what a romantic story," Irina said, clutching Boris's arm when her feet slipped on a cobblestone.

Boris said, "Whenever the missing right hand was mentioned, he used to say, 'Galina is my right hand.' "

"He had good reason to say that," Irina said.

"Later, Kalinets had a great career. He served as a factory director, then as a deputy Minister. In 1937 he was picked up one night by the KGB, which was the NKVD at that time, with thousands of others, those legendary warriors of the Civil war."

"What happened next?"

"Kalinets and Galina had connections among the top brass. She tried to find out what he was accused of. Some friends of theirs in the NKVD told her she must renounce him, as the Party expected every Soviet citizen to behave."

"The mores have not changed much," Irina said. They wanted me to renounce my father."

"Yes and no," Boris said. "Their basic approach has not changed, true. But in '37, if your father was arrested and you didn't renounce him you went to jail. Often one went to jail even after having renounced a condemned relative. Nowadays they may choose to leave you alone; that's what they are apparently doing with you. Galina refused to renounce Kalinets. In fact she vouched for him, asserting him to be a devout Party member, an admirer of Stalin, an unbendable communist, etc, etc."

"I can see what happened next," Irina said. "They jailed her didn't they?"

"Yes. In June '37. For nineteen years."

"I see. Until the *big rehabilitation* by Nikita Khrushchev in 1956."

"Right. She survived nineteen years of camps and prisons. Kalinets never reappeared from the Gulag. He was shot almost at once, in '37."

"But what had Galina been sentenced for, officially?"

"At that time people never saw a judge. They just announced the term, usually ten years and in rare instances some absurd 'crime' definition was give. In Galina's case there was no trial, but she was told her crimes were two fold: first, being the wife of an 'enemy of the people,' and second, belonging to the 'bourgeois' class before 1917."

"But her ten-year term ended in '47."

"Yes. But in '47 all those victims of 1937 who remained alive were advised that their term was doubled. No reason given."

"This mass re-education of citizens in jails has certainly been the greatest achievement of our workers' state," Irina said bitterly.

"Yes," Boris said. "As a result everybody's love for our government has become overwhelming. Let me tell you one more story which you may find improbable. In one of the camps Galina met that young White officer who once spared her life. He was not young anymore 18 years later. But she recognized his face. During those few seconds his gun was aimed at her, his face was carved in her memory. It was the same man beyond a doubt. What you think was he doing there?"

"What inmates do in a camp," she said. "Work, starve, die."

"He was not an inmate. This White soldier was now the camp commander with the rank of a Captain in the NKVD."

"Boris, it is a fable."

"Galina went to talk to this man, to tell him that she had recognized him. Do you now understand what a crazy and naive woman she is? She had no idea whether he concealed that he was once a White officer. As camp commander he just had to move a finger and she would be shot. But as I've told you, she always has assumed everybody was a 'good person'."

"Since she is alive then her assumption was correct."

"More than that," Boris said. "The Captain turned out to work under his real name and his past was known. This was one of the paradoxes of Stalin's time. A devout communist jailed, a former White officer working in the NKVD. At the same time thousands of former social-democrats, and those who happened to aid the Whites, and scores of innocent citizens were shot without any court procedure. The selection of victims was irrational. A madhouse.

"As it happened, the camp commander and my aunt fell in love. He assigned her to work in a kitchen and saved her. But as it happened so often in those years, a group of the NKVD officers were jailed. Nobody ever learned the reason. She survived, he did not."

They climbed up a hill, the dark silhouettes of low

houses were set dimly against the lighter sky already speckled with shimmering stars.

"An amazing story," Irina said, "Even though millions suffered through it in those years."

"True. In 1956 when she was released, I was in an orphanage. My mother died in '55 when I was four years old. This children's home was a hell. Always hungry. Sometimes it re-emerges in my nightmares and I feel as if I'm strangling. Galina managed to locate me in that orphanage in Likhoslavl and she adopted me. We lived in Kalinin where she was allocated an apartment. All her decorations had been returned to her and a pension approved as to a fully exonerated Party veteran. My grandaunt is very intelligent but she is unable to admit that all she had been fighting for turned out to be shit. She still believes that she fought for justice and a better world. She believes it was Stalin who betrayed the Party. And now she believes all the trouble is in the Kremlin with inept leaders. The system, she believes, is splendid."

"Very common attitude," Irina said. "It's the easiest ways to cope with the disgusting reality."

They found themselves on the top of a hill where the street ended. A small house sat on the hill's crest. "That's where aunt Galina lives," Boris said. "After I obtained my room from the University, Galina traded her apartment in Kalinin for this house. Everybody thinks she accepted a lot of money for her Kalinin apartment. Nobody accepts it at the face value. In fact, she did not take any money as it would be against her principles. She wants to look at the beauty of this land. Tomorrow you will see how magnificent this view is, the lake with forest-covered islands in it. In summertime thousands of tourists come to see Lake Seliger.

"Maybe, she is asleep," Irina said.

"I have always thought Aunt Galina never sleeps."

Boris knocked at the door. Instead of inquiring who the visitors were Galina Roksaeva opened the door at once. Boris and Irina blinked when a lamp hanging under the low ceiling shone into their eyes.

Aunt Galina stood tall, her eighty-year-old face strong, her posture erect, her slender neck bearing her white-haired head gracefully. Her blue eyes sparkled in an astonishingly childlike manner.

"Boris! At last!" she said, her voice sounding young. She stared at Irina. There was no curiosity in this stare, only a calm inquiry. She moved her eyes to Boris, then again to Irina. Her eyes displayed comprehension as if confirming that she understood who the girl was. She smiled as she moved her spectacles to her high forehead.

Then the old woman made a slight movement towards Irina and before she understood the reason for her response, Irina moved likewise towards the old woman. They hugged each other.

"I knew it should be this way," Boris whispered to himself, watching the two women embracing each other.

What did they have in common? Nothing, if judged by documents or by common sense. Everything, if judged by how they moved spontaneously towards each other, obviously attracted to each other from the first glance. They continued to hug each other not wanting to end their embrace.

The morning of Tuesday, December 6, brought a gay play of sunlight on the low ceiling of Galina's house. The bitter aroma of hot pine tar and smoke wafted over the room. Boris pulled the blanket away from his face, turned his head and saw Irina squatting at the stove feeding it short pine logs. A few logs already cracked in the stove, flames beating from inside the iron cast shutter.

From the floor he stared at Irina's legs without stockings. Light from the stove quivered on her knees, her white silky skin taut on the relief of her calves. She did not see his glance as he remained motionless, wishing to prolong this moment of joy forever.

Then she turned her face towards him. She caught the direction of Boris's stare and she glanced down at her legs. She did not move for a while as though caught by a camera.

Aunt Galina walked in and Irina straightened up. Boris tossed the blanket aside and sprang up and it was Irina who now stared with curiosity at the long muscles of his thighs. Her eyes slid over the bulging erection hidden by his white sport trunks. Her cheeks flushed slightly and she looked with understanding straight into his eyes.

He knew that regardless of what he was doing on behalf of her father and despite being 13 years older, she was attracted to him. Attracted not only as a friend and intellectual peer but in a purely physical sense.

He embraced his grand-aunt, kissed her cheek and leading her, made a tour of a dance around the kitchen. The old woman laughed and kissed him on the forehead. She released herself from Boris's embrace, turned to Irina and said, "I suspect that these kisses and hugs are actually intended for you, Irina."

Irina smiled bashfully.

"Now, my children," Aunt Galina said, "What will you have for your breakfast? You know, I eat so little, mainly cabbage and potatoes. I grow them in my kitchen-garden. I buy only milk when available and bread. You young people need something more substantial. Sorry, there is nothing in this house to offer."

"Don't worry, Auntie," Boris said. "I'll go to the *bazar* now, to get some food."

Before leaving the house, Boris pointed out the window. "Irina, look at this beauty," he said. The hill dropped from the strip of land at the house's wall. Small wooden houses were scattered over the arc-shaped slopes of a dale fringing the shore.

The lake had frozen fully after the recent snowfall. Lake Seliger was a giant plate of bright-blue ice. In the middle of the lake was the island with tile roofs of the buildings hidden behind the trees.

"Golokomlya," Boris said, pointing to the island. "There is no access to it for regular citizens. People think there is a plant building atomic bombs. Others believe there's a station watching American satellites. Natural assumptions, but these rumors are false. They never would place an atomic plant or anything of this type in the line of direct vision from a town. Moreover, in the wintertime there is no water barrier, one can reach it on ice."

"So, what is there?" Irina said.

"A mental hospital," Boris said. "apparently, they don't want people to know what is going on there. The beautiful island of Golokomlya is off limits for everybody but the patients and mental hospital personnel."

In the *bazar* square, people, mainly women, swarmed at crude plank benches. Behind the benches, *kolkhoznik*s in winter garb, shawls, *tulups*, and *valenki*, stood, rocking from foot to foot, their hands tucked under aprons. On the benches, piles of green cabbage rolls and brown potatoes sat. Wooden barrels stored sour cabbage and dark-green pickles, giving off the aroma of dill; baskets filled with pyramids of eggs and chunks of meat sprawled among bright green leaves of burdock.

None of these could be found in stores. The *kolkhozniks* produced this food but not on the collective farms. They supplied the *bazar* from the tiny strips of land they were allowed to work for themselves.

The sellers stood there in their winter garb watching the townpeople contemptuously. Most of the lookers just scrutinized the food and sniffed its smells. Few of them bought anything but potatoes and cabbage. The prices were too high.

Five rubles for a kilogram of sinewy beef. Six rubles for a kilogram of fat, greenish pork. Four rubles for a lean bluish chicken which looked as though it had died of starvation.

Boris looked at the meat for a while. First, he would buy eggs. A dozen went for two-fifty. And butter. Five rubles a kilo, but he would take only hundred grams. After that, he would consider meat again.

A short man in an odd gray cap touched his sleeve. The black pupils of his eyes shifted fast back and forth from the people swarming around to Boris's face. The cap the man wore, mockingly called "airplane," indicated that its owner was a Georgian. Two more men in similar "airplane" caps with scarves around their necks huddled behind a bench. They sold oranges, the fruits of their blessed, warm Georgian soil.

"What's the matter?" Boris said.

The Georgian made a sign inviting Boris to follow him. "You wanted cockle-shells, dear comrade," the man said with an obvious Georgian accent. Boris, perplexed, stared at the man. The Georgian pulled his hand from his pocket and opened his palm. A five-beam Red Star lay there with a golden ring and small rubies around its center. The Red Star Order.

"Well, comrade, I give it away. Just for nothing," the man said. "Do you want it? One, two, three and give me the answer."

Boris continued to stare at the star in silence, and the man said with an air of annoyance, "Say something, comrade. You've come fifteen minutes earlier than agreed. In such deals one comes on time, not earlier, not later. Not good, dear comrade."

Then the expression on Boris's face apparently told the Georgian that something was wrong. He looked Boris up and down. He gazed at Boris's bare head, at the stubborn curl of russet hair. Then he shifted his eyes towards Boris's shoes. Moved his eyes along Boris's raincoat. Apparently, he had concluded now that Boris was not the man who was expected to appear.

He closed his palm and the Red Star disappeared in his pocket. "They said he would be an intelligentsia man, without a cap," he murmured, but he did not try to walk away. He stayed right in the *bazar* next to the two other Georgians, his eyes scanning the crowd, his hand in his pocket.

For a while Boris stayed where he was. He could not decide what to do.

The Georgian said something to his partners. They looked at Boris and started removing their oranges from the bench, putting them into two big wooden valises which sat next to their feet.

Obviously, these people might have possessed some clue to the chain of sinister events Boris had witnessed in Bologoe. They would depart in a few minutes uneasy because of the mistake. There was no way he could stop three of them. He had to explore the sole available option. He turned and walked rapidly to the *bazar* square's corner where the Militsia station was situated.

In the low-ceilinged room of the station an iron stove glared red, flames humming behind its half-opened shutter. A Lieutenant sat behind a counter, his uniform cap pushed low, his big teeth in a half-smile.

"Comrade Lieutenant," Boris said, "In the *bazar*, there is a man selling a Red Star Order. Please, hurry, they may get away."

The officer gazed at Boris, "Your passport, citizen," he said without any sign of being impressed. He leafed through Boris's passport, studying every page.

"From Kalinin? What are you doing in Ostashkov?"

"Visiting with my aunt. Comrade Lieutenant, they may flee. Please."

"Calmness, citizen. Nobody can flee from the Soviet Militsia. The aunt's name and address?" He wrote down Galina Roksaeva's address in a big journal.

"Comrade Lieutenant, they are leaving the *bazar*, hurry."

"Don't you teach me what the Militsia must do," the officer said, his smile disappearing now from his face. "Description of the man you accuse of speculating with medals?"

"I think he is a Georgian . . ."

"You think? Or you know?"

"I don't know, just his accent and cap."

"If you don't know, shut up. Tell me only what you know. First, are you drunk?"

"No, I am not. Look, I was almost killed last week in Bologoe by killers who steal medals."

"Bologoe? Do you have an aunt in Bologoe, too?"

"No, I happened to be there on business."

"What kind of business?" the Lieutenant said.

"Does it matter? We talk here while those medal sellers are getting away."

"You seem not to understand how you must behave. I think I should test the alcohol in your blood." He pressed a button. A short curve-legged Militsioner walked in.

"This Tarutin," said the Lieutenant looking into the passport. "I think he is either drunk or insane. I've decided to detain him. If he is not drunk, I think we better send him for a sanity test."

"But, comrade Lieutenant," Boris said, "I have not done anything wrong. I have only reported a man offering a Red Star for sale. He called it a cockle-shell."

"Cockle-shell, you say? I believe, we must check you. Yes. As to those alleged Georgians, the Militsia will take care of them. Yes, we will."

The Militsioner led Boris through a narrow corridor into an empty smelly room with bars over a dirty window. It contained a table and a tripod-legged stool.

"Now, take off your clothes," the Militsioner said. He sat down on the stool and picked his nose. Boris hesitated.

"In the event of resistance," the Militsioner said in the same emotionless tone, "You will be handcuffed. Nothing wrong, citizen, just a regular check. Better do what you're told."

Boris slowly took off his coat and shirt. He felt a strange indifference now, like some force he had no control of was taking over his actions. This Militsioner was just a screw in a machine. It would be absurd to argue with a machine.

He took off his shoes, socks, underpants and obeying the Militsioner's sign, put all his clothing on the table. The best way to get it over with seemed to be to follow their procedure. He did not think of the medal seller anymore, he only wanted to get out of this place.

The Militsioner unlocked a closet in the wall. There was a black cubicle with a narrow bench screwed to the wall. The Militsioner pointed to the dark interior of the closet. "Into the box!" he said and yawned. Boris looked at the Militsioner in hesitation. Naked, his body covered with goose-flesh, he felt now completely impotent. He shrugged and stepped into the box and sat down on the bench. The Militsioner slammed the door.

In the darkness red and violet spots danced before Boris's eyes. Then his eyes adjusted and he saw faint gray chinks between the box's door and the wall.

Outside the box, the Militsioner whistled a currently popular song as he searched Boris's belongings.

Then Boris heard the Militsioner walking, the door banged and silence descended upon the dark box.

They would check Aunt Galina, Boris thought, Maybe the university in Kalinin. But how long would he stay in this black box, his knees hard-pressed by the thick door, his eyes trying to discern something through the chinks?

Chapter 28

Yosif Markovich Magidov understood what jail was all about in the few hours after the door of his cell banged behind him for the first time.

The screeching sounds of keys in heavy locks had made it ultimately clear that his world was limited to the cement strip two steps wide and five steps long. Around him were four walls with a narrow window in one of them. A grating made of black-painted steel bars was cemented across the window.

A small barrel stood in the corner, its cover held together by two nailed crossbars did not hamper the stench.

The stinking barrel in the corner, the immense thickness of the wall, the checkered patterns of bars in the window's embrasure, even the remnants of thousands of flies on the wall, were features of a jail one may have anticipated to meet in this place. But, if he wanted to define what jail was all about, his definition would be "clangs."

The clangs were what he could not ignore.

Since he had neither paper nor pen he had but one

choice to work his formulas in his mind. He even enjoyed keeping his calculations clear in his head. This extra effort even provided some unexpected advantage, by not relying on paper he was forced to do his calculations with a caution he never had to exercise before. In a strange way it made his understanding of his theory's development crisper and deeper than ever.

The clangs were what his willpower could not cope with.

The guards wore soft felt boots so that inmates never heard their footsteps. At any moment a guard could approach without a sound and peer inside through a peephole. The footsteps was the only thing in this place which did not make a clanging sound. Over and over again a resounding iron clang thundered somewhere.

One never knew what each clang meant and this riddle of the sounds was a strain on every nerve of each inmate in a solitary cell.

The prison doctor walked into the cell soon after Magidov's arrival he had the scarlet nose of a drunkard. He looked around the cell, grinned and said, "Alone? It may be boring at the outset but it's only the first ten years that are hard."

He left the cell and the door banged. Then Magidov heard more jangles, thuds, clangs as the doctor continued his march through the cells. This time, the meaning of the sounds was known, nonetheless even these banging jolts strained Magidov's senses.

Yes, jail meant clangs.

Three times a day guards distributed meals. Breakfast at 6 am was invariably a chunk of a tar-like bread, a bowl of hot water and a teaspoonful of sugar. At noon a bowl of hot water with a handful of barley grains passed as soup and a spoonful of hard porridge. At 6 pm, another bowl of soup.

On the third day his trousers had become loose on his waist.

Once a day a guard unlocked the door and made a sign to the inmate to pick up the barrel. Hardly lifting the heavy stinking barrel he followed the guard to a huge lavatory with hundreds of oval holes in the cement floor. Since he was kept on the investigators' order, in a solitary cell, Magidov was also alone in the lavatory. During the fifteen minutes he was in the lavatory he exercised.

Somewhere deep inside there was an anxiety for his Irina. Because there was nothing he could do for her he pushed this anxiety deep into his subconscious.

On the morning of his fifth day in jail, Tuesday, December 6, the door of his cell opened and a guard, in a sloppily fitted uniform appeared. Glancing at a piece of paper, he said, "On letter M," and when Magidov did not answer, apparently not understanding what the guard wanted, the latter said, "How long in jail?"

"Four days and a night."

"*Green*. When asked by a letter, say your full name, clear? So, on letter M."

"Magidov, comrade, Yosif Markovich."

"There are no comrades for you here, detained Magidov. You must say 'citizen Superior,' and only if permitted to talk, clear? Now we go. I follow you. Keep the hands behind the back, no talk, no looking sideways, clear?"

They walked along the dark corridor. "Stop," the guard said in a low voice, his breath on Magidov's neck. After several seconds the guard tinkled his keys and he said, "Ahead!"

He led Magidov into a small room without windows. There was a black telephone on the table and a small box with a button on it. One wooden chair stood behind the desk, another screwed to the floor at the door about five steps from the desk. The guard stayed at the door. Magidov sat down on the chair located at the door.

"Up!" the warder barked, his face displaying a genuine disgust.

The door opened and a short, slightly stooped man Magidov remembered from the house search, walked in. He signed a paper held by the guard and waved his hand in dismissal.

The investigator sat down, placed a black folder on the desk, then crossed his hands over his chest and looked at Magidov who was now seated.

Magidov saw wit and intelligence in the investigator's gray eyes, distinguishing him from typical members of the judicial profession Magidov happened to meet earlier.

"Good morning, Yosif Markovich," the investigator said. "My name is Artamon Artamonovich Sergeev and I am an Investigator of the City Prosecutor's office. From now on we will work together with you until the case is completed. You must understand I am your friend and it is in your best interests to work with me. As a mature person I hope you will do your best to aid the investigation."

Sergeev's words were what Magidov would expect from a typical investigator. They almost dispelled the first impression made by Sergeev.

"Thank you, Artamon Artamonovich," Magidov said. "I look forward to many pleasant and rewarding hours with you. Just, I am afraid, as being with you would bring such an immeasurable pleasure to me, I may be tempted not to expedite the investigation just to prolong the pleasure. Then he grinned touching the five-day-old black beard on his thin chin.

Sergeev paused, leafing through the papers in his folder. "I regret, Yosif Markovich, your defiance but I appreciate your wit and character," Sergeev said. "Unfortunately, the situation you and I are in is not conducive to jokes. He looked straight into Magidov's eyes then turned his eyes aside feeling uncomfortable.

"Well," Sergeev went on, "my duties require me to start with formally asking you your name, birthdate and other personal data. Tell your full name and all the aliases you have ever used, if any."

Magidov nodded. Then he answered Sergeev's questions and Sergeev wrote down his answers on numbered sheets of paper which he fastened one by one in a black folder.

In about half an hour, they were done with this part of the procedure. Magidov read and signed all the pages filled out with the questions and answers.

"Good, Yosif Markovich," Sergeev said. "And now, let's talk regarding the substance. On that Sunday evening, when Baev was found dead I understand that you testified to Lieutenant Nifontov that you came to the University building at about eight-thirty. Do you wish to change your testimony now?"

"No! I am sure you will find proof that I've told the truth."

"I would like to assure you, Yosif Markovich, that I want very much to unearth the truth."

Magidov stared at Sergeev, baffled by the sincerity in Sergeev's voice. The eyes of the two men met. Then both lowered their eyes. They felt some imperceptible change in the emotional atmosphere. Magidov lifted his eyes a couple of times as if studying his interrogator.

"To help me, Yosif Markovich, try to recall something which could be verifiable, like some event which occurred beyond the university building between eight and eight-thirty, and in which you took part."

"Oh, sure," Magidov said, his voice again acquiring

the tone of a faint jesterishness. "Yes, there was an event. In the tram on my way to the university between eight and eight-thirty on that Sunday, I solved a differential equation of the second order. You want me to write down this equation for you?" He stopped, he saw an expression of pain on Sergeev's face.

For a while, Sergeev remained silent, looking at his papers. Then he said, pensively glancing at Magidov, "*Verbum sat sapienti est.*"

"Oh, the golden Latin!" Magidov said. "*Alma mater! Ars longa, vita brevis! Et sic de similibus, etcetera, etcetera, etcetera.* How very pleasant to learn that one can find educated persons among the servants of our judicial system."

The telephone on the desk rang. Sergeev sighed and picked up the receiver. "Yes," he said. His face showed disappointment. "Yes," he said once more and laid down the receiver. He looked at Magidov, sighed again, then pressed the button of the desk.

The guard walked in. He signed a piece of paper, then stopped at the door and looked at Magidov's face. "Yosif Markovich, I have some business to attend to. Some of my associates will talk with you now. I want you to realize, however, that *I am* in charge of your case. *Remember* that, please." He walked out.

The guard stood silently at the door, his hands at his sides. Not a sound could be heard in the empty room. Minutes ticked by. Gradually Magidov huddled in his chair. He tried to think of his theory, fragments of formulas obscurely emerging and disappearing again in this drowsy mind.

It was obvious that Sergeev tried to convey some message to him, but he did not understand what kind of a message it was. From time to time he opened his eyes and saw the guard still frozen in the same pose at the door, the rolled-up piece of paper in his hand.

Magidov's half-nap was interrupted by the sound of the door opening. A big man walked in smoking a cigarette and holding an ashtray. He signed the paper and the guard left. The big man sat down. He started reading papers in the folder left on the desk by Sergeev. From time to time he glanced at Magidov, finished one cigarette and immediately lit another. Loops of blue smoke floated slowly across the small room.

It took an hour until the big man finished reading the file, a pile of cigarette stubs in the ashtray.

"So, citizen Magidov," the big man said. "It is the time for you to stop your stubborn disavowals and tell the truth. I think you are an impudent bastard. You have used comrade Sergeev's kindness but it will not work, Magidov. Either you admit your guilt at once or I make mincemeat of you." He stared in silence at Magidov. The latter did not react in any way.

"You seem not to be interested in my words, are you? What is that you think about?"

"I am thinking whether it is reasonable to use a third approximation when solving the Schroedinger equation for the case of three particles."

"Ah, scoffing at me, boasting. Education you have, you pig," the big man interrupted.

"No, I just thought you were genuinely interested," Magidov said in a tone of innocence.

"Do you know what would happen to you if this was in the fifties? We would beat information out of you in 10 minutes."

"You would enjoy the comeback of the fifties, wouldn't you," Magidov said.

"You fucking idiot, do you think we do not possess means to break you down? You pig!" the big man shouted. He jumped to his feet, made several fast steps towards

Magidov and his big hand, clutching a cigarette, swung over Magidov's head. Magidov jerked his head aside.

"Ah, you see, I have not yet touched you, and you already piss into your pants. I can make mincemeat of you, pig." He walked back to the desk, opened the folder. "I am listening, Magidov, spill out your story. And I warn you, only the truth."

Magidov remained silent. The big man waited with a pen in his hand. Then he sighed, laid down the pen and banged his fist on the desk. He shouted, "You fucking swine, son of a whore, I will show you how to scoff at interrogators." His fists hit the desk a couple of times, then he pressed the button. The guard walked in.

"Take him away, I can't stand him," the big man shouted.

They walked along the corridor, Magidov again leading the way. Before they had reached the corridor's corner, the guard said, "Stop." He unlocked a big door.

Heat and noise struck Magidov. This was a big room, with three levels of bunks full of people smelling of sweaty bodies and dirty rags. A heavy urine stench from a giant barrel almost knocked Magidov down. Sweat glistened on pale bodies many covered with tattoos.

There was no free place on the overcrowded bunks. Magidov leaned against the dirty wall and estimated the cell's population at about 200 men. Many sat embracing their own knees, heads down, immersed in grave thoughts.

The heavy door banged over and over again. A guard appeared, shouted a letter, and an inmate shouted a name in response and walked out. It happened eight or ten times during the hour but it did not seem to create any free space on bunks.

Magidov closed his eyes. He expected this change in his situation to be the first step on the long road to attempt to break his will. He was prepared.

He was not worried about the second interrogator, the shouting man with big fists. He felt he could cope with his rudeness, curses and threats. Sergeev seemed to be a much more formidable adversary. And strangely enough, Magidov was confident that Sergeev tried to convey some message when he emphasized the word 'remember'—to remember that Sergeev was in charge of the case. Could it mean that Sergeev was advising him to ignore what the other interrogators might say or do?

After several hours in the big cell the door banged once more and a guard shouted, "On letter M."

The guard led him again to the same small room. The same big man sat there at the desk, a cigarette in his mouth.

"So, pig, have you come to your senses? I really don't believe you will ever tell us the truth. Yours is a nation of liars and traitors," the big man said.

"How wonderfully you match your position," Magidov said. "With the grace of a rhinoceros. You must have earned scores of awards."

"You swine's litter, dog's shit, stinking *Zhid*, I let your intestines out, you—you—" the big man shouted, hitting the desk with his fist. "Tell me about the tools you used to kill Baev."

Magidov did not answer. The big man waited for a while, then hit the desk again. He jumped up, approached Magidov and his huge fist swung in the air. This time Magidov did not move. The big man's fist flashed in front of Magidov's eyes but did not hit him. The interrogator returned to the desk. He shouted again, hit the desk with his fist, approached Magidov over and over again, his heavy hands swinging in the air next to Magidov's face. He demanded answers about the tools used for Baev's murder. He swore. He cursed Magidov and all the Jews in the world. It continued for another hour.

At the moment when the big man hit the desk especially hard, the door swung open and another man entered. He wore a gray suit, a lemon-yellow tie and spectacles in gilded frames. "Calm down, Demko," he said. The big man stopped shouting. The guard came in with a glass of water for the big man. Demko drank, wiped his mouth and walked out. The man in gray suit sat down in the chair.

"How are you feeling, Yosif Markovich?" he said, his voice bearing signs of empathy. "I apologize for the improper behavior of associate investigator Demko. Such methods are strongly forbidden. Do you want some tea?"

"I want associate investigator Demko back here. I have enjoyed his performance," Magidov said.

"Oh, Yosif Markovich, I understand your feelings. It is hard for you to trust me. I don't request that you trust me blindly. Just drink some tea and relax. And we will talk a little, and you will tell me only what you want to tell. And you will see that I write down every your word exactly as it will be said. Fair enough?"

"And who you are, if I am permitted to inquire?" Magidov said.

"Well, I am also an associate investigator but I am here as a member of a team aiding Artamon Artamonovich Sergeev who is in charge of this case. So, what about tea? With sugar! And, albeit I am not sure I'll succeed, I may try to get for you a sweet roll."

"Since you have not mentioned your name, I'll call you Ivan Ivanovich. Fair enough?" Magidov said. "So, Ivan Ivanovich, the law permits you to detain a suspect without formally presenting him with an *accusation conclusion* for not more than 72 hours. Whereas I am here for the fifth day I have not been confronted with a formal accusation."

"Oh, very good. You are right, Yosif Markovich. You could've been a good lawyer. There is such a law, indeed. But, there is another clause in the same law that says 72 hours unless a Region Prosecutor deems it proper to prolong it for 72 hours more."

"And then for 72 more, and so on and so on?" Magidov said.

"Well, more or less."

"I see," Magidov said. "It is indeed a convenient law. I fathom, though, the Prosecutor wouldn't bother to delay the compilation of a formal accusation if you had any real evidence against me. Hence, you hold me here without justification."

"Well, Yosif Markovich, our socialist system of justice is based on different concepts. For us, there are much more significant factors than the concept of a guilt versus innocence, or hard proof versus circumstantial evidence. Also, we do not accept the bourgeois concept of the presumption of innocence."

"I realize that guilt and innocence are a purely politics-related notions. If a person is useless for the Party goals, it is prudent to consider such a person guilty."

"Well, you exaggerate, you exaggerate. Oh, here is your tea and roll." The warder came in carrying a tray. Magidov nodded and took the glass with tea and the roll.

"Now, Yosif Markovich, man to man, just tell me, how you happened to kill Baev. Was it self-defense? If it was, it would serve as an important *mitigating factor* in the incriminating procedure; it would make your guilt less serious. More important, your voluntary confession would drastically change your situation. Daily walks in the yard, better meals. And visits from your relatives, I promise you. What is more important, our courts take into account an openhearted confession and a sincere repentance."

"Nice to know this, Ivan Ivanovich. But I had nothing to do with Baev's demise. I didn't even know he was killed or when and how. Sorry, I can't help you."

The investigator shook his head in a disapproval. Without any sign of impatience, they talked in this vein for another hour.

Then the telephone rang. The associate investigator picked up the receiver. "Yes," he said. "Well, Yosif Markovich, I must leave. Demko will replace me now. I am sure he will not behave as rudely as before. Try to understand his situation. He must produce results. If you don't tell him anything he has no results and he will be reprimanded."

The guard walked in, the rite of signing the paper was properly executed and *the good guy* in gray suit disappeared. The guard assumed the attention pose at the entrance. Almost at once Demko walked in.

"Do we drink tea? Sweet? With a roll?" he shouted. "And have you earned this tea?" The guard took the glass and the remnants of the roll and walked out. The big man hit the desk with his fist.

"Now, you bastard, how did you murder your dear comrade Baev!" He continued shouting, hitting the desk with such force that a chip of wood off the desk's edge. "You'll see, scoundrel, because of you, this desk is damaged. You will pay to compensate for the damage."

Magidov did not answer. He yawned and lifted his eyes to the ceiling. The big man continued shouting and swearing and hitting the desk for another hour.

Then the telephone rang. The big man picked up the receiver. "Yes," he said. Once again the rite of signing the paper was performed, then Demko left and the guard assumed his attention pose.

Sergeev came in and sat at the desk. He remained silent for several long minutes, then he said, "Yosif Markovich, I have some news, not very encouraging for you. We have thoroughly interrogated every tram driver who happened to be on duty on that Sunday evening when Baev was killed.

We have shown your photograph to them. None of the drivers recognize you."

Magidov did not react. He just stared at Sergeev and the latter lowered his eyes. Then Sergeev said. "There is another point, Magidov. You insist that you came to the University building after eight pm. If so, how did you walk into the building? The entrance door was locked from inside."

"Finally, a relevant question," Magidov said. "I don't know what you know, but I know that the door was not locked. Usually this door is ajar all the time. On that evening, strangely enough, it was not ajar. It was almost closed, but it was not locked."

"So, what you maintain really is that the other witnesses have lied," Sergeev said. "The janitor has testified that she personally locked this door. This testimony is corroborated by other witnesses."

"Maybe she did lock it. Maybe somebody unlocked it afterwards."

"None of the people in the building have admitted they had ever approached the door," Sergeev said.

"Naturally enough. Who might want to unlock the door? Only somebody leaving the building. And whoever had left the building before the Militsia's arrival, is apparently not among those you have interrogated."

"It sounds logical, Yosif Markovich, but it is only your surmise. Not facts."

"True. Well, if you are trying earnestly to understand what has happened, I'll tell you about some facts which are relevant to your question about the door."

"What is that?"

"On that Sunday evening there was a snowfall, just a light fall of snowflakes. When I came to the University entrance there was fresh snow powder on the ground."

"Well, what has it to do with the door?"

"There was a string of footprints on the virgin layer of fresh snow, just a single string of footprints. Somebody had walked out a few minutes before I came. Since the snowfall continued for another hour the footprints soon disappeared under the subsequent snow layers."

"So, you imply that some man or woman had unlocked the door from inside, left the building and then shut the door but did not pull it close enough to get it locked. And this happened at some time between eight and eight thirty," Sergeev said, still avoiding Magidov's eyes.

"Yes, that is what I imply. But not a man and not a woman."

"Then what?"

"Judging by the footprints it looked like a child, somebody maybe ten or twelve years old."

PART 5

Chapter 29

WITHOUT LIGHT AND SOUNDS IN THIS BOX BORIS FELL ASLEEP. His knees ached and the lack of air and the chill woke him. Each time he opened his eyes there was the same blackness.

Then he woke up once more and there were no gray chinks of light any longer. All was black. The entire day was over, this Tuesday, December 6. Could they have forgotten about him?

A door banged. The chinks faintly glowed and two voices sounded. Apparently, a Militsioner had led some man into the room. The Militsioner ordered the man to undress. The man swore calling the Militsioner a pederast. A slap sounded and the man moaned. Then he swore again and the Militsioner shouted, "Fucking scum, I'll beat the shit out of you."

The door banged again. Evidently one more Militsioner came in. Thuds and the policemen's hard breathing and the man's groans and curses filled Boris's heart with chilling anguish. A lock clicked. The door of another box next to

Boris creaked. The policemen loaded the man into it and slammed the door. Then the policemen left.

For a while, the man in the adjacent box continued moaning. Gradually, the moans subsided. Then he knocked at the plank wall separating the two boxes. "Is there anybody?" the man said hoarsely.

"Yes. Who are you?" Boris said.

"A thief or a *frier*?" the man said.

From Artamon's stories, Boris knew that in the *Fenia*, the thieves' jargon, the word 'frier' meant a person not belonging to the thieves' society.

After short hesitation, Boris said, "I am just a man."

"*Frier*," the man in the next box said matter-of-factly. "Hey, *mujik*, make up to smoke."

Mujik, which meant peasant, was another *Fenia*'s word for a non-thief.

"To smoke? How?" Boris said.

"I teach you," the hoarse voice said. "Just put the baccy under the bench, understand? Then we bang on the doors, you and me, until the pederasts come. They will unlock the boxes and beat us up. Then I'll sneak into your box and you'll take mine, understand?"

"Crazy," Boris said. "I don't have anything to smoke. Even if I had, how could you smoke in this box? And what if they will not let us switch boxes, just beat us up and put us back? You don't mind being beaten?"

"A *frier* is a *frier*," the hoarse voice said. "A thief is not afraid of those pederasts. They beat me up anyway, it is nothing for me. So, make up a baccy, won't you?"

"I do not smoke."

"Pederast!" And the hoarse voice swore.

A couple of hours later, a Militsioner unlocked Boris's box.

Spots of light danced before Boris's eyes, made by the

weak yellow glare of a small lamp. The Militsioner pointed at the pile of Boris's clothing and told him to dress.

As they had not returned his watch to him he managed to look at the officer's wristwatch. It showed a few minutes after seven. Did Irina and Galina know his whereabouts?

He did not ask the Militsioners about his watch and documents. The fastest way to get out was to wait patiently, letting them proceed at their own pace. Any attempt to expedite the procedure would just jeopardize the prospects of his leaving.

The officer handed a folder to the Militsioner.

"Let's go, Tarutin," the Militsioner said.

"What do you mean?" Boris said feeling that his heart dropped again into a chill. They seemed to have no intention of letting him go. "Haven't you checked with my aunt? Or with the University? Where are we going?"

"Much to know—to die early," the Militsioner said.

They walked out. Chilly wind breathed into Boris's face, making him shiver. The sky was clear, giant stars shimmering over the low roofs of the buildings surrounding the dark *bazar* square, now deserted.

A van, the infamous "black raven" used for transporting prisoners within cities, stood next to the Militsia station. It's sides bore a deceiving title, "Meat." The Militsioner said, "In, Tarutin."

The engine revved up, then the van bounced and leaped forward. Boris could see a small window in the back door. Dark silhouettes of houses flashed by, rare street lamps on poles, trees and segments of the sidewalks. Then houses and trees disappeared, replaced by a dark flat expanse which stretched all around.

They drove on ice across the lake. So, the Lieutenant of the *bazar* Militsia station had apparently made good his threat and arranged for Boris's examination in the Golokomlya mental hospital.

The man in the hospital's reception room had thick hands, wide shoulders and a reddish scar across his cheek. Despite his white smock he looked more like a jailer than a hospital attendant. He signed a paper. The Militsioner rolled the paper up, shoved it into the sleeve of his greatcoat and walked out.

The man with the scar looked Boris up and down. "A dissident?" he said, unlocking an iron gate. It was like entering a wire cage.

"I don't know why they have sent me here. It's just a misunderstanding," Boris said.

"It's always a misunderstanding. You fucking intelligentsia people. Don't worry, you'll be all right here. If you behave, understand?"

"But, comrade, no doctor sent me here. The Militsia cannot judge one's mental health."

"Well, I see why you are here. You are a philosopher." The attendant grabbed Boris's arm and twisted it behind his back, the man's leg in a heavy boot knocking under Boris's knee. As Boris started to fall the attendant's hand squeezed Boris's chin and mouth; the next moment Boris's head was jammed between the attendant's knees cramping Boris's earlobes painfully. The attendant held Boris for a few seconds then spread his knees and let Boris loose.

For a while, Boris lay flat on the cool linoleum, the attendant's black boots hovering before his eyes. A fury cramped Boris's heart. He knew he could grab the attendant's boots, jump on him, make him scream in fear. But he knew that it would create an uphill fight with the entire omnipotent system. He had no right to start this fight here. Irina, Valushin, they needed him. He had to get out of here as soon as possible. He waited until his rage subsided then he rose slowly.

"It was just a warning, understand?" the attendant said. "I used to be a wrestling champion, understand? I can bend down three bastards like you at the same time. Let's go, I show you your room."

There were six beds in the room with bars across the window. The attendant tossed a crumpled gray gown with torn sleeves on Boris's bed. Boris changed into the gown and sat down on the bed.

As long as the attendant stayed, four out of the five other people in the room sat frozen on their beds. The fifth man did not pay attention to the attendant. He lay flat on his bed, his lips moving slightly.

The former wrestling champion walked out taking Boris's clothing. The people in the room relaxed. Three of them sat cross-legged on their beds.

One more man, his hands holding the flaps of his gown on his stomach, approached Boris. "Listen, they all are crazy," he whispered, his thumb waving at the other inhabitants of the room. "Beware, they all work for the NKVD."

"NKVD? You mean, the KGB? There is no NKVD nowadays," Boris said, instantly regretting his attempt to reason with a man who was supposedly mentally disturbed.

"You are right," the man said. "I just wanted to test you. But they are crazy! I've reported it to the doctor."

"Have you? And what did the doctor think of that?" Boris said.

"The doctor works for the NKVD. They watch me all the time. Please," the man lowered his whispering voice even more. "Are they watching me now?"

Boris glanced at the four people in the room. "No," he said, "They are not looking at us at all." He clambered onto his bed and pressed his back to the wall.

Another man approached Boris. He was in his late sixties. "Excuse me," the man said, "May I ask you a question?" And, without waiting for Boris's reaction, the old man whispered, "Are you Stalin?"

"No, I am Tarutin," Boris said.

"Oh, again the same story. Each time they bring in somebody new, I hope it will be Stalin at last. I am tired. Oh, how tired I am, keeping watch!"

A piercing scream sounded somewhere a few rooms away. Everybody in the room shuddered nervously. The scream gradually changed its tone, fluctuating from a high-pitched shriek to a low growl and again converting into a thin squeal.

"It is in the section for the violent," said the only man who seemed to have no fear of the attendant. "I gather, you are here for the same reason as I am," he said, sat up on his bed and extended his hand. "My name is Fomichev. I can see you are a sane man. Don't be afraid of these four people, they are quite harmless."

The scream continued, waves of shrill sound intermingling with animal-like growls.

"I am Tarutin," Boris said. "How long have you been here?"

"One week. You see, I am under investigation by the KGB. I am the headman of the Valdai community of the Adventists."

"That's why you are under investigation?"

"The third time," Fomichev said. "Twice before they just sentenced me to terms in jail. Now they say only a lunatic can be so stubborn as to adhere to *religious superstitions*. Therefore I am here for an examination. My Lord is with me, either in a jail or in a madhouse. I can pray to my Lord everywhere."

Boris said, "They certainly do not like believers but not every believer is in jail, isn't this true?"

"Yes, that's right. I have committed, in their view, a number of crimes. One is that in our community we teach our children to love the Lord. But in state school they teach children there is no God. So we refuse to send our children to the state schools."

"I see now," Boris said. "That is what they will never tolerate."

"True. And, the second crime of ours is that we refuse to register our community with the State Authority for Religious Cults."

"I understand about children. But the registration—" Boris said.

"The Authority for Religious Cults is a Department of the KGB. If you register with them, they usurp the right to approve a minister for the community."

"Approve or appoint?" Boris said.

"True, to appoint. And every minister they appoint—"

"—Is a KGB officer," Boris finished.

"Quite true. Some churches, like the Russian Orthodox church, prefer to accept KGB-assigned priests. They are allowed to function under strict supervision. Their freedom is limited but they avoid harsh persecutions."

"But yours is not among those churches," Boris said.

"No, ours is not. We are loyal citizens, though. We pray for the state and the government. We obey the government and all the laws."

"And that is why they hold you in jails and psychic wards, isn't it?" Boris said.

"God knows, it is. And what has brought you to this place, Tarutin?"

Some feeling told Boris he could trust this man. He told Fomichev about his weekend in Bologoe, about Magidov and about the Militsia in Ostashkov.

For some time, Fomichev apparently digested Boris's story.

"God has directed you to get close to your death in order to wake you, Boris," Fomichev said. "Your life has been full of vanity, an empty life, not the life God has planned for you. It is noble to fight for an innocent man, but unselfishly, as God wants you to do. You are doing this in order to gratify your flesh through this Jewish woman."

"You're right, her body drives me mad. But it is not as simple as it looks. Irina and her father dream of leaving this country for good. They have started some actions towards this goal. If Magidov were set free this would be a step to their departure. And if they depart I shall never see her again."

"God teaches us a good action is a reward unto itself. Still, if you dig deeper isn't there a hope that if her father is set free they will change their minds and stay?"

"I don't know," Boris said.

"I feel I must fight for Magidov's exoneration and for this girl, whatever the outcome."

"Good, Boris," Fomichev said. In this madhouse you are given a chance to review your whole life. Don't miss this chance. Good night, God bless you."

The next morning, Wednesday, December 7, an attendant appeared in the room's door at about seven am. "Tarutin, to the doctor," he said.

The doctor turned out to be a young man in his middle twenties. The high collar of his white smock was held by a huge pin: the silky blond mustache looked glued rather than grown naturally. He looked at Tarutin and waved him to a chair.

"So, Boris Petrovich, how do we feel today?"

"We feel great," Boris said.

"Good. Do you have questions?"

"Not at this time," Boris said.

"Hmm. Usually, people in your situation ask why they are here."

"And would you answer such question?" Boris said.

"Sometimes, sometimes. So, do you know why you are here?"

"I don't," Boris said.

"Well, you seem to have had some misunderstanding with the Militsia, correct?"

"Quite so. I believe it was a misunderstanding. So, maybe you will now clear up this misunderstanding and I shall depart with thanks?"

"Aha!" the doctor said. "You don't want to find out the doctors' opinion on the state of your mental health, do you?"

"So far, nobody ever told me that my behavior seemed suspicious in regard to my mental health."

"Ah, Boris Petrovich, every patient says the same thing. No mentally disturbed person has ever admitted to be mentally disturbed." And the doctor chuckled, being obviously happy with his statement. He wrote something in the file open on his desk.

"Well, what is your opinion of my mental state, doctor?"

"As hard as you may find it to believe, Boris Petrovich, it is obvious that you need some relaxation. And the best place to get it is here. We will take care of you until you are completely right."

Boris felt that hot sweat on his face and armpits. He forced himself not to show his anger. He knew about dissidents who were systematically destroyed by drugs in prisons run by the KGB. But why was he selected for such treatment? He had not yet done anything that exposed him to the KGB.

He stayed silent. The young doctor watched him, waiting for a display of rage that would justify drastic measures. Very quietly Boris said, "Very well, doctor, you know best. May I ask you what kind of healing procedure you contemplate for me?"

"Well, you have no need to know our methods. However, I am going to prescribe moderate doses of Haloperydole or of Aminazine as sedatives."

These two drugs were known as the KGB-psychiatry tools for crushing dissidents' willpower. Why did this young man want to subject Boris to such a treatment?

The temptation to beat up the young misfit flashed in his mind. He suppressed it. That would provide them with perfect proof of his mental instability. He did not move. The doctor wrote something in the file, apparently his prescriptions. The door opened and one more man walked in.

Boris glanced at the new arrival. He saw a man in his early forties wearing a white smock. Behind thick glasses his gray eyes seemed unnaturally large. Suddenly he remembered. This was doctor Litvin.

He saw the doctor making an almost imperceptible sign. His sign asked Boris to pretend not to recognize him.

Doctor Litvin extended his hand and the young doctor, handed over the file. Doctor Litvin leafed through it and said, "Thank you, I will handle this case myself. You may go." The young man half-bowed and left. Doctor Litvin sat down.

"So, this is indeed a small world," he said. "Fate loves jokes. How are you, Tarutin?"

"I am well, Doctor, Not to mention that your young colleague wants to subject me to Haloperydole."

"Forget it. He is an enthusiastic adherent of some over-popular methods of the Soviet psychiatry. Do you know what your file contains?"

"No."

"They have written that you were detained by the Militsia . . ."

"I was. True."

"For hooliganism. You attacked a Militsioner, tore away

his shoulder-strap, shouted insults at the Soviet Army and the Party and threw a stone at the Militsia station's window—"

"Did I? Didn't I kill anybody? Or plant a bomb in the Moscow subway?"

"You did not. But what you've allegedly done is sufficient to lock you up in jail for a few years. Instead, they sent you here for examination. Smart."

"Smart? It is the most preposterous thing because—"

"Because you have not committed any of these horrible crimes?"

"It is all lies."

"I know, Tarutin. Were it true they would've roasted you. Punitive psychiatry is reserved only for special cases. In this place you could be put away without a need to prove anything. Now, why do they want to get rid of you? I am sure, you've poked your nose in some of their private affairs."

"Cockle-shells," Boris said.

"I don't know what you mean. You are lucky that I happened to walk in. We have over 800 patients. It is impossible for me to watch every one of them."

"So, this young man was free to destroy my mind."

"Of course your ultimate fate would've been decided by a commission in one month. This commission's policy is not to repudiate the decision of a doctor-in-charge."

"But what the devil has he found in my mental state . . ."

"Listen, Tarutin." Doctor Litvin unfolded the file and read, "Diagnosis. Languidly progressing schizophrenia. Severely disordered perception of reality. Prescribed: Haloperydole, three times a day, for ten days. In the case of a violent reaction, cold wraps and straightjacket."

"My God," Boris said. "But why?"

"My friend, one of the sections of this hospital is under the direct supervision of the KGB. This young doctor has gone through a probationary service in the Serbski institute in Moscow."

"KGB officers first and doctors second. I've heard about it, doctor."

"My dear physicist Tarutin, sometimes I feel ashamed to admit I am a psychiatrist. Virtually everybody can be diagnosed as schizophrenic."

"At a psychiatrist's whim?" Boris said.

"On a KGB order."

"I see. And your young doctor?"

"He has grown up applying these quasi-medical diagnoses to dissidents."

"Well, doctor, what will you do now?"

"Destroy these sheets with your so-called diagnosis and replace them with my conclusion that the examination has proven your sanity."

"Thank you, doctor."

"Now, my dear physicist," Litvin said, "I am afraid we have no transportation for you. Probably not until late afternoon. Would you accept my invitation to spend some time in my quarters?"

"I would love to doctor, but my family's worried. I must hurry. I will walk over the ice."

"My God, Boris! Alive and well," Irina said, relief glistening in her eyes which were circled by dark shadows. She leaped over the threshold and grabbed Boris, her cheek touching his chin. He felt the resilience of her firm breasts. He hugged her back. His thigh sensed the touch of her hips and he pressed his lips to her neck.

Aunt Galina tousled Boris's hair and turned her face away.

The conversation with Fomichev the Adventist re-emerged suddenly in Boris's mind. "He has pried into my heart, this believer," Boris thought. "What shall I do if she leaves the country?" He released Irina. For a long while she kept hugging him. She released him finally but she did not hide her longing for him.

Boris said, "I am worried about Valushin."

"I have been worried about him, too," Irina said. "He has been locked up in your room for nearly two days now, without food."

I must take a plane to Kalinin if there is one at this time. Let's collect all the money we can from every hole to pay for the ticket. In a few days I'll receive my salary. Until then for all three of us, it's water and bread."

"And some potatoes," Aunt Galina Roksaeva said.

Chapter 30

THE SMALL PLANE JUMPED LIKE A GRASSHOPPER ON THE unpaved airfield. The entire plane shook madly.

With only twelve seats in the plane the passengers pressed their faces to the tiny windows and stared at the lake.

It would take a little over one hour to cover nearly one hundred and twenty kilometers between Ostashkov and Kalinin. In about fifteen minutes, however, Boris realized that he wouldn't endure these incessant jolts without developing severe nausea which would last for another hour after the flight.

The rest of the passengers watched as Boris crawled from his seat and stretched on the plane's floor. The chilly floor shook mercilessly under his back, but in this position he was invulnerable to the nauseating effect of the jolts and falls.

He had only five rubles left. The twenty-kilometer ride in a taxi from the airport to the city center would cost at least that much. Fortunately, there were a couple of passengers with suitcases and they would share the taxicab and the bill with him.

He ran up the stairs, then along the corridor.

"I am here, Zhenia," he shouted pushing the key into the lock. He flung the door open.

The room was empty.

He stood at the door, gazing at the sofa and the cabinet and the rug on the floor as if the lanky figure of his technician could reappear miraculously after a long enough stare. Then he saw that the window was not closed; a piece of paper, glued across a chink, was stirring slightly.

He leaned on the sill and glanced at the sidewalk four stories down and at the iron pipe next to his window. This pipe served as a ventilation duct for the students' canteen located in the basement.

The distance between neighboring hoops, about one meter, would allow a man with above-average strength to crawl down the pipe. It would be a challenge matching the determination of a skillful cliff-climber.

Or of a desperate man. As he had expected, Katya did not know anything. During Boris's absence, Valushin had never knocked at her door. The janitors knew nothing about Valushin.

There was no doubt in Boris's mind that Valushin was driven by his thirst for alcohol. His dexterity must have been enhanced by his desperate quest for anything containing a trace of alcohol. This must have enabled him to descend on the pipe.

Boris ran out heading to Valushin's hut.

He crossed the bridge over the Tmaka and passed a couple of fishermen, then entered the maze of the curved by-streets. He opened the door to Valushin's hut. The hut was empty.

Now he walked rapidly to the University. Thanks to Ada Ryzhik, all his classes yesterday were taken care of.

But today, on this Wednesday, he was expected to start his classes at eight am.

Valushin was not in the Magnetic lab. A group of students worked there with the big magnet, the group Boris was scheduled to supervise with Valushin assisting. Rakov, an Assistant Professor from the Department of Technical Physics, was substituting.

Rakov, his face covered with sweat, was reading the magnet's manual. When Rakov saw Boris his face showed his relief.

"Have you seen Valushin?" Boris asked.

"No!" Rakov said. "I am fighting here with your magnetic mysteries. Glory to God, you are back." He left and Boris took charge.

The circuit did not work. Boris quickly found the error in the wires' connections. In a couple of minutes the magnetic loop appeared on the oscilloscope screen.

It was an exciting feeling for Boris to observe these elegant hysteresis loops with the two straightlinear segments on both sides of the loop. He had developed the experiment several years earlier and it was one of the experiments most loved by students and one that the faculty loved to demonstrate to visitors. As the students watched the patterns on the screen, fascination sparkled in their eyes.

But Boris was upset. What could have happened to Valushin? He could hardly concentrate on the students' questions as they felt his absentmindedness.

Finally, the bell rang. The students ran out and hurried to the canteen. It was four o'clock. Studies were over. The Evening division would start at six.

He had to see Ada Ryzhik to thank her for replacing him with Rakov. She occupied a tiny cubicle in the remote corner of the fourth floor and was always there.

"Oh, Tarutin, I rescheduled all your classes."

"Ada, you are a sorceress of scheduling. A living computer."

The hunchback's face displayed pleasure. "Boris, you were supposed to be here at eight."

"I know, Ada. Sorry, I did not have the freedom of choice."

"Don't tell me, Boris. After you left my apartment, I thought about your words, remember? That by giving you Starkova's address I might have helped to save an innocent man. It was not hard to guess who you had in mind. You know, nobody notices Ada Ryzhik. Ada Ryzhik notices everybody."

"I notice you very well, Ada."

"You are not everybody, Boris. I thought, you might need more free time. So, this morning, before classes started, I had an emergency plan prepared in the event you needed more free time."

"Ada, you are a great woman," Boris said. "But how about my Department Head and our Dean?"

"Boris, your Department Head Vernov is happy if he doesn't know about anything irregular."

"And Gavrik?"

"Something has happened to our Dean. He ordered me to cancel all of his classes. He has been behaving unusually."

"You mean, he has abandoned his habit of watching everybody?"

"He has not been watching anybody during the last several days. Something else is on his mind. This morning, he wanted to see your schedule. Then he went to your lab but you were not there. He did not ask a single question about you."

"So, he has learned about my absence."

"Boris, he behaved as if he did not notice your absence.

He seemed to be interested only in your man, this alcoholic—"

"Zhenia Valushin. But Zhenia was not in today either."

"True," Ada said. "Then Gavrik came here and asked me about Valushin's address.

"When did this happen?" Boris said.

"He asked about the address before the recess."

Ada pulled aside the curtain and pointed at the window. "When I am tired of all these thousands of schedules I look through the window. You can see the main entrance from my window."

"Yes," Boris said. "So, what have you seen today, Ada?"

"Your Valushin. He was here, in the building, a little more than an hour ago. I saw him leaving. He went towards the Tmaka."

"I know. His home is over the Tmaka bridge. But he seems not to have arrived home. He must have been looking for a drink somewhere."

"Soon after Valushin had left, Gavrik ran out," Ada said. I have never seen him in such a rush. He sped up towards the Tmaka."

"What did you say, Ada? Gavrik? He followed Valushin? I better run, Ada."

"But Boris."

"Not now, Ada." He ran out.

In the lobby, Klava Turova stood at the stairway, her green eyes lit up with gaiety, a smile dimpling her soft cheeks.

"Where have you been, Boris? I keep looking for you in the lab. Nobody seems to know where you are."

"Zhenia Valushin? Have you seen him today?" Boris said.

"Yes, I have seen him. About an hour ago on my way here. I had just crossed the bridge over the Tmaka and met your Valushin. He looked half-mad, his eyes rolling. He did not know anything about you. Boris, how about coming this evening to see me."

"Klava, we'll talk about it later. Tell me, when you met Zhenia Valushin, was anybody following him?"

"Following? I don't know. The street was deserted. Shortly after I had passed Valushin I saw Gavrik. He walked in the same direction—towards the bridge."

"Could the shadow you saw on your glass door the evening when Baev died and you were with Talin—"

"Still jealous, Borenka?"

"No! Could it have been the shadow of Gavrik?"

"But we saw Gavrik arrive in the building later, didn't we?"

"Gavrik was in the building when Baev was killed. I don't know how he managed to get out without being noticed. And Zhenia Valushin is the only man who saw Gavrik running in the corridor that night. So, could it have been Gavrik's shadow?"

"I don't know. Of course it could've been. Where are you running to, Boris? I am coming with you."

About twenty minutes later Boris and Klava walked into Valushin's hut. It was still deserted.

Klava, let's go back over the bridge. Show me where exactly you met Valushin."

They rushed down the same path and crossed the Tmaka bridge again. From the bridge, it took them five minutes to get to where Klava met Valushin. If Valushin had continued his walk, the only path he could have taken would lead him over the bridge.

Then Klava showed the place where she met Gavrik. If Gavrik followed Valushin and was walking fast and Valushin hobbling, Gavrik would have caught up with Valushin a little earlier than the bridge.

Boris and Klava returned to the bridge. Two fishermen sat on the bridge's edge, their feet dangling over the water, their rods quivering in the vapor rising from the river.

Boris approached the fishermen and described Valushin. They had not seen anybody meeting either Valushin's or Gavrik's description.

"Where the devil could he have gone?" Boris said. "In his state all he could think of is vodka. Or anything containing alcohol like varnish or perfume."

"That reminds me of an unpleasant event this morning," Klava said. "Somebody stole a flask with ethanol from my lab."

"Ethanol? *Spiritus vini*, as my friend Artamon would say."

"Yes. In the Electron Microscopy, we have some alcohol allocated to clean samples. It is strictly accounted for, every drop of it. Each time we use some we fill out a form; we need three signatures certifying it was used for experiments. When I came to the lab today there was one flask missing. A quarter of a liter of pure alcohol."

"Excuse me," one of the fishermen said. "You talking about a flask. If you mean the one I found, I did not know it was yours." He pointed at a small pail of the type fishermen use to hold freshly caught fish. An empty pyrex glass flask lay in the pail.

"Just as I arrived it was sitting at the water's edge. As I found it I thought it was mine. Useful at home. You can make tea in it. I don't want anything stolen though, I am a worker. Take it."

Klava sniffed the flask. "It still smells of alcohol," she said. "It looks exactly like our flasks."

"I don't like it, Klava, I don't like it," Boris said. "If Zhenia finished off the ethanol in this flask, where is he?"

"I am scared," Klava said.

"Please, Klava, go to the University and wait there. I must see my friend Artamon Sergeev."

In half an hour, Boris was sitting in Artamon's office on the third floor of the City and Region Prosecution building.

"I am glad you are here, Boris," Artamon said. "Why did you choose those awful words about the *hour of truth* in our relations? You know me, I am trying to be honest. Within the system. If I succeed and become a Prosecutor one day, I shall be able to do a lot of good. To achieve this level, I must play by their rules."

"If the rules of the game require condemning an innocent man, it is a game I wouldn't want to partake of," Boris said.

"Listen, Boris," Artamon said. "After I interrogated Magidov I had the gut feeling he was telling the truth. I have no proof, just a feeling. You know, this is not a trivial case. The decision to prosecute Magidov has been made on a very high level. I am just a small screw in this case, formally in charge but actually powerless. If I told my bosses about my feeling they would deride me for non-professionalism, then kick me off the case and my status would be impaired irreversibly. If, however, I found real proof of Magidov's innocence I would be willing to risk telling my bosses about it. And the outcome of such a venture would be far from clear."

"I regret I fell on you when I came to you with Irina. It's just that she suffers and I can't help her. And I remember my father was also condemned for something he never committed."

"*Abusus non tollit usus*," Artamon said. "A misuse of a law must not abolish the use of the law."

"Now my technician, Valushin, had disappeared," Boris said. "I am afraid something happened to him."

"Experience has shown that gut feelings are often more

reliable than direct proof," Artamon said. "Tell me more about it."

Twenty minutes later they stood on the bridge over the Tmaka where a few fishermen gathered. "Attention, comrades," Artamon shouted and the heads turned to him. "I am Sergeev, an Investigator of the City Prosecutor's office. Here is my certificate. I need your assistance in a matter of importance."

The fishermen abandoned their rods. Nobody would ignore a request from the Prosecutor's office.

Artamon explained that he wanted them to scatter along the shores. They lowered their rods into the river's streams and moved them slowly, sensing anything unusual that could be uncovered on the bottom of this shallow river.

"I've found something," a man said. He walked into water, crouched and pulled something from the stream. It was a woman's purse and empty. The man laid it at Artamon's feet. Another man fished out an old rusty pan, next came a pot without a neck.

In about twenty minutes a pile of objects were placed at Artamon's feet. There were toys, remnants of books, a leg of a desk and a sack full of sand. Then one man fished out a plastic bag, its neck was tied tightly with a thin rope.

"It is not what we are looking for," Artamon said. "Please, continue the search."

Boris took the bag. It was filled with sand. Then he untied the rope.

There was a hammer inside, a type found in any carpenter's shop.

The hammer was almost dry. The rope had been tied tightly enough to prevent water seeping into the bag. On the hammer's face some dark liquid could be seen.

"What is that on the hammer?" Boris said.

Artamon glanced at the hammer indifferently. Then his

face changed when he held it close to his eyes. "I think it is blood with some hair in it."

"Hey, look here," another man shouted. He stood knee-deep in the river next to the bridge trying to drag something heavy out of the river. Other men joined him. Before they had finished Boris knew what they had found.

In a few more minutes the body of Valushin lay on the snow. His hand, stiffened by death, clutched an empty, drenched paper tube, the remnants of a cigarette without tobacco.

They stood there waiting for the Militsia under the winter sky which had already become dark.

"Such a talent, gone just like that," Boris said.

"I know you liked him very much," Artamon said. "One more victim of vodka. Apparently he was dead drunk when he was crossing the bridge and fell into the river."

"You may be right," Boris said. "As for the alcohol, a flask with ethanol was stolen today from a lab and an empty flask was found under this bridge."

"Hence," Artamon said, "it is a plausible guess that in his desperate quest for alcohol, Valushin managed to break into the Electron Microscopy lab, unless somebody helped him."

"If you are alluding to Klava—" Boris said.

"Boris, you know better. It is not my habit to allude except when I have some evidence. I don't have any now."

"Artamon, I know that when Valushin walked from the University to this bridge Gavrik was following him. He might have seen something. Why don't you question Gavrik?"

"Not that fast, my friend. I am neither on friendly nor neighborly terms with your Gavrik so I can't question him casually. As to an official interrogation, I am only in charge of the Baev death investigation not this poor drunkard's drowning. Moreover, whatever you think of Gavrik, he holds a high rank in the Party and in the KGB. You can't simply summon such a bigwig for an interrogation."

"He may know something about the last half-hour of Valushin's life."

"Well, Gavrik will not flee anywhere. Go ahead and unearth whatever facts you can. Just do it with discretion. If you discover information which might provide an excuse for interrogating Gavrik as a witness, we may try it."

Chapter 31

ON EVERY THURSDAY THIS SEMESTER BORIS HAD TWELVE hours of classes. This Thursday there was no technician to assist him.

Everything went wrong this Thursday as if some nasty spirit, delighted by the disappearance of Valushin, made every device in the lab go awry.

The copper wire in the big magnet coil burned out and replacing the coil took two hours of hard dirty work. The oscilloscope, held together by Valushin's miraculous hands, emitted a thin whistle and then burned out.

Locating the burned throttle in the oscilloscope's box and scrounging the labs for another took one more hour.

But he was glad to be busy with these mundane jobs. While his hands held the soldering iron, wires and pliers, his mind was free to mull over the last few days. He tried to reconstruct the missing links in two chains of events: one the mystery around the murder of Party Secretary Baev, and the other, the murders in Bologoe and the medals hunters.

His preoccupation with fixing devices in the lab saved him from meaningless chatter with people who heard of Valushin's death and came to offer their condolences.

There were only three people he wanted to talk with: Klava Turova, Jildibek Musaev, and Ada Ryzhik.

He went to see Klava during the first recess.

Students surrounded the tower of the electron microscope. Despite the students' curious stares Klava hugged Boris, her full breasts pressed against his chest.

"Boris, I may have been the last person to see Valushin alive."

"I know, Klava," Boris said. "You could not have known."

They walked into a small windowless chamber adjacent to the microscope room used as a storage area.

A cabinet with a red-painted, iron door and a heavy brass lock was in one corner of the chamber.

"Is this where the alcohol is kept?" Boris said.

Klava nodded. She hugged Boris again, but he felt that despite her sadness and despite the student drone in the next room, the hug had stirred sexual excitement in her blood. This excitement was transmitted to Boris from her body which felt hot even through the smock she wore. He had to make an effort to keep his mind on his purpose.

"So, there are three doors on the way to the alcohol," Boris said. "One from the corridor to the electron microscopy lab. Another from the lab to this cubicle. And a third on this cabinet. And all three have locks."

"Right, Boris. Somebody unlocked all three of them."

"Klava, did you ever forget to lock any of three doors?"

"Hey, Boris, you should know better."

"We all are human."

"Boris, I could have forgotten to lock one of them but not all three. Besides, the door from the corridor to the lab and the door from the lab to this chamber both lock by themselves. They just click and that is it. But this hanging lock must be locked with a key."

"Who has a key?"

"Only I have it."

"Only you?"

"Well, the janitors have a key to the outer door. They come in every few days to mop the floors, but they can't open this cubicle, not to mention the cabinet."

"Yet a flask with alcohol disappeared."

"All three doors were locked as usual, Boris. Whoever took the flask had duplicate keys as there was no sign of tampering with the locks."

The veil of a light snowfall had softened the familiar contours of the university building. Boris walked around the university backyard. Two brown-painted back doors, one in the left and the other in the right wing of the building faced a low barracks sitting on the opposite side of the unpaved backyard.

On the Rector's order the back doors were kept locked to eliminate the endless outflow of purloined items from paper to typewriters.

If chief janitor Musaev unlocked the back doors even once, he could lose his job.

Musaev valued his job highly because a chief janitor was entitled to an accommodation in the barracks in the backyard. If he lost his job he would be kicked out with his wife and nine daughters.

Nonetheless, he once dared to take the risk, when he helped Boris move a drunken Valushin through the back door.

Jildibek Musaev, despite his Moslem origin, did not shun drinking. It was his affection for vodka that made Musaev sympathetic to Valushin's misfortune.

Boris walked into the barracks where Musaev lived.

One of the hinges on the door was half-loose. Boris pushed the screeching door.

Musaev was sitting on the floor working: he supplemented his salary by repairing shoes for the neighborhood people. His wife was rolling dough on a table as his daughters watched.

Musaev abandoned the shoes and got up. He shook Boris's hand. "Thank you for coming, comrade Tarutin," Musaev said. "It is an honor. You, all," he turned to his wife and daughters. "Thank comrade Tarutin for the honor." Musaev's wife bowed three times, but the daughters just smiled and nodded.

"Whatever your eye falls upon in this home, is yours, comrade Tarutin," Musaev said solemnly pointing at his dingy furniture and at his daughters' smiling faces. Boris nodded, also in a solemn manner. Musaev made a gesture inviting Boris to sit down on a sofa.

Boris waited a couple of minutes, paying tribute to the host's custom. Then he stood up and said, "May we talk outside, Musaev?"

Musaev put on his cotton-padded coat and they walked out.

"I would like to ask you about keys, Musaev," Boris said.

"I would like to know about the keys myself, comrade Tarutin." Musaev seemed a little more drunk than usual. He moved his face close to Boris, his fingers clutching Boris's raincoat.

"My dear, my dear comrade Tarutin, you are educated man and I am fool. You explain me about those keys. Baev was an angry man, but he knew order. He was like Stalin. Everything was in its place. And where are his keys now? And where is his dress jacket? Vilen Trofimovich Gavrik said I'd imagined this jacket. Yes, I am drunk and I am a fool. But I saw the jacket. With all those decorations on its chest."

"What you are talking about?" Boris said. "Which jacket? I wanted to ask you only who may have the keys to the Electron Microscopy."

"It doesn't matter. All the keys were in one bunch. Baev, carried a master key. That opened every door. And keys to every cabinet and closet."

"Baev had all the keys?" Boris said. "But he is dead. Since he can't have stolen the flask with alcohol, yesterday—wait, where are Baev's keys?"

"That is the question I keep asking," Musaev said. "After Baev died they looked in Baev's pockets. All over his office. But where are the keys? I tell you. Whoever killed Baev took his keys."

"But who could have the keys now?"

"I don't know. I am like a soldier obeying orders. When they told me to keep the keys, I kept them. When they told me make a master key for Baev, I did. They told me, never unlock these back doors! So, I've never unlocked."

"Comrade Tarutin, Boris Petrovich. *They* are doing something to put me in jail with these damned doors."

"What are you talking about, Jildibek?"

"*They* are now using these back doors. I see *them* from my place," and Jildibek waved his hand towards his barracks.

In the speech of low-educated people like Musaev, the word 'they' could refer not only to several persons, as the Russian Grammar would require, but to a single person of high esteem.

"Who is *they*?" Boris said.

"Gavrik, Vilen Trofimovich," Musaev said.

"Gavrik? Was he using the back door?"

"Yes. Also, he is the one who said there was no Baev jacket and no decorations. I am a fool and a drunk but I am not an imbecile. I saw the jacket with all the medals. Whoever has the keys has the jacket and the medals."

At one o'clock Boris was back in the magnetic lab. Pieces started to fall together in his mind. All he had learned from Valushin, from Klava Turova, from Ada Ryzhik and from Jildibek Musaev seemed to point in one direction. Gavrik! Valushin saw Gavrik run in the corridor with a bag in his hands. Ada Ryzhik and Klava Turova saw Gavrik follow Valushin. Musaev saw Gavrik use the back door, the door Gavrik could have used to leave the building after Baev was killed and after Valushin saw Gavrik in the corridor with a bag.

Boris knew from Artamon's many stories that any number of pieces of circumstantial evidence, confirming each other, were often chains of unrelated coincidences. Still, he could not overcome the feeling that Gavrik was connected to the death of his best friend and fellow KGB man, Baev.

But what disturbed Boris even more was the possible connection between the bizarre events and what Musaev said about Baev's uniform jacket covered with decorations. Somebody stole the jacket. The man who had the key to Baev's office was the Dean, the Acting Party Secretary, former KGB officer, Baev's friend and colleague, Vilen Trofimovich Gavrik.

Boris tried to recall what he knew about Gavrik. Nearly nothing. And what connection was there between the medals on Baev's uniform, the medal sellers in Ostashkov, the Ostashkov Militsia and those murders in Bologoe?

To solve the riddle, Boris needed help. His friend Artamon Sergeev could provide this help but solving this riddle could cost Artamon Sergeev his career.

After twelve hours of classes when Boris walked out, he saw the tiny figure of Ada Ryzhik huddling in a shawl. She was waiting for him.

"You fled so fast, Boris, I had no chance to tell you that when Baev was killed, I was in the building. Alevtina, the janitor, knew I was there."

"She did?" Boris said.

"Alevtina met me in the toilet before the Militsia arrived. She told me that twenty minutes before Baev was found dead. Nobody likes the Militsia so I asked Alevtina not to tell anybody she saw me. She agreed. You understand, nobody would ever think that with my hands I could've slain Baev. I left the building before the Militsia arrived."

"Did you unlock the entrance door?"

"That's what I wanted to tell you."

"So, you opened the door but did not lock it, right?"

"Yes. I walked out of the building and I was a few steps away when Magidov appeared from the side street. It was about eight-thirty. I saw Magidov cross the street and walk in. He did not notice me. You know, this man is always immersed in his thoughts. He does not notice anything around him, especially such a tiny thing as Ada Ryzhik."

"But Ada Ryzhik notices everybody. You are a great woman." Boris bowed to the hunchback and kissed her cheek.

She walked away, a tiny limping figure, leaving a string of footprints on the fresh snow. They were small, as if a child walked there, somebody ten or twelve years old.

Responding to Boris's knocks Artemon opened the door of his apartment, holding a bottle in his hand.

"Blessed by everybody coming here," Artamon said. "Especially my friend and patron, Boris, I miss you, old pirate."

"I owe you, Artamon, remember? A ski tour. Why don't we go on Saturday? Not a regular tour but a luxurious ski tour around Lake Seliger. How about that?"

"Boris, you are a genius. now, my friend, what else? Your eyes are saying you've not yet finished your speech. Spill out what is on your heart."

"There is a small problem. My salary is due on Monday, so would you lend me twenty rubles?"

"Happily. Even thirty."

"Great. Then, I'll go to Moscow tomorrow and scrounge for food. A ski tour is only as good as the food one has in a rucksack."

"Boris, my friend, you are incapable of lying. You wouldn't spend a whole day in lines in Moscow stores. And you wouldn't drag a valise with meat, cheese and eggs on an overcrowded train *for yourself*. You wouldn't do it for the two of us either, ski tour or no ski tour."

"Well, Artamon, I will spend a whole day in lines in Moscow food stores. I will drag a valise with meat, cheese, and eggs with the money you lend me. I'll drag it in the overcrowded train, but you're right, it will not be just for the two of us. We'll take this food to Ostashkov. Whatever you suspect are my intentions, I promise you the ski run of your dreams."

"I read in your eyes, Borka, that you don't give a damn for a ski tour. You want something from me, don't you? You want to use this opportunity to convince me that I must question Gavrik. Ah, what's the difference! We'll go! We'll go, Boris, even though the daughter of the man under my investigation is in Ostashkov, with or without skis."

"Thanks, my friend."

"And now I'll disclose to you a professional secret, Boris. The forensic lab has reported that the blood and hair on that hammer matched Baev's blood and hair."

Chapter 32

ALEVTINA ARRANGED HER AFFAIRS NICELY. HER JOB AS A doorwoman at the University was very convenient. The shift was twelve hours long sitting in the lobby. The break between shifts was two days and nights. The salary was sixty rubles per month. Her passport was stamped "Employed, Kalinin State University", thus she was a legally working person.

She was a very lucky woman. Once or twice a week she replaced an elevator woman in Moscow. Aunt Pasha, who was actually nobody's aunt, had a side business. A lucrative one. From her in-law who served as a clerk in the big *GUM* store, she learned when imported lingerie was expected to arrive, thus Pasha could lay her hands on the lingerie before it reached the counters. She took the lingerie to the toilets in Moscow railway stations where she sold her merchandise to provincial women who came to the capital vying for different goodies. They were happy to buy the nice pieces at even ten times the official price.

For this business Pasha needed time during the day. Alevtina did not receive money for working in Pasha's elevator. Instead, she enjoyed the use of a cubicle built under the stairway for the elevator attendant.

On this Friday Alevtina was to travel to Moscow and work several hours in the elevator and in the evening on her own business. Alevtina woke up when it was still dark in order to catch the first train.

She took her worn brown purse and checked her season ticket to Moscow.

Warming up as she walked, she passed the University building, then new apartment buildings, eight of them exactly alike with four floors and four entrances each, where Alevtina hoped to acquire an apartment when the old one was demolished.

As always, Alevtina managed to arrive at the terminal when the electric train was already at the platform. She proceeded to the first car knowing that she wouldn't have to walk so far when she arrived in Moscow.

Alevtina fell asleep rapidly her hand resting on her purse. She never forgot that inside the purse was her passport, season computer ticket, three rubles and the key.

About twenty minutes before Moscow, noisy swarms of suburban folks fought for every available space. Alevtina opened her eyes and lowered her legs from the bench. Presently the concrete platform ran along the windows where a black wall of bodies was ready to assault the opening doors. A woman in a dirty white smock sold rolls, coffee and sandwiches. As always, Alevtina bought a herring sandwich and a cup of coffee.

She had to hurry because as usual the train was half-an-hour late. Pasha would be waiting impatiently.

Alevtina could not afford to lose the peevish vixen's

cubicle. Pasha only had to whistle and many people would whirl around for the cubicle. Without it half the business would fly in the sky.

Alevtina rushed to the subway, dived into its roaring hole and squeezed into a car. After riding an escalator up an endless tunnel, she came out in the very heart of the central district of Moscow. Alevtina's thoughts were far away. She dreamed of how she would earn more money than usual and manage to take care of her teeth.

She would like to pay for teeth without money, but in her district dental clinic all the dentists were female and she could not roll under anybody.

Pasha, a long shawl on her head, was dressed to run. They nodded to each other and Alevtina walked into the elevator's cabin. This day-shift was excellent.

Around noon Alevtina went into the dining room next door where she bought soup with noodles, cabbage salad and two slices of bread. The cashier, Nadia, was a friend so Alevtina received her check without waiting in line.

Alevtina and Nadia took turns using Pasha's cubicle for quickies. Nadia was better off, of course: she had an apartment in Moscow and her husband was a lathe operator. But Nadia's life had its flaws. She could not work late and was always afraid to show the men the trail to her apartment. Nadia was young and pretty and her stockings had no darned spots. During a scant hour after her shift in the eatery, she managed to get at least one client before running home to her husband. Alevtina, a free bird, could hunt for clients until midnight, in time for the last train.

Just after Alevtina came back to the elevator, Aunt Pasha ran in pale and scared before she was due. She had scarcely managed to escape a Militsia round-up where Policewomen in plain clothes had stormed the terminal toilets tearing bags from everybody's hands. They drove sellers and buyers into dirty corners to search under their skirts and blouses. Pasha broke through the police line and ran out leaving behind bags with garments, mohair rolls, knitted hats. Alevtina now had more time for prostitution. It would be a good evening.

It was chilly outside by the time she was ready to go home. The snow had hardened. Her shoes slid still she walked fast. The forty rubles she had earned this day moved her much closer to her goal, fixing her teeth. She was a lucky woman.

In the terminal, people swarmed everywhere. A Militsioner watched them solemnly. She glanced at the wall clock and knew the local train had already left.

At the counter at the express train window she handed over ten rubles. The cashier glanced with a faint curiosity at Alevtina.

The train rolled with a howl. In one of the cars, on a bench, Alevtina slept. She moaned in sleep, a pain in her mouth where a client had hit her. Her head swung, knocking the wooden wall. She did not hear how the car's door banged. Then somebody stood over her.

"Alevtina, what the devil has happened to you?"

She opened her eyes. "Boris Petrovich." She looked a Tarutin, valise in hand. A valise, apparently with food from Moscow stores. She half-opened her mouth, her bloody tongue hardly moving when she said, "I am fine." And tears appeared in her eyes.

"I'll be right back," Boris said. He left his valise and walked along the aisle. Then he was back, a moistened handkerchief in hand. He lightly touched Alevtina's lips with the handkerchief.

"You know, my father was a doctor," he said. "So easing pain is in our blood." Indeed, she felt better at the touch of Boris's hand.

"Sorry you have to wait an hour till Kalinin. There we'll do something better."

In Kalinin, Boris found a night taxi. They crawled into the taxi with Boris's valise and Alevtina's bag. At the entrance to Alevtina's yard, Boris told the taxi driver to wait. He led the woman into her room.

Two girls stared with widely opened eyes at the swollen lip of their mother.

"Relax, Alevtina."

"I am fine, Boris Petrovich, it will cure before my wedding."

In fifteen minutes he was back in Alevtina's room. The taxi had taken him to a night-emergency pharmacy and back. He had some pills with him and an ointment. He carefully applied the ointment to her lips. She felt the pain subsiding even more.

"Just take these pills, one now and one in the morning. And on Monday, go to a doctor. Good night."

"Comrade Taluntin," she said, moving with an effort her swollen tongue. "Thank you. God will repay you. I want to tell you something. Your gal's father, he is innocent. On that Sunday, when Baev died and we waited for the Militsia, I had the door locked as you told me. Ada Ryzhik opened it. She did not know anything about Baev. I thought, why not save her from talk with the Militsia. She is a hunchback, marked by God. I told her what had happened and she left the building before the Militsia came in."

"I know, Alevtina. Ada has already told me. She opened the door, and that was how Magidov walked in."

"Yes, Boris Petrovich. After Ada had left, I noticed she

failed to close the door fully. Magidov walked in but did not lock the door either. Why should he? Then I saw it being unlocked and I locked it again. You told me to keep it closed. Excuse me, I had been afraid to tell about it before."

"Thank you, Alevtina. You, in your post at the entrance, you can see a lot of things."

"Yes, comrade Taluntin. I know, it was Gavrik."

"What do you mean?"

"On Wednesday, when your man—"

"Zhenia Valushin?"

"Yes. I saw him leave the building, he looked awful. He was looking for vodka. And then I saw Gavrik run into the *Electron Microscopy*. Then Gavrik ran out with a flask."

"The flask!" Boris said. "That is how Valushin got the alcohol. Gavrik gave alcohol to Zhenia."

"I think so, too. Gavrik had this flask in his hand when he ran after Valushin. Please, I am saying this only for you."

"Thank you, Alevtina. If the official investigator questioned you about it, would you repeat what you've told me now?"

"I don't know. Gavrik is such an important man. If I had no daughters. No, please, he can make mincemeat of me."

"Not if we prove him guilty."

"God will punish Gavrik, without me. I don't know anything, please."

He walked down the dark empty streets. The bits of information he had collected fell into a consistent picture. Each clue alone would not constitute proof. In their totality, however, they provided a pattern as to what actually happened.

To find out exactly what happened and prove it he

needed Artamon Sergeev's full-scale cooperation. On their trip to Ostashkov he would have a chance to share with Artamon the information he had accumulated. Maybe this would be his last chance to reverse the direction of the sinister events.

Chapter 33

Boris, Artamon and Irina burst into Galina Roksaeva's house. They brought with them the cold wind and freshness of the forests; their skis and poles tumbled into a corner as they shook the snow from their shoes.

A slab of *Yaroslavl* cheese, with large holes on its spongy cheeks, next to a neatly laid pyramid of hard-boiled eggs. And a plate full of meat cutlets stood next to the vodka. The thirty rubles which Artamon had lent to Boris had produced the anticipated result.

They sat around the kitchen table, their faces rapidly becoming crimson in the house's warmth. They had not talked during their ski run. The investigator seemed ill at ease in Irina's presence. Many shadows hung over the relationship of these three people. The shadow of Magidov in jail and the shadows of Artamon's superiors, and the shadow of Artamon's inner struggle between his life-long dream of becoming a Prosecutor and his fear of losing Boris's friendship.

It was during the five-hour trip on a bus from Kalinin to

Ostashkov, that Boris shared with Artamon all the information he managed to acquire in the course of the last several days. Artamon listened with the utmost attention sorting out the information, separating facts from surmises.

"This information may be significant," Artamon said. "But as far as Gavrik's involvement goes, there are two important factors missing."

"What is the first one?"

"Lack of motivation," Artamon said. "If Gavrik were instrumental in Valushin's death by supplying Valushin with alcohol or by pushing the drunkard into the river, it would mean Gavrik wanted Valushin dead. Why? Your guess is Gavrik considered Valushin a dangerous witness. But Gavrik would've considered Valushin a dangerous witness only if Gavrik had killed Baev. And this is where the lack of motivation comes in. Why would Gavrik kill his close friend and colleague?

"Because we don't know his motivation, does not mean he didn't have one," Boris said. "You've told me many stories about seemingly non-motivated murders."

"Yes, Boris, and that is where the second missing factor comes in."

"I am all attention."

"The murderer's personality. His psychological profile. All you know about Gavrik is that he is an ultimate bureaucrat. And he is ignorant in Physics. Granted. Scores of nasty overseers and bureaucrats and illiterate people stroll around never even killing a chicken."

"Isn't this a double standard?" Boris asked. "Magidov, a Jew and not a Party member, is being held in jail even though there is no indication that he might be involved in Baev's death. As for Gavrik, a whole mass of evidence is not enough to summon him for interrogation. Even as a witness!"

"You are right, Boris. What you've said is at the very

core of our judicial system. You know, a few years before the Bolshevik upheaval in 1917, the Russian judicial system had become fairly liberal, hence the Bolsheviks eliminated it as 'bourgeois.' The new courts were supposed to make decisions based on the unwritten 'revolutionary law.' At that time, just belonging to the 'intelligentsia' could mean a death sentence. Not much proof of guilt required. Certainly, we have come a long way after those years. There are many written law codes now, but the 'revolutionary law-consciousness' has never lost its impact on our judicial system."

"I know this, Artamon. More often than not, some secret *instruction* may weigh more upon a court's decision than the officially proclaimed law of the country."

"True. Not only a secret instruction, but just a phone call, say, from a Party committee. And that is why, my friend, there is a drastic difference between the attitudes of the law towards Magidov and towards Gavrik."

"And that is why you refuse to interrogate Gavrik."

"What I refuse to do, is to fuck up this affair by falling on Gavrik without being fully confident he can be squeezed into a confession."

At the table in Galina Roksaeva's home they sat in silence, a bowl of hot potatoes steaming on the scrubbed table's surface.

"Everything will work out, my dear friend," Artamon said.

Boris waved his hand in a gesture of defeat. After spelling out the evidence he had nonetheless failed to gain Artamon's cooperation.

Rolling a hot potato in his fingers, Boris said, "This damned Gavrik, how could I find out anything regarding his psychological profile?"

"Who is this Gavrik you are talking about?" Galina

Roksaeva said, lifting her eyes from the dish in which she was mashing a potato with a fork.

Nobody answered.

After a while, Galina Roksaeva said, "You know, we old charcoals, we don't usually keep in mind what happened a few minutes ago. Our minds are like sieves. What we remember—"

"—is what happened 100 years ago. The longer ago, the better the memory. You've told me that more than once," Boris said.

"That's right," Galina said. "And that's why I am asking who this Gavrik is. Is his first name Maren?"

"No, Auntie," Boris said. "If you once knew some man by the name of Maren Gavrik, he was not our Gavrik."

"I knew a Gavrik, yes. This one I am talking about, his name was Maren which stood for *Mar*x-*En*gels. Mar-en. He grew up in an orphanage and he was given his name there. Acronyms were very fashionable at that time. Revolutionary names. One boy there was given the name of Yovist, which stood for *Yo*sif *V*issarionovich *St*alin."

"As a matter of fact, our Gavrik seems to have also such a name," Boris said. "I guess, it stands for *V*ladimir *I*lyich *Len*in. V-i-len for short."

"That is what I wanted to know, my dear," aunt Galina said. "Maren Gavrik had a brother who grew up in the same orphanage. Vilen Gavrik. So, that's him. A butcher."

"A butcher?" Boris and Artamon said, abandoning their potatoes.

"I knew him in 1954 and '55. He was a young man at that time, about twenty-three or twenty-five. So, now he must be over fifty."

"Our Vilen Trofimovich Gavrik is a little over fifty," Boris said. "So, what did you know about him? And why have you called him a butcher?"

"Because there is no better word," Aunt Galina said. "Do you want the whole story?"

"I want the whole story, Auntie," Boris said. "Not about Maren. Just about Vilen Gavrik. I am afraid these reminiscences are not of the sort you love to revive in your mind."

"If we forget we let it happen again," the old woman said. "I am ready to talk. One request, though. Please, do not make any comments. It is hard for me to talk if I am interrupted. I lose the line. My age takes its toll."

"Not a single interruption," Boris said, staring at Artamon and Irina. They nodded.

"It happened in East Siberia, in the *Ozerlag*," Galina said. "It is an abbreviation for 'Special Closed-regime camp.' Mail designation was Post Office box ZhSh-420. Ozerlag was a whole chain of camps, each one with one to 10,000 inmates. All over, there were about 150,000 inmates in the Ozerlag.

"It's campsites were so called 'zones,' usually bare, fenced-in rectangles, surrounded by the Siberian forest, *taiga*, stretched along the Taishet-Lena railroad for 200 kilometers.

"The mood among the *Gulag*'s bosses was uncertain as Stalin had already passed away. Everybody expected changes. On the surface, everything seemed to remain as when millions of innocent people perished in the Gulag. Starvation. Hard labor. Arbitrary punishments. Nonetheless, a faint smell of what would become Khrushchev's *rehabilitation* of 1956, was in the air. Some of the most notorious Gulag monsters were waiting for a sign to indicate what the new shape of the Gulag should be.

"There was a Captain Kvashnin in the Ozerlag known for forcing women undress and dance in snow naked and barefoot. He used to call it 'Making a Bolshoi Ballet.' In 1954 Kvashnin began to ease up.

"In this atmosphere of uncertainty two new camp-warders, Maren and Vilen Gavrik arrived, transferred from Kolyma camps. Vilen Gavrik never swore and never shouted at the inmates. He rarely used punishments like putting an inmate into a cold cell. He seemed to be a an emotionless bureaucrat without much zeal for his job.

"I worked in the camp kitchen at that time. At noontime we loaded big cast-iron bowls with soup onto a platform and a tractor hauled this platform to worksites. There we distributed meals among the inmates who worked with timber. One day we came with soup to one such worksite. We had to enter the work zone through a gate. We were told to wait outside. First, a big pile of logs had to be hauled out from the zone.

"Our tractor with the platform stopped beside the road and obstructed the view of the road as it was seen from the guard tower. A young inmate, about 20, could not resist the temptation. Hiding behind our tractor, he sneaked out from the fenced-in zone. We saw him crawling in the trench along the road.

"It was a desperate attempt. But you can hardly imagine that irresistible thirst even for one minute of freedom, which made many inmates attempt to escape against insurmountable odds.

"This young man succeeded only for a few minutes. As soon as he realized that a guard had discovered him beyond the fence, he gave up. He lifted his hands. He stood in full view at the entrance to a barracks next to the zone's gate.

"And then Vilen Gavrik appeared. He glanced at the prisoner who stood there hands up. Without hurrying, Gavrik walked to a group of inmates working with timber. He picked up an axe and walked slowly towards the escapee. Gavrik made a sign for him to walk into the barracks. The young man obeyed. Gavrik followed.

"We heard a thud. Then Gavrik reappeared from the barracks, axe in hand. There was blood on it.

" 'The swine attacked me,' Gavrik said. 'He will never do so again.' And he smiled. We knew that as soon as they entered the barracks, Gavrik struck the man's head from behind.

"Then Gavrik went back to the inmates' group and laid the axe on the snow and calmly walked away."

After a long silence, Boris said, "That's why you called him butcher?"

"For the lack of a better word," Galina said. "There was a persistent rumor that Vilen Gavrik often volunteered to execute inmates sentenced to death by the camp's court. The executioner's identity had always been kept secret. But I believe there is no smoke without a fire. And if you could've seen the smile on Gavrik's face after he reappeared from that empty barracks, you would easily believe that he might enjoy being an executioner."

They sat in silence, not touching the potatoes which cooled down gradually. Then Artamon clapped his palm at the bottle's bottom. The cork shot out. Artamon poured vodka into the glasses.

"To justice," he said, clinking his glass with those of his partners.

"To *real* justice," Boris said.

Artamon grabbed Boris's hand and squeezed it forcefully.

"To real justice," he said.

Irina clasped her glass. "To real justice," she said.

They gulped vodka. Then Irina, Boris and Artamon bit into the potatoes. After a ski run, nobody in the world would refuse a meal, with or without vodka.

Chapter 34

"Please, Vilen Trofimovich, take a seat, make yourself comfortable," Artamon Sergeev said meeting Gavrik at the big oakwood door of the investigator's office.

"I am here to fulfill my duty as a witness," Gavrik said, his thick fingers resting on his knees. "Though I am surprised that you have summoned me. First, because I did not witness comrade Baev's death. I came later when the Militsia was already interrogating suspects. The only thing I can do is to characterize the people allegedly involved in this heinous crime. You know, Rodion Glebovich Baev had been my best friend." And Gavrik touched his eyes with his hand.

Sergeev nodded sympathetically.

"Anything you can tell us will be most appreciated, Vilen Trofimovich," Sergeev said.

"And, second," Gavrik continued, regaining his quiet composure, "as you know, my duties are multiple. Besides official duties, of which you may be aware, I also have some unadvertised duties, and let me assure you they are by no means less important."

"I understand very well, Vilen Trofimovich. To justify my request for your coming, I may tell you that because of the seriousness of the crime under investigation, I have been instructed by the Region Prosecutor to explore every angle, however remote it may seem. Characterizing the people allegedly involved, as you have offered to do, may be invaluable. Therefore, I, on the one hand, apologize for the necessity to invite you here. I prefer not to use the word 'summon.' And, also, I promise not to hold you even a single minute over the unavoidable minimum. On the other hand, I shall be extremely grateful to you for any information you could possibly supply."

"Then let us start," Gavrik said.

"Thank you, Vilen Trofimovich. I would like to offer you tea. We don't offer it to ordinary witnesses. But you are not an ordinary witness. You are, I would say, an older colleague. I just want you to feel as comfortable as—"

"Well, tea with sugar and a roll," Gavrik said.

Sergeev picked up the receiver. "Comrade Demko," he said, "Comrade Gavrik has kindly accepted our offer to have a cup of tea. With sugar. And a roll. Do it fast, please. I must fill out a form which is a requirement of the law," Sergeev said. "You are expected to answer formal questions regarding your full name, address, occupation, and so on. You know these formalities."

They were in the middle of the procedure when there was a knock at the door and a man with a tray walked in. He was a big man with thick hands and wide shoulders.

"Comrade Gavrik, meet my assistant, Associate Investigator Demko. Demko, this is Vilen Trofimovich Gavrik our special witness."

Associate Investigator Demko did not say anything. He sized up the special witness and the gloomy expression on

Demko's face did not change. He settled the tray on a small wheeled table.

"Demko serves a very useful purpose," Sergeev said when Demko left. "Just his appearance makes many reluctant witnesses more talkative. You understand I mean witnesses not of your kind."

Gavrik stirred sugar in his cup. He touched the cup, as if probing the tea's temperature.

"Are you a tea fan?" Sergeev said.

"I am." Gavrik sniffed the tea.

"I thought you must be. Since you served in the Gulag in East Siberia where a strong tea is the most valued commodity."

Gavrik smiled, his thin lips sawing deeper into his cheeks, the permanent blue shadow around his mouth darkening.

"You mean *chifir*," Gavrik said condescendingly. "In camps it was called chifir. Not tea. Chifir is made by boiling a fifty gram of tea in half a liter of water. It is as black as tar. After several gulps your eyes pop out. That's the stuff!"

"Do you want me to ask our people to make a chifir for you?"

"Nonsense! We are not in Siberia. Just proceed as time is precious."

"I did not want to interfere with your drinking tea. If you are done—" Gavrik nodded, Sergeev picked up the receiver. "Comrade Demko," he said. "Comrade Gavrik has finished his tea. Please take away the tray."

Demko appeared, took the tray with the cup and walked out.

"Now, just for the sake of the procedure, let me reiterate the data we have registered," Sergeev said. You are Gavrik, Vilen Trofimovich."

Somebody knocked at the door. Sergeev lifted his eyes from the desk. "Come in," he said.

Demko entered, carrying a packet. Sergeev nodded and pointed at the wheeled table which stood next to Sergeev's desk. Demko unwrapped the packet. His wide back obstructed the view of the wheeled table from Gavrik. Then he walked out.

"So, again, you are Gavrik, Vilen Trofimovich—"

Although Gavrik's face was turned to Sergeev, his eyes squinted at the wheeled table. What Demko had placed there was a half-a-liter flask made of pyrex. A small cardboard tag hung on its neck. Gavrik turned his eyes from the flask back to Sergeev. He coughed slightly. Sergeev glanced at the flask, then at Gavrik, shrugged and turned his eyes again to the desk.

"You are Gavrik, Vilen Trofimovich—"

Somebody knocked at the door.

"Come in," Sergeev said.

Demko entered the room with another packet. Sergeev nodded and pointed at the wheeled table. Demko unwrapped the packet and walked out. What he had left on the wheeled table was a hammer, the kind that could be found in any carpenter's shop. A plastic bag lay on the wheeled table next to the hammer. The hammer and the bag had cardboard tags attached to them.

"I hope this is the last time they will interrupt us. You are Gavrik, Vilen Trofimovich—"

Gavrik turned his eyes to the door as if expecting one more knock. Indeed, a knock followed. Gavrik chuckled nervously. Two men walked in carrying a stand with a cardboard shield. A big square-shaped piece of white paper was tacked to the shield which the two men placed on the stand next to Sergeev's desk and left. Gavrik stared at the stand. Drawn on the white paper was a primitive map of a meandering river with the word "Tmaka" next to it. Two short parallel lines crossed the river with the word "bridge" next to them. Three long arrows which started at the map's corners and pointed towards the bridge, crossed the map. At the arrows' starting points the words appeared, "witness 1," "witness 2," and "witness 3."

"So, you are Gavrik, Vilen Trofimovich," Sergeev said. This time, nobody knocked at the door and Sergeev, slowly, thoroughly pronouncing every word, read all the numbers, names and other data registered in the form. Gavrik did not interrupt him. His eyes turned time and again to the map.

"And now, Vilen Trofimovich, using your own words, please tell whatever you consider relevant to the murder of your—"

The telephone rang. Sergeev picked the receiver. "Yes. Yes," he said. He returned the receiver to the cradle, looked for a while at the silent special witness and then said, "Vilen Trofimovich, because of some unexpected development I must leave for a while. In the meantime, my associate Demko will continue this conversation."

Demko walked in. Before leaving the room Sergeev stopped next to Gavrik, gazed at him, shook his head and finally walked out.

"So, these are the things," Demko said, staring at Gavrik.

Gavrik coughed and said, "I actually don't have much time. Can we continue this—mm—conversation some other time?"

"Have you ever served in the army?" Demko asked, his tone bearing clear signs of disdain. "Well, don't answer, I know your career. In the Gulag. Then, transferred from the Ministry for Internal affairs to the KGB. During your last four years with the KGB, you served in special detachments. Then retirement from the KGB. Assignment to the missile institute. Finally, transfer to the University. Your career implies you must understand what an order of a superior is. My superior, Investigator Sergeev, has ordered me to stay with you until his return. So, what significance may it have whether you do have or you do not have time?"

"Do you understand who are you talking to?" Gavrik said, his voice low and his cheeks paler than usual.

"Do you understand that you are in the Prosecutor's office?" Demko said, lifting his big body from the chair. "Do you realize that we implement the orders of the Region Prosecutor? And the Region Prosecutor is subordinate only to the Prosecutor General of the USSR. Do I have to teach you, citizen Gavrik, such elementary concepts?" He walked closer to Gavrik and peered at Gavrik's face. Then, suddenly in a very low voice, he said, "And if needed, I can make mincemeat of you. And nobody in the world would as much as wink." And he shook his big fist next to Gavrik's face. Beads of sweat appeared. He did not say anything.

In about half an hour, the door swung open and Sergeev walked in. He stopped next to Gavrik, stared at the latter, shook his head and then walked to his chair. Demko stood behind Sergeev's back.

Sergeev pressed a button on his desk. The door opened again and one more man walked in. This man wore a gray suit and a lemon-yellow tie. He carried a tray. It looked like the same tray used to bring tea for Gavrik. A cup was on the tray. A cardboard tag was attached now to the cup.

"Report the results of the examination," Sergeev said solemnly, looking at Gavrik.

The man with yellow tie pointed at the tray. "The examination has shown that the fingerprints left on this cup are identical with those on this flask and on the handle of this hammer, which, as has been established earlier, was used to hit the late Baev on his head." The man with yellow tie laid a sheet of paper on Sergeev's desk and walked to the door.

Sergeev stared silently at Gavrik. Demko stood silently behind Sergeev's back. Gavrik wiped his face with his sleeve. After a very long silence Gavrik said, his voice wheezing, "I understand now, it is a trap."

"Come on, Gavrik," Demko said. "With your background and experience, what you are saying sounds ludicrous. We are all soldiers of the Party. Artamon Artamonovich, let me interrogate citizen Gavrik," and Demko flexed his arms. Sergeev made a gesture as if appealing to Demko to be patient.

"Maybe citizen Gavrik has some questions," Artamon said.

"Yes," Gavrik said. It was an effort to move his very dry tongue. He pointed at the map drawn on the stand. "What is it on there? Which witnesses?"

"That is what you better tell us, citizen Gavrik," Sergeev said. "You are a long-time associate of the *organs*. You must know that our courts take a voluntary confession very seriously. As well as sincere repentance."

"Which court?" Gavrik said. "The only court I may be subjected to is the internal court of the KGB."

"If we transfer you to the KGB," Sergeev said. "This will be decided upon by the Party."

Long silence ensued. Then Sergeev said, "So far, in this preliminary stage, I may be able to suggest a deal, Gavrik. We have all the information we need to prove everything. But it is a lengthy procedure. It may take time. During this time you will have many conversations with Demko. Many! And during this time we will keep you deep down. Shall I teach you how such things are done? It may take a week or a month or three months, until we round up everything properly. Which we will do ultimately. It will happen with or without your cooperation. Or, if you wish, you have a chance to save us time and effort and in this way to improve your situation. To this end, you just tell us everything yourself. On your own initiative! Nobody would ever learn that we've nudged you to confess. As to this stuff," he pointed at the map and the wheeled tray, "I promise you it will not appear as something we uncovered. No, it will appear as the material obtained as a consequence of your voluntary confession and wholehearted cooperation. After that, you tell us whether you prefer to stay under our jurisdiction or the KGB's."

Gavrik again wiped his face with his sleeve.

"Let me talk to him a little," Demko said again.

Sergeev looked pensively at his associate. Then he said, "Well, I'll leave you here but don't push him, let him consider his options. I'll be back in an hour, Gavrik," and he stood up from his chair. Demko smiled and flexed his arms.

"No," Gavrik said. "Don't leave me with him. I have decided. Please, don't forget, I have come to you voluntarily and I am telling everything sincerely. All I want is to assist the investigation. I will write down everything myself."

Sergeev made a sign and Demko left the room.

Gavrik was unable to write, his hands trembled and all he could produce was scribbling. After a few attempts, he gave up. He started talking and Sergeev wrote down his confession.

When they had finished, Sergeev read every page he had written. Then he looked at his wristwatch. A few minutes after one pm, Monday, December 12.

"To summarize your confession, Gavrik, you had a quarrel with Baev, on Sunday, November 27. This quarrel started because Baev disliked you personally and had threatened to force you into premature retirement. In the course of this quarrel, Baev insulted you rudely. When you answered in kind he, in his rage, tried to hit you with a hammer. In self-defense, you wrested the hammer out of Baev's hand. In the heat of this fight, trying to divert his blow, you hit him on the head inadvertently. He fell dead. You panicked. Then you decided to conceal what had happened to confuse investigators. You dragged Baev's body to the mechanical lab. You set his body under the impact tester and replaced the potentiometer to have enough time to escape. You took the keys from Baev's pocket, placed the hammer into a plastic bag and ran out through the back door. When running in the corridor to the back door you saw Valushin staring at you. You rushed to the Tmaka and threw the bag with the hammer into the water.

"You decided that you had to silence Valushin but there was no opportunity to do so until last Wednesday. On that day you located Valushin in the University building. He seemed to be in a gruesome state, desperate to get some alcohol. You unlocked the cabinet in the electronic microscopy lab and took a flask of alcohol. Then you followed Valushin. You caught up with him a few steps before the Tmaka bridge. You offered him alcohol in exchange for the promise that he would never reveal that he had seen you running in the corridor with a bag. Valushin grabbed the flask eagerly. He drank the alcohol and got deadly drunk at once. You decided to assist him reaching his home. You walked together over the Tmaka bridge and suddenly he lost equilibrium. You tried to support him but failed to prevent his falling into the river. You rushed from the bridge in fear. This is what you've said, correct?"

Gavrik nodded, his face showing some relaxation.

"Good," Sergeev said. "You see, there is not a word

in this document about the fingerprints, about witnesses. I have not asked a single question regarding these facts. As I have promised it will be presented as your voluntary confession, submitted by you on your own initiative, before we had collected any other proof or testimony against you. It is very prudent of you to have made this confession and it is very much to your advantage. Now, please, sign your testimony."

Gavrik's hand still trembled. He hesitated, the pen in his hand dithering over the page.

"What is the matter, Gavrik? You understand that every word you said has been recorded. Look." Sergeev pulled out a drawer and displayed a microphone with a black wire snaking into the drawer.

Gavrik sighed. "Shall I get a special treatment?" he said. "All my life I have served the Party interests."

"It is very probable," Sergeev said pensively.

Gavrik's trembling hand scribbled his signature. First he signed the last page and then, in a backward sequence, every page, until he reached the first page of his testimony. Sergeev picked up the sheets and fastened them, one by one, in a black folder.

Chapter 35

SENIOR INVESTIGATOR IGOR KONSTANTINOVICH LOPOUKHOV sighed and weighed the black folder with Gavrik's confession in his hand.

"As a lawyer, I appreciate what you have done, Artamon Artamonovich," Lopoukhov said. "As a communist I am horrified. You know very well the level where the decision has been made regarding Magidov. You have been there yourself." He shook the folder. "This is like thunder from a blue sky."

Sergeev nodded after each of Lopoukhov's comments.

Lopoukhov plunged into motionless silence. Then he opened the folder and read every page again.

"The first and most important question, Artamon Artamonovich. Who knows the contents of this file?"

"Only myself and Gavrik," Sergeev said.

"Are you certain?"

"I am, Igor Konstantinovich."

"Well, at least you have displayed the necessary caution," Lopoukhov said with the evident relief. "Now, before we proceed, just between us, how did you manage to crack him? Have you used any special squeezing technique?" A genuine curiosity sounded in Lopoukhov's voice.

"As you see, Igor Konstantinovich, this is a voluntary confession, Gavrik's own initiative. Although it seems to be corroborated, *post-factum*, by a number of testimonies, we certainly did not have in our possession any proof which could've been used to press hard on Gavrik."

"Yes, you may not necessarily have had hard proofs," Lopoukhov said. "We both know that if a skilled investigator has a reasonable confidence that the suspect is guilty, such a skilled investigator can easily stage what would appear to the suspect to be undeniable proof. And such a technique will often squeeze a suspect into a confession. And I am prone to believe you are a skilled enough investigator."

"I have good teachers," Sergeev said looking straight into Lopoukhov's eyes. Lopoukhov gazed at Sergeev for a while. The latter did not turn his eyes away.

Then Lopoukhov said, "So, again, is it true that nobody but you knows exactly what Gavrik confessed to? Good. Hence, if a decision up there," he pointed to the ceiling, "is made to ignore this document or to alter it in an appropriate way, there will be no reverberations among the lower echelon of our staff?"

"Right," Sergeev said. "the only problem which I can foresee in the event of a possible alteration or complete elimination of this document is Gavrik's resistance to such a development. He has already digested the hardest part of this situation. To start playing a role again may be beyond his spiritual power. Why don't we try the reaction there?" And Sergeev also pointed at the ceiling.

"Are there any copies of this?" Lopoukhov said, shaking the black folder again.

"None whatsoever," Sergeev said firmly.

"Well, what is your impression of this Gavrik?" Lopoukhov said.

"He was a little arrogant at the outset. Afterwards he looked like a bunch of grapes after all the juices had been squeezed out of in a winery press. I think he could not bear the burden of what he had done."

Lopoukhov looked at Sergeev suspiciously. "It sounds strange," he said, "for such a seasoned KGB professional. Of course, in such a situation I abstain from undertaking any steps on my own. We will report all this to the Prosecutor. But I have a feeling something is wrong in your story, whatever your reason may be for presenting it in a specific light. For now, we will report it to Gnida."

Sergeev nodded silently.

Region Prosecutor Filip Ivanovich Gnida stared at the black folder opened on his desk, and his narrow long face, with a black goatie quivering on his almost non-existent chin, expressed disbelief. Then he raised his brown eyes, deeply set under a low forehead and said in a tone of a deep pain, "How could you allow this to happen? This could be a disaster. At least you have had enough brains to keep it between Gavrik and the two of you. That is if you are hundred percent positive nobody knows what this contains," and he shook the black folder. "Is there any copy of it?"

Lopoukhov and Sergeev both shook their heads energetically.

"I can't make a decision in this matter on my own. We must consult with the *obkom* immediately. Does the KGB know about this story?" Gnida asked looking at Lopoukhov. The latter looked at Sergeev.

"I have not told anybody about it," Sergeev said. "I went directly to Igor Konstantinovich. Gavrik is still in my office. Officially he is there as a witness. He can be allowed to leave if you decide so, Filip Ivanovich."

"You are crazy," Gnida said. "To let him go! What if he is mentally unstable? He may start disseminating this story all over the city. No, keep him there until a decision is made. I'll be in touch with the region Party committee immediately. In the meantime, not a word to the KGB that we have Gavrik in our custody."

"Yes, Filip Ivanovich," Lopoukhov and Sergeev said in one voice.

"Well, my friends," said Misha Berkin, the technical aide to the First Secretary of the region Party committee, *obkom*. "Now tell me exactly what happened to such a straightforward affair. It takes a special talent to fuck up such a beautiful design."

Region Prosecutor Gnida, Senior Investigator Lopoukhov and Investigator Sergeev sat, elbow to elbow, on a sofa in Misha's personal office. Misha's open eye surveyed them, while his second, almost closed eye, seemed to look at the ceiling. All three visitors shrank under Misha's glance as if trying to become as inconspicuous as possible. Gnida handed the black folder to Misha.

Misha opened the folder but, unlike Gnida and Lopoukhov before him, he did not read it meticulously. He just leafed through it, grasping quickly the essence of Gavrik's testimony.

"Do you believe it?" he asked. "Your opinion, Prosecutor."

Gnida turned his eyes to the ceiling and said, "I think, as Magidov has been defined by the *obkom* as the murderer, that's all what we need to know."

"Good," Misha said. "Yours is the right attitude. But this is not the answer to my question. Lopoukhov, your opinion."

Lopoukhov raised his eyes to the ceiling and said, "I

am prone to think that Gavrik is mentally ill and all this is his imagination. As to the actual murderer."

"Sergeev, your opinion," Misha interrupted.

"Gavrik has told the truth. He killed Baev," Sergeev said. "He has lied in details. I don't buy his story about self-defense and all this stuff. Regarding Valushin, I am afraid Gavrik pushed him into the river."

"The Party is not concerned with the demise of every alcoholic," Misha said. "What the Party is concerned with is Baev's murder. We must evaluate the possible danger to the valuable lives of the region leaders. You stay here while I see if I can talk to Ivan Platonovich." He walked out to talk with his boss, Ivan Platonovich Korytov, the First Secretary of the Region Party Committee.

"You are too smart for our profession," Gnida said to Sergeev. "If you had the proper understanding of the situation, you would never allow this to happen. A qualified investigator must be always in control of the investigation process. Not to let an idiot confess unless his confession is in the best interests of the prosecution. I don't know if you should be allowed to work even as a notary."

Lopoukhov nodded approvingly.

"And you, Senior Investigator Lopoukhov," Gnida continued. "You have committed a serious political error by recommending Sergeev for a highly responsible assignment in the Prosecutor's office. You will bear responsibility as a communist for this gaffe."

Lopoukhov nodded again, and his face acquired a grave expression. "Yes, Filip Ivanovich, you are absolutely right. I must reconsider with the utmost seriousness, all my activities and analyze my grave mistakes. I will do my best to regain the Party's and your personal trust."

Sergeev remained silent. His eyes expressed tiredness.

"So, that is it," he thought. "I did not succeed in

becoming Count Monte-Cristo, so I must requalify myself as a janitor." So did he cite mentally this quotation from the popular novel "The Golden Calf" by Ilf and Petrov. "I may have saved my friendship with my only friend, Boris. Though, I am not even sure of that. What I am sure of is that I never shall be a Prosecutor. All I have as a consolation is Gnida's remark that I am too smart, not too stupid. What I need at this moment is a bottle of vodka. However cautious I tried to be is of no consequence any more. But why have they been so fast in falling on me? So far, they can easily suppress any evidence of Gavrik's confession, if they wish to. It is not too hard to imagine what will happen to me if they learn how I squeezed Gavrik into confession." His mind seemed to be in complete disarray when Misha Berkin walked in.

"Well, comrade lawyers," Misha said, his open eye surveying the three men whose faces expressed stress, fear, and uncertainty.

"Comrade Korytov has agreed with my opinion. He asked me to convey to you the Party's appreciation of a job well done. It is very important that we have been able to discover the real extent of the devious plot against our Party and, more specifically, against our dear comrade Baev. It seems evident that the Zionist, Magidov, managed to corrupt even a KGB man. Magidov has succeeded in converting Gavrik into a blind tool of the Zionist machinations. Magidov designed this murder and Gavrik implemented it. The Party expects you to prove it. Is the Party's opinion clear, comrades? Especially you, Sergeev, you are expected to show your skill by completely untangling the Zionist plot. But no fuss around the city! This affair must be kept strictly hush-hush. You will advise the KGB now that Gavrik is in your custody. They will probably demand Gavrik's transfer to the KGB. You will refer them to us. We will know how to handle it. Do you understand, comrades? Refer them to the *obkom*!" He stressed his last words.

"What a brilliant move!" Region Prosecutor Gnida said when the three of them walked out of the *obkom* building. "This is what the leading role of the Party means."

"Indeed, it is a brilliant move," Senior Investigator Lopoukhov agreed. "Now this case has acquired a new dimension. Artamon Artamonovich, discretion, discretion and discretion!"

Artamon Sergeev felt inclined to agree that Misha's move was brilliant. It had changed Sergeev's status in a matter of seconds, from that of an impertinent smartass who had fucked up a beautifully designed case, to an efficient implementor of the Party's will, and a promising investigator who has been instrumental in discovering a devious anti-Party plot.

The two abrupt changes in his situation, one being a sudden fall into the abyss of career failure and the other, an upsurge in his status and reputation; both changes being caused by forces completely beyond his control.

He had no way of knowing what the motivation was behind Misha Berkin's "brilliant move" approved by the region's Master. He surmised that the Party bosses had grasped an opportunity to gain additional leverage against the Region KGB.

"Well done, Artamon Artamonovich," Prosecutor Gnida said. "Arrange a search of Gavrik's apartment. Prepare my order, I'll sign it at once. Book Gavrik at once and put him in the special ward. Warn the prison authority, no information to anybody regarding Gavrik. Complete isolation! Igor Konstantinovich, you will call some of Rashkov's deputies in the KGB, and tell them that Gavrik is detained as a suspect in a serious crime. Don't elaborate. Refer them to the *obkom*. I am sure they will call me. Then I'll take care of them." The region Prosecutor slapped Sergeev on his shoulder.

"So, I am in the saddle again," Sergeev thought, walking along the Volga to the Prosecutor's office. Light wind carried snowflakes so he raised the collar of his gray coat. "But what shall I say to Boris? Even after taking such a risk and escaping disaster and having the confessed murderer in custody, all this has failed to ease the fate of the condemned Jew, Magidov. What shall I say to Boris and to the beautiful girl whose legs have driven him crazy?"

PART 6

Chapter 36

FOR TWO WEEKS IN KORYTOV'S MANSION, ALLA HAD BEEN in a state that had the quality of a bizarre half-dream. Every morning, waking up, she could not comprehend reality. Her slim body huddled under a linen sheet on Korytov's immense bed; or was it a hallucination and she would wake up again where there was no such house with its numerous rooms and invisible servants?

Then she awoke fully and knew this mansion was the reality. And the ache between her thighs was real; Korytov gave it no chance to subside. Every evening Korytov repeated the ritual of the first day.

Obeying Korytov's demand, she gently rubbed her fingers over his gradually swelling flesh; then he would pull her over his knees until she straddled him. With his face contorted in ecstasy he thrust himself between her legs, closing his eyes and moaning. But he never repeated those words, "Oh, Sonia, Sonia," which he had shouted on the first night. From the second day, he had whispered her name, "Alla, Alla, my little Alla."

In the daytime she was mostly alone. The shadows of servants flashed from time to time somewhere on the margins of her vision. She ate very little, even the oranges in the big bowl lost their appeal.

When she felt hungry she walked into a big dining room.

A wheelcart would appear holding a dozen dishes and pans with cold and hot food. She seldom saw the person who pushed the cart through a door in its far end. She now realized that invisible eyes watched her at all times, taking care of her needs and wishes.

Aunt Masha, the housekeeper, asked Alla every morning whether the girl had any special desires regarding either meals or entertainment. Yes, she wanted all of it. But then she discovered she did not want anything. She started reading, but in a few minutes the book invariably appeared either boring or incomprehensible.

Everything seemed to have lost its taste for Alla because she knew that in a few hours Korytov would be coming back from his office.

She felt nauseated when Korytov's wide-jowled face emerged in her mental vision. But she knew, nonetheless, that what he was doing with her every night was something she was born to enjoy. Somewhere deep inside, the anxiety of those copulations with the old pig co-existed with a persistent hunger to sense again the thrust of a man's flesh.

Several times a telephone rang when she was in Korytov's bedroom. He would point at the door and she would leave his bedroom. Afterwards, he would walk to her room and ask her to join him again. Then once the telephone rang when they were couplet. He hated the interruption so he made a sign for her to stay.

His passion for her seemed to grow into an obsession. If

a telephone rang he talked now in her presence, obviously hating to part with her for even a few minutes.

In a few more days, in order not to lose the continuous touch with her body, he started using a device enabling him to talk without lifting the receiver. She could hear not only Korytov's words but the other speaker as well.

The same man made all these calls. His name was Misha. He talked about things Alla did not understand. The words "Central Committee," "Rashkov's skullduggeries," "Kurchin's tricks," sounded in almost each of these conversations. Unwittingly she had been memorizing sentences, words, names, dates, not understanding what they related to.

Then the evening of December 13 came. Korytov arrived much earlier than usual. He walked into Alla's room and made his usual scooping gesture. For two hours he tried stubbornly, craving desperately for what was evidently beyond his capacity. "What shall I do tomorrow?" he moaned.

Tomorrow came with a heavy snowfall. Close to noon there were noises of arriving cars with footsteps echoing in the hollow of the glass-covered dome.

Alla walked into the corridor and looked through the window. Two cars stood next to the entrance. A couple of big men unloaded them, carrying heavy suitcases into the house. Ksenia Sidorovna, Korytov's wife, must have come back from her trip abroad.

About four o'clock the door to her room opened. A squat old woman with colorless hair stood there, and behind her shoulder, the tall figure of Arkady, the chauffeur.

Alla stood up. Ksenia Sidorovna moved her bleak blue eyes from Alla's head down over the girl's budding breasts slightly bulging under her white cotton blouse, then along Alla's waist and narrow hips, then along Alla's legs. She gazed at Alla's calves for a long time. Then, without saying a word, she turned and walked away.

The evening came, and the raspberry-colored light of her table lamp fell on the rug and the chair. She was still huddling in the chair, intermittently napping and waiting for something to happen.

But nothing happened and nobody bothered her. And then she heard a muted roar of an engine and knew that Korytov was home.

She opened her door cautiously. The corridor seemed to be empty. She approached the door of Korytov's bedroom. She pressed her ear to the door but it hid sounds well.

In the same cautious manner, she walked back. She stepped into her room but before she had closed the door the thud of another door jerked open made her freeze where she stood.

This thud had come from the door of Korytov's bedroom.

Korytov's voice was unusually shrill, "I want the girl to stay here! Is it not enough that I have endured *you* for all those years? You have everything any woman in the world could dream of. I may one day be a Secretary of the Central Committee. You know what responsibility rests on my shoulders! Have I not earned the right to a little relaxation?"

And a woman's voice answered, calmly, with a sinister self-confidence, "I don't give a damn for your titles, Ivan. Where would you be without my brother Stepan who made it to the top and dragged you up with him? Now, you have a full-fledged brothel and I don't care. But not in my house! And not with adolescent harlots!"

It was still dark on this morning of Thursday, December 15, when a loud knock woke Alla from her nightmarish half-sleep. Arkady, the chauffeur, stood in the door. He ordered her to dress. Then he ordered her to put her belongings together. In a couple of minutes she had in her hand the same bundle she had brought with her when she came here two weeks earlier.

They walked out. Arkady pointed at the back seat of his Volga sedan. Her bundle in hand, she crawled inside.

Arkady drove very fast, ignoring red lights and stop signs. Half-turning to the back seat, he handed Alla a folded piece of paper. "Your ticket to Samarkand," he said.

She made just one step on the sidewalk and the black Volga sedan with the obkom's plate leapt onto the snow-covered road, hurling yellow snow balls from under its wheels. Alla shook the dirty snow off her clothing and wiped it from her face.

In the tunnel, she touched the hard square inside her skirt. The folded three-ruble bill, her emergency fund given to her by her mother in Samarkand, was still there.

She walked along the platform, shivering in her coat which suited the mild winters of Samarkand but seemed inadequate for Kalinin.

The mansion, the old man raping her every night, the huge dining room, all this had suddenly become unreal. Only the faint remnants of the ache between her legs proved that all this had indeed happened to her.

All she needed now was to embrace her mother, her strong, unbending, beautiful mother who would know how to heal whatever wounds Alla might have suffered.

The salty drops crawled down her cheeks. Swallowing them, she walked along the platform, then boarded a car.

A man in a railway uniform stood over her. "Who you travel with?" he shouted. "Mother, father, who? Ticket inspection."

Alla produced the ticket she had received from Arkady. The inspector unfolded it, clucked his tongue and, peering at Alla's face, asked, "Where are you traveling to, girl?"

"Samarkand. To my mother."

"That's what I see. Your ticket is good through Moscow to Samarkand. Your train from Moscow departs at six today. Then why are you in this train? This is a loop-route train to Rzhev, through Ostashkov. You are moving away from Moscow not to Moscow. Your ticket is not valid here. In accordance with the railway statutes, you must leave the train at the next stop and pay penalty. Twenty-five rubles." He put his foot on the pallet, placed a cardboard plank on his knee and started filling out a form.

Alla squeezed her hand between her waist and her skirt. She pulled out the three ruble bill, unfolded it and showed to the inspector. "This is all I have," she said.

He stopped writing, looked in disbelief at the bill and said, "That is all you have for the Moscow-Samarkand trip? How old are you? Thirteen? Traveling on your own? If we let you get out at the next stop, how will you get back to Kalinin or Moscow?"

"Well, I think we can overlook for a couple of hours that you have no valid ticket. At any rate you have paid for a ticket to Samarkand which you cannot use anymore, worth 20 times more than this trip. The state has not lost a kopek. We will let you stay until Ostashkov. There is a Militsia station at Ostashkov terminal; let them take care of you.

"Just be prepared. Our mail shuttle will take seven hours to reach Ostashkov. I have a daughter, just like you."

Ostashkov station's windows glowed gloomily.

The ticket inspector, for a farewell sign, touched Alla's shoulder and walked out of the Militsia room. The Militsioner was an old man. Alla remained in the semi-dark waiting hall of the Ostashkov railway station.

"We must arrange for your transportation to your mother.

The state will pay for it. I think tomorrow early in the morning I'll put you in this same mail shuttle back to Kalinin. Let the region Militsia authority take care of your trip to Samarkand."

"You spend the night there in the waiting hall. Ten benches, choose any you like, sit or lie, as you please. No worries. Do you understand?" He waved his hand towards the waiting hall.

As far as he was concerned, the affair has been closed.

* * *

On Sunday Boris and Artamon left Ostashkov for Kalinin. Boris promised to keep Irina posted on any new developments in her father's case.

Boris said he and Irina would probably be better off addressing letters *poste restante*. The post office at the railway station seemed to be the most convenient choice.

At the earliest, Boris could have written his first letter on Monday. If sent Tuesday morning it would arrive on Thursday. Irina forced herself to wait until the last hour the post office was open to increase the chance that a letter had arrived.

But there was no letter for her.

She would be here again tomorrow. She walked from the train station post office window and several men waiting at the ticket counter followed her with their stares.

She was already at the exit door when something flashed through her mind. She saw something without really noticing what it was. Yes, a couple of legs. Real runner's legs. While her mind was far away, her eyes had caught sight of these legs.

She turned around and made a fast survey of the hall. Yes, there they were, runner's legs with powerful calves—long, sculptured, shapely—and with graceful supple ankles.

The owner of these runner's legs kept her feet on the bench, hugging her knees with her hands, her head downcast so that her face was almost buried in her knees. Then Irina realized this was a child of maybe 14 or 15. What could this lone child be doing here at this time?

Irina took several steps towards the street. Then she turned her head again. Something defenseless and hopeless manifested itself in these thin hands embracing legs born to run.

Irina walked to the girl. "What are you doing here?" she asked. The girl lifted her eyes full of tears.

The girl stared at Irina with wide-open eyes. First, her stare expressed only remoteness. Then it changed, and Irina felt that the girl was suffering desperate loneliness and desired to trust whoever would be nice to her and willing to help.

She sat down next to the girl. "Tell me what you're doing here at this time," Irina said. And the girl told her story, her eyes sparkling in a display of attraction to Irina who had immediately won the girl's trust.

Aunt Galina looked amazed when Irina came back from her excursion to the post office with a young girl. The old woman did not need many explanations. Yes, certainly, Alla could stay in her house. Tomorrow they would think of something to help this girl. In the meantime, tea, potatoes and eggs would be a proper meal for this evening.

Chapter 37

A KNOCK AT THE DOOR WOKE BORIS. IT WAS STILL DARK. "Comrade Tarutin, a telephone call for you. They say it is urgent." The janitor, with a shawl covering her disheveled gray hair, stood in the door yawning and shielding her mouth with her hand.

Boris shoved his legs into his pants, buttoned his shirt and rushed to the stairway. He jumped down three stairs at once, and then, to make it even faster, sat on the railing and slid down. Panting, Boris picked up the receiver.

"Boris? Irina speaking. From Ostashkov. I know that on Friday you have no classes so you might have decided to come here."

"Yes, I'll be in Ostashkov this afternoon."

"That is why I am calling you this early. Stay where you are, Boris, I'll be in Kalinin shortly."

"Where are you talking from?"

"There is a very kind woman here, a doctor, only three blocks from your aunt's house. She happened to treat the director of the telephone station here so she has a telephone in her house. Your Aunt Galina knows her."

"What happened? Why are you coming?"

"I can't tell you on the phone, do you understand?"

Of course he understood. Every telephone in the country was supposedly monitored by the KGB.

"I have borrowed some money from this doctor," Irina said. "We will take a plane and be in Kalinin at eight."

"What do you mean by 'we'?"

"Once you urged me to have patience, Boris. Now, be patient for a couple of hours." She hung up.

He stood at the window in the small building of the Kalinin air terminal. The tiny airplane landed, then the propeller stopped and its door slid sideways.

There she was and his heart stopped. She was walking along the asphalt path to the terminal, valise in hand, the same valise Boris had used to bring food from Moscow. Her legs, long, beautifully muscled, and more magnificent than he remembered. She came closer and her dark childish eyes made his heart beat faster.

Then he saw a young girl who seemed to accompany Irina. A tall girl, thin, with the long sculptured calves of a runner. The girl carried a bundle. Irina dropped the valise and leaped into his arms. For the first time she kissed him full on the mouth. When they pulled apart she said, "Boris, meet Alla Shumilova. This is Boris Petrovich Tarutin."

"No, just Boris, please." He shook the girl's hand. It was fragile, childishly bony. She looked quite ordinary. No, there was something in her eyes showing experience and grief, something not quite fitting her age which probably was not more than fourteen.

"We must arrange for Alla's trip to her mother," Irina said. We could not do it from Ostashkov so it was enough of a reason to come here. Alla and I will go back to my apartment. The hell with my neighbors."

"That is one thing Artamon can do," Boris said. "Toss a little thunder over your neighbors' heads. They will quickly develop an immense respect for you. I'll talk to Artamon today, so your neighbors will not bother you."

"There is something else I want to tell you," Irina said. "When we get to my place, we'll talk about it."

"Boris, be prepared for a surprise," Irina said. "How many poems of Pushkin or Lermontov do you know by heart?"

"I don't think I ever counted. Why?"

"Name any poem by Pushkin or by Lermontov, or by Tyutchev, or Fet. Not something completely obscure, but not something which is studied in schools as an obligatory item."

"Let's see," Boris said. "How about 'Three Palms' by Lermontov? It is well known but not obligatory in schools. Why?"

"Well, Alla," Irina said. "Do you know 'Three Palms'?"

Alla nodded.

"Now, listen and wonder, Boris," Irina said. "Show him, Alla."

The girl smiled bashfully. Then she started, "In sandy plains of the Arabian land, three proud palms grew high. A spring broke out among them, purling, from the futile soil—" The taxicab rocked on the rough pavement as the girl recited the entire poem.

"Now, Boris, something else, if you wish," Irina said.

"You mean, Alla would know by heart—"

"Hundreds of poems and stories and names and—"

The taxi driver turned his head. "You must take her to the region competition of young talents. She may win a good award. I see now, she is not your daughter."

* * *

Everything in Magidov's apartment was in the same mess as on the night they came to pick up Irina's documents.

They settled in the kitchen. Irina placed a tea kettle on the electric range as Boris brought a board holding a dozen medals, the prizes won by Irina. He fastened the board to the window thus shielding the broken glass.

"So, what is it you could not talk about in the taxi?"

"Let's talk in my room while Alla watches the kettle."

"Alla has a miraculous memory, as you have seen," Irina said. "She thinks her memory is mechanical, that is, she remembers easily whatever she hears."

Boris smiled. "She will understand it one day."

"She stayed for two weeks in the house of Korytov."

"Korytov? Oh, you mean, *the* Korytov, the region Master."

"Yes," Irina said. "She was a guest invited by Korytov."

"How did she wind up in your lap?"

"To make a long story short, the Korytovs kicked her out."

"And what was her crime?" Boris asked.

"There was a crime committed. This old bastard Korytov forced her into his bed. Every night for two weeks."

"My God. How old is she? It is statutory rape."

"She will be fourteen next April."

"But Korytov is married, isn't he," Boris said.

"He is. During those two weeks, Korytov's wife happened to be abroad, disguised as a working woman."

"That is how they always make up their delegations to these international gatherings—"

"—where they condemn imperialists and Zionists and praise the Kremlin's peacemakers," Irina finished. "This Korytova woman came home two days ago and somebody in the house tattled, so she kicked Alla out. She gave Alla a ticket to Samarkand where Alla's mother lives but Alla took a wrong train and I ran into her accidentally in Ostashkov station."

"But what induced you to pick her up?"

"The first thing was her legs," Irina said.

"Legs? So you understand why I singled you out from the crowd at the train station."

"With two differences. The first is that with me and Alla, what counted was not that the legs were female, I caught sight of legs *born to run*."

"And the second difference?" Boris said.

"The second difference is that in a few minutes it was not legs that counted. Tell me, Boris, is there a chance to bring Korytov to justice for rape?"

"Are you serious? The region Master is above the law. Any attempt to press charges against him would mean serious trouble for the plaintiff. Probably a placement in a mental institution."

"I know. It is such an outrage," Irina said. "Korytov kept Alla in his bedroom every night. She happened to overhear his telephone conversations. Alla understood very little of what he was talking about but with her memory she remembers these talks. Last night I talked with your Aunt Galina about my father's case and we mentioned Gavrik. When Alla heard Gavrik's name she said this name had come up in those telephone conversations."

"And Alla can repeat those telephone calls word for word."

"Like Lermontov's poem. Right, Boris."

"What secrets have you learned?"

"Somebody by the name of Misha had been telling Korytov about the developments in what he named 'Magidov-Gavrik case.' "

"Then you already know about this new development," Boris said.

"I do. Do you want to know the gist of what Misha said?"

"I can hardly wait."

"As this Misha put it, he 'sold' Gavrik to the KGB," Irina said.

"That is the exact expression Artamon used to describe what had happened with Gavrik."

"The second thing which transpired is that the *obkom* has their own man in the KGB and Misha runs that man. This *obkom* spy is an investigator by the name of Mordin and he is in charge of Gavrik's case. Mordin has been reporting daily to Misha."

"And then Misha calls up Korytov to report."

"By transferring Gavrik to the KGB—done at the KGB's request—Misha made it clear that the *obkom* did the KGB a favor and a reciprocating favor would be expected."

"It's exactly what Artamon surmised," Boris said.

"Mordin is to report to Misha whatever occurs in the case."

"So the *obkom* would be on the top of events."

"Right. Mordin reported that Gavrik *cracked* on his first day in the KGB."

"Whatever crimes a KGB officer commits, its rule is to cover up for their man."

"Not in this case. Baev was also a KGB officer and of a higher rank than Gavrik."

"So they would not forgive?"

"Right. Gavrik knew what he could expect from his colleagues and gave away whatever they wanted to know—"

"—To save himself from harsher treatment," Boris finished.

"The first question they asked Gavrik was why he used the impact tester. Gavrik has put forward a theory behind his action. You see he considers himself an expert in executions.

"Gavrik explained he has always been in favor of beheading those sentenced to the death penalty. Gavrik maintained that decapitating criminals is the genuine Russian way from time immemorial."

"He was right," Boris said. "As you know, there is still the 'Lobnoye mesto,' this huge round-shaped stone in the Red Square in Moscow. That is where heads were chopped off, until a couple of centuries ago."

The gist of the story is that he considered the impact tester the closest thing to a guillotine. By using the tester he almost fulfilled his life-long dream of executing somebody on a guillotine."

"Did these investigators think of sending Gavrik to a psychiatric examination?"

"No," Irina said. "He is not a dissident. Gavrik admitted that he knocked Baev out using a hammer. Then he dragged Baev, alive, to that impact tester. He readjusted the timer to have time for an escape."

"Yes, it is all consistent. I believe Gavrik pushed Valushin into the river."

"They are not interested in Valushin's death," Irina said. "There are some other curious things about Gavrik's confession. They wanted to know his motive. It seems that Baev and Gavrik held the helm of an organization which sprawled over many regions. It consisted of former convicts who served their terms in the camps where Gavrik and Baev served as warders. In this organization Gavrik had a higher position than Baev, whereas in the KGB, Baev held a higher rank. Apparently, Baev did not like this situation and attempted to take over the organization. As Misha put it, following the rules of a murderers' gang, Gavrik just had to kill his rival."

"Irina, did Misha say what this organization has been doing? Why do former convicts obey Gavrik?"

"He did not talk about it. Misha reported that during a

search of Gavrik's apartment a large number of medals were discovered including those belonging to Baev."

"I expected it."

"The KGB is furious. You see, Gavrik even had Militsia officers in his organization which he kept outside his KGB connections. That is what they are not prepared to forgive."

"And what about your father?"

"The region Prosecutor receives briefings from the KGB and *obkom* and he even asked Misha whether it was the time to release my father. Misha answered that nothing would happen to Magidov if he spent more time in jail."

"They want to present your father as a mastermind behind Gavrik's crimes."

"I believe my father can't fit their script. They have the murderer, don't they. Boris, I think you have done a great job. Without you, Sergeev would never have gotten a confession from Gavrik."

"I've done it for myself as much as for your father. Irina, I don't believe they will release your father without additional pressure. And I have an idea."

"Tell me about it," Irina said.

"I have to talk to my friend Galaunov. He has connections among the dissidents in Moscow. Some of them are Jews fighting for emigration permits. Some others are just craving for democracy. Others, like Galaunov, are Russian nationalists. Whatever their convictions and desires are, some of them manage to get in touch with foreign correspondents in Moscow."

"Oh, I see now. Is it possible?"

"If the information about your father reached the West and some of the radio stations like the Voice of America, Radio Liberty, Deutsche Welle, BBC, had broadcasts about him, it might help. Our friends do not like a fuss regarding their noble work. Also, maybe some scientific societies or the groups monitoring human rights violations would take up your father's cause. He is a first-class scientist and he has not committed any crime."

"You have given me new hope. If only you could get in touch with those correspondents. Now, do you want to listen to Alla repeat those telephone conversations? Maybe you could find out something I've misinterpreted. I am not an expert in crime investigations."

"Neither am I except from what I've learned from Artamon's stories. But you are right, *one mind is good, but two are better*. Let's listen."

After he had listened to Alla repeat the telephone calls between Korytov and Misha Berkin, Boris said, "Irina, I can't add anything. You've interpreted it most intelligently. Which gives me an opportunity to respond to the two differences between my perception of female legs and yours. When I saw you in the station your legs singled you out from the crowd. But my admiration for your magnificent runner's legs is only part of it."

Irina smiled and sparks of joy flickered in her eyes.

"Do not apologize," she said. "I see nothing wrong if a man admires female legs."

"Well, I am also aware you have also something here." Boris topped Irina's forehead. "And I like it very much."

She hugged him.

Chapter 38

FOR OVER 20 YEARS, MISHA HAD BEEN IN THE CLOSEST proximity to the centers of unlimited power. Still, he could never forget his father's unhappy ethnic origin. Because of his father's origin, Misha Berkin had been permanently foretasting a sudden collapse of his career.

Misha's ingenuity and quick mind which he placed at Korytov's disposal had kept him afloat. He knew that one blunder or if something happened to Korytov or if the Party decided with or without a reason that even a single half-Jew in the Party apparatus was one too many, Misha would become a non-person. In his tumultuous life as a power broker, Misha could never fully enjoy all those luxuries his position had provided.

Once a month Misha spent a morning at the theater. From the theater he headed to the KGB.

Lieutenant General Rashkov, the Chairman of the Kalinin region KGB, sat behind an old-fashioned desk. A large painting hung on the wall behind Rashkov's head depicting a man with a goatie and burning eyes. This was Felix

Dzerzhinsky founder of the *Cheka*, the first incarnation of what after a number of transformations, through the OGPU, NKVD, MVD and MGB, had become the KGB.

Also in the room was investigator Mordin, the *obkom* spy in the KGB.

Misha would not be surprised if Rashkov knew Mordin was the *obkom*'s spy; Misha would not be surprised if Mordin had held the assignment with the consent of his KGB superiors. After over twenty years in the epicenter of inter-Party intrigue Misha would not be surprised by anything.

What Misha had to discuss with Rashkov was not for anybody's ears. After the exchange of greetings Misha said, "Excuse me, Timofei Georgievich, if you need to talk with comrade Mordin maybe I should wait outside?" It was a figure of speech implying that Mordin get out at once.

"Well, Timofei Georgievich," Misha said, "One good turn deserves another. I have made my move, now it's your turn."

Rashkov remained silent. His unblinking eyes remained immobile behind the thick glasses of his old-fashioned pince-nez.

The boss of Stalin's secret police, Lavrentiy Beria, used to wear pince-nez. Some of Beria's henchmen had also acquired the same kind of eye-glasses.

Misha had studied Rashkov's career as soon as Rashkov was appointed the chairman of the Kalinin region KGB. Rashkov had been one of those professional secret police masters who had survived the deaths of several consecutive heads of the secret police.

Looking now at Rashkov, Misha could feel the thoughts flowing through Rashkov's head. "This damned Yid, would he dare to show his insolence in *my* time I would flay him alive. A stinking lousy aide dares to set conditions to a KGB general!"

But Rashkov did not say anything. Only a pinky of Rashkov's hand slightly tapped on the desk betraying his inner strain. He waited until Misha would say what he wanted as the price for Gavrik's transfer to the KGB. And Misha told him.

Misha's boss Korytov seemed to be in the most depressed state Misha had ever seen. After Ksenia kicked out that 13-year-old girl, the old woman did not want to speak to her husband.

Ksenia, Korytov's wife and the sister of a big shot Kalyazin, was Korytov's main asset in the inner-Party joustings. If Ksenia ceased to serve as a link to her brother it could have the gravest consequences. The Gavrik affair seemed to offer a solution to placate the old woman.

A few months earlier, Rashkov's wife had appeared at a celebration wearing a ring with a huge blue diamond. She wore it to impress the wives of the region's big shots. Where did the diamond come from?

To solve the riddle, Misha had explored all of his sources of information. The answer turned out to be fascinating.

Yes, this was a genuine stone from India. In the time of Catherine the Great, Prince Potyomkin had presented this diamond to the empress. The gem was part of the Csars' treasury.

The diamond remained in Lanskoi's family until the revolution. In 1917 the last Prince Lanskoi fled Russia and smuggled out his gems.

The collection had been sold. The blue diamond turned up in the possession of a gem dealer in Amsterdam. It remained there for many years. Last year the blue diamond had disappeared. Now Misha understood when the stone reappeared on the finger of Rashkov's wife.

Misha felt self-confident. First, Rashkov owed Misha a favor. Second, if Misha hinted he knew that Rashkov had appropriated a national treasure for his personal use the old KGB general would give up the diamond with a smile on his thin lips.

And Korytov would present it to Ksenia as a gift. If the old bat did not melt at once and her fury subside, Misha did not know anything about women.

"There are vicious rumors, Timofei Georgievich," Misha said, "regarding Potyomkin's diamond which your people have heroically retrieved for our Motherland."

Rashkov's pinky stopped tapping the desk. He did not say anything.

"Of course, Timofei Georgievich," Misha continued. "We in the *obkom* treat these rumors as malicious gossip.

Rashkov's eyes remained unblinking.

"Well, Timofei Georgievich, we understand that you have some respectable reasons for having this diamond temporarily in your personal custody. There is the opinion that it would be expedient to place this diamond where it belongs and the *obkom* is willing to assist you in this. The Party will take care of all further actions in regard to this gem."

Yes, Misha's expectations proved correct: the old KGB master did not show the slightest emotion. He did not smile though, he just pressed a button on his desk.

When the diamond was finally in Misha's hands, he felt a strange emptiness in his heart. This achievement would cost dearly; now Korytov instead of Rashkov would be in possession of a national treasure and Rashkov would have leverage over the *obkom*. Who knew what the future held in store?

When Korytov saw the diamond his eyes showed excitement. Yes, this bauble must mitigate Ksenia's fury. Once again his aide had demonstrated a supernatural ability to find a solution to any problem.

Misha ordered lunch in his personal office. A servant in white uniform wheeled in a cart with a dozen dishes. Then Misha was alone in his office. He walked to a wall safe and fetched a small book from it.

Misha leafed through the book slowly. The strange characters fascinated him. The book had been confiscated from Magidov. At Misha's request, this textbook of Hebrew for Russian-speaking beginners was sent to the *obkom*, to let Misha take a look at the *incriminating evidence*.

One of the telephones on Misha's desk rang. It was connected with an anti-bugging device and had direct access to Misha from outside circumventing his secretaries. Few people knew the number of this telephone and one of these was Mordin, Misha's spy in the KGB. Misha picked up the receiver.

"Number forty-four reporting," the voice said. It was intentionally distorted by an electronic device.

"Number eleven listening, forty-four," Misha said.

"Please, the verification number." Misha gave his seven-digit code number. Mordin responded with his eight-digit code number. Then Mordin started reporting.

"There are some disturbing developments."

"Go ahead," Misha said.

"I have interrogated a few people who were at the university on the night of Baev's murder," Mordin said. "I have discovered that there is a man, the supervisor of Valushin who has been investigating the case on his own. His name is Tarutin. He is also a close friend of investigator Sergeev. So, Sergeev may have been leaking sensitive information to this Tarutin."

"Your estimate of the damage," Misha said.

"Extremely serious. This Tarutin seems to know about some critical knots of the entire affair."

"Do you know why Tarutin is interested in collecting this information? Do you have a file on him?"

"No file. There is a file on Tarutin's father. The father died in jail while under interrogation in 1953. Exonerated post-mortem."

"I see. What else?"

"Tarutin's mother died in 1955. At thirty-eight. Heart disease. Apparently aggravated by her husband's arrest."

"I see," Misha said. Has Tarutin been harboring anti-Soviet feelings because of his parents?"

"Possible. Also, he is on friendly terms with Galaunov."

"Oh, Galaunov! Is that the Lenin prize laureate who's been rubbing elbows with dissidents in Moscow?"

"Right. I have unearthed some facts explaining Tarutin's activities in a simpler way."

"Go ahead."

"Evidently Magidov's daughter is Tarutin's girlfriend."

"Aha! It makes sense."

"I suspect Magidov's daughter knows everything Tarutin has dug up. It is an extremely dangerous situation. Just look at the following scenario. Tarutin may share his knowledge with Galaunov. Galaunov can share this knowledge with those dissidents he meets in Moscow."

"I understand, forty-four," Misha said. "Very sensitive information can be leaked abroad. Yes, it is very serious."

"Number eleven, we must silence Tarutin and Irina Magidova. You understand that if interrogated by my organization they may disclose some facts which would be better kept between the two of us."

"I see your point," Misha said. "I shall consider our options. Tell me the exact names and addresses, forty-four, and thanks for a job well done."

Misha Berkin closed his eyes. He leaned against the cushion of his rocking chair. His intuition, actually some subconscious calculating apparatus, was doing its invisible and silent work, sorting out all the option available, their possible ramifications, risks, advantages and drawbacks.

It took about an hour of deep meditation before Misha opened his eyes and picked up the phone and called Mordin. Misha went through the routine of code exchange, then said, "Number one, I am seeking your approval for an extraordinary operation."

"What the devil is the matter?" Korytov said.

"Do you want details?"

"No, no, Misha. Just the general flavor."

"A serious danger has emerged which could ruin the entire Gavrik-Magidov case. An urgent action is required to cut off some channels through which the information can leak out."

"Well, Misha. I see. If it is urgent, you have my authorization for the actions you deem proper. You may act in my name."

"Thank you, number one," Misha said.

For his next call, Misha used the same telephone.

"Number eleven calling," Misha said.

"Thirty-three listening," was the response of the man who was in charge of *special operations*. They went through the code exchange.

"Thirty-three, this is an emergency. You shall start operation A-1. Do you understand?"

"Yes, number eleven. We shall start operation A-1."

"The names and the addresses are—" And Misha gave him the names and addresses of Boris Tarutin and Irina Magidova.

"You shall report the implementation immediately. Remember, everything must look like an accident," Misha said.

"That is what our operations are all about, number eleven.

"Good luck, number thirty-three," Misha said.

After having given an order of the kind Misha had just issued, some people in Misha's position would drink vodka, trying to kill with alcohol the bites of conscience. But he had an aversion to vodka. He was, though, a connoisseur of high-quality wines. He kept in his office bottles filled with Kindsmarauly brought directly from Georgia, and a selection of superb Moldavian table wines.

Today the wine had no effect on the invisible animal with sharp teeth, Misha's conscience. To Misha's annoyance he discovered it had been stubbornly hiding deeply at the bottom of his steel-hard heart.

Chapter 39

It was about eleven a.m. on Friday, December 16, when somebody knocked at the door of Magidovs' apartment.

"I hope this is not my lovely neighbors again," Irina said. She went to open the door. Boris heard a male voice which seemed familiar to him. And then, accompanied by Irina, a man walked in, holding in hand a musquash fur cap. A surprised Boris recognized Doctor Litvin of the Golokomlya mental hospital.

"I have been looking for you," Litvin said.

"How the devil could you possibly know that I was here?" Boris said.

"I didn't know. I went to the university and I got the impression everybody knew where to look for you."

"You mean—"

"It was very simple, my friend. I asked a janitor where your room would be. She said there would be no point in looking for you in your room since you had left the building a couple of hours earlier. She said I should look you up in the quarters of some young woman, the daughter of Professor Magidov. You see, Boris, nothing goes unnoticed."

"You are right, doctor," Boris said. "Our every step is exposed to curious eyes."

"And every word to curious ears," Irina said.

"I guess you are Magidov's daughter," Litvin said.

"She is," Boris said. "Now, doctor, in what way can I assist you?"

"I have come to Kalinin to meet my superior in the region's health authority. Since I was here anyway, I decided I might as well attempt to find you. I believe, I possess some information which you may want to know, Tarutin."

"Alla," Boris said. "Would you please pick up some book for yourself, there, in the larger room, and read it for a while? Thank you. I hope it will not take long. Doctor, we can speak here now, I don't hide anything from Irina."

"I would be a bad psychiatrist if I could not have guessed it myself, my friend."

"Then, doctor, please proceed," Boris said.

"Tell me, Boris, does the name Fomichev mean anything to you?"

"Yes. I spent a night in your hospital, with this man. I think he is quite sane."

"Yes, he is," Doctor Litvin said. Apparently you trusted him more than you trusted me."

"I thought we had all the time in the world at our disposal. After you released me, I had only one wish, to get out of there."

"Let me explain Irina," Litvin said. "Fomichev is headman of some religious community in Valdai. This group has been refusing to register with the State Authority for Religious cults. They have also been bringing up their children in the spirit of their beliefs.

"Fomichev was sent by the KGB to our hospital for an

examination. Of course, he is sane. But! As soon as I declare Fomichev sane he goes back to jail and draws a minimum of five years in camps. It is his third arrest."

Irina said. "So, you just keep him under observation."

"Well, I have some ideas," Litvin said. "But it is Fomichev's life. The decision must be his. The KGB demand a definite medical conclusion; either Fomichev is sane, then welcome back to jail, or sick and he would have to stay with us for as long as needed to cure him. He would be considered cured only after renouncing his *religious superstitions*.

"I am telling you this to show you the mutual trust developing between myself and Fomichev. I let him work in my office sorting out files and he came across an unusual case."

"Aha, here we are," Boris said.

"Yes. A little more than two weeks ago a patient arrived in Golokomlya who had been sent from Bologoe. Ah, I see, you are curious. Yes, a Captain Nikiforov of Bologoe Militsia sent him. Does it mean anything to you, Boris?"

"It does, doctor," Boris said.

"Three days after this man's arrival," Litvin continued, "the same Bologoe Militsia sent a letter requesting the immediate return of this man to their custody."

"Have you complied, doctor?" Boris said.

"No, we are not subordinate to the Militsia."

"So, he is still with you," Boris said.

"Right. Now another letter arrived, demanding his return. Well, I have talked with this patient who said His nickname is Guran."

Boris said. "Do you know about Guran's nefarious activities in Bologoe?"

"That is why I am here. Fomichev had been handling Guran's file.

"The file shows he has been suspected of numerous murders, and robbing the victims of their medals. I asked Guran how he used these medals. He laughed and said there was a whole organization and he was just a small screw. These medals are sold all over the country. The organization is headed up by a man nicknamed Plague."

"Aha, doctor!" Boris jumped to his feet. "Did he tell you the real name of Plague?"

"No. Guran said this bunch of murderers and robbers consisted of professionals, men who served terms in camps where Plague had been a warder. There is no way to get out of Plague's gang because he has in his possession files of criminal activities of his henchmen. He can put any one of them back into jail. Everybody in the gang believes that Plague has KGB support."

Boris and Irina exchanged glances. "Boris, do you think this Plague can be Gavrik?" Irina said.

"It is very probable."

"Who the devil is Gavrik?" Litvin asked.

"He is the man who killed Baev."

"I see. It jibes with what Guran told me about Plague," Litvin said. "Well, that is about it, my friend. I am leaving now, back to Golokomlya. Be very, very cautious. I am afraid you have not been cautious enough. You have exposed your friendship with this beautiful girl at the time her father is being roasted. This has certainly been reckless on your part and not at all beneficial to her as well. It takes great moral courage to ignore the rules the citizens of this country are supposed to follow."

Doctor Litvin left.

"The doctor is right," Irina said. "You are in danger, Boris. Drop your involvement in my father's case before it is too late."

"No, Irina, justice cannot be ignored, so for me there is no retreat. I must hurry to see Galaunov. With the help of some foreign correspondent we have a chance to wind up ahead of the possible disaster."

"Boris, I am scared," Irina said.

He kissed Irina not as a friend but as a lover. They stood frozen for a while, then Irina freed herself slowly, her eyes wet with happiness.

Boris said, "I am going to Artamon, to see what he may advise, then to Galaunov. I love you, Irina. I know it is not the proper time to ask you to marry me. But in the event something happens to me I wanted you to know."

She hugged him. He moved his hand over her hair, then he freed himself reluctantly from her embrace and she whispered, "And I love you, Boris."

Chapter 40

WHEN BORIS WALKED INTO SERGEEV'S OFFICE, ARTAMON was sitting at his desk. To Boris's astonishment, Artamon, who never smoked, was holding a cigarette in his lips as he turned his eyes towards Boris. The sad expression of Artamon's face, the corners of his mouth downcast, did not change.

"It does not help," Artamon said, showing Boris the cigarette. "*Ex nihilo nihil fit*. Alas, in the office I may not drink vodka. And vodka is the only thing which could help me at this time. Now, Boris, let's take a walk.

They walked slowly along the Volga quay. Now, in the middle of December, rough bluish ice covered the river. Only in the very center did a black current of water flow between serrated edges of ice.

Artamon said, "Walking here we are visible to anybody whoever might wish to watch us. Since our relationship is a matter of record what counts is nobody can overhear us."

"Do you imply that you have become a target of eavesdropping?" Boris said.

"That is what I imply, my friend. Yes."

"Because of your discovering Gavrik was the murderer?" Boris said.

"Yes," Artamon said. "We took a risk and we have lost the game, my friend."

"It may have been a game for you, Artamon, or your bosses, but not for Magidov. Not for me."

"*Fronti nula fides*. For me, Boris, it *was* a high-stake game."

"But why would they want to eavesdrop on you? Didn't you duly report everything to your superiors? Didn't you obey orders?"

"I took the risk of squeezing Gavrik into a confession," Artamon said gloomily. "Despite the decision of the *obkom* to make Magidov the culprit, I assumed Gavrik would stay in my hands and the entire affair would be under our control. Alas, the day after Gavrik confessed he was transferred to the KGB. I don't know why the *obkom* did so as it is contrary to their decision to entrust our office with this case."

"Isn't *obkom*'s policy just the whim of today's master?" Boris said. "And what is going on in the KGB?"

"In the KGB the case is in the hands of investigator Mordin."

"Do you know anything about this Mordin?" Boris said.

"Mordin is dumb. As a lawyer, Mordin is illiterate. But in the KGB it doesn't matter. What they do have are unlimited resources and determination and they are not concerned with the letter of the law.

"Mordin has been informing everybody about what they call now the Magidov-Gavrik case. Which means two things which have a direct bearing on my well being and yours."

"Which are?" Boris said.

"One is to infer that I have been not as close-mouthed with you as I could be."

"I see. And the second thing?" Boris said.

"Your activities as a self-appointed investigator."

"Oh! I have certainly transgressed the limits of a good Soviet citizen. I have tried to unearth the truth on my own," Boris said.

"What will happen to you?" Boris said.

"Who knows? Maybe move me to small mundane cases. Maybe kick me out of the Party. I wouldn't even be surprised if nothing happened. In the meantime, I feel like I am hung between heaven and earth."

"I understand, Artamon. Would you listen to some news, anyway? I have obtained some additional information."

After Boris finished telling Guran's story Artamon said, "I am sure Plague is Gavrik. There just can't be two separate underground organizations on such scale, both involved in trading medals. As it happens, I can hardly make use of it now. But the more I know, the better I am equipped to handle the situation. Now, my friend, let me warn you. You must be concerned with what it means for you."

"You mean the danger of Mordin learning about my investigation?"

"Right. I don't know what you can do about it. Just, be cautious. If you could somehow go away for several months, say, to Siberia. It wouldn't guarantee anything but sometimes it helps."

"I won't. But I am going abroad with the information about Magidov."

"Abroad? Oh, you mean to have it broadcast to gain

support of some human right organizations like those monitoring compliance with the Helsinki accord?"

"Yes."

"My friend, the situation, as I perceive it is very grave. Trust my intuition, if they decide to crush you down they will try some covert trick. That is why it may help if you just move somewhere. They don't want the rumors about Baev spreading all over the country."

"Artamon, your speech has convinced me. The best course would be to make as much fuss as possible," Boris said.

"So, you take the risk—"

"It can backfire. Granted! It is a shame to reveal to the world that we are unable to handle our own affairs."

"Of course, Boris. I feel the same way."

"If it were just me, Artamon, I might think about fleeing to Siberia, but, if I leave the region who would help Magidov? No, I must stay and an appeal for help from abroad seems to be the only way to help him."

"Well, Boris, I hope your crazy attempt will not backfire. My friend, whatever the outcome I love and admire you. I am glad you have been my friend. And don't judge me too harshly as I am not *ad unguem* a complete coward. I am merely not a hero, Boris."

Boris found Galaunov sitting on his desk, his feet resting on a chair. Glasses in broken frames, fastened with a piece of a copper wire. He was staring at a chalk drawing on a blackboard of a device for a friction coefficient's measurement. Galaunov had been one of the world's leading experts on physics of friction.

When Galaunov saw Boris, he removed his glasses, his blue eyes sparkling.

"Boris! Welcome," he growled. "Do you want to join

me again for a ski run? You're invited to stay in my parents' hut so we can set out as early as possible. And there is always fresh milk waiting for you."

"Thanks, Nikolai, but I have to stay in town. But I must talk to you."

"You are involved in all kinds of strange activities. But first, your scientific research. I will not leave you alone until you start another research project."

"I'm occupied with more urgent things, Nikolai."

"My God you are stubborn."

"I want to ask you something, Nikolai. Last time you said that you could foresee two choices for Jews in Russia. One is to leave this country for Israel, and you are in favor of granting permission to every Jew who wants to go there."

"Right, Boris. And, if you remember I have talked about another option."

"That any Jew considering himself a Russian must be accepted as a Russian, right?"

"Yes. My approach is not based on religion, race or blood."

"And how about a third choice?"

"Like what?"

"If a Jew does not want to leave this country because his ancestors have lived here for centuries. But he wants to stay a Jew as he was born and prefers to live in Russia. What about this version?"

"I consider it unnatural. A person who wants to remain a Jew, should move to Israel. However, if a person chooses to live in Russia, then he must accept our culture, habits, and attitudes."

"Here is the line separating our attitudes," Boris said. "I feel that everybody is entitled to choose where he wants to live, particularly if he wants to remain in the place he was born."

Galaunov laughed bitterly. "Boris, do you understand what the word Nation means? Nation is a living organism. Any alien body inside an organism inevitably causes a disease. Every organism strives to either digest or expel an alien body."

"If you compare a nation to a biological organism you arrive at dangerous conclusions," Boris said, which means different parts of a biological body cannot move in different directions without destroying the body. That's nonsense! Your analogy, if applied to a nation, would mean that any dissent is a disease."

"Boris, if you consider me a bigot."

"Of course not, Nikolai. Otherwise I wouldn't be here now. We need your help, your connections with dissidents in Moscow."

"Tell me about it," Galaunov said.

Boris told him about the latest development in the Gavrik-Magidov case. And about Alla's story. And he asked whether Galaunov would help or would he set out on a ski run this weekend as usual.

"My ski run will have to wait until next week. I'll go to Moscow tomorrow. I'll take this girl Alla there and put her on her train to Samarkand. What an outrageous story! Now, do you need money to buy clothing for this girl?"

"Irina has given Alla underwear, a sweater and a blouse. We'll give her enough money for the three days of travel. Just talk to the conductor. You know, five rubles would do it. He'll look after the girl during the trip."

"No problem," Galaunov said. "Then, I will be looking for people in Moscow who can get in touch with a foreign correspondent. You understand, Boris, I cannot guarantee success. These people live under such precarious conditions."

"Can't you go directly to a foreign correspondent?"

"My God, no." Galaunov said. "It is hard to approach a foreign correspondent."

"Because of their fear of the KGB?" Boris said.

"Well, true, they are usually more afraid of the KGB than we are. It takes time and effort to develop a mutual trust with a correspondent. That's why it's best to approach a correspondent through somebody who has earned credibility in the eyes of this correspondent."

Boris said, "Recently, I discussed with Talin books about our country published abroad by these correspondents."

"I read a few of them," Galaunov said. "They spend three years in Moscow living in a comfortable apartment, buy the best food in special stores and observe the *poor but warm-hearted* Russian people. They go home and write books about Russia. They mention condescendingly that Russians are the same as Americans except that the best of us do not understand how to respect differing opinions."

"As for respecting differing opinions," Boris said, "I am afraid, there is a grain of truth in these correspondents' observations. We are not accustomed to impassioned discussions. We in Russia have been using fistfights rather than discussions."

Galaunov laughed and said, "Yes, my friend, in our country the fist is still considered the best argument among the rulers as well as the dissidents."

"How do you to get these books? I have never even seen one."

"I borrow them from the same people I am going to look up in Moscow tomorrow," Galaunov said. "You understand, these books circulate only in the underground. One may draw a few years in jail for having such a book."

How will you locate people who have access to foreign correspondents?"

"Tomorrow is Saturday," Galaunov said. "So, I will look them up in the one place they gather on Saturdays. "Arkhipov Street in Moscow."

Chapter 41

GALAUNOV, ALLA, AND IRINA STOOD ON THE PLATFORM, at the entrance to a car of the electric train Kalinin-Moscow. Soft snowflakes descended slowly to the platform's asphalt. Boris ran out of the station hall door and handed a box to Alla.

"Some candies to sweeten your journey," Boris said.

A resounding voice roared the usual unintelligible mumble at the departure of the train.

Galaunov and Alla stood on the landing of the moving car, Alla bent forward staring until Boris and Irina's figures disappeared.

Once in the car, Alla unwrapped the package. There was a box with assorted candies. Alla handed the open box to Galaunov who took one piece. Alla hesitated, indecisive, then she selected a sugarplum ball.

In Moscow they found an empty locker in the terminal, and left Alla's belongings there. They walked from the terminal building to Komsomolskaya Square.

"We'll send a telegram to your mother," Galaunov said. "Arrive home Tuesday 6 pm. Alla."

While Alla filled out the form, Galaunov took a place in a queue snaking in front of the telegraph counters. Then they crossed the street and walked into an eatery named "Russian Tea."

"This is one of the best places in Moscow, for lunch," Galaunov said. "They serve a delicious dish called 'Meat-in-jar.'"

They ordered, and the "meat-in-a-jar" appeared in 20 minutes. It was served hot in a ceramic jar. On the top was a thin, flat cake. Underneath was a steaming broth with a beautiful aroma of meat, laurel leaves and pepper.

"Listen, my girl," Galaunov said. "We still have a few hours before your train departs. I suggest you watch a movie. In the meantime I shall attend to some business. Then we meet in front of the cinema, how about that?"

"I prefer to stay with you," Alla said. "I shall not stand in your way."

After walking a few blocks they turned left and then right. It was a short street and looked as if it had only one block. Then Alla saw a crowd next to one particular building. But it was not a line gathering at store entrances; the crowd consisted of many small groups from three to ten people in each.

They talked to each other quietly.

"Here we are, Alla," Galaunov said. "This is Arkhipov street."

"Arkhipov street? What is so special about this street?"

"The only officially operating synagogue in Moscow is situated on this block," Galaunov said.

"Synagogue? What is a synagogue?" Alla said.

"Do you know what a church is?"

"Yes, it is where the believers pray. In Samarkand there is one church. I have never been there though. And there is a mosque in Samarkand. Do you know what a mosque is?"

Galaunov laughed. "Yes, I do," he said.

Alla stared at Galaunov, astonished. Galaunov laid his hand on her shoulder. "Since your mother is Jewish it is funny that I have to explain to you about the synagogue. It is more sad than funny. A synagogue is like a Jewish church."

"So, all these people have they come to pray?" Alla said. "Are they all Jews?"

"I think so," Galaunov said. "Except for some KGB's stoolies who disguise themselves as Jews. Most of these people are not here to pray.

"Outside the synagogue Jews of all ages gather every Saturday to discuss their problems. Mostly, how to get out of Russia."

"Why do they want to get out? Where do they want to go?"

"Some want to go to Israel, others, to America."

"To Israel and America? Those are such awful places, capitalists oppress the people there."

"You have good teachers."

"If they want to get out of the USSR, why are they permitted to gather here?" Alla said.

"The KGB thinks it is easier to watch these in one place than in many different places."

"I would never agree to leave our country," Alla said.

"Neither would I," Galaunov said. "But these people have their reasons. Now, Alla, I see the man I want to speak to. Do you understand you must never tell anybody that you witnessed my conversation with this man."

Alla stared at Galaunov with wide eyes. After a long pause, she said, "I will not tell anybody."

Many of the people on Arkhipov Street knew Galaunov well.

There were a number of long term "refuseniks" here, people who had been refused an exit visa for no understandable reason.

What evoked Galaunov's admiration was that few long-term refuseniks had yielded to the KGB harassment, and many refuseniks, after years of struggling, had succeeded in getting visas. Others had been imprisoned, many held scientific seminars in their apartments, they taught and studied Hebrew and they cultivated contacts with foreign correspondents.

Galaunov noticed the man he wanted to meet. Like Galaunov, Professor Vorsky was also a renowed specialist in Physics of friction. He had repeatedly applied for a visa for seven years, all this time without a job. He had been jailed, beaten, vilified and slandered at gatherings and in the press. But nothing seemed to destroy his determination.

Galaunov had been on friendly terms with Vorsky since their student years. It was a mystery to Galaunov, how this former professor and laboratory head, winner of numerous scientific honors, had been earning his living.

When Vorsky noticed Galaunov, he nodded slightly and made an almost imperceptible gesture with his hand. Galaunov answered with an equally faint nod. He took Alla's hand and they walked down the street. When they reached the next corner Vorsky emerged.

"Now, Alla," Galaunov said. "Please stay at this corner. As long as there is nobody in that side street, don't move. If you see somebody approaching start walking towards us."

"Don't worry, I'll be your sentry."

"You don't want this child involved, Nikolai Ivanovich," the refusenik said, "so I assume it is something sensitive.

How is your life as a Lenin prize laureate with the heart of a Russian nationalist?"

"My life is more or less happy, my friend. Unlike you I am at home. What I am here for concerns a Jewish physicist who wants to leave Russia. He is in jail in Kalinin. Would you help get the information about him to the West?"

"Tell me about it," the refusenik said.

Galaunov told the story of Magidov, Irina and Tarutin. When he had finished, Vorsky repeated the names of to be sure he had gotten them correct.

"Nikolai Ivanovich, usually it is not advisable to rely on one person's word when such a story is being made known abroad. But this time it comes from you, and I trust you. I shall do my best. If I am lucky, this information will reach the West in eight to twelve hours. I hope I shall complete the task before I am in jail again. I am afraid it may happen at any hour."

"Thank you, my friend," Galaunov said. "I wish I could be of more help to you, but you wouldn't accept money from me, would you?"

Vorsky smiled. "I have never doubted I may rely on you, Nikolai Ivanovich. Thank you, but I am perfectly well off. My regards to Glafira."

"And mine—to your wife and boys."

The refusenik walked away and disappeared behind the corner. Galaunov and Alla walked in the opposite direction.

Alla and Galaunov stood on the platform. A crowd's buzz floated from inside the terminal. Late passengers dragged their suitcases on the dirty snow.

"You'll be home soon, Alla," Galaunov said. "Please, let us know you have arrived. Write me a letter. And remember, you'll always have friends in Kalinin. You are welcome at any time."

Alla did not say anything. She held Galaunov's hand, her aquamarine eyes staring at his face.

"You know I don't have children. But if I did I wish I had a daughter like you." He said these words and bit his tongue.

Galaunov remained motionless on the platform, until the clangs of the train which had left the station completely subsided. He would go back to Kalinin now and report to Boris about the results of his mission.

Chapter 42

THE TRAIN CARRYING ALLA AND GALAUNOV TO MOSCOW disappeared behind a turn; Boris and Irina left the station and headed to the University.

"I have missed so many classes," Irina said. "They may use it as a pretext to kick me out of the University. My only hope is my professor, Oleg Nikiforovich Talin, who has always singled me out as his favorite student."

"Which means you are excellent in English."

"I have been trying," Irina said.

"Then he may cover up for you."

"Unless he is too scared by my father's story."

"I know Talin well," Boris said. "Of course he is scared because his own situation is far from secure. But Talin despises this madhouse."

Irina said, "Of course Talin would never admit it openly but it is no secret that he reads smuggled English books."

"Not to mention," Boris said, "that he listens to the BBC and Voice of America in English. Talin has access to information."

"Which may make him better informed but no less scared."

"What I mean," Boris said, "were it in Talin's power to decide, your father's story would induce Talin to forgive your truancy. The question is how much your dean learned about your absences through his stool-pigeons."

"I'll just walk into the class and see what will happen."

"Fine," Boris said. "Meanwhile we cannot do anything more today. We have to wait until Galaunov tells us the results of his trip."

They walked into the University building.

"I'll meet you after your classes," Boris said. Irina smiled, waved her hand and disappeared behind the door to the English classroom. Boris waited for several minutes but Irina did not walk out.

Boris crossed the street and walked until he was in front of the dorm.

A white ambulance van stood, next to the dorm entrance, big red crosses on its sides, engine idling. A bulky man in a white smock and the bearing of a circus wrestler stood leaning against the van's back door.

As Boris walked into the entrance hall the janitor saw Boris and her eyes opened wider. Boris had the impression that the woman wanted to tell him something. He shrugged and started climbing the stairs.

"Comrade Tarutin," the janitor said in a very low voice. Boris turned around.

"Yes, Auntie, do you want to tell me something?"

The janitor remained silent, only her eyes seemed to glow. Boris waited but the old woman did not speak.

"Is it something about this ambulance?"

The janitor shook her head slightly. Perplexed by her odd behavior Boris ran up the stairs.

He approached his room and as he was about to insert

the key in the lock he stopped. He sensed the odor of tobacco smoke from his room.

Artamon's warning emerged in Boris's mind. "*They would probably opt for a covert trick.*"

Boris put the key back in his pocket, turned and walked down the stairway.

Before descending the stairs he stopped. In the middle of a bright day, in the university building full of people, what could they do to him? And if he fled now, where to? Should he run away as a hare from a fox because of some vague feeling of jeopardy? Was he not in his own country? They did not grab people just like that any longer. Boris turned again and walked to his door.

He tried the knob of his door, but it was locked. Boris inserted his key into the lock and as the door opened the odor of tobacco smoke wafted from his room. Angry, he yanked the door open and stepped in.

He saw three men, two on his sofa, one with a cigarette in his mouth; the third man stood at the window. All three of them were a good deal taller and heavier than Boris.

The man who stood at the window squeezed a small rubber ball. On the floor lay a folded stretcher like those used in ambulances.

Boris's eyes had grasped all this in a fraction of a second. Before he could make another move, the two sitting men jumped up from the sofa. One of them, in a quick, dexterous motion, slid between Boris and the door.

"What the devil are you doing in my room?" Boris said.

"Comrade Tarutin, Boris Petrovich?" the man at the window said in a low voice.

"And who are you?" Boris said. The two men grabbed his hands, twisted them behind his back as the third man leaped towards Boris and forced the black rubber ball into his mouth.

Powerful hands turned his body forcing it down on the sofa. He felt a rope tying his legs together.

The rubber ball cramped his tongue but he did not feel any fear. He watched as if from some observation point outside his body.

Still holding Boris's hands firmly, they skillfully took off his coat and jacket. While one of the men rolled up his shirt sleeve, Boris saw a syringe in the man's hands. Then he felt the bite of a needle in his upper arm. Burning heat spread from the spot of the injection.

They continued to hold his hands firmly. Minutes went by. The burning sensation in Boris's arm gradually subsided. Then he started feeling dizzy. One of the men glanced at his watch.

"A couple of minutes more to be on the safe side," the man said in a very low voice. Then he put a cigarette in his mouth.

Boris saw blue rings of smoke floating above the man's head. A few more minutes passed. The man with the cigarette glanced at his watch.

"That's it," he said. "I think he's ready."

The heavy weight on Boris's legs vanished. Somebody's hand pulled the rubber ball from his mouth.

Boris could not move his tongue. A numbness encompassed his whole body. The figures of the three men seemed to be veiled in a grayish fog, but his mind was clear. He had been drugged but he felt content, as if what was occurring to him was of no significance. Two men lifted the stretcher and the third man opened the door.

* * *

He had lost the feeling of time. How long had he been

in this van, inside a dark garage? Maybe minutes? Or hours? Or maybe days?

He had fallen asleep one more time, when a sound woke him. Apparently, a gate opened; he heard the roar of a car rolling into the garage. The stench of exhaust fumes reached him. The car's engine snorted and then its sound died. A strip of light fell on the mat glass of the van's back door. Then footsteps approached the van. Its back rolled open.

The light beam struck Boris's eyes, and through the motley spots dancing before his pupils, he discerned dim figures which seemed to be the same big-framed men in white smocks. Two of them climbed into the van. Then they hauled in another stretcher with a body on it which they placed next to Boris.

Before the men closed the van's door, Boris's eyes, still dazzled by the light beam, saw the bulge of white plaster over the mouth of the person on the second stretcher.

Even before his mind had consciously decoded the meaning of the curl of auburn hair, the gracious line of the nose and the shadow on the sunken cheek Boris's heart shrank in horror. This woman was Irina.

PART 7

Chapter 43

MISHA BERKIN WAS ON THE TOP OF ALL EVENTS IN THE Party Central Committee. To survive and succeed, a Party *apparatchik* must be permanently informed about trends.

One of the secrets of Misha's twenty-year-long survival in the Party *apparat* was his uncanny ability to zero in on the best possible shadow figure, to enlist this man as his link to the highest level of the hierarchy and to cultivate this relationship.

Misha used many different techniques to maintain his link's willingness to supply information. Above all, however, Misha favored one method proven through centuries in every form of society. It was what the Russian tradition had sanctified under the irreverent name of bribe.

Misha felt everybody could be bribed but the bribe must suit the desires of the particular individual.

In the Central Committee Misha's link was a man madly infatuated with fishing and vodka. To accommodate this innocent passion, Misha had experts in the Caspian Sea select from daily catches, samples of large sturgeons. Kept alive, in special containers filled with sea water, the sturgeons were transported 2,000 kilometers, from the Caspian sea to Kalinin. Here they were kept in a special pool waiting until Misha's link would arrive for his next fishing endeavor.

The beauty of this arrangement for the Moscow man was that Kalinin was located next door to Moscow yet it was in another administrative region. Thus the man from Moscow could escape on any Sunday to his beloved sturgeons and vodka; it took less than an hour on a helicopter from Moscow to Kalinin. Since his hobby took place beyond the Moscow region, nobody in Moscow ever saw him in his favorite state of intoxication.

It was Saturday afternoon and Misha was not expecting any drastic developments in Moscow at this time. He had called up his link because it was his iron-clad rule not to miss a single day in his vigil.

"Hello, number eleven," the man in Moscow said. "There is news. You will not like it."

Misha remained silent. After a pause, the Moscow man continued, "As of Monday, number zero will have been sent *to where Makar had never driven calves*."

Misha's heart dropped. "Number zero" was how they had been referring to Korytov's big shot brother-in-law in the Central Committee, Stepan Kalyazin. The common adage *sent to where Makar had never driven calves*, in this case meant dismissal. It meant a civil death. A plunge into nothing. A Party official on Kalyazin's level, once dismissed would become a non-person.

Kalyazin, and by default, Korytov, were not members of the new Master's inner circle. But Misha expected the old fox Kalyazin to survive and eventually to thrive under the new master. Without Kalyazin on top the fate of Korytov had been sealed as well.

"Are you still listening?" the man in Moscow said.

During these few seconds of digesting the sudden news from Moscow, Misha's mind went through a rapid analysis of his options. His decision was instant. There was no longer a way to save Korytov from dismissal but there could still be a chance to make his collapse less painful. And Misha owed it to himself in the first place to try cushioning Korytov's fall.

"Thank you, twenty-two," Misha said. "I'll secure a letter from number one with a request for immediate retirement for health reasons. Would you try to get this request honored?"

The man in Moscow knew that "number one" meant Korytov. After a short pause the Moscow man said, "Yes, it may be a good idea. Of course this letter must arrive today through telex. And it better be supported by good evidence of sincerity."

"I understand," Misha said. "I'll try to arrange for appropriate evidence of our sincerity."

"You better do it," the man in Moscow said. They both knew what might have served as an "evidence of sincerity." Sturgeons would no longer suffice to cushion the imminent Korytov's and, hence, Misha's fall. Yes, this time it had to be something really valuable.

Misha replaced the receiver and leaned back in his rocking chair. He closed his eyes and let his mind mull over the situation. There were several things which had to be done. Misha's mind listed them quickly in the order of importance as he knew he had only 36 hours to do the job.

Fifteen minutes later when Misha opened his eyes, there was a complete plan ready in his head with a clear-cut schedule of sequential actions.

He started with a call to Korytov. The region Czar and Lord turned out to be busy with a couple of female stenographers.

Misha knew that Korytov's attempts to substitute his stenographers for the 13-year-old girl did not work. Under usual circumstances Misha would never interrupt Korytov's entertainment. More so since these whores were reporting to Misha whatever happened between them and Korytov.

Today everything changed.

And for the first time in 20 years, Misha felt defiance and anger thinking of Korytov. Were it not for his paternal ancestry, Misha thought, he could have been a political figure in his own right. Even though Misha knew that his career was about to collapse he felt a semblance of relief. The worst event he had always feared had finally occurred. This turned out to be easier than permanent foreboding.

And even more than relief, the inglorious end of Korytov's career brought a gloating satisfaction in Misha's heart. This end was a just reward for the old fool.

But Misha's feelings were one thing, his sound judgment something altogether different. He would do what he could to save Korytov and thus himself from the consequences of the new upheaval in the Party.

Misha walked from his office into the narrow corridor. Here to his right, was the entrance to Korytov's private office with its chain of rooms hidden behind sliding partitions.

Misha dialed the code number on the device hidden in a wall recess and the heavy partition rolled back into the wall. Misha walked into the Lord's sanctuary.

The first room Misha walked through was empty. A telephone on the desk blinked red. Misha stopped at the next door and listened. He heard some muted voices. He knocked. The sounds of the voices vanished. The silence lasted for a few seconds. Then Misha heard Korytov asking, "Who is there?"

"Berkin. Dress yourself before I walk in. And you,

girls get out at once," Misha said loudly. "At once!" he repeated.

He waited half a minute and then pushed open the door. He saw Korytov with his pants already on but still barefoot and without a shirt. Korytov's face displayed a mixture of perplexity, embarrassment and fear. The half-dressed women grabbed their clothes and scampered out.

Korytov stared at Misha. The mere appearance of his aide in this place warned Korytov that some catastrophic event had occurred. He waited, his hands quivering.

"*Finita la comedia,*" Misha said.

Korytov did not speak any language except Russian. Unlike Misha, Korytov had never been a theater fan or a book reader. But the old man seemed to have understood its meaning. Tears appeared in his eyes.

"Kalyazin is out," Misha said. "Now dress and I'll tell you what to do. And don't try to deviate from what I tell you. Your only chance to soften the blow is to follow my instructions exactly." And without waiting for Korytov's answer, Misha walked out.

Back in the first room, Misha took the seat at Korytov's desk. He waited, looking at the twinkling lights on the telephones. In a few minutes Korytov walked in.

"Take a paper and a pen," Misha said. "And write down what I tell you. Write it legibly; it would be better not to type it as the typist could spread rumors prematurely. And check with me on the spelling of every word."

Following Misha's dictation he wrote a letter of resignation addressed to the Central Committee of the Communist Party of the Soviet Union.

"You wait here," Misha said. "Don't answer the telephone, do you understand? I'll be back in a few minutes."

Misha went to his communication room. He arranged for a telex to Moscow and then walked back to Korytov's inner office.

"Now, a couple of other things," Misha said. "One is, I suggest that you request an apartment in the compound for special pensioners. Vacate both the Big *Dacha* and the apartment on Prospect Mira at once. You may still get an apartment of your choice in the special pensioners' compound and I believe you may be left alone there. Otherwise, on Monday you will be kicked out and whatever is assigned as your new residence would depend on a somebody's whim."

Korytov moaned. Misha waited.

"How can I?" Korytov said, his voice distorted in pain. "Ksenia! She would not agree to move out on our own."

"You forget that Ksenia's opinions are of no consequence any longer," Misha said. "She is Kalyazina, isn't she? And being Kalyazina today is something different from what it was."

Korytov's body shook uncontrollably.

"And now," Misha said, "where is Potyomkin's diamond?"

"I gave it to Ksenia yesterday," Korytov said, more tears appearing in his eyes.

"You must take it back immediately. Immediately! Will you do it or you want me to handle it?"

"I'll do it," Korytov said hurriedly. Amid the debris of his career the old man would enjoy the chance to repay all the humiliation he had suffered at the hands of his wife during the long years of their miserable marriage.

"Yes, Misha, you're right. Give the damned diamond back to Rashkov, let him choke with it."

"Back to Rashkov?" Misha said. No, there's a better place for this diamond. Our lives depend on it."

"You know better, Misha," Korytov said.

"As soon as Rashkov finds out about your resignation," Misha continued, "he'll remember the diamond. But he will not move a finger until he knows the diamond's whereabouts."

"Right, Misha," Korytov said.

"And when he finds out," Misha said, "he will never mention its existence, or it will backfire."

"You know better," Korytov said.

"Rush now. Don't come back without the stone, do you understand? I have to make some calls to destroy traces of some decisions we made recently. Otherwise the new Master may make mincemeat of us."

"Misha," Korytov continued in trembling voice. "Will you be able to bury all those decisions?"

Misha looked at Korytov. "Yes," he said. "Unless you have done something stupid of which I have no knowledge. Have you?"

Korytov hesitated seemingly.

"Don't be foolish, spill it," Misha said sternly.

"I don't know," Korytov mumbled. "Misha, this girl, Alla Shumilova. She listened to our talks over the phone. I hope she paid no attention, but I don't know."

Misha frowned slightly as he digested this new information.

"Where is the girl now?" Misha said.

"I think on a train or maybe already in Samarkand. Yes, she was supposed to take a train to Samarkand on Thursday."

"So, I'll have to take care of this as well," Misha said. "Now get the diamond, and fast. Comb your hair before you walk out. And re-button your shirt properly."

Back in his office, Misha called up his link in Moscow.

"The letter from number one has been telexed," Misha said. "Please check if it arrived. I don't want complications because some fucking piece of paper went astray."

The Moscow man just grunted.

"The evidence of sincerity will follow," Misha said. I

have a request though. I'll bring it to you myself on Monday. Would you trust my word?"

"In this situation nobody's word can substitute for real evidence." The voice of the Moscow man sounded slightly irritated now.

"If you do not have it by Monday afternoon," Misha said, "you still have time to cancel arrangements for number one's retirement. It is my last request."

"But not later than early afternoon on Monday," the man in Moscow said drily.

Misha's next call was to the man in charge of *special operations*. The telephone in that man's office rang but nobody picked up the receiver.

There was no answer at the man's home either.

Misha did not know how "special operations" such as the one with Boris Tarutin and Irina Magidova were implemented. What Misha did know was that in view of the news from Moscow the operation had to be stopped. If it was not too late.

If he could not stop the operation the Militsia and the Prosecutor's office would conduct an investigation and conclude it was Misha's design—that he was the directing hand.

Before Misha received the news from Moscow, he had been confident that his man in charge of the operation would create a fatal accident involving citizens Tarutin and Magidova.

The news from Moscow had altered the entire situation. Beginning Monday, Misha would no longer have strings to pull and events could go awry. And there would be no lack of witnesses who would love to point a finger at Korytov and Misha. He had to pave Tarutin.

Since he could not reach the man in charge of the operation Misha had to stop in himself.

The door of Misha's office opened and Korytov's figure

appeared. Without entering the room Korytov extended his hand. There was a small box in it.

Misha stretched his hand and his boss made a few irresolute steps forward until his extended hand touched that of Misha. The box slid into Misha's palm.

Misha opened the lid and stared for a while at the enormous diamond. Sparkles of red and blue flames burned in its bottomless blue depth.

Chapter 44

The first place Misha had to examine was Boris Tarutin's room. If Boris was still home, Misha could hide Tarutin and his girlfriend until the operation was called off.

Misha told his chauffeur to wait at the curb and walked into the university building.

At the janitor's desk, a girl-student was sitting. It was close to 10 pm and visits to the dorms were only allowed until eight pm. Misha displayed his certificate and said, "*Obkom*. Where is assistant Tarutin's room?"

"Room 409, fourth floor."

Misha trudged up the stairs. When he reached the fourth floor he stopped to rest before walking to room 409.

Misha reviewed the numbers and deduced that room 409 must be the fifth to his left.

He looked and saw the fifth door was ajar. Two men stood next to it talking to each other.

Misha recognized one of these men, investigator Sergeev

of the city Prosecutor's office. He did not know the second man.

Sergeev's face was turned half-away so that the investigator did not see Misha. The blond-bearded man did not know Misha Berkin.

Misha remained close to the door trying to overhear the conversation between Sergeev and the tall man.

"That is why I am worried about Boris," Sergeev said.

"I am worried too," the bear-like man said. I just wanted to report to Boris about my trip to Moscow."

Sergeev said, "he is not here. Obviously something irregular has happened. The door in not locked, tobacco ashes on the floor and Boris never smoked."

"What if we ask neighbors about Boris?" Galaunov said.

"We may try," Sergeev said. The footsteps of the two men approached the kitchen.

Misha Berkin glanced around. There was no place for him to hide. He picked up a pan from the nearest table and took a place behind the two women waiting for their turn at the gas range.

With his back to the door, he saw vague reflections of Sergeev and Galaunov in the window pane as the two men appeared in the kitchen.

"Excuse me, comrades," Sergeev said in a loud voice. "Do you know Tarutin, room 409?"

Several faces turned to the door.

"He is sick," one of the women said. "An ambulance took him away."

Another woman said, "Maybe he was just drunk."

"What are you talking about?" the first woman said. I know Boris well; he is not a drinker."

The first woman said I saw Boris's face when they took him on a stretcher. You could see he was really sick. Cheeks burning, eyes muddy."

"When did it happen?" Sergeev said.

"A few hours ago," the woman said. She then looked suspiciously at Misha Berkin and at the pan in his hands.

"What are you doing here?" she said. She put her pan on the floor and crossed her plump hands over her formidable bosom.

Misha smiled. "I am a relative of the Bogomilovs," he said in a low voice. "Visiting with them." The woman stared at him now with the increased suspicion. "From Murom?" she said.

"From Murom," Misha answered. He waited for Sergeev and Galaunov to leave. He had learned enough, now he wanted to sneak out unnoticed by Sergeev.

He failed to do so. Sergeev had recognized Misha Berkin of the *obkom* but could not believe his own eyes.

"Comrade Berkin," Sergeev said, astonishment ringing in his voice.

Again, Misha's decision was instant. It was imperative to stop the operation with Tarutin and his girlfriend. Misha's quick mind had realized immediately how these two people could become instrumental in stopping operation A-1.

Misha turned around to face the two men.

"You both are Tarutin's friends, are you not?" Misha said setting the pan back on the table.

Galaunov and Sergeev glanced at each other.

"Nikolai Ivanovich, meet comrade Berkin, of the *obkom*," Sergeev said. "Comrade Berkin, this is."

"Professor Galaunov," Misha said. "I know. Everybody knows our region's Lenin prize winner. Let's get out and not disturb these nice women."

They walked into the corridor; Sergeev's and Galaunov's faces were puzzled.

"Now, comrades, if you want to extricate your friend Tarutin from his predicament, we must hurry."

Galaunov said. "Is he in some hospital?"

"That is what I am going to find out," Misha said. "Trust me."

Sergeev, with a pensive expression on his face, touched Galaunov's sleeve and said, "I believe, Nikolai Ivanovich, we shall accept with gratitude comrade Berkin's offer. Comrade Berkin, I won't ask any questions, just tell us what to do."

Misha's car, with the *obkom*'s license plates, rushed through intersections ignoring red lights. At a big iron gate Misha waved his certificate through the lowered window of his car. This was a guarded compound where privileged men assigned to covert jobs of special character, lived with their families.

Misha leapt from the car, ran to the entrance and knocked at one of the doors on the second floor. There was no answer.

"The man we are looking for," Misha said to Sergeev and Galaunov, most probably went to his *dacha* with his wife and children. Devil knows where this *dacha* may be."

"Comrade Berkin," Sergeev said. "There are just a few possible locations where such people may have a *dacha*. It must be a cluster of *dachas* and an unmarked road leading to them and a guard on duty at this access road. Your certificate, comrade Berkin, must serve as a pass to enter these places. So, what is the man's name?"

"I may not tell this man's name," Misha said.

"Then why the devil have you requested our assistance?" Galaunov growled. Sergeev touched Galaunov's sleeve as if appealing to him to calm down. "Comrade Berkin," Sergeev said. "I assure you I and Nikolai Ivanovich will forget this man's name as soon as we locate him."

Misha said, "The man who lives in this apartment is the only one who can tell us where Tarutin is. Well, it doesn't matter any more," Misha said after a long pause. "This man's name is Tigranyan."

The beams of the car's headlights danced on the rows of poplars lining the asphalt strip of road. The car, a Volga sedan, rattled and screamed on the road's curves.

"Faster, my boy," Misha said to his chauffeur. The speedometer's pointer crawled up to the one-hundred-twenty kilometers mark.

"It must be soon, to the left," Sergeev said, when a pole with a number on it flashed by. "You better slow down so you won't miss the access road."

"That's it," Misha and Galaunov said in one voice. To their left an asphalt strip deviated from the main road. The car's light-beam rocked on the bushes of bird-cherry, their naked twigs black against the background of a snow-clad hill.

Then a chain-link fence rose up from the darkness, with a closed gate across the road. The chauffeur pressed the brakes and the car's front bumper stopped a few centimeters from the gate.

"This is where your assistance comes in," Misha Berkin said.

"You mean, we have to break through the gate?" Sergeev said. "Comrade Galaunov may be indeed handy for such a task."

"By no means," Misha said. "I know something about such compounds. I live in one myself. Behind this gate, in about fifty meters farther on the road, there must be a second gate and a booth. If we honk, a guard will come here. But he will not allow us in unless we display a special pass.

"But in your position," Sergeev said. "wouldn't your certificate open every door in the Kalinin region?"

"I may have some influence over some events in this region, true," Misha said, "But I can do this over the phone from my office. In the field, my certificate does not mean much to such people as guards at gates."

You mean," Sergeev said, "my status as an investigator."

"Yes," Misha said, "You've got it. These guards understand the authority of an investigator of the Prosecution office. It's next only to the KGB."

"Then what can my role be?" Galaunov said. "A professor at the university."

"We don't know what kind of a situation we may encounter," Misha said. "Maybe, somewhere down the road—"

"—We will need to impress somebody with the Lenin Prize winner title," Sergeev finished.

"Right," Misha said. "Comrade Sergeev has taken the words from my mouth. Now please, give them a good long honk," he said to the chauffeur.

Soon a man's figure appeared behind the gate. The guard in a sheepskin *tulup*, stayed behind the gate waiting silently.

Sergeev half-opened the car's door and said, "Do you have Armenians living here?"

"I don't know if they are Armenians or Turks or who knows what," the guard said. "It's not my job to know."

"I am an investigator of the Prosecutor's office," Sergeev said. "Here is my certificate. I order you to answer my question to the best of your knowledge under the threat of a criminal prosecution. It is a State affair. Is a person by the name of Tigranyan living in this place?"

The guard's tone changed. With a hint of an apology, he said, "Comrade investigator, I don't know the names. They show me their passes when they come in or leave. I just check the photographs against the faces."

"But you must have a list of all the *dachas'* inhabitants," Sergeev said. "Where is it? You better assist us otherwise you may be accused of obstructing the investigation."

"Let me see your certificate," the guard said. Sergeev crawled out of the car and approached the gate. The guard fetched a flashlight from his pocket. He read the certificate. Then he directed the flashlight at Sergeev's face, comparing it with the photograph.

"I can't let you in on my own, without a pass. No exception, these are my orders, comrade investigator. What is the name you want? Tigranyan? I'll check."

He walked away into the darkness. Sergeev returned to the car and closed the door.

The engine continued idling and the four men remained silent. Minutes went by.

The guard's figure appeared again in the beam. He approached the gate and said, "There is some Armenian name on the list. Arutunyan. Is that who you want?"

"No. Let's hurry to the place off the road to Torzhok," Sergeev said.

The car roared again on the main road, this time back to Kalinin. The clock on the dashboard showed a quarter to twelve.

The clock showed twenty after twelve when they rushed into the city. The car's roar, reflected from buildings, thundered in the empty streets.

They drove along the Volga, crossed the bridge and continued their mad run westward along a tram railway. In 15 minutes they passed the tram's end station and dashed onto a country road, past a sign, "Torzhok 60 km."

It was about two o'clock when they noticed a side road.

At about 15 minutes after two they stopped in front of another chain-link gate crossing the road.

It was about twenty minutes before three when they drove back to the main road after they had found that no Armenians had *dachas* in this cluster.

"Well, there is only one more place I know of," Sergeev said. "Off the road to Staritsa, south-west of Kalinin. Unless comrade Berkin knows more than I do."

"I know only the places where the *obkom*'s people have *dachas*," Misha said. "Tigranyan will not be found there. Let's try that place off the road to Staritsa."

"Gasoline," the chauffeur said. He pointed at the gas level guage. The tank was almost empty.

"Then, first to the *obkom's* garage," Misha said. "Either you fill the tank there or we take another car."

Sergeev said, "In the motel they have a gas station for foreigners. They may allow us to fill our tank there."

The Volga sedan rolled into the motel's driveway. They rang a bell and a yawning woman in a shawl appeared.

"What do you want at this hour?" the woman said.

"Gasoline."

The woman said, "Our gasoline is for our guests only."

"Look at this, mother," Sergeev said, displaying his certificate. "Prosecutor's office. A state affair. I order you to assist us in filling the tank of our car. Immediately!"

The woman stared at the certificate. "Why didn't you say so at once? Take seats in the lobby. I'll wake somebody to help you."

"Ready," the chauffeur said five minutes later. It was three-thirty when the Volga sedan rolled out of the motel's driveway onto the road.

They approached the tram's end station when an ambulance van appeared on the otherwise deserted street. It moved from the town toward the road to Torzhok. In the sedan's headlights big red crosses on the van's sides glared for a moment and then the van sank in the night.

"Where could they be going?" Galaunov said. "This is

the end of the town. Ambulances do not serve the countryside."

"Maybe," Sergeev said, "some doctor works in Kalinin but live in Mednoe. He may be just going home after a night shift in a hospital."

It was close to four o'clock when the Volga sedan slowed down at the gate of the last *dacha* cluster, southwest of the city.

By four-thirty the man named Tigranyan, with house shoes on his feet, a trenchcoat thrown over his shoulders, appeared at the compound's gate. In the headlight's beam, his prune-like black eyes looked without any expression at the sedan with the chauffeur and three other people in it.

"We have spent the night looking for you," Misha said through the lowered car's window. "Where are Tarutin and the girl?"

"What girl?" Galaunov said. Sergeev touched Galaunov's sleeve. "No questions," he whispered.

"What do you mean where are they?" Tigranyan said. "Everything is going according to the plan."

"You must stop A-1," Misha whispered, leaning out of the car's window. "Hurry up!"

Tigranyan stuck his head into the car's window and looked at the clock on the dashboard. "Four-thirty," he said. "I am afraid, it is too late."

Chapter 45

ONCE AGAIN, A SOUND OF AN OPENING DOOR WOKE BORIS. A triangle of light fell on the van's back door. A flashlight beam struck his eyes. He sensed Irina's movement next to him and heard her moan. Figures of men appeared on the background of the van's door. He thought there were three of them. The men sat down on the van's left-side bench and placed their feet on Boris's body. The engine roared. The gate squeaked and the van rolled out of the garage.

To Boris's left, he sensed the warmth of Irina's body, while on his right, a chilly touch of the night frost crawled gradually deeper under his shirt. His back had been freezing, the chill flowing through the stretcher's canvas from the van's floor.

The van rocked again as if descending from the road, rolled a few seconds on what seemed to be a non-paved surface, and stopped. The lieutenant opened the van's back and clambered out. He would have to wait until his confederates stole a car from the motel.

The Lieutenant and the chauffeur exchanged a few words.

They talked about the weather. They seemed to be glad that there was enough snow on the ground which would certainly be good for the winter-crops.

Then the driver said, "Comrade Lieutenant, why won't you let me do it, tonight? Last time you assigned Baranov to drive the hit-car; isn't it my turn to get a bonus?"

"Don't worry, your time will come," the lieutenant said. "I promised this night to Baranov."

They remained silent now. Then Boris heard remote footsteps. "Who the devil can be walking on the road at this time?" the lieutenant said.

"Look, there he is," the driver said. "Without the Volvo, walking."

The footsteps came closer.

"We couldn't do anything with the Volvo without making a lot of noise," the man who came on foot said. "This Volvo has some damn protection on its door, it would take drilling to open it."

"It is four-thirty now," the lieutenant said. "We are behind schedule. Is Baranov waiting in the parking lot?"

"Yes, comrade lieutenant."

"The noise of our van may attract attention. You better run like crazy, and come back with the Volkswagen."

"Yes, comrade lieutenant," the third man said.

After a while the roar of an approaching car made the glass in the van's back door vibrate slightly. The car slowed down and swerved off the road. Its engine stopped abruptly, then the thud of a slammed car door sounded.

"Now, boys," the lieutenant said, "we do not have much time. Dawn will be coming soon. So, let's do everything neatly.

"But what about our hundred-gram of vodka?" one of the men said.

"Sure," the lieutenant said. "It is your sacred right. Just, do it fast. Baranov, fetched the bottle."

A bottle was uncorked.

"Uh, damned stuff," a voice said. "Good. I feel better now." They took swigs from a bottle."

"Done?" the lieutenant said. "So, start with the woman."

The back door of the van swung open. It faced the Eastern sky and a pale sign of the approaching dawn quivered. Then the dark figures of the men obstructed the view. The men had left the door open and carried Irina away from the van.

Then Boris heard a thump, as if a body fell on the ground.

"Drag her here," the lieutenant said. "Yes, this way. And don't shudder, keep yourself composed. The first time it is always a little scary. Just think about your bonus."

The men returned and pulled the stretcher with Boris out of the van.

They carried Boris toward the road. They dropped the stretcher and Boris fell onto the frosty asphalt. The cruel jolt stunned him for a while.

As far as Boris could see, he and Irina had their feet towards each other their bodies at an obtuse angle forming a chevron.

Now, boys, hurry up! Baranov, into the car! Everybody else watch! Go!"

Boris heard the roar of the engine. On the fringe of his vision he saw the silhouette of the Volkswagen. It rocked, climbed back onto the road, and made a U-turn.

"Comrade lieutenant, lights," one of the men shouted.

Quick, drag them both aside."

Powerful hands clutched Boris under his armpits and feet. Panting, two men ran heavily toward the forest, carrying Boris with them, then they let Boris fall into a ditch full of snow. The other two men carried Irina to the other side of the road.

The ditch was not deep enough to cover Boris's body. His head was partly above the edge of the ditch. He saw the bright lights of an approaching car. Judging by the sound the car was moving at a very high rate of speed and in a few seconds it would flash by.

The beam of the approaching car threw a cone of light on the ambulance van, the red crosses on the ambulance's sides glittering.

"Comrade lieutenant, they're braking," a voice shouted.

"Away from the road! I'll take care of them," the lieutenant barked.

The car stopped a few steps from the van's location. Its doors swung open on both sides.

"In the name of the Party," a voice sounded. Then Boris saw men running from the sedan towards the ambulance.

There was something unusual about the figure of the man who ran ahead of the others. Boris realized that the man wore a trenchcoat, but his legs were naked, and he wore house slippers.

"Lieutenant Andronov, it's me. Where are the subjects?"

"Colonel Tigranyan," the lieutenant said, his voice expressing astonishment. "Lieutenant Andronov reporting. The operation is in progress. Due to an unexpected complication there is a delay in the schedule. The operation will be completed in—"

"Stop, lieutenant. Call your people off. It was simply a test. Do you understand? A test of your preparedness. Release the subjects at once."

Boris could not walk by himself. Sergeev and Galaunov helped him into the car.

When his powerless body leaned against the back seat the beam of a flashlight fell on Irina's face. She slumped onto the car seat next to Boris.

"How are you feeling?" Sergeev said, staring at Boris through the opened car's window.

"Fine," said Boris.

"There was never a danger to your lives," a man standing next to Sergeev said.

"This is comrade Berkin," Sergeev said. "Of the *obkom*."

"Remember, please," Berkin continued. "This was merely a test! Thank you for playing your role so skillfully."

Chapter 46

WHEN MISHA TOLD TARUTIN AND IRINA THAT THERE WAS never any danger to their lives, he was following Party practice of never admitting the truth about covert actions. He did not expect them to believe the "test" version. Nor did Misha expect that Tarutin and Irina would keep quiet about the experience. So Misha concocted a new scheme.

From Torzhok road, Misha's chauffeur drove them all home. It was six in the morning when Misha arrived in the *obkom*.

He watched the faint lights on the telephones. He could not comprehend now that in 24 hours he wouldn't even be allowed to enter this office.

Close to seven he gave up his attempts to rest. He switched on the lights and started making calls.

Some of his calls were made within the city of Kalinin, others to Samarkand. People owed favors to Misha and today he would request they pay off those old debts.

While making his third call in Kalinin, Misha learned something of interest a KGB man, after listening to Misha's instructions, told him that an invitation had arrived from Israel for Yosif Markovich Magidov and his daughter Irina. The Post office would not deliver a letter from Israel to Magidov so it forwarded the envelope to the KGB.

Misha could have completed his plan without the invitation but it simplified the procedure he had designed. It did not matter that the invitation was only for the Magidovs. Misha chuckled when he added Tarutin to the Magidovs.

He made all his calls. It was all arranged.

* * *

Somebody hit Boris's head cruelly, over and over again. He tried to cover his head with his hands. Then he woke up, his heart pounding heavily. He was gasping for air.

Nobody was hitting him. He was alone in his room, lying on his sofa. Boris had slept the whole day as well as through the night. His backbone ached. He tried to stretch to alleviate the pain but he couldn't seem to relieve the cramped muscles and overstrained bones.

The bangs were real though. Somebody was knocking on his door persistently. "Tarutin! Tarutin! Wake up! Urgent matter!"

Boris got up, still dizzy, and walked to the door. A Militsioner stood in the corridor.

"Citizen Tarutin?" the Militsioner said. "You must go at once to the region Authority of Internal Affairs. I'll show you the way."

"What do you mean? Am I arrested?"

"No!" the Militsioner protested vigorously.

The Militsioner apparently had noticed that Tarutin was not quite well. "Calm down, citizen. Nothing to be concerned about!"

"What am I summoned for?"

"I don't know, citizen. I don't know. Just, the department which is summoning you has nothing to do with arrests or criminals. Hurry! They are waiting for you."

"May I have a cup of tea first?"

Boris splashed cold water on his face. Then he rubbed his face with a rough towel and started feeling better. The Militsioner waited patiently, not trying to hurry him. After Boris has swallowed a few gulps of hot tea and bitten at a chunk of bread he felt almost normal.

On the Volga's left bank they entered the yellow three-story building of the region Authority of Internal Affairs. On the second floor a sign read "Passport Department."

They walked into the corridor. And then Boris saw a woman's figure in a claret-red coat with a heap of auburn hair. A lone figure in the deserted corridor sitting on a bench, her beautifully shaped runner's legs with the knees exposed. Before his eyes had recognized her, his heart told him it was Irina.

Sadness had bent down the corners of her eyes.

She touched Boris's arm. A faint spark of joy flickered in her eyes.

"Did they tell you what we are here for?" Boris said, holding Irina's hand.

"They told me I am to meet my father here. And you?"

Boris had no time to answer. He heard the sound of an opening door and Irina's face lit up with excitement. She leaped past Boris. Boris turned. Professor Yosif Markovich Magidov stood there as Irina embraced him and pressed her face to his shoulder.

Magidov's face looked shrunken. His eyes had sunk deep under his high forehead. Then Boris realized that Magidov's curly brown hair had been shaved clean in the jail.

Two men in uniform appeared at the door. One of them glanced at Magidov and said, "Yes, I accept him, here is my signature. Now, unlock the manacles."

"What a devilish invention, these manacles," he said. "The slightest move causes them to shrink and bite into one's flesh. I managed to be cautious until Irina appeared. I jerked my hands then inadvertently and nearly crushed my wrists.

The officer said, "Imported stuff. Americans supply these handcuffs to us."

There was nobody else in the corridor except for the three of them. Magidov took a few steps forward and Irina took his hand.

They took seats on a bench which stood alongside the windows lit gray by the approaching dawn.

"Did they tell you what are you here for?" Irina said.

"No," Magidov said.

"At least they have not deceived Irina," Boris said. "They told her she would meet you here. I wonder why I am here."

A few hours ago Boris and I were just a thread from being killed."

"No!" Magidov said. "My God, why?"

"We don't know," Boris said, "We are pawns in some game. I suspect our being here now is a continuation of that game."

One of the brown-painted doors opened. A woman appeared in a Lieutenant's uniform.

"Citizen Tarutin?" she asked looking at Boris. Boris nodded. She turned her eyes to Magidov. His clean-shaven skull apparently told her that this man was indeed the one she expected to meet here. Irina's identity seemed to be obvious to her.

"I am Lieutenant Petrova," she said. "Come in, citizens."

They entered the office and took seats in front of her desk.

Lieutenant Petrova opened the top folder on her desk.

"I am authorized to inform you, citizens, that your applications have been approved." Her eyes circled the faces of the three people. They exchanged glances.

"Which applications, may I ask?" Magidov said.

"Your applications for a visa to leave for Israel."

The three people stared at Petrova in disbelief.

"Is it a kind of a joke?" Boris said.

Petrova did not bother to answer such a stupid question.

Magidov turned his face to Irina. "Ira, I see that while I had been in jail an invitation has come from Israel."

"No, Papa," Irina said. "I know of no invitation."

"Then how come they accepted your application? Their rules require that an invitation must accompany—"

"Papa, I never filled out an application. How could I even think of it when you were in jail?"

"Then," Magidov said, "it seems to be something mysterious. Citizen Lieutenant, would you explain—"

"And what about me?" Boris said. "I never applied for a visa to Israel."

Their words did not seem to make any impression on Petrova. "Citizens," she said, "My task is to announce the decision. When and how you have applied for a visa is not what I am entrusted to discuss. The visa will be issued in a few minutes and it will be a joint visa for the entire family. One visa for all three of you."

"The entire family?" Magidov said. "The three of us? Do you imply that Tarutin is a member of our family?"

"Yes, citizen Magidov," Petrova said. "That is what the documents show." She displayed an oblong piece of paper. Astounded, Boris saw it was a marriage certificate dated a month earlier. It stated that citizen Tarutin Boris Petrovich and citizen Magidova Irina Yosifovna had registered their marriage in the Section for the Registration of the Citizens' Status of the Kalinin city council.

"Congratulations," Magidov said staring at his daughter.

"What kind of a joke is this?" Boris said. "Of course, Irina is a wonderful woman and I love her. It hardly justifies registering her marriage to a man without asking him."

"You mean—" Magidov started.

"One month ago," Irina said, "I was not even acquainted with Boris."

The Lieutenant's flat face did not change. "You can't dispute these documents," she said. "They are official. So, you will get your visa and leave our country today."

"Regarding leaving our country," Boris said, "I have never thought of it. The fact is you are kicking me out of my country. Please, show me my application for a visa.

"My task is to announce the decision and deliver your documents," Lieutenant Petrova said. Anything contradicting these documents did not exist for her. "Do you refuse to accept your visa?" she said.

"We accept it," Magidov and Irina said hurriedly in one voice. Boris remained silent.

"It is a family visa," Petrova said. "You cannot leave without Tarutin."

Boris still remained silent. Petrova waited patiently. Then she said, "Stay here, I'll be back momentarily."

She left the room.

"Papa, let me explain," Irina said. "Boris saved your life. He helped me while you were in jail. He fought on your behalf. He uncovered the real murderer. I guess that is why he is not wanted any longer in this country." Her voice trembled and tears glistened in her eyes.

"The real murderer?" Magidov said.

"You don't know! Gavrik killed Baev," Irina said.

"And he killed Valushin," Boris added.

"My God! I see," Magidov said. He stayed silent for some time. Then he continued, "We must decide what to do with this sudden chance to get out of the country. A chance to emigrate. I think, if we miss it now it will never occur again. Boris, I don't want to discuss your feelings towards your country. I understand your anger. It's natural. But, if you want my opinion you have only two options. One is to join us now. And then you will take this country with you in your heart, as millions have done before. Remember Bunin, Nabokov, Sikorsky, Timoshenko."

Magidov continued, "If you refuse to accept the visa, Boris, then they will make mincemeat of you here. And us, of course."

"You are right," Boris said. "I am angry." They manipulate people's lives. He picked up the marriage certificate from the desk. "Luckily they decided to marry two people in love with each other . . ."

The door opened and Lieutenant Petrova walked in.

"Colonel Smolokurov, Chief of the Department, wants you to proceed to his office," she said.

The colonel's office was three times as big as that of Petrova. Four windows faced the Volga.

"Citizens, you are right in noticing that the procedure with your visa was not quite conventional. I understand that you, Magidov, and you, Magidova, have no objections against this arrangement. There was invitation from Israel sent to you after all. It wouldn't have been sent without your request."

"We accept the arrangement," Magidov said. "Why do you forcibly add Tarutin to our family?"

Colonel Smolokurov wrinkled his face slightly, as if in a friendly disapproval. "Come on, Magidov," he said. "Why such expressions! I must tell you that it is the three of you or none of you."

A heavy silence ensued.

"Why do you make waves, Tarutin?" Colonel Smolokurov said, "It will do no good."

Boris turned to Irina and took her head. "Will you marry me—I mean, for real?

"Yes, my love. We owe your our lives as well as our hearts."

"I accept the arrangement," Boris said. Magidov's and Irina's faces relaxed. Irina laughed suddenly although tears still glistened in her eyes. She held Boris's hand and squeezed it nervously. Magidov covered his face with his palms.

"Very good," Smolokurov said calmly. "Irina Magidova-Tarutina, please surrender your passport to Lieutenant Petrova. And you, Tarutin, your passport and military card. Now, we have taken care of your tickets. Lieutenant Petrova will deliver them to you together with your visa. Your train to Vienna will depart today at three pm from the Bielorusski station in Moscow. Our man will accompany you to Moscow and help you to board the train."

"Colonel, what about the payment for the visa? I have heard it must be a considerable amount,"

"No payments in your case," the Colonel said. "Now, please tell us which belongings you would like to take with you. We will dispatch Militsioners to your residences, to bring your personal items." Smolokurov took a piece of paper to write down the list of their personal effects.

Irina laughed nervously.

"I want my personal photographs," Magidov said. "They were taken to the prosecutor's office after the house search. And my pads with calculations."

"I want my runner's honors and certificates," Irina said. "And my runner's shoes. They are now in the apartment of doctor Bronsky. I'll give you the address."

"No problem with that," the Colonel said calmly. "And what about you, Tarutin?"

"I want the photographs of my parents. They are on the wall in my room."

The colonel nodded.

"Then, I want paintings. I have in my room a number of paintings. They are stored behind the cabinet."

Smolokurov's face changed. He seemed to mull over Boris's request. Then he said, "I am sorry. Paintings cannot be taken abroad without your paying a levy. Now, if those paintings are of good quality, the levy may be well beyond of what you are able to pay. Also, a commission of experts must evaluate the paintings. It would take several days to arrange for such an examination. But you must leave today. I am sorry. Whatever else, not paintings."

"I am also sorry, Colonel," Boris said. "If you could have me married to Irina without my participation then you must be able to arrange for a document allowing me to take the paintings. These paintings have never been exhibited or registered anywhere officially."

Irina and Magidov looked at Boris sadly. Irina's hand trembled noticeably. In the silence they waited for Smolokurov's reaction. He sighed and picked up the telephone.

"Comrade Berkin," he said. "I apologize for bothering you at this hour. Tarutin wants to take some paintings with him. Ah? But we have instructions. Excuse me? I see. Yes, comrade Berkin. To remove every obstacle. I understand, comrade Berkin."

He replaced the receiver. He looked at Boris, and Boris thought the colonel's glance displayed a sudden curiosity. "You must be satisfied," Smolokurov said. "You may take your paintings with you. You'll get a certificate that your paintings have been checked out and permitted to be taken abroad. Now, until the Militsioners bring your things, Lieutenant Petrova will take you to our canteen for breakfast."

A waitress, young, and pretty, brought a tray with butter, milk, warm rolls and a jar, with strawberry jam. She unloaded the tray, walked away and reappeared with another tray holding four dishes with steaming meat cutlets, rice and beans. Finally two pots with tea and a tray of pastries. Neither the Magidovs nor Tarutin ever had access to a privileged canteen.

"With all this food before me, I feel as if I am already aboard," Magidov said.

They ate silently for a while.

"Boris," Magidov said, "Why did you take the risk with your bluff regarding the paintings?"

"I owe it to Valushin," Boris said. "He always dreamed of having his paintings exhibited."

"Since it was impossible to exhibit them in this country, you want to do so abroad" Irina said, understanding his feelings. "I just can't believe it's true," Irina said. "I feel like I'll wake up and it will vanish. All those other countries, Israel, America, do they really exist? In a couple of days we will get rid of queues and lines, forever. Boris, I am sad that you are not really happy."

"I am the last of the Tarutins," Boris said. "We have been a part of this country for centuries. And now they kick me out, as garbage."

All you have had here you can find elsewhere. Plus freedom, which you have not had here."

"And what about my friends, Irina? I leave all of my friends behind. And my Grand-aunt Galina. She will have to pass away alone, without anybody around. As to our future, Irina, I suspect that the West, has its share of scoundrels and idiots."

Lieutenant Petrova appeared in the entrance to the canteen.

"Magidov family," she said, "Proceed to my office, your documents are ready. I need your signatures and then you'll check your personal belongings. Follow me."

Chapter 47

AT NINE AM ON MONDAY, DECEMBER 19, SECOND SECRETARY of the Kalinin region Party committee Kurchin appeared in the door of the office where First Secretary Korytov was waiting behind his empty desk.

Korytov knew this was to be his last hour in this office.

Kurchin coughed and said with extreme solemnity, "Comrade Korytov, Ivan Platonovich, I am authorized by the Central Committee of our Party to take over the duties of the First Secretary of the Kalinin region Party Committee, effective immediately. The Central Committee has informed us that you have submitted your resignation. It has been accepted and approved by the Central Committee. Please surrender all the keys to rooms, safes, gates and the like which may have been in your possession. Then you will be driven to your former residence. You will be informed in a due course about the procedure for vacating said residence and about your transfer to another residence."

Korytov coughed and said, "Thank you, comrade

Kurchin. I am supposed to deliver Orders and medals today at ten o'clock, to the best people of our region."

Kurchin shook his small head. "The Party never misses anything, comrade Korytov," he said. "I am entrusted now to perform this important task and I will deliver the decorations."

He waited in silence for a while, then he continued. "The Party thinks you should start your earned rest at once. So, please surrender the keys and proceed to the car."

Through the window of his office, temporary First Secretary of the Kalinin region Party Committee Kurchin watched the black Volga sedan roll out of the *obkom*'s back yard, carrying away the deposed master. Tomorrow he would not be entitled even to this one car.

Kurchin's secretary walked in.

"Congratulations, Vladimir Kronidovich," the secretary said.

Kurchin frowned. He knew that he had no chance to get the position vacated by Korytov. Kurchin's csardom was for a few days only.

The hall was full of people who wanted to witness the ceremony. These decorations were signs of recognition. Kurchin spoke, "—of the contribution made by the best sons and daughters of our great Soviet people to our historical victories on our way to the radiant future of mankind. Our orders and medals are the signs of Glory!"

The obligatory thunder of applause followed. Then Kurchin continued, evoking admiration on the part of those who sat in the several front rows; they saw clearly that Kurchin, deviating from the custom of the Party leaders, did not use a prepared text. The devil ran his speech from his head! And this speech was by no means worse than any other speeches of Party leaders. Like any of such speeches, it was *politically mature*, void of any information and clearly indicating when an applause was due.

"Now, the names will be announced and the recipients should step forward, to accept the Orders and the medals," Kurchin said finally. The audience droned in excitation.

"The Order of Lenin is awarded to comrade Rashkov Timofei Georgievich—Order of Lenin is awarded to—"

One by one, the people who were awarded the decorations ascended to the stage to receive the signs of Glory from the Motherland. The thunder of applause roared and roared, without interruption.

On the black market, an Order of Lenin would draw from three to 4,000 rubles, 30 to 40 times a monthly salary of a physician or teacher. The Order of the Red Banner about 2,000. Every decoration had its price in the officially non-existent underground market. Prices depended on the amounts of gold, silver and gems used to make them.

Chapter 48

THE MEETING WHERE THE MEMBERS OF THE REGION ELITE accepted their decorations, had its function in Misha Berkin's plans. Misha knew that everybody who was *somebody* in Kalinin would be at this meeting for about three hours. Three hours would provide the crucial time span for the completion of Misha's design. When the region's rulers started taking inventory of the new situation created by Korytov's abrupt disappearance, it would be too late for them to stop the actions Misha had set in motion.

Until the completion of the meeting, Misha could still use his prerogatives of a man speaking in the name of the *obkom*.

Misha ordered his chauffeur to drive him to the Military airfield in Migalovo, a 20 minute ride. At the gate Misha displayed his certificate, was immediately admitted and the chauffeur drove him to a special section where airplanes and helicopters were always ready for the *obkom*.

The commander of the special section knew Misha personally. But adhering to the procedure the commander checked Misha's certificate. It was valid. He relayed Misha's request for a helicopter.

The green-painted helicopter trembled at the hangar's gate and its whistling blades merged into a quivering circle. The pilot handed Misha a pair of earphones which were supposed to both muffle the deafening roar and enable the passenger to communicate with the pilot if need be.

The flight to Moscow would take about forty five-minutes.

Misha saw a train crawling slowly in a south-eastern direction towards Moscow. This was the local electric train Kalinin-Moscow. It should be carrying the Magidovs and Tarutin. In less than two hours, this train would arrive in Moscow.

Misha would have prefered to kick out the "Magidov bunch" on a plane but no tickets to Moscow-Vienna flights could be obtained on such short notice.

Misha had also telephoned contacts and some people removed Alla Shumilova from the Moscow-Samarkand train at Kzyl-Orda. At the same time her mother was to be told that her daughter was taken off the train because of a sudden illness.

The old woman would be put on a plane from Samarkand to Kzyl-Orda. There mother and the daughter would be told they must leave the country. The operatives would make sure the Shumilovs arrived in Moscow in time to bard the Moscow-Vienna train.

After all the old former scout Shumilova was born Pitkina. Her parents were Jewish. It would be correct to send them to Israel. Some day in the future the Shumilovs might even grow to be grateful to Misha for their forced emigration.

Thinking now about the operation which he had set in motion and which, if not interrupted by Rashkov's henchmen, would result in the Magidovs', Shumilovs' and Tarutin's emigration from the USSR. His main incentive for organizing this exodus was his need to avoid spreading information that could adversely affect his own situation.

His actions in the "Magidov affair" was transformed in his mind into an arrangement for the five people's "escape" from Russia which he helped to implement out of his "humanitarian" impulses.

A practical man, a man of expediency rather than of ideology, Misha never attached much significance to the *Marxist theory*. Misha, nevertheless recalled the frequently cited Marx's utterance, "One's being determines one's consciousness."

The helicopter landed on a special airfield in Moscow, where 50 identical helicopters lined the asphalt strip. He thanked the pilot.

A taxi took Misha to the center of the huge capital. He climbed up the wide granite stairs leading to the oakwood door of the somber, eight-story gray building where some of the departments of the Party Central Committee were located.

The cool emptiness of the huge entrance hall, with its traditional marble columns, seemed to fit a luxurious mortuary rather than the center of the ruling machine. From an internal telephone booth, Misha dialed his *link*'s number.

It had been an understanding between Misha and his *link* that their meetings should take place in an inconspicuous way. Misha did not request a *propusk,* a pass to enter the building. It would be registered in a log book and leave a trail of Misha's visit.

When the Moscow man took the telephone and heard Misha's voice, he asked, "The evidence of sincerity?"

"Uh huh," Misha said.

"Wait there," the man said.

In a few minutes Misha's *link* emerged from the elevator. They walked to a hall corner.

He said he could devote no more than two minutes. Misha looked around. Nobody watched. Misha brought from his pocket a small leather box and handed it to the *link*. The man lifted the box's lid. His tired eyes glistened in amazement.

"Genuine?" he asked, his voice showing his respect at the enormous value of the "evidence of sincerity."

"Potyomkin's diamond," Misha said. "A national treasure."

"I see. Well, the Party will take care of this item."

"So, how about me?" Misha said.

The man from Moscow frowned. "I can't promise anything. Korytov will be left alone even though he does not deserve the pension to which he is entitled officially. But you—"

The Moscow man paused. Then his pale lips curved in what could be considered a smile and he added, "Could you not have been more careful in selecting your father? You could've been an important person in the Party *apparat*. But you understand, the Party must preserve the utmost flexibility in using its *cadres*. In your case this flexibility would be impaired. There are many functions you cannot be assigned to. My best advice is talk to the KGB people. They can use you. Try it. Now, I must hurry."

The helicopter shook incessantly. In the cabin's corner, Misha huddled, his face flabby his eyes not seeing the copter's shadow running over the dark mass of tress and the snow-coated fields.

He thought about the advice to try his luck with the KGB. This man in Moscow could not have known that Misha's relationship with the Kalinin region KGB made it impossible for him to seek a new assignment through the local KGB people. He probably could try it in some other region. Whatever his prospects in such an endeavor might have been, it was clear that there was no place any longer for Misha Berkin in the Party *apparat*. All they would allow him to do was some dirty work as a small spider within the KGB system of all-embracing cobwebs.

He had no schemes to plot, no fights to fight, no traps to fear any more. His last plot was over, and his last fight had been lost irreversibly.

A mirror hung on the wall of the helicopter's cabin. Misha glanced at his reflection. He saw his pale-blue eyes, his roundish face with the prominent temples and his slightly upturned broad nose; all this was his legacy from his mother, a Russian peasant. He seemed to have not inherited a single facial feature from his Jewish father.

Misha stood up, opened the door and jumped out.

Chapter 49

At 5 am on December 21, the train Moscow-Vienna rolled slowly towards the border between Czechoslovakia and Austria. The attendant knocked on doors announcing that everybody must be awake for the border crossing procedure. This train, on its way from Moscow, had already crossed two borders, Poland and Czechoslovakia.

But now, the train was approaching the real border between the Kremlin empire and the rest of the world.

Boris walked from his compartment into the car's corridor. In the gray twilight, he watched the sand slope slowly floating past the train.

His mind returned to the events of the last two days. Soon after their train left Moscow they discovered that Alla Shumilova and her mother had also been forced to leave their country and were traveling in the same car. When Alla saw Boris and Irina, she leapt to Irina and hugged her, the girl's eyes full of tears.

Sonia Shumilova, Alla's mother, seemed to be stunned by the abrupt overturn of her life.

She did not yet know how to cope with the sudden loss of her decorations; following the regulations she had not been allowed to take abroad her numerous wartime orders and medals. For years these decorations had been an inseparable part of her life. She was a heroine of the great war.

She was completely at a loss; she had not the slightest idea of what she would be doing abroad. Her emigration meant the automatic cancellation of her war time pension. With deep grief she left behind two dear graves, one of her son Igor and one of her husband Vasily.

Then there was the custom-house in Brest. The passengers had to drag all of their baggage from the train to the custom hall. The baggage of the "Magidovs family" consisted mainly of Valushin's paintings.

The custom inspector was puzzled when he saw that these five people had not been carrying much baggage with them. Usually, the people who were allowed to emigrate, tried to carry with as much of their belonging as possible.

He checked the paintings thoroughly. He was disappointed not to have found anything to justify hassling these emigrants. He noticed a small blue-and-red badge on Boris's chest, the sign of a mountaineering instructor. He grinned and demanded the surrender of the badge. Boris shrugged and unpinned the badge from his lapel. The customs man attached the badge to his jacket and they got back on the train.

None of them had ever seen carriages like the luxurious cars of the Moscow-Vienna train. The compartments had only two beds each, all polished wood and glittering brass and mirrors. Boris shared a compartment with Magidov, and Irina had a compartment all for herself. The Shumilovs occupied one compartment.

Stretching out on his soft and springy upper-level bed,

Boris thought that the fake marriage certificate had erected a new barrier between him and Irina.

He remembered her glances at him, especially on that sunny winter morning in Aunt Galina's house, in front of the cast-iron stove where the pine logs crackled in tongues of flame. And how she had hugged and kissed him when he came back from the Golokomlya mental hospital. And how she jumped from the truck's cabin to the platform to be with him. And many other episodes which showed that she loved him. They operated under the stress generated by her father's suffering in the jail and by the uncertainty of their future. This stood in the way of their fledging mutual passion. But now her father was free would the affection remain? He knew how he felt about her. Did she really feel the same about him. The preposterous marriage certificate made it awkward to display any feelings between them.

Or could it be that he had misread her feelings? Maybe she was just waiting for his move?

In a strange way the presence of her father also made Boris uneasy. Magidov, who had always been a very silent man, had changed. He talked with Boris for hours, as if compensating for the long days of his forced silence in jail. And, although Magidov was 12 years older than Boris, a feeling of being peers had developed between them in the course of this trip, particularly since both were physicists. And this feeling of being a peer to Irina's father made Boris feel much older than Irina, belonging to another generation.

The eastern sky glowed pink now. The train slowed down even more. And then the passengers, who were sticking to the windows now, saw that the train crawled slowly through a giant gate. A wide strip of bare soil, dug over, stretched on both side of the gate. The "forbidden zone."

* * *

As the train pulled gradually westward and the gate slowly floated back, they saw that two tall fences, made of several layers of barbed wire, now stretched along the train on both sides of the railway.

The train stopped. The gate behind it closed. The train stood now in a giant wire cage.

Entangled within this fence's wire interlacement, guard towers spiked to the grayish morning sky. Powerful search lights, machine-guns, and flame throwers hung in garlands on the towers' multiple levels.

Soldiers appeared from nowhere pouring into the giant wire cage. They rushed aboard the carriages and clambered on the carriages' roofs. They went through car corridors, compartments, toilets. They looked under the benches and over baggage racks. They knocked at the car walls with heavy hammers. Not a fly could leave, without permission.

"Isn't this cage a symbol of the entire world east of this fence?" Magidov said. "Man is now in a wire cage. The USSR is 22,000,000 square kilometers of a prison surrounded by a barbed wire fence."

An officer who had been watching the work of his soldiers, overheard Magidov's words. He said through his teeth, "Instead of letting such scum go, I would cut your stinking throats. Hitler made one mistake, he did not finish off all of you."

"Thank you," Sonia Shumilova said suddenly. "Your words, citizen officer, have made leaving Russia much easier for me."

The gate on the western side opened. The train trembled and started moving westward slowly. The giant fence with its spikes of sinister towers could be seen now in its menacing endlessness, stretching from horizon to horizon. Then the last car rolled out from the cage and the gate closed behind the train. The wheels' rattle accelerated gradually.

"We are free!" Irina shouted, laughing and crying at the same time. "We are free!" She hugged her father. Magidov glanced at his watch.

"Remember this moment," Magidov said. "It is seven am, December 21, the time of our leaving prison."

Irina turned to Boris. She held the marriage certificate in hand. "Boris, as my husband I insist you share my compartment—or do you wish to tear this up?"

Boris took her in his arms and kissed her.

Magidov said, "I give you both my blessing. And after she is exhausted by this honeymoon—hurry back—we must talk some more."